THE HOUSE AT BALNESMOOR

Summer on the moorland, and Norman Lang makes a gruesome discovery near his idyllic country retreat that will forever taint his existence and take his already tormented wife to the brink of madness: he finds the bodies of not one, but two, Glasgow schoolgirls buried among the heather roots. The estate agent had certainly kept that one quiet. . .

Inspector McCaig's investigation into the tangled, clandestine lives of a remote highland community leads him to believe the killer may yet strike again, so expediency is vital. As he hones in, McCaig begins to recognise the usual portents: the fatal fusion of youthful passion and neurosis gone murderously awry. And he knows this deadly confusion may still reign inside the killer's twisted mind. . .

THE HOUSE AT BALNESMOOR

Hugh C. Rae

·BLACK· DAGGER ·CRIME·

First Published 1969
by
Coward-McCann, Inc.

This edition 1999 by Chivers Press
published by arrangement with
the author

ISBN 0 7540 8540 6

British Library Cataloguing in Publication Data available

Printed and bound in Great Britain by
Redwood Books, Trowbridge, Wiltshire

Part One

ONE

The moor drowsed under the hot Sabbath sun, tawny and shabby like the flanks of an old lion. A wavering heat mist suggested that it stretched like the ocean to an infinite horizon, but from the lawn of the house only a mile or two of its vast acreage was visible. A crust of heather, peat-hag and broom rose to a line of low hills flat and faint in the distance. Beyond the ridge a plateau narrowed gradually and dropped down into the valley of Lannerburn twelve straight miles away. From the bottom of the track at the garden's end Lang could not look on to the moorland. A steep shelf of rock and the debris of dark red earth jutted above him and only the ragged edge, the heather crust flocked with insects and butterflies, showed. The rare spring drought had burned all colour from the earth, but with an hour of rain the wilderness would sprout up bright and it would be summer. Lang up-ended the wheelbarrow; rubbish cascaded to the bank. The ache in his back gripped his spine wickedly and he grunted, straightening. The intricate shadows of the thicket offered him shade and he crouched down to rest for a moment and think of the pleasurable afternoon ahead; a deck chair, the newspapers, maybe even a small glass of lager to cool him down. In the branches overhead a finch fluttered, oddly silent, as if trapped. Lang watched it, smiling.

His gumboots pressed gently against his haunches and, sighing, he unbuttoned his waistcoat. He had done a fair morning's work, cutting deep into the regiment of coarse weeds which stormed his garden fences. He was almost ready to stow away his tools and enjoy a spot of idleness. Throughout his working life he had dreamed of just such a day as this. Satisfaction tightened his innards, and he grinned and winked at the finch again as if it could understand his feelings. A whisper of traffic on the village road drifted up from behind the house, a safe distance away. The sound was hardly less hazy and somnolent than the imprecise spirals of song which the larks gave out as they rode the warm currents of air above the moor. More like August than May it was; the summer would surely fulfil the promise of the spring. Lang was content with his anticipation. The grinding years, the scrimping and saving years it had taken to gather enough cash to buy this place suddenly all seemed worth it. He glanced over his shoulder at the house as if to make sure it was really true. The lingering doubts which had lasted the winter evaporated : there was no better way for a man to pass the evening of his life than close to nature. Once he got the garden licked into shape he could settle back and let the whole place look after itself. It was not an easy task he had set himself; the previous owner had let the place run to seed. Lang couldn't understand it. How could anyone stand back and watch the moor creep closer, reaching out to reclaim the fine lawn and the flower beds. Lang tutted and pushed himself stiffly to his feet. Slovenly devils, he thought, as he attacked the mound of rubbish again. Throughout the wet winter months, of necessity devoted to indoor improvements, he had sustained himself with plans for the garden. His prime ambition was to extend the green lawn all three hundred yards to the fence, and thus to enhance the value of the property, though he had no intention of selling. He lifted an armful of weed stalks, leaves and broken branches and dropped them on top of the pile in the grate which he had built from stones and strips of old iron unearthed from under the brambles. He tramped the pile down then sprinkled it with paraffin from the can, dribbling the blue liquid into the newspapers at the heart of the bonfire. Leaning back cautiously, he struck a match and poked it deep into the kindling. Pale flames ran along the tiny twigs, igniting them in passing. An instant later the first gentle whisper of the fire roared up, crackling as the dry wood caught. The transparent shimmer of heat drove upwards into the clots of rubbish and leaf thatch. The flames dampened into chalky blue smoke, billowing in shapely curlicues, drifting through the thicket well away from the house. With a twitter of anxiety the finch fled from its makeshift cage and swooped off to the shelter of the trees.

6

Though he had chosen the site with care, Lang tended the bonfire vigilantly, walking round and round it, tidying straggling creepers and pushing down the swelling core. He was mindful of the dangers of brush fires in this unusually dry season and the proximity of the house doubled his caution. The crude hearth was far enough from the bushes which overshadowed the track, high on the earthy bank, to be safe. Just off to his left the vegetation was dense, dense enough to absorb the dirty droppings of the hikers and Sunday car trippers who came this way : not many of them really, for the true moor path was a half mile off through the gate by Johnstone's farm. It was only courting couples, lovers, who visited this dead-end with any frequency, it being dark and private enough to hide their sinful behaviour. Lang had discovered beer cans and wine bottles in the bushes, even in his garden, other things as well, dirty things. It angered him that such folk impinged on his property, soiling it, and the prowling sounds of the cars at night roused his temper. More than once this last month Jenny had had difficulty in persuading him not to storm down with a flash-light and make trouble. Perhaps his wife was right : what they got up to in their cars wasn't really his business. Any young lass who came out here with a man knew just what she was in for. Still, they should cart their dirt away with them, keep it to themselves.

The fire burned steadily, purling rich smoke up across the moor where a faint drift of noon-time breeze rubbed it slowly into the innocent blue sky. Lang sighed once more, rubbed his hands on his thighs, lifted the handles and trundled the empty barrow down the lane and through the rusty iron gate into his garden. The sunlight was not strong enough to glaze the long lounge window, but it powdered it with mellow pink and edged the shadow of the kitchen gable across the garage wall. Through the faint sheen of light Lang could see nothing in the room, but as he approached the toolshed Jenny opened the kitchen door and came down on to the path. Her flowered dress hung too far below the knee to be fashionable but Jenny had never made any pretence of being that; the memory of youthful days which the style awakened in Lang was worth more than any smart modernity. A woollen cardigan draped around her shoulders leaving her arms bare. Her silvery hair lifted over her ears to show the Celtic ear-rings which he'd given her last autumn to mark their fortieth wedding anniversary. Lang regarded his wife with a trace of wariness, a habit occasioned by her illnesses and bouts of depression. Today, however, she appeared rested and calm. The marks of the neurotic spells, which had scarred their last years in Glasgow, were fading away. That was the country for you, Lang thought; by the end of the summer she'd look ten years younger. He smiled at her, nodding as she gestured at the table on the lawn. He pushed the barrow against the shed, watched her adjust the striped canvas awning over the table, then walked to the tap to wash his hands. Standing out from a post, the tap was one of the special features of the 'grounds' which Galbraith the estate agent had stressed. Ruefully Lang recalled how floridly the agent had described the tap as if the thing was a triumph of hydrodynamic engineering and not just a place to fit the hose. Still, he hadn't been taken in by any of Galbraith's double-talk. He'd even managed to beat the agent down two hundred on the initial asking price. He laved his hands under the tap, dried them on a torn towel and went to join Jenny at the table. She was pouring tea from the pot into the cups on the tray.

'Don't overdo it, Norman,' she said. 'You've the whole summer ahead of you.'

Lang nodded. 'I'll be stopping soon,' he said. 'My back's twingeing a bit.'

Characteristic fastidiousness made him button his old tweed waistcoat and fasten the stud at the neck of his shirt before he took the teacup. Jenny perched on the edge of the camp chair, a faint dust of face powder discernible against the fine grain of her skin. A teaspoon clinked daintly on the china rim as she stirred in a sweetener and a drop of milk.

'How are you getting on?' she asked, almost formally.

'Oh, fine,' said Lang. 'I'm thinking once I've cleared it all, I might pick up a few raspberry canes for planting.'

'I thought you were going to grass it.'

'Fruit bushes would be nice,' said Lang.

'They're so expensive, Norman, aren't they?'

'We'd save in the long run,' said Lang, 'You could make jam.'

'It's cheap enough in the shops,' said Jenny.

'But it's not like homemade.'

8

'Sit down, Norman,' the woman said.

'I'm mucky,' Lang said, looking at his stained corduroys. 'I wouldn't want to mark the chair.'

'It'll clean,' Jenny said. 'Sit down.'

Lang nodded again. Much of their contact was composed of these almost deferential nods, as if constant movements of the head were necessary to confirm their interreliance. Holding the saucer in his palm Lang lifted the teacup with finger and thumb and sipped the weak honey-coloured liquid thoughtfully. He gazed out over the moor. The breeze stirred in the trees behind the house, sudden, brief and lively, diminishing again as it skittered across the heatherland, twisting the hanging curtains of warm air, snatching smoke from the bonfire to draw away like ghostly pennants. When the wind dropped the silence was intense : no sound and no movement anywhere in the panorama. The clean taste of tea and the faint fragrance of wood smoke had an analgesic effect on Lang. He felt soothed, relaxed and contented, more contented at that exact moment than ever before. Then it was over; a crack opened, fissures spread out like a web and the sphere of his happiness, which he had laboured so long and hard to construct, shattered like a glass egg.

'*Norman!*' The strident note in Jenny's voice brought him whirling round. Her face was lifted, the folds of skin beneath her chin hanging from the suddenly sharpened jaw. '*Over there.*'

He turned again. His muscles, tortured by the rapidity of the movement, stabbed pain down his thighs. But he paid no attention to it. As the breeze sloughed again, coming over the house like a tide, he glimpsed the tatter of red flame, strong even in sunlight, whipping up from the thicket.

'My God !' he said.

He dropped his teacup and ran. Even before he reached the gate he could hear the sound of the fire rampaging through the underbrush. Ironically, his own small bonfire had disintegrated. A fragment of it, a glowing skein of ash, floated up to entangle itself in the shrubs. Flirtatiously the little wind died only to strike up again instantly from another quarter, sucking flames back across the track to meet him. Lang covered his cheek with his forearm as the blast scorched him. He danced this way and

9

that along the path, impotent without a weapon to beat back the blaze.

'Norman.'

He glanced back. Jenny was scurrying down the slope of the lawn, waving the sacking. Behind her the house was still serene, and a fresh wave of fear shifted into him. He ran to meet her, shouting incoherent instructions.

Though the sacking was damp, when he flapped it around the fringes of the fire the material caught and quickly charred, flakes of burning canvas floating round him like black snow. At the heart of the blaze the undergrowth had welded itself into an incandescent white blob. When it fell inward, searing out a blast of heat and a fountain of sparks, the ground all around was left naked and tarry, and Lang dared to go forward. He smashed down the crisp ribs of the bushes with the sack, blotting the air with soot particles and smoke. Choking, he retreated again only to notice that flames were running out from the demolished thicket, groping through the tussocks into pockets of fresh tinder. Cursing, he hauled himself through the skeletal remains of the overhead branches, hearing them snap and feeling their hot cores sting, swinging his head like a tethered bull, hopelessly confused. Jenny's voice gave him something to cling to and he lumbered down on to the track again, stamping out scallops of flame as he went. Two yards from the boundary fence she stood with the hose in her hands wearing an expression of abject apology as if she blamed herself for the tube's shortness. How she had fitted and unrolled it so quickly Lang did not know, but in control of himself once more he hopped over the rail and grabbed the plastic nozzle from her. Smoke billowed overhead, racing Jenny across the lawn, as she hurried uphill to the tap. A minute later water brought the hose alive. It was as limber as a snake in Lang's fists, the coils flicking out straight on the grass. He could just discern Jenny by the shed jamming the ring against the tap with her fingers. Feebly at first, then with increasing force, water trickled from the nozzle. At last a thin tubular jet went curving over the fence and fell splattering on to the nearer reaches of the fire.

Soon the thicket was a black and dripping cave, with fire smothering itself in the earth, living red only in the stubble and contorted tree roots. Lang jerked the hose up, piercing the emptiness where the holocaust had raged, watching intently

10

as the smooth curve dashed into spray against the trunks and rained down on the area. The scorched ground was criss-crossed with rivulets wending among the treacly litter into the gullies and on to the track, thickening into mud. Lang laid the hose, still pouring water, on the grass and stepped over the fence to survey the damage. The back of his right hand was tender where the fire had kissed it and his spine ached, but he trudged over the whole wide area three or four times searching for and smothering any small sparks which the wind might reignite. Only then did he go back up to the house to find Jenny.

She was slumped in the deck-chair, one hand across her bosom, her face puffy with exertion and excitement. She stared up at him but could not speak.

'It's all right,' he told her, just as she began to weep. 'It's all right, dear. It's all over and done with. I put it out.'

She went on crying, without a sound. He was just considering how best to comfort her when Johnstone's Land-rover bounced on to the track and drew up sharply at the bottom of the garden. He watched the farmer leap the rail and stride over the grass, then patting Jenny abstractly on the shoulder, went down to meet him.

'What the hell's been happening then?' Johnstone shouted. He was tall, young, well-fleshed, with jet-black hair and brows, thunderous-black. His nose was prominent like a honed blade and his lips thin. Lang had had few dealings with the man, though he was their nearest neighbour, but, for some intangible reason, he distrusted him. Now Johnstone was angry, but the fact that his anger was justified did not lessen Lang's belligerent response in the least.

'The thicket went on fire' said Lang. 'I put it out.'

'How'd it get started?'

'The wind . . . .'

'Did y'start it yourself then?' Johnstone demanded.

'I was burning some rubbish,' Lang said. 'It's out now though, don't worry.'

Johnstone spread his legs, thick under the torn breeches and heavy in the boots. He towered over the elderly man. 'Jesus, y'could've had the whole place up in smoke.'

'I'm sorry,' said Lang. 'It'll not happen again.'

'The whole bloody place,' said Johnstone. 'Is your wife hurt then?'

11

'Shock,' said Lang. 'She's all right otherwise.'

'We'd better take a look down there,' said Johnstone.

'I have done,' said Lang. 'It's quite safe now.'

'I'll just have a look for m'self, if y'don't mind,' growled Johnstone. 'Valuable beasts I've got in those fields.'

Reluctantly Lang followed Johnstone down to the track and helped the grumbling farmer set up a longer length of rubber hose and sluice down the hedgerows. The thicket was totally destroyed. Johnstone kicked his way around it, pausing only to point with his toe at the wispy shell of a nest stuck with the bodies of two infant birds, like little charred sausages. Lang nodded contritely and felt sad at the sight. But he was glad when Johnstone wound up his hose and drove off in the Land-rover. Now he could perhaps put the incident behind him, mark it up to experience, and salvage some of the afternoon. But it was too late; Jenny had one of her attacks, a mild one, so he had to prepare and serve lunch himself. It was almost evening before things were back to normal. By that time the sky had clouded over, rain, brought stealthily by the wind, massed gloomy and low over the moorland. Depressed by the waste of a day, Lang went early to bed.

Jenny was asleep, doped by one of her pills, and slept through the storm, but Lang heard it; the sibilant hiss of rain sheets across the roof, the drum of drops flung solidly against the window, the gusty ferocity of the gale pushing round the house on its way to the open moor. Usually a storm only increased his sense of security, for the house was snug and tight, but tonight it made him restless. He listened to it for a while then pulled the quilt over his head and burrowed his ears deep into the pillow. The rain rattled away, rising and falling like a tide, and the wind buffeted the building. A gnawing apprehension would not let him sleep. He told himself again and again that rain was a good thing; it would put the fire out completely. But even that logic was no consolation and did not comfort him. It was well into the small hours before he slipped tensely down into sleep.

Monday's lunch was simmering on the kitchen stove, and a rich aroma of baking scones came from the oven. Jenny seemed to be herself again and the tribulations of Sunday forgotten. So Lang was surprised to find himself rooting out his gumboots

12

and sitting down to pull them on. When Jenny asked him where he was going, he could not tell her, nor could he give her a valid reason for going out. He had never been one to act on impulse and his only explanation sounded so stupid that he would not admit it even to himself. That blackened scar on the bank, shiny as coal with the rain now, drew him out of the cosy lounge. He had stood by the window peeking at it, again without reason, infected by curiosity, and an urge which, by lunch-time, he just had to satisfy. A more boyish person might have used it simply as an excuse to get out in the rain, to splash among the floods, squirms of brown mud at the gate, but not Lang : all traces of boyishness had long since been ground out of him. He was annoyed at the queer obsession which tugged him from shelter.

The clouds had shape, lying in bands of bruised blue-black, and the wind veered, dragging ragged edges of rain forth and back across the hag-like thorn brooms. Like ebony the burned branches stood out sharply against the liquid running surface of the bank. Rivers gushed from channels under the soil, pushing reddish sludge on to the waterlogged track. When he thought of it later he fancied he had gone directly, unerringly, to the place, but it was not so : there was no mystic certainty in the discovery. The accident was a casual coincidence.

Aimlessly he wandered into the middle of the clearing where yesterday the thicket had buzzed in the sun, clumpy and overgrown. There he stopped, irritably chiding himself for being foolish enough to come out of the house on such a dismal day, bored with the silly spirit which had prompted the excursion. He felt rain drip from the brim of his cap, heard it *pock* against his oilskins, and blew it away from the tip of his nose. He turned to plough back to the garden gate, kicking the brittle stumps out of his way, awkward in the soft blunt gumboots, slippery with mud. He kicked again then stopped. He was looking at it now. In the gulf between sight and recognition lay his final chance of escape, but it was a false opportunity for he had no real control over that region of his mind. His frown tipped the cap over his eyes and he pushed it back, stooping slightly. The rain hissed around him, wetness falling on wetness, merging swiftly, the saturated charcoal twigs holding a necklace of clear drops on their underribs. He began to think he knew what it meant, what it was, and the image

13

rammed itself hard against his brain, so that its imprint was to remain with him precise and sharply defined ever after. He took a step closer.

It was not a root exposed by the actions of fire and water, though it had the gnarled, knobbled shape of a root, a large root slicked with spidery fungus and pimpled with decay. But just where it jutted out of the earth was a joint, and the joint was white, dead calcic white with every crumb of dirt washed off. Even then he might have passed it off, pulled back, grunted and gone home. But there was cloth too, a fringe of material pasted around the joint, nailed by the weight of the banking. His boot went forward, the rubber explored the shape, nudged it, pushed it to the side. It resisted. He pressed it again and the end of the object jerked abruptly out of the dirt. He bent closer, then flinched, stepping back, withdrawing his foot, stepped back again, gaping. His arms rose stiffly to balance his body against the slippery run of the slope. His mouth opened wider. The breath he drew was tainted with the sickish sweet smell and he emptied his lungs with a roar. Wheeling, he crashed down the banking. When he opened his jaws again he was shouting, bellowing tormentedly as if the very fabric of his soul was being ripped in two. He was still bellowing when he reached the house and Jenny flung open the kitchen door.

TWO

The body had been there a long, long time : there was no hurry now, no desperate rush to comb out clues. Anything material which had survived the elements would not be lost to them now. It was possible that, if the killer was a local man – why should he be local, why even a man – he would show some signs of panic. Still, that was a hell of a long shot and Chief Superintendent McCaig did not have enough of the amateur left in him to set any store by long shots. He faced the window of the lounge and peered over the darkening landscape at the figures grouped round the trench like participants in a pagan rite. The vans were off to the left, ambulance, press boys' buggies, ranging round out of view behind the house. Thank God, they'd dug the kid up at the edge of the moor and not

14

somewhere out in the middle. That would have been fun, lugging gear, pissing about in the clag ten miles from a tea urn and a warm fire, dickering with walkie-talkies like an army captain. Anyway, they weren't going to find much down there that they could use, not after ... well, the corpse had been in the ground for bloody months, it took no expert in pathology to tell that. He would put his men through the motions in that direction, just in case, but lean his own, not inconsiderable weight, on more tangible factors. It wouldn't take that long, once Glasgow stuck its finger in the pie, to find out which one of the dozen Missing Persons was missing no longer, then he could work out the concentric circles of investigation; an exercise in statistics. He had the happy knack of depersonalising reports, and discovering the weakness in the order, the gap in logical pattern through which, with sufficient forces, he could focus his attack like a laser beam. It wasn't instinct, but experience which told him that this poor bloody victim was going to lead him a merry dance. He was getting a bit too damned fat to dance these days; this county executive post was turning him gradually into a vegetable.

Reflected in the long glass before him he could see the spectral figures of Ryan and Blair flanking the hang-dog wee man who'd stumbled across the grave – Lang: his house, and not a bad piece of property either, perched on the edge of the Balnesmoor. He studied Lang's image carefully but felt no sympathy for the elderly man, just as he felt nothing yet for the nameless girl they'd dredged out of the dirt. He flicked his gaze towards the kitchen where the tremulous whistle of a boiling kettle was cut off promptly on its rise to shrillness. Tea, thank God; he was hungry, too.

A camera flashed, vivid in the gloomy afternoon light. He blinked, and listened to the voices behind him. It would do no harm to let Lang think Ryan was the boss, the man he must answer to, while he stood back in the warm room relating the spoken words to the dreich operation out yonder on Balnesmoor. Ryan was good at these interviews, had just the right kind of persistent warmth. He knew how to push down gently, cloaking his insistence with sympathy. McCaig had wondered more than once if perhaps that sympathetic tone was actually genuine. He listened, motionless, to Inspector Ryan's questions, Lang's answers. Blair flipped over a page in his

15

notebook and the sound, trapped in a lull of voices, was like the side of a house falling.

'You must have had some reason for going down there this morning,' said Ryan, 'or do you like ploutering about in the rain, Mr Lang?'

'No,' said Lang. 'I don't. I was curious.'

'Oh yes, about what?'

'How much damage there was.'

'Didn't you see that yesterday' said Ryan, 'when you and the farmer looked over the place?'

There was something abnormal in Lang's tension, and McCaig sensed it. It wasn't that he was distraught or sick at what had happened, the feeling was of resentment, antagonism. McCaig had experienced it often enough in his days with the Glasgow C.I.D. to recognise it now. There was something lying just under the surface which, he hoped, Ryan would be skilful enough to extract. Still, it had been a shock to them both. Christ, the wife had melted to jelly by the time they got a doctor to her. It had taken a mighty heavy dose of sedative to knock the old dear out and get her out of their way.

Lang was answering. 'I was too concerned yesterday with putting the fire *out*. Then, my wife wasn't herself after it.'

'Must have been unsettling,' murmured Ryan. 'I suppose you were worried in case sparks spread to the house.'

'Of course I was,' said Lang. 'It's my own house, you know, cost me a pretty penny, and none of your mortgage nonsense about it either.'

'It's certainly a nice place,' said Ryan. 'Isn't it, Sergeant?'

Blair nodded obediently. 'Very nice.'

'But what'll it be worth now, I wonder,' said Lang, 'after this.' He glared at each of the detectives in turn, as if he held them personally responsible for the tragedy.

That's it, thought McCaig, that's what's got the bugger's back up; he's worried about the house-price dropping. Perhaps Lang was one of those types who buy a place cheap, devote a lot of sweat to decorating and improving, then flog it again at a fat profit. There was quite a gang of them at that with the old tenement flats in Glasgow; nothing illegal about it of course. Ryan had the same notion.

'Were you thinking of selling then, Mr Lang?' the Inspector inquired.

16

'Certainly not. I'm here 'til I die,' said Lang.

'How long have you been in Balnesmoor, in this house?'

'We looked it over April last,' Lang answered, 'bought it in May, but we never took possession until July, Glasgow Fair Monday, and it was September, after my retiral, that we moved in permanently.'

Blair took note of the dates in neat shorthand which seemed to flow from the pencil with a dexterity the big hand should not have possessed.

'Would you know,' said Ryan, 'how many owners there were before you?'

'I think it was three. Galbraith'll have the records.'

'Is that Robert Galbraith, in Lannerburn?' Ryan asked.

'Yes,' said Lang. 'All I know is that I took over from a family called Herron.'

'Herron,' said Ryan nodding slowly as if in response to a massive profundity. 'What did you do, Mr Lang?'

'Eh?' said Lang. He was comically dour and McCaig suddenly placed the type – he was the spit of one of the old-time Scottish panto comedians, big squashed nose, streaky grey moustache and round protruding chin; only Lang's voice was high, not husky and granular with bawling down the hecklers in the back of the gods.

'Before you retired?' Ryan explained.

'I was cashier in Welfords the printers, in Glasgow,' Lang replied. His mouth tightened with pride. 'Head Cashier. I was there all my working life, after I got out of the army – First War.'

'Do you have children?' said Ryan.

'No,' said Lang. 'We never had a family.'

McCaig sensed that Ryan was looking at him now, trying to attract his attention. The rain was easing now and in the distance away over the moorland, brighter weather spread like a streak of margarine against the sky. McCaig swung round and walked the length of the lounge, past the bookcase, the T.V. set, the doorway and took up a stance by the standard lamp behind Blair. The suite was modern, imitation Danish.

'Can you see all right, Sergeant?' McCaig asked.

'Sir,' Blair replied, equivocally.

McCaig placed his thumb on the button of the lamp, under the shade. He stared at Lang. 'All right?'

17

Lang nodded his assent, and light flooded the corner of the room, over Blair's notebook. Without stooping the Chief could easily read the clean Pitman's.

'This house must have cost quite a bit,' he said. 'Did Welford's pay well?'

'I saved,' said Lang grudgingly, 'and I'd an endowment policy.'

'What drew your attention to the body?' said McCaig abruptly.

'I don't know. It was just the leg.'

'You touched it?'

'I told you, I pulled it out with my foot,' said Lang. 'I just kicked it and it came away.'

'You knew right off what it was?'

'Not at once.'

'How soon?'

'When it came right out of the ground.'

'Is the track at the foot of your garden used much?' McCaig asked.

'In summer, folk use it to go on to the moor,' said Lang.

'I thought the access path was over by Johnstone's farm?' said McCaig.

'Folk think this lane goes somewhere, then when they see it doesn't they just ... I don't know what they do – go back I suppose.'

'What sort of people?' said McCaig.

'Hikers, picnickers, bird-watchers.'

'Children?' said McCaig.

'There was a party from a school, with a teacher, last autumn. They all went up on the moor,' said Lang.

'Really!' said Ryan. 'Which school?'

'I don't know.'

'How long did they spend up there?' asked Ryan.

'An afternoon.'

'You ... watched them?' said McCaig.

'I saw them,' replied Lang, 'but I didn't watch them. They went up the path by the farm. Maybe Johnstone watched them.'

'None of them came down this way?' said McCaig.

'Not to my knowledge,' said Lang.

'They didn't call at this house?'

18

'Why should they?' said Lang.

'Asking for milk, or a drink,' put in Ryan. 'You know what kids are like, they think everything's free in the country.'

'No,' said Lang, 'they didn't come here.'

'Perhaps your wife talked to one of them,' McCaig suggested.

'Jenny didn't.' said Lang. 'I was here all day. I'm here every day. We've never been farther than the village since we came to Balnesmoor.'

'Your wife does the shopping?' said McCaig. 'And you stay here alone?'

'Never,' said Lang – McCaig felt he had got the point. 'Jenny's not able to carry heavy bags, so I go with her – always.'

'Other children must come up on the moor too,' said McCaig. 'Village children, don't you ever see them?'

'The odd one,' Lang admitted, 'in the distance, but then we haven't been here a summer yet.'

'Anyone else use the track?' asked McCaig.

Lang sucked his moustache. He put his small hands on his knees and deliberately focused his attention on the hearth rug. 'Couples.'

'Courting couples?' said Ryan.

'Yes,' said Lang. 'And a bloody nuisance they are, with their motorcars, and litter in my garden.'

'Where do they park?' asked Ryan.

'All along the track.'

'Often?'

'Weekends mostly,' said Lang. 'WE can hear the cars stopping, loud when the wind's off the moor, and see the lights from the windows.'

'Now, is there only one at a time or groups of them?' said Ryan. 'I mean cars.'

'Usually just one or two, but lately there's been up to half a dozen. It must be the good weather,' said Lang.

'Or the spring,' Ryan added. 'Do they park near each other?'

'I'm not sure,' said Lang. 'No, I think they keep well apart.'

'Do you ever hear anything?' said Ryan.

'Like what?'

'Cries or shouts?'

19

'Laughing sometimes,' said Lang, adding bitterly, 'It's disgusting. It annoys my wife.'

'But they don't really make a nuisance of themselves,' said Ryan. 'Do they?'

'I suppose not,' Lang admitted reluctantly. 'But it's still disgusting.'

'Ever notice anything peculiar about them?' said Ryan.

'I don't spy on them, if that's what you're driving at,' said Lang angrily. 'And you saying they don't do any harm. They did harm to that girl you found out there, didn't they: right in front of my house.'

'It's out of the way,' said Ryan quietly. 'The bushes give good protection.'

McCaig was suddenly impatient with Ryan: no need to explain anything to this little bugger. He could work out reasons for himself, or read it up in the *Express* like the rest of the country. And if he wanted to be paranoic about it then he could go on thinking that fate had picked him specially for the business. He had no time to placate anyone with reasons, though some of the philosophical nuts that hung round the fringe of every crime could have done so – Derek could have done so, for instance, but then that was the kind of character his son had turned out to be – whether he got it from his mother or not, McCaig was too much of a realist to say. Balnesmoor was a natural place to dump a carcass anyway; where the devil did Lang expect the body to turn up – Lannerburn Main Street, wrapped in pink ribbon? Before Ryan could console the old man with reasons, McCaig said brusquely, 'That's all for the time being, Mr Lang.'

Lang scrambled quickly to his feet and, holding one hand to his buttocks as if in pain, jerked his head at the window. 'Have you taken it away yet?'

'Not yet,' said McCaig.

'It's difficult to move,' said Ryan, standing too.

McCaig pulled upon the door to the kitchen. The Welfare woman was caught in the act of infusing tea. He paused, moving his bulk to let Lang see what was happening in the kitchen, but Lang was gaping out of the window again. Ryan touched him on the elbow. 'Cup of tea, Mr Lang?'

'No, thanks.'

'Do you mind if we . . .?'

20

'No,' said Lang distantly. 'Go ahead.'

McCaig went into the kitchen as Ryan explained, 'It's a dismal afternoon, Mr Lang, and we haven't got a mobile canteen up here yet, for some reason. We won't bother you much after this.'

Lang said nothing but, protectively it seemed to McCaig, followed them into the kitchen. The woman from the Welfare Centre – the doctor must have brought her in – was grimly setting out biscuits on a plate. McCaig helped himself, then lifted the hot cup. Blair stuffed his notebook into his pocket and edged towards the dresser. McCaig could tell by the expression on the old joker's face that he objected to them using his kitchen as a café : or maybe he thought policemen shouldn't eat while they were on a job : or maybe that they shouldn't have any stomach to eat after poking about a rotten corpse. Well, this would be a lesson to him in the art of professional crime detection.

'I hope your wife's all right,' Ryan was saying, sipping his tea, his saucer held like a gentleman.

'She's highly-strung, you see,' said Lang. 'I thought coming to the country would help her.'

'I'm sure it will,' said Ryan.

'Fat chance now,' said Lang, 'with what's happened. Listen, how long will you be down there in my garden?'

'After the body's gone,' said Ryan amiably, 'we shouldn't be too long.'

'That depends,' said McCaig. 'There's a possibility we might find others.'

'Other what?' said Lang sharply.

'Bodies,' said McCaig. 'We don't know yet that she's the only one buried at the bottom of your garden.' He gulped a burning mouthful, and supped up the residue of the sugar with his tongue. 'Sorry, Mr Lang, but it's a fact you'll just have to face : that bank down there might be thick with them. And we just won't know for sure until we dig.'

'God in Heaven,' said Lang weakly and sat down on the chair Ryan pushed behind him. 'I never thought of that.'

Lang made a point of being at his wife's bedside when she came awake. It was late in the evening now and the promise of a break in the weather had been false. The sky was again

21

clotted with black cloud and rain fell relentlessly on the house and the moor, obscuring the low hills. Lang switched on the bed lamp, trying, for the woman's benefit, to pretend that the sounds of police activity outside were inaudible. He left her momentarily to close the curtains, then returned on tip-toe. She lay on her back still as a wax dummy, with her hair all unkempt and her pupils dopey and disorientated with the dregs of the sedative. She clutched the blankets to her chin, the knuckles almost as white as the washed bone which he could not put from his mind, brittle too. He did not speak, waiting for fear to flood her face and tell him how much of the day's happenings had trickled back into her memory. He did not have to wait long. Her fingers picked at the stitching of the blanket, a start of tears swimming on to her lashes.

'It's all right, Jenny,' he said. 'I'm here.'

'Did they . . .'

'Yes. They've taken it away now.'

'Who was it?'

'I don't know,' he said.

'Was it a child, Norman?'

'I really don't know. Nobody knows yet.'

'Who was she?'

'It's too early for them to tell, Jenny. Try and go back to sleep.'

'I can't.'

'Try.'

'I can't,' she said despairingly.

'Are you hungry?' Lang said.

The violent gesture shocked him, and her hand bit into his wrist with a strength he would not have credited to her, a cruel force. 'Tell me who she was?'

'Nobody knows yet, nobody,' he assured her. She held on to him, dragging herself up on the prop of his arm. Her skin was colourless, not even white now but transparent, her eyes sunken and red. Her spasm of fury was pitiable but Lang could only respond with impatience. 'Lie down,' he said.

'How long has she been out there?' Jenny said.

'Nobody knows I tell you. Lie down.'

She struggled to swing her legs from the bed but he blocked her with his body. 'I want to look,' she was shouting. 'I want to look and see.'

22

'Stay where you are.'

'You don't want me to look,' she snapped. 'Why not?'

'There's nothing to see,' he lied.

'They're there, I can hear them.'

'Just police.'

'I want to see them.'

'*No*.'

'When will they leave us alone?'

'Tomorrow.'

'Promise,' she said.

'I can't exactly promise,' said Lang, 'but . . .'

'Let me up.' She struggled against him. 'I want to see them.'

Lang drew back from the bedside. 'All right, Jenny,' he said. 'If it'll make you happy.'

He whipped back the curtain from the window, then courteously offered her his arm. She ignored him, sliding her haunches over the side of the mattress and planting her thin stick-like ankles and ugly feet on the carpet. Staggering slightly, she crossed to the window and, holding her arms soldier-straight by her sides, examined the dusk outside. Though the corner of the lounge shielded her from a view of the main centres of activity, she could see the shapes of the cars and the round eyes of the lamps. Lang, at her shoulder but not touching her, was astonished to notice a young constable on guard at the kitchen door. Was he being held prisoner in his own house? Anger roared in him. He jerked his fist as if to wave a threat at the burly young man. Then he realised that he was being protected from the newspapermen who hung about the fringes of the lawn like shabby carrion crows. He suddenly found himself able to pick out all the pressmen, for they and they alone were idle. They leaned or stood about, mere shapes in the early dusk, chatting, smoking. One was alone, nearer than the others, hunched inside a pale mackintosh, his bottom resting on the top wire of the fence. He looked wet and miserable but patient, and that patience was horrible for Lang to behold. Even as he watched, another of them climbed stealthily over the fence and stole up the grassy slope, knelt in the wet and raised his camera. They were photographing the house : his house. Then there was another, a third and a fourth, turning, attentive, like animals catching the scent of game. They were all turning round now to stare at the

23

house. Then one of them waved, and he saw that they were waving at her, at Jenny, and with disgust saw her raise her naked arm, the robe slipping down it like loose skin, in response.

'Come away,' he said. 'I told you there was nothing to see.'

'So many of them,' she said. 'I must talk to them.'

'There's plenty of time for that,' he said. 'Anyway, I told them everything. You can't help them.'

'How do you know?' she said. 'How do you know what I can tell them?'

He yanked the curtain chord savagely and dropped the curtain across her. Gripping her elbow he drew her towards the bed. 'I want to talk to them tonight and get it over with,' she said, resisting feebly.

'They'll still be here tomorrow.'

Her voice was crumpling at the edges like a leaf of paper in a hot oven. 'I want to do it *now*.'

'There's no hurry,' he said.

'You won't get rid of them until they talk to me.'

'Yes, yes,' Lang said.

She stopped resisting and sank her knees on the bed, her head lifted as if the thought had entered her between the shoulder blades like an invisible knife. 'It's not them,' she whispered. 'It's her we'll never get rid of.' The instant the weeping broke Lang pulled her round and cradled her head awkwardly against his cardigan. He tried to press her lips against his chest to stop the words coming, but it was no use. 'No, no, no,' she cried. 'We'll never get rid of her now, never, Norman, never, never.'

Soothingly he patted her, but said nothing. Somehow he could not bring himself to deny what she had said.

THREE

Doreen English, unheard of for twenty months, fell into the category of pretty teenagers who annually boosted the long list of persons missing from home. There had been an investigation, of course; the Glasgow C.I.D., prodded by bewildered parents, did every routine thing they could do to trace her whereabouts.

24

The press had shown no interest. Reporters were shrewd enough to anticipate public reaction to such a banal old story; a quick glance over the resumé, and at poor Doreen's photograph, and the average citizen would slyly grin, chalking it up as just another case of teenage wanderlust, or maybe just the lust without the wander at all. Nobody, the police excepted, bothered too much with a missing girl. But hand up a ravaged corpse and public curiosity was instantly aroused, hunger for information inexhaustible.

Inspector Ryan sat at the corner of the long table. He was older than he looked, for his smooth complexion and neatly-trimmed fair hair gave him an appearance of almost childlike naivety. But the stresses of seventeen years of county police work, eight with the C.I.D., and the raising of three kids in off-duty hours, had marked him in subtle ways. He had no store of sarcasm, and his frankness, a tentative quality far removed from the blunt guile of most detectives, puzzled his co-workers in headquarters and would probably hold him at his present rank for the rest of his life. Ryan knew it too, but accepted the situation without rancour : no leopard, he had no spots to change anyway.

All the top brass of the county were at the table, and of the three detectives from Glasgow even the humblest outranked Ryan. McCaig sat at the top, like a chairman at a board meeting. Occasionally he would rise to make a point on the huge map of the county which hung from the wall behind him. The atmosphere in the room was strange; Ryan, who had been through his share of murder cases – pub stabbings, a wife killing, a couple of robberies with fatal violence – could remember nothing like it. The usual air of frantic, super-charged efficiency was missing; yet the calm purposeful tone of the discussion did not quite veil the excitement and anger of the senior men. With death there was always anger, though sometimes it was cloaked in cynical ruefulness, or even sorrow. But often there was excitement too, the tongue-lolling pleasure of the hunt, though every policeman, bred in a tradition of dourness, did his best to disguise it. This was the mainspring of the work, the art which, even when dealing with violent death, bred its own satisfactions. The spur was seldom the thought of ultimate justice, triumphs of deduction, arrest and conviction, but personal, and being personal, never pure.

25

McCaig dryly read the preliminary post-mortem report. It had reached him just after dawn, the two Edinburgh professors having laboured in the tiled chambers of Lannerburn Mortuary throughout the night to prepare it. At a steady two hundred words per minute the Chief read out the forensic analysis and compared it with details in one of the nine folders on his desk. Nine girls between the ages of fourteen and seventeen, nine sets of parents, relatives, friends, nine homes across six counties : months, years of anguished hoping all suddenly brought to the block, false leads and teeter-totter faiths balanced now between the file in McCaig's right hand and the folder in the left. Doreen English : there was no doubt. The dental report clinched it. Doreen English; a person again, baptised by science, the decaying lump of flesh and bones moulded into the shape of a girl with a history and a meaning.

Manual strangulation : positive.

Pregnant : probably negative.

Sexually assaulted : probably not.

Vague – not vague but medically cautious. Every officer in the conference room was shrewd enough to reinterpret the doctors' careful qualifications into clear-cut answers. For the immediate purpose of the investigation, it had to be Yes, or No. To the ordinary policeman the miracle of forensic deduction was no more than an essential act of faith. Even to those who had witnessed the unearthing, there could be no memory of that thing that had come out of the ground. The girl would be created by them, almost like a character in fiction; they'd never known her in life, but would now, in their way, know her better than ever her father had. Ryan tried not to think of the man and the woman in the room, being forced, for their own peace of mind, to identify the object under the cloth. Even handling the clothing, cleaned and pressed but somehow dead too, and, of course, tainted, would be an indescribable ordeal.

Items for identification :

Sheepskin coat – *Missing*.

Handbag – *Missing*.

Black patent leather shoes, size five.

Grey woollen skirt : 'St. Michael's' Brand.

White nylon, ribbed sweater : 'St. Michael's' Brand.

Underclothing : brassiere, white cotton panties, and nylon stockings.

Not much, Ryan thought, for a cold November morning. He fiddled around with the thought and tucked it away; McCaig's voice went on tapping out facts. The parents were on their way from Glasgow, but the body had been clothed and the clothing tallied and it was only a question of making formal identification. Apparently McCaig wasn't going to wait. As far as the boss was concerned, the dead girl was Doreen English.

Ryan opened the stapled folder in front of him and studied the photographs again, while absorbing the gist of McCaig's remarks. Even in plain school uniform no one could mistake her for a child. They certainly grew up fast these days. He wondered if Jean, his own daughter, would be a woman at sixteen; hard to believe looking at her now, just ten years old. Doreen's smile was confident, a bit smug – all three of the shots showed it quite unmistakably – with a glint of a female cunning in the eyes. She obviously knew what make-up was, and how to use it, and the school blouse with its tie discarded and top button open was a pretty potent weapon. Yes, the whole pose was valid and quite consistent with the emerging picture of a girl with secrets, secrets a shade darker than the usual reel of teenage dreams. He could see why Glasgow had perhaps been a wee thing slack, reluctant to take the fond parents' word that Doreen was an angel and would never just *Run Away*. Odd bits of gossip corroborated the theory that she'd gone off of her own free will, whispers from classmates and friends of 'somebody', straight accounts of conversations in which Doreen had confessed herself 'sick of living here'. The pattern of a liaison was contained too in the multitude of answers which the detectives had recorded : the weekly beat club had served Doreen as a cover. 'No, hasn't been here for months', the convenor said; yet, that's where her parents supposed she was every Sunday night. The 'special' girl-friend had loyally provided excuses for lost afternoons, evenings, whole days, when Doreen was off on her own with her 'mysterious stranger.' Well it looked now as if the mysterious stranger had killed her. Certainly the mysterious stranger had to be found. She hadn't run off with him to London, or Manchester or Liverpool. After all, she hadn't dyed her hair, changed her face with powder and paint, sunk into the pool of casual shop-assistants or waitresses or small-firm typists and taken on a whole new 'free'

27

personality under the wing of her anonymous lover. She had never been given the chance. Whoever he was, and whatever he had promised her, he had gained her trust sufficiently to bring to the surface all the innate female skills of deception. That Saturday morning, Doreen's plans were vague; shopping, the pictures in Glasgow, a night at the dancing with the loyal lying chum. That she had arranged to go dancing on Saturday evening meant nothing, except that the mesh of her lie was narrow. McCaig's assessment was scrupulously fair, containing few hypotheses not bedrocked in fact. Doreen English had made opportunities cunningly, deliberately setting out to forestall detection. She had woven her falsehoods so cleverly that even the police could not pick them loose. And the man, assuming it was a man, had never been traced. Would he be now? He would have to be now! Doreen English, born and raised in a good, respectable, lower-middle class home in a suburb of Glasgow, educated by the Corporation and the Church of Scotland Sunday School, had wound up forty miles away as a decomposing corpse, three feet eight inches under the soil of Balnesmoor.

Questions: Ryan noted them down. Had she come here of her own accord; by bus, by car? Had she been brought here alive and killed; killed elsewhere and brought here dead? Why Balnesmoor? Because her lover and probably her killer lived here, or knew the place, or picked the spot at random? Impulse, or premeditation? Motive sex, or the threat of exposure, or the thumbscrew of a demand, or just possibly a panic pregnancy. Maniac, or fool? Did he kill because he loved, or could not love? Was the act of administering death a substitute, or just plain attractive? Take your pick! Ryan watched McCaig shift his arm slowly and slide another folder from the left-hand pile. He knew what was coming, knew what was on McCaig's mind and was surprised that the Chief had the nerve to throw it in to the midst of all these experts. Another one.

'This is the file of another missing girl, Anna Ewart', said McCaig. 'Same age to within a month, approximately the same basic pattern. She went missing from home in March of last year, fourteen months ago, again on a Saturday morning. She hasn't been traced. And she lived in Craigiemill too; yes, the same district, fifteen minutes' walk from Doreen's house.'

28

'We didn't miss that trick, you know,' said the Chief from Glasgow. 'We moved on that one.'

Saw it in the papers, thought Ryan, but all played down. If the girls had been three years younger they'd have carved themselves headlines three inches thick. Man trouble again.

'Nothing doing,' the Glasgow Chief went on. 'The Ewart girl had already broadcast the fact that she was ready to chuck it all up and head for London. She even admitted she'd a boyfriend.'

'But didn't give details?' asked McCaig.

The Glasgow detective shook his head. 'Nary a word.'

'Young or old, they know how to keep their mouths shut when it suits them,' McCaig said.

'You think she's up there too sir?' asked Inspector Sellars, a county man.

'I think she might be.'

'Any others?' Glasgow asked.

McCaig shrugged. 'It's too early to say. The other files don't relate to the schedule of facts. The similarity between Doreen and this other one,' he wagged the second folder, 'this Anna Ewart, are just too damned close for comfort.'

'You want to dig?' the Chief Constable enquired.

'Yes.'

'We'll be howking up the area anyway,' the Chief Constable said. He looked weary even at the thought, as if he would be handling a spade himself. 'So we might as well seize the chance.'

'Fine', said McCaig.

Ryan noticed how he had taken over, as was his due, the organisation of the operation, using his territorial advantage to display to these upper echelon officers his whole bag of tricks.

'Now, it's the man we want, the mystery man that we *think* Doreen was seeing on the sly.' said McCaig. 'If you, Bill, handle the Glasgow end of it, since you've been on the case already, we'll undertake the county.'

'It may not be Glasgow *or* Lannerburn,' said the Glasgow Superintendent.

'Looks like it though,' the Chief Constable said.

Ryan felt himself nodding, face down, in agreement. It did look like it, especially if McCaig's theory about the second body proved true. But, my God, Balnesmoor was a hell of a big place,

29

and there wasn't nearly enough evidence to support the scant supposition that the lover, the killer, had struck twice, let alone used the same dumping ground for his pair of corpses. A rarity indeed, a blue moon day – McCaig playing on a long shot. There were two ends to the case, the pick-up point in the Craigiemill suburb, and the grave here in the county. But hundreds of thousands of acres of Scotland's rough country, quiet country, were convenient to a car. Why Balnesmoor particularly, and, if Anna Ewart really was victim number two, why necessarily Balnesmoor the second time too? Ryan sighed, loudly enough to draw a cold glance from McCaig.

Five minutes later the Supers and the Chiefs moved into the Operations Room to work out details of the deployment of police and auxiliary helpers. McCaig lingered behind.

'Don't agree with me?' he asked Ryan. Sellars stood by awaiting instructions too, his eyes bland, not looking at anything. 'Come on, tell me you don't agree.'

'No, I do agree,' said Ryan without meekness. 'But it's a bit far to go yet.'

'Maybe,' said McCaig. 'From you, Inspector, I'd like the report from the farmer, Johnstone, then you can delegate Blair to the other houses in the immediate area of the moor, and get down to Galbraith and find out about the previous occupants of that house. A handy place, that house, to do the dirty in, hm?'

'What about Doreen's parents?'

'Yes,' said McCaig, glancing at his watch. 'Sellars, you'd better dash down to the Mortuary right away, and see them through. It should be just a formality.'

'Yes, Chief,' Sellars said. Then, as McCaig hurried out of the conference room, muttered under his breath 'some bloody formality.'

'I'm glad it's not me', said Ryan.

Sellars wrinkled his lip. 'He wouldn't send you', he said.

'Why not?'

'You've got kids of your own.'

'I've done it before, often,' said Ryan.

'One like this?'

'No,' Ryan admitted. 'Not ever one like this.'

'Then be thankful it's me', said Sellars.

Plucking his raincoat from the rack, he went out. He had the

30

hang-dog reluctant slouch of a man who knows that in the next hour he will suffer emotions which are too raw to be soothed by professional objectivity. Ryan was glad he'd been allotted the farm – damned glad.

The tang of new cheese wormed its way through the heart-shaped holes in the corner cupboard and permeated the whole kitchen. Like most farmhouse smells it was just a shade too strong to be appetising. Even the woman had an odour about her, but that particular niff didn't make Ryan purse his lips in distaste; it was sexual, the natural perfume of a female, warm. He could almost feel the warmth coming off her, from under the thick dressing gown. Some farmer's wife who still trotted about at ten-fifteen in a dressing gown! Her hair was long, flowing in a chestnut haze over her strong shoulders. She had the build of a farm lass all right, but none of the thick, dowdy ruddiness which the erosion of hard manual work about the house and yard usually imparted. The kitchen was straight traditional, the real thing, kail-yard without romance. There were none of the modern appurtenances which almost every other mains in the county boasted. By the look of it Johnstone's wife was still obliged to do her cooking over the open fire. No, there was a small Calor Gas stove over by the sinks. The length of threadbare carpet on the stone-flagged floor flapped in the draught from under the door. In the winter it must be freezing. How did they keep warm? In bed! That woman in a double bed would keep any man warm. The magnificent body and beautiful hair placed her apart and added a sinister note as if Johnstone had maybe abducted her from some lord's hall and was keeping her in the mains against her will, a prisoner. Her features were large, regular and handsome, and the eyes, for a person of her reddish colouring, very dark. Impish too, they chimed with the sensual manner she had of holding herself and the frank look she gave him, almost appraising. She stood by the table, arms folded, the dressing gown not quite held together by the sash so that he could see the line of the cotton nightgown where her thighs pushed it out. She must have just got up. Maybe that was what Johnstone had at midmorning instead of toast and tea – lucky devil. Ryan tried not to stare at her too obviously and concentrated with great seriousness on the man in the chair opposite. The attraction of the wife

31

somehow put him at a disadvantage with the husband, and he steeled himself to bully a bit, more McCaig's style of questioning than his own. Johnstone was a figure to match the scene, big and tough, whetted down by the labour and the climate. Yet he seemed quick enough in the wits and rapped out answers to most of Ryan's questions without hesitation.

'How did the fire start?' Ryan asked.

'He was burnin' rubbish,' said Johnstone, 'an' the wind stole up an' spread the sparks. He had it near out when I got there. Stupid bastard could've fired the whole place.'

'Do you know the Langs well?'

'He keeps himsel' t' himsel', and so d'we for that matter. They never come down this length.' said Johnstone.

'Do you go down the track much, past his house?'

'Seldom.'

'How about you, Mrs Johnstone?' Ryan asked.

The woman shifted a little closer to her husband, but the movement was not defensive. Johnstone crossed his knees. He was just in from the byre, in a denim shirt with a pair of broad ex-army braces supporting his stained flannels, the boots caked with rich brown flecks of dung, straw-ticked.

'I've no need to go that way,' the woman replied.

'You don't think Lang deliberately fired that bush?' Ryan said.

'For what, b'Christ?' said Johnstone.

'He may have been thinking of clearing the bank.'

'Ach never,' said Johnstone. 'It was an accident – carelessness.'

'Dairy cattle you're on here, is it?' Ryan asked next.

'Ay, it is.'

'Who uses the access path?'

'Trampers, trippers, townie riff-raff,' said Johnstone. 'It's too rough t'be popular though.'

'Schools?'

'Only twice, yet, said Johnstone. 'They never came in the yard though. I never spoke t'any of them. Did you, Edna?'

The woman shook her head.

'Who had the house before Mr Lang?' said Ryan, maintaining his policy of switching topics.

'The Herrons – man, wife, two bairns, girl 'n' boy.'

'Did you know them at all?'

32

The woman replied. 'Well enough. She'd come over for her milk and butter and an egg or two at times. The kids liked the animals.'

'And before the Herrons?'

The woman paused; it seemed to Ryan that she would have preferred her husband to answer, that at the moment she avoided turning her eyes down to him only by an effort of will. The impression was vague, but he took note of it. Sergeant Blair, Ryan had almost forgotten about him for he sat behind the Inspector, cleared his throat. The wife started. 'The Coopers,' she said. 'They used it only at weekends, a country place for them.'

'Cooper,' said Johnstone with undisguised bitterness, 'was stinkin' rich. He only came out here an' bought the place so's he could give his wild parties without anyone bothering about the noise. They'd run them bloody parties through from Friday night 'til Sunday. Christ, when the wind was in the east we could hear them singin' and laughin' an' birlin' away like a bloody coven.'

'That kind,' said Ryan, nodding : the outskirts of Lanner-burn was peppered with them, absent owners, weekenders.

'D'y'know that the woman would stot about the garden in her scud,' said Johnstone. Sweetie-wife, thought Ryan, you enjoy having something to tattle about. Gossip seemed indecent coming from such a big man. 'Bare ! Once they all did it; bare as bloody babies.'

Ryan could imagine that scene too, the long garden with its coiffured lawn, the airbeds and probably gross, middle-ageing naked bodies stark white in the sun, giggling and daring but turned modestly belly down. 'Cars lined up all the way to the main road. I never knew,' said Johnstone, ambiguously, 'where they all slept.' *Nouveau riche*, Ryan expected, who'd probably built the house as a gimmick with some of the excess cash from a lucky, or shady, transaction. Probably the weather hadn't suited their idea of fun. He'd have to track them down, of course, for questioning. Where would they be now? Sunning it in one of those cheap villas in Spain possibly.

'You weren't asked over to any of these parties?' he enquired.

'No,' said Edna Johnstone promptly.

'You were never in the house?'

33

'What would the likes of me be doin' consortin' with the likes of the Coopers?' said Johnstone.

'How about you, Mrs Johnstone?' Ryan asked.

Yes, he'd been right; there was something uneasy here, as if a couple of his last questions had touched a nerve.

'Mrs Johnstone?'

'No, not me either,' she said.

But the husband's response hinted that she was lying; Ryan had the feeling that she was lying under the man's prompting. The more he thought about it, the more sure he became that he had stumbled across one of those secrets which bloom inside marriage like weeds in a hothouse. He hesitated, wondered if he should go on tweaking away at this point, or switch to a new tack. They were going sullen on him, both of them. She tugged the gown tighter around her. Her breasts were opulent. Even Blair was conscious of them, slightly embarrassed, twisting the pencil in his fingers, broodingly. Ryan cleared his throat. 'Did any of the Coopers' friends spill over on to the moor?'

'Sometimes,' said Johnstone. He wanted to be unco-operative but the tale was too good. He burst out, 'Ay, there was one, a grown man an' all, used t'fly a kite up there.'

'Really!' said Ryan, holding in a smile. He glanced at the Sergeant, but the comic image did not seem to impress Blair at all. Ryan recalled the times last autumn when he had pranced across the field behind his bungalow twitching the string of the home-made box kite which his children, with surprisingly little prodding, had got him to make for them. The billow of the wind in his hand, the slough and swoop of it, the liveliness amused him too. Still, he wasn't being eccentric, he had fatherhood as an excuse for enjoying himself.

'Any idea who the guests were?' said Ryan.

'Why should we?' snapped Johnstone.

'I thought they might be local.'

A fairly lengthy pause, and Johnstone said, 'No. Never knew any of them.'

The idea stirred in his mind, like a hedgehog turning under its winter leaves. Maybe the carefully disguised animosity between the Johnstones had something to do with the Coopers, or one of their guests. Edna Johnstone was a handsome piece, and, unless he had wrongly interpreted the look in her eye,

34

fond of company. On the other hand, she may have rebuffed all advances from the wolves at Cooper's parties, but done so with such reluctance that her husband's jealous nature had been pricked anyway. Something like that. Conjecture! Just what connection the Johnstones' domestic trials and tiny defensive intrigues had to do with Doreen English, Ryan could not for the life of him imagine. Perhaps he should have been a private dick after all – McCaig had flung out that insult once – he seemed to have an unfortunate knack for rooting out the grubby junk of personal relationships. Really they were impossible to avoid, those small deceptions. Sometimes though one would lead to another in a casual chain which, in conjunction with the ticking of the police machine, would direct them to a vital piece of information – the link between a killer and his victim, perhaps. Fragments, Ryan told himself, just crazy little bits and pieces; nothing to get excited about. Yet, he knew the woman was lying. He challenged her directly. 'Did you know any of the guests, Mrs Johnstone?'

'No.' Quite emphatic. Too emphatic. 'No, I never.'

'Thank you,' said Ryan.

Slightly puzzled by the sudden end to the interview, Blair got to his feet.

'Is that all y'want t'know?' said Johnstone.

'For the moment, thank you,' Ryan told him.

He worked the latch and pulled the door open. The wind hurtled wetly against him, buffeting his coat against his thighs. Even Johnstone shivered and cupped his big fists over his shoulders. Ryan let Blair go out into the yard, then turned and peered back into the kitchen. Edna Johnstone, the gown flapping wide and loose, swung round from the mantelshelf, a cigarette on its way to her mouth.

'What did you say Cooper's first name was?' Ryan called amiably.

'Jack,' said the woman, then bit her lip.

'Thank you,' said Ryan politely. He went out, closing the door carefully behind him.

Bullying gusts of wind pushed the Hillman about, and Ryan was relieved that Blair was along to do the driving. He had never learned to feel comfortable behind a wheel, and on a day like this the back road from Balnesmoor to Thane was too exposed for comfort. The strip of tarmac ahead of them was

35

like a black river, fringed by pale spikes of dried winter grass
on both verges. A hare, still streaked with its snow-coat, shot
across in front of them. Blair sat forward, the gleam of the
hunter in his eye.

'Big one,' he said.

Surface water hissed under the tyres and the wipers strained
to keep the windscreen clear. Ryan sat low in the front seat,
smoking a cigarette. He did not see the animal's dash.

'She was that,' he said.

Blair glanced at his passenger, frowning. Ryan went on, 'I'll
bet she's a hell of a handful though.'

'What?'

'Johnstone's wife.'

Blair laughed, and shook his head. 'Ay,' he said. 'I'll bet she
is.'

'There's not many like her in the county.'

'Maybe it's as well,' said the Sergeant, still chuckling.

FOUR

'Yes,' said Galbraith jovially. 'The house, that's a marvellous
bit of deductive reasoning. Very conveniently situated for
hanky-panky. None of my clients did it though, I'll tell you
that.'

The estate agent wore a rich, dark tweed suit, thrown wide
across the jacket to show off his shirt front which was a very
pale pink. His maroon tie had minute red foetuses worked in to
it and the knot was big and generous, elbowing the buttons of
the collar. Galbraith, in complete possession of the office,
sprawled back in his chair, brown well-polished shoes balanced
on the rim of the metal wastebox, restlessly tipping it about
without ever letting it topple over.

'Do you know where the former owners are now?' said
Ryan.

'Of course, of course,' said Galbraith. He grinned and
pushed a king-size filter into his teeth. 'If you want to hide out,
never fall into the hands of a good estate agent, that's my
advice.'

Not yet thirty, in spite of the makings of a bow-window belly and thinning hair, Galbraith gave the impression of being a man on top of the world. Ryan had long since given up envying his kind, the kind who had everything, health, youth, money, security, and responsibilities to nobody but themselves. Galbraith had the proper upbringing at the best schools in the county, and was probably highly successful with women – or men, as the case may be. The business had dropped right into his lap, readymade; about the only readymade thing Galbraith had ever owned in his life. When the old man – only sixty-one – dropped down with his mandatory coronary off the fifth tee of the Radleigh main course and died before his caddy could even get the umbrella up over him, Galbraith, at twenty-four, had inherited the lot, except for his step-brother's legal portion. All this Ryan remembered quite well from accounts in the local paper and from general chat about the county. The step-brother, never a county man in any sense of the word, probably had some stake in the agency but by that time he was already set up in the whisky business and obviously didn't give a damn about the housing trade. In spite of dour prophecies from neglected relatives that he was too brash and inexperienced to make a go of running the concern, young Galbraith had contrived to prosper. He was brimful of confidence, carefree and, after a fashion, charming, but these qualities grated on Ryan like a chalk on slate that wet afternoon. The faint flush on the agent's cheeks was probably the result of too much booze, and it gave Ryan some satisfaction to envisage the eventual nemesis of a rotting liver lying in store for him in the not too distant future.

'I hope,' Galbraith was saying, 'you'll try not to make *too* much fuss around the place. I'd hate the tone of the district brought down just when I've started selling the idea that it's a weary business-man's paradise.'

A venomous retort burned on Ryan's tongue but he held it tactfully back. 'I just want details about the property, Mr Galbraith, if you'd be so good.'

'The old ranch, hm?' said Galbraith. 'Fair enough, I suppose. All right then,' He consulted a sheet of paper on his desk.

'Seems you expected us?' said Ryan.

'I'm not daft, you know,' said Galbraith with a grin. 'Ready?' Blair nodded and Galbraith read off the words on the

37

sheet. 'My father owned the land. He put the house up in the winter of 1960/61. Architects were Ross & McFadzean of Edinburgh, builders Logie of Lannerburn whose premises are five doors down from here.'

'Yes, I know,' said Ryan.

'Of course, you're a local man,' said Galbraith. 'I forgot. Anyhow, we offered the property for sale through the usual channels, asking seven-and-one-half thousand pounds, in May, 1961, the beginning of the month. And it was purchased shortly after by Mr Jack Cooper at the stipulated price.'

'You built the house first, then sold it?' asked Blair. 'Is that not a bit unusual?'

'Very sharp, Sergeant,' said Galbraith. 'Sure, it's not considered good practice to build then sell, not with single properties. Different with estate work, but that's another story.'

'Was there a reason for building then, somebody who backed out, or what?' Ryan asked.

'Yes,' said Galbraith. He lifted his brows with silly apology. 'Me.'

'Can you explain what you mean, please?' said Ryan.

'The old man put the place up for his beloved son, me, I mean, because he was hoping I'd get myself married to this young lady I was ... affianced to at the time. He liked her, my old man did, very much. In fact, just between us three, he picked her out for me. But ...' Galbraith spread his hands helplessly as if the broken engagement had been an act of God and not deliberate choice. 'I chickened out at the last minute.'

'I see,' said Ryan.

'Yes, I was too young to marry,' said Galbraith. 'Now I'm too wise.'

'You got the money from the sale, though?' asked Blair, pretending to scrutinise his notes as he spoke.

Some of the humour went out of the agent's face and he answered curtly. 'That's right.'

'Your father ... didn't object?' asked Ryan.

'He gave me the damn' place,' said Galbraith. 'It was mine to sell.'

Ryan nodded, and watched Blair reduce the conversation to a shortform or two.

'Tell me about Cooper?'

'Well, he wasn't short of money,' said Galbraith, 'that's for sure. He carried out a lot of rather expensive improvements on the place, hired a gardener and that sort of thing. Of course, he was working a fiddle with the mortgage, bringing in some tax relief he probably wasn't entitled to. I don't know much about it.'

'How did he make his money?'

'Heating; crashed in on the central heating boom. He tried to talk me into giving him contracts for some of our business in that line, but, of course, I didn't.'

'Why do you say "of course"?' Ryan asked.

'We were all tied up with Innes, across the Square; still are for that matter. I believe in trading with local firms wherever possible.'

Ryan knew why too. Galbraith was the big man in the county pool and he could crack the whip over the small contractors in Lannerburn in the matter of prices and contract dates. Perhaps he even owned a part of Innes's. Ryan didn't ask though, but pushed on with his inquiries about Jack Cooper. 'I'm told the Balnesmoor house was only a weekend place for him?'

'Sure,' Galbraith agreed. 'A place to impress his friends with, and in. Once you have three "tellys" and two cars the next step is either a power-boat or a country house. Cooper preferred the country house thing.'

'He lives in Glasgow, doesn't he?'

'Yes, that's where his offices are.'

'Were you ever at one of his parties?' said Ryan.

'Just one,' said Galbraith, mulling over the recollection. 'It wasn't my style really. In fact, it was pretty hairy.'

'Pretty . . . hairy?' asked Ryan.

'Oh, you know,' Galbraith explained, 'too many jumped-up gentry, bookies and bar-owners, and that sort of thing, none of them really in my age-group.'

'You like them younger?'

'Sure,' said Galbraith with great frankness. 'I like them fresh. But don't put me down as a chap's hungers after schoolgirls. I like them fresh, but I like them with bumps on, if you see what I mean.'

'What can you tell me about the kind of people who went to his parties?'

'Nothing. It is all of six years ago, remember,' said Galbraith.

39

'I was but a callow youth in those days, and not terribly observant.'

'How long did Cooper have the house?'

'Almost three years.'

'And his reason for selling?'

'Profit,' said Galbraith. 'He couldn't resist grabbing a nice fat profit. The cost of good property has doubled in the last few years, and Cooper saw the chance of making a tidy little bundle by selling. He could have hung on, but I think he was frightened that prices would stop rising.' Galbraith shook his head. 'He should have known better. My God, the spiral still shows no sign of tailing off.'

'How much profit did he make?'

'I'm not sure I should divulge that kind of information,' said Galbraith coyly. Ryan waited, saying nothing and finally Galbraith told him, 'Well, I suppose you're police and could get it out of me anyway if you really wanted it – a couple of thousand. He could have made more if he'd hung on.'

'Do you know where Cooper lives now?'

Galbraith lifted a sheet of foolscap and passed it on to Ryan. 'I thought you'd want to know that. Beat you to it. It's all there in black-and-white.' Ryan folded the paper without looking at it and slipped it into his breast pocket. 'It's Glasgow,' Galbraith continued. 'But he has another nice little place – not so little come to think of it – up in Lochbury, a cottage this time. Bought it for an old song about two years ago. He must like the county.'

'Why did he sell one to buy another?'

'I'm only theorising now,' said Galbraith, 'but he probably needed some solid capital to help him expand at the time he sold the Balnesmoor place; then when the crisis was over he picked up the Lochbury cottage. It's a shrewd move, because it's bigger and has secluded grounds, about half an acre. It probably gave him plenty of scope for shaping it up as he wanted and making the government foot the bill. They're up to all the dodges these days, chaps like Jack Cooper.' And you too, son, thought Ryan.

'Now about the Herrons?' he said.

'Family group of four – large mortgage. Herron was with the B.B.C. in Glasgow at the time, but he gave that up and struck out on his own, writing or something. I really don't know much

40

about them. Anyway, he was only in the house for a couple of years, then he sold it off again and moved back to Glasgow. He said it was for the childrens' education but personally I think he just bit off more than he could chew and had to give the place up for financial reasons.'

'Where are they now?'

'The last address I had for him is on the sheet,' said Galbraith.

'Lang?'

'Well, you've met him,' said Galbraith. For a moment Ryan thought the agent had said it all, but he continued, 'He moaned on about the price of the house, and argued about the cost of fittings and repairs with Herron, mostly through me, but he wanted it, wanted it very badly I should say. I advised Herron to stick to his guns and we got what we asked for it in the long run. Herron didn't do too badly out of it.'

'Inflationary spiral,' Ryan suggested.

'Sure.'

'Thank you,' said Ryan, and got to his feet.

Galbraith got up too. 'Going, are you? I'm disappointed. I thought you'd be bound to ask me where I was on the night of November twentieth.'

'November twentieth,' said Ryan. 'Why?'

'That's when the girl went missing.'

'Was it?' said Ryan.

Galbraith clucked his tongue against his teeth, and lifted a newspaper from the bundle on a chair by his desk. 'Don't you lot keep in touch? Look, it's headlines.'

Ryan glanced at the black heading, and the photographs. Galbraith held the paper against the light from the window. 'Was she really as gorgeous as that?' he asked.

'I only saw her dead,' said Ryan, 'and she wasn't pretty at all.'

Galbraith shuddered theatrically. 'Gruesome.'

Ryan took the paper from Galbraith's hand and stared more closely at the front page, then he folded it and held it up. 'Mind if I keep it?'

'Be my guest,' said Galbraith. 'Plenty more where that came from.'

Behind the serving hatch of the headquarters' canteen Moira appeared. Rubicund with ill-temper, she slammed down the

41

plates of pie and beans. She had flat features, stone-grey hair, and resented the operation which had caught her unprepared.

'You're not being over-generous with the beans today, lass,' Blair said.

Ryan pushed off discreetly before the cook could sear his eardrums with her reply. The small room was thick with smoke and the mutter of male voices, the clatter of cutlery and cups. He wished he had accepted Sandy's suggestion that they make a quick snack in the Lannerburn café. But he still had the ridiculous leftover guilt of a young constable that one of his superiors would nab him pinching a break during duty hours. He slid his tray on to the table under Sellar's nose. The Inspector glanced up and pulled his cup back to make room for Ryan and Blair. Blair was grinning, ruefully shaking his head at the roasting old Moira had given him, but when he looked down at Sellars his smile vanished. Busily, Ryan cleared the tin tray of dishes and propped it down by his shin. He arranged the meal, poured sauce on the pie and cut through it. Sellars watched the forkful of meat come up and into Ryan's mouth.

'They made positive identification,' he said.

'Been a poor do for McCaig if they hadn't,' said Blair, carving up the brittle pie crust.

'Bad, was it?' asked Ryan, food in his cheek.

'Pretty bad,' said Sellars. He lit one cigarette from the stump of the one before, and inhaled. 'Where were you?'

'Johnstone's farm.'

'And?'

'He wouldn't confess,' said Ryan. 'Ever met his wife?'

Sellars almost managed to leer, but it came out lopsided and unconvincing. 'I've seen her once or twice.'

'And not at the Women's Guild either, I'll bet,' said Blair.

'She was at the cattle show in Glenbuck last year,' said Sellars.

'Did she win anything?' Blair asked.

'She's got the build for it right enough,' said Sellars.

'Any of your dirty stories about her?' said Ryan.

Sellars, sipping his tea, culled his store of obscene tales. 'Nup,' he said at last. 'But I could easy invent some if it's stimulation you're after.'

'I could do that for myself,' said Ryan.

'*You!*' said Sellars. 'You've been married so long you've forgotten what ...'

'All right, all right,' said Ryan quickly. 'I meant I'm interested in them both. They're a funny pair.'

'All farmers are funny,' said Sellars, whose father and two brothers happened to be dairymen. 'It's all that animal husbandry as does it.'

For several minutes the men ate in silence, and the tension which the cross-talk had eased from Sellars brow returned. His eyes had a hollowness, distant, and he pinched and worried the tip of his cigarette with his teeth. He was dark and swarthy, almost simian, several years younger than Ryan and not long made up from Detective-Sergeant. Behind him he carried the full weight of training at the best police college in the country, but the lapses between the academic theory of crime and reality still caught him wrong-footed at times.

'Are we off to Glasgow then?' said Blair, pushing his plate away.

'Why not?' said Ryan. 'I'd rather do them on my own than shove more than we have to over to Glasgow Branch.'

'Who're you after?' asked Sellars.

'The house owners, character called Cooper and a family, Herron. They were the ones in residence when the girl got the chop.'

'I remember Cooper,' said Sellars. 'He's got a place up in Lochbury now.'

'That's him,' said Ryan. 'I don't suppose you were one of his weekend nudists.'

'Oh, ay, I heard about that,' said Sellars. 'Orgies of freckled flesh. Put Johnstone's cows off the milk, did it?'

'I don't know about the cows but it didn't help Johnstone's blood pressure any,' said Ryan. 'I'll be interested to meet Cooper.'

'Will you?' said Sellars. 'As a student of life, or because?'

'Because,' said Ryan.

'You won't find many madmen in his class,' said Sellars. 'If they kill anyone it's for profit.'

'Come on now,' said Ryan. 'You can't dazzle me with your generalisations.'

'I suppose I shouldn't,' said Sellars. 'But if you ask me this is one of those psycho jobs, and he'll be bloody hard to find.'

43

'It's too soon to tell anyway,' said Ryan. 'What time is it?'

'Two o'clock, five past,' said Blair.

'Where's McCaig?'

'Up with the diggers,' said Sellars. 'Where I'll be in ten minutes.'

'Do you think McCaig's making an arse of himself?' Blair said.

Sellars shook his head. 'Nup. I think he's right.'

'And there's another one up there?' asked Ryan.

'Somewhere underground,' said Sellars, 'But I doubt if we'll find her.'

'Unless McCaig gets lucky,' said Ryan.

'Mind you,' said Blair, 'he's not often wrong.'

'Unfortunately,' said Sellars, 'but I hope he is this time. I hope to God he is.'

FIVE

The Herrons now lived in a new block of flats tucked discreetly amid the mansions of Glasgow's south side. It was almost four o'clock before Blair and Ryan reached the building, but luckily Herron, a freelance journalist and scriptwriter, was at home, and Ryan was able to question husband and wife together. Though their concern and eagerness to help were genuine, the Herrons gave Ryan no new information, merely corroborating statements already made by Galbraith, Lang and the Johnstones. Herron was quite frank about his reasons for leaving Balnesmoor; Galbraith's guess was right, money had been the problem. If Ryan had hoped that one of the Herrons might have noticed something on the track or the moor which would constitute a lead, then he was disappointed. He left the flat before five to drive across Glasgow to Cooper's city address.

The close leading to Cooper's flat was a great echoing Victorian vault with yellowing tiles and curving brass-studded banisters. The residence showed its class in the stained glass windows which tinted the light on each landing. Until he had shown his credentials and explained the exact purpose of his call, Mrs Cooper kept him on the door mat. Finally satisfied that he was a real policeman, the woman admitted him, Blair following, into the house. The vast lounge was fitted with expensive but tasteless furniture. A blazing cocktail cabinet, spindly lamps with embroidered shades, a cluster of grape-like bulbs in a ceiling fixture gave the effect of almost blinding brightness. Over the fireplace – glossy brown unconvincing plastic logs above three electric bars – hung a huge spit-and-toothpaste painting, only a shade flatter than the image on the T.V. screen which flickered soundlessly in a corner. Madge Cooper struck Ryan as only an extension of the room : bright and vulgar too, pneumatic breasts accentuated by a tight black dress under which her roll-on made noticeable ridges on her plump thighs. Her features were pretty, china-doll-like, but the mask of cosmetic preparations gave the impression of grime. Here, thought Ryan, was a woman who hadn't quite caught up with her hubby's aspirations, doomed to chase not just the chimera of respectability but the faster hares of breeding and station. In trim hipsters, blue wool shirt and crimson slippers, Jack Cooper leapt up to greet them.

'Can't say I haven't been expecting you.' He pumped Ryan's hand. 'Sit down, sit down. Drink?'

'No thanks.'

'On duty, eh?' said Cooper. He was small, rotund, with thick lips and bushy grey hair. In spite of youthful gear he must have been pushing fifty, his vigour probably for show. His eyes had a glaucous glint and his tan was dry and tended to yellow down the jowls. Spectacles sat on top of the *T.V. Times* on a table by his armchair.

'It's about that place we had up in Balnesmoor, right?'

'Yes,' said Ryan.

'Sit down, sit down the both of you,' Cooper urged while his wife clinked bottle to glass in the altar of the cabinet. The overstuffed sofa clutched at the detectives' haunches like the soft petals of a carnivorous plant.

'Comfortable, eh?' said Cooper.

Ryan and Blair nodded in unison, holding themselves awkwardly upright with their elbows.

'I suppose young Galbraith turned up my address?' said Cooper. 'You'll not have my name on your wanted list?'

'You never know, Jack,' said Mrs Cooper, laughing asthmatically.

45

'We'd like you to answer a few questions, if you will,' said Ryan.

'Fire away,' said Cooper.

Ryan led the Coopers through the dates of purchase of the Balnesmoor property, and the batch of questions which had become standard in the case. They answered him long-windedly, referring each to the other throughout, conferring and confirming, Ryan imagined, almost like a couple of fly-boys taking the micky out of a beat constable. The act was well rehearsed, but not comic; it dawned on him only gradually, settling his ire, that it was not a put-on for his benefit but the manner in which the couple always conversed. Both Cooper and his wife were drinking. She propped on the arm of her husband's chair holding his arm around her waist with one hand, the glass in the other. To denote caution and deep thinking each had a single individual mannerism – the woman batting her eyelashes, the man thrusting out his under lip. At long last Ryan got them round to talking about the parties.

'Ay, we had some rare times' said Cooper, shaking his head wistfully. 'Didn't we, Madge.'

'Terrific,' said Madge. 'It's the place, the country.'

'Got a better hideaway now, of course,' Cooper went on, 'up in Lochbury : bigger, more guests can stay over. The ranch was just that bit too cramped, wasn't it, Madge. I'm a man's likes to have a few spare beds to shake down any of his guests who have a bit too much to drink. Am'n't I, Madge?'

The woman arched her plucked brows in grotesque agreement. 'Still, we did all right out of the sale,' Cooper continued. 'He's bloody good at his job, Galbraith, damn good. He'd tell you about me, I suppose?'

'That's right,' said Ryan. 'Did you have many ... guests at these weekends?'

'In my business you make a lot of friends. Anyway, we're the mixing kind, Madge and me, aren't we dear?' said Cooper. 'It's heating I'm in. You'll've heard of the firm?'

'What sort of people attended your parties?' asked Ryan. 'Did you know them all personally, or were there many of the "friend of a friend" kind?'

'See what y'mean,' said Cooper. 'See what y'mean. No, we knew them all, with maybe one'r two exceptions now and again.'

46

'Any local people?'

'What, Balnesmoor? No,' said Cooper.

'From anywhere in the county?'

'Well – Galbraith,' said Cooper. He took his arm from around his wife and cupped his cocktail glass in both hands. 'Galbraith was the only one. Listen, inspector, what're you driving at?'

'It's his job, Jack, just his job,' the woman said.

'All right, Mr Cooper,' said Ryan. 'I'll be frank. I'd like to know just how well you knew the people who used your house at weekends. Whether any of them might . . .'

'Here, here,' said Cooper, 'that's a bit nasty, isn't it?'

'. . . any of them might have brought along a girl without your being aware of it.'

'Not a chance,' said Cooper. 'Anyway, it's mostly an older crowd we hang about with. We're not a pair of old fogies, mind, but my friends are about our age, most of them.'

'Young at heart,' added Mrs Cooper.

'You didn't invite the neighbours over?'

'What neighbours?' said Cooper.

'The Johnstones, for instance?'

'Farmers!' said Cooper; that was Ryan's answer.

'Are you quite sure you'd recognise everyone who spent a weekend or even a day, out at your place?' Ryan persisted.

'You mean the dead girl?' said Cooper, gravely. 'She was never in my house.'

'I've some photographs here . . .' Ryan began, but Cooper cut him short.

'Saw them in the newspaper,' he said. 'That's the first time I ever laid eyes on her, definitely.'

'Yes,' said Ryan, 'but the press copy wasn't up to much. These are much clearer : perhaps . . .'

'I'll look at them,' Mrs Cooper announced, reaching out for the manilla envelope on Blair's knee. Ryan removed the blown-up shots from the stiffener and passed them to the woman. She hesitated. 'They're not . . .?'

'They're from the family,' Ryan explained.

'Poor bastards,' said Cooper, sitting back.

The woman took each card by a corner and examined it. Ryan studied her reactions, hoping for some tell-tale sign of recognition. Though Mrs. Cooper's expression registered several

47

concurrent emotions none of them tallied with guilt or surprise. She handed the photographs across to her husband, who sat them on his knee, put on his spectacles, cocked his head, and leafed through the thin sheaf. 'Looks a lot older than sixteen to me,' he remarked. 'Doesn't she, dear?'

'A pretty wee thing though,' said Mrs Cooper. Ryan thought he detected tears in her eyes, but she rubbed her lids with her thumbs before he could be sure. He waited until the couple returned the photographs, then asked, 'Did you ever see her before?'

'Positively not,' said Cooper.

'Mrs Cooper?'

'No, I never did,' she said. 'But I hope you catch the swine that done it. Hanging's too good for him.'

'Now,' said Ryan patiently, 'I wonder if you can supply me with the names of your visitors.'

'What for?' asked Cooper suspiciously.

'In case they saw anything ... untoward, while staying with you in Balnesmoor,' Ryan explained.

'Have you got t'go bothering them?' Cooper said.

'I'm afraid so.'

'It's a tall order,' Cooper said. 'What can we do about that now, Madge?'

'I could ...' said the woman. Cooper thought over her unfinished proposal, then gave his sanction with a curt nod. She slipped off the chair and crossed to an antique bureau which dressed an odd corner by the window. With frank curiosity Ryan and Blair turned to watch her. She opened an inside drawer, brought out a thick, leather-bound book and carried it over to the hearth.

'Three years's a long time,' said Cooper as his wife gave him the book. He riffled the pages thoughtfully. 'I suppose a lot of them'll have moved. Still.' With a decisive gesture he tossed the book into Ryan's lap. 'They're all listed in that, most of them who came up.' Ryan greedily closed his hand on the volume.

'Lucky for you I send a lot of Christmas cards,' said Mrs Cooper. 'I hope it's some use to you, but I have my doubts.'

'We'll see,' said Ryan. 'I'll let you have it back as soon as possible.'

'We only had respectable folk at our house,' the woman said.

'I expect it's one of those sex maniacs you're after, some spoiled wee laddie running wild.'

'The system's at fault,' said Cooper. 'I blame the system. The kids today are spoiled rotten. I hope you get him.'

'I hope so too,' said Ryan. He handed the address-book to Blair who tucked it carefully into the envelope.

'Listen,' said Cooper, leaning forward, 'have you police got something up your sleeves you're not letting dab about?'

'What makes you think that?' asked Ryan carefully.

'I can read between the lines,' said Cooper. 'Do you think it's a local man?'

'We've no idea,' said Ryan.

'How about her lover then?'

Ryan hadn't seen the evening papers but he was certain McCaig would not release that kind of detail, just yet. Perhaps the press had dug up some flack from the files of reports, scant though they were, of Doreen's disappearance. He could soon find out. He said, 'How do you know she had a lover? It's not in the press.'

Cooper sat back and grinned smugly at his wife.

'I told you, Madge, didn't I? Right away, I said she had a lover.'

'Jack!', admonished Mrs Cooper.

'How do you know?' said Ryan.

'Experience,' said Cooper. 'It's the way she looks in those photographs. I said to Madge here as soon's I saw the *Express*, that girl's got a naughty look in her eye.'

'You shouldn't speak ill of the dead,' said Mrs Cooper. For an instant Ryan expected her to cross herself. Instead she scowled at her husband. 'It's not proper, Jack.'

'He knows what I mean,' said Cooper. 'Don't you, inspector? She was carrying-on, wasn't she? One thing about young girls, they can't fake that look.'

'Thanks for your . . . help,' said Ryan hastily.

He got out of the flat before Cooper could pump him further or irritate him with pompous theorising. At least they'd got one good thing out of the afternoon's graft – the address book.

As they drove off, swinging north east for the boulevard, he took the envelope and pulled out the book. He flicked through the thin leaves, scanning the names written there in a neat,

49

large, almost childlike hand – Madge Cooper's probably : the society hostess.

'Think he's in there?' asked Blair.

'Who knows?'

'Strikes me he might be.'

'Come off it, Sandy, you know better than that.'

'If he knew the house and the moor at all before he killed her, then ...'

'Balls,' said Ryan sharply. He was tired now and hungry and wanted only silence on the hour's drive back to headquarters. 'All this book means is work, bloody hard work. It could've been anybody in the county.'

'A local,' said Blair. 'Well, maybe the Chief's caught him by now.'

'Balls,' said Ryan again. This time Sergeant Blair took the hint and shut up tight for the rest of the journey.

He had Blair stop off in Balnesmoor, and walked down to the digging area, hoping to find McCaig and perhaps get off until morning with a verbal report. It was almost full dark now, but the sky had cleared. A milky iridescence away over the hills silhouetted some of the groups, making them seem small and ineffectual against the vast black blankets of scrub. Over the thicket and its surrounds arc-lamps glared down from high positions on the tailgates of Electricity Board wagons. Reporters and photographers still milled about and it took Ryan some time to ascertain that McCaig had left the scene. Sellars was up in the bracken at the moor's edge, stooped over a riddle through which a constable poured spadefuls of harsh earth from a ragged and apparently random pit hacked out of the undergrowth. Ryan did not go up, but threaded his way back through the crowd and headed for the Hillman at the roadend. Knowing McCaig, he'd be another couple of hours in the station making out his reports.

He was worn thin, and snappish; and this only the beginning of the case. Another week, at least a week, of long days and short nights, of snacks grabbed on the wing, and it wasn't even his own case. No, he was off on the rim somewhere, just another minion on the perimeter of the wheel which hubbed around the operations' room, around McCaig. He did not envy the Chief his administrative responsibilities; he knew in himself

50

he could not bear them as well as the boss. Yet he envied McCaig his chance to stand at the centre of a big operation like this assured that any satisfaction going would fall on him. Satisfaction, God, what a daft word to use, even to think of, in connection with a killing. Now who, barring another policeman, would imagine that personal emotions were involved? Maybe the killer would; he too pulled his triumph out of evil. Perhaps, just perhaps, the sensation he had when his hands came back from a throat was not too remote from a detective's when a shard of evidence fits at last, and you know you have him, the one, the man, nailed under law.

Ryan glanced up at the ranch-house. The curtains were drawn, even in the kitchen. Except for the policeman hovering dutifully around the lawn, the place looked deserted. Perhaps the Langs had got off their marks. More likely the lucky devils were upstairs in their beds asleep. Either way they were lucky; it had happened to them, but it was over, and they were free to do just what they liked. He thought longingly of his own bed, and Jean, and groaned softly to himself. If Ryan had paused for a moment longer at the corner he would have seen the light in the bathroom of the house go on, and known that whatever else the Langs were doing they were not asleep.

SIX

Though she had vomited once just after he had got into bed, before midnight she had stumbled down into deep, rasping sleep. Lang knew she was deep by the way her mouth hung open and her head lolled back on the pillow. He could always tell when she was only dozing, or, for some queer reason of her own, feigning slumber, because there were muscles in her neck which she could not voluntarily relax. Only when her head gave a couple of spasmodic leaps then slackened off, as if a wire had suddenly snapped, was she right over. He lay rigidly by her side, listening to the low now but still audible growling of the unfamiliar traffic on the track. After a time he too slept.

In the morning, however, it seemed she had set her foot on the road to recovery and the tension in him sloughed off

51

leaving only a residue of irritation. But he was careful not to impose upon her and, in spite of his hunger, settled for a snack at lunch time. It was mid-afternoon when the mood, or the illness – even now he didn't know what term to use – crept over her again. She placed herself deliberately in the most uncomfortable chair in the house, sitting erect, hands folded in her lap, her back to the window. Afraid of rousing some other noisier manifestation of this malaise, Lang crept about on tiptoe. Sometimes the desire to shout at her was very strong, for he needed someone upon whom to vent his ire and suppressed anxiety. They were still out there, hordes of them, swarming all over the landscape. If he had not been afraid of relinquishing the last vestiges of his privacy he would have gone down among them : but if he started consorting with them they might worm their way into his house. They were just the kind to impose on a citizen. Anyway, he'd done his civic duty, given them all the help he could; and arguing with them would do no good. He crept out of the lounge into the kitchen for the tenth time in an hour. His departure appeared to pass unnoticed by the woman in the chair. The remains of his meagre lunch still adhered to the plates on the draining board, cold ham crinkled at the edges with the heat. The kitchen was hot, for the sun was back again today, bright and hot, and birds were whillowing and chittering on the trees outside. He scooped the wasted ends of meat into the can beneath the sink and crashed dishes into the basin, He stopped, guiltily, and peered back into the lounge, but Jenny was as motionless as a statue. Very gently he closed the door between the rooms, then stepped to the tiny side-window and lifted the cotton curtain. Neck craned, temples pressed against the glass he inspected the flanks of the moor.

Still there, a whole army of them. Madness! Lang screamed the word to himself without opening his mouth. Rank bureaucratic madness! The creature had been dead for nigh on two years but they couldn't seem to grasp that they'd find nothing out there now. They were only making a show, a circus, an exhibition for the news and T.V. people, to fool a gullible public into thinking that they knew what they were doing. Carting away all the damned rubbish of the day, tatty old jackets and shoes, and bottles and lengths of iron; they wouldn't find any clues now. Disturbed, the wild things which had their homes in the banking, made off with darting scuttles which, because it was diversion, caused the men nearby to shake their spades and shout. That morning a giant rat had galloped up his lawn and shot off round the back of the shed; no saying where it was digging in now. Oh, yes, he'd known there were rats in the banking, you expected that in the country, but why should they be routed out and chased into his property. They'd be in the house next, gnawing at the furniture, making their filthy messes on the new floors. But worst of all was the terrible effect of the rabble on Jenny. She wouldn't even begin to recover until they packed up and went away for good. It was positively dangerous to her health to have them out there all day, nights too, to remind her of the dead girl. One careless mistake had turned up, and set askew, the nice comfortable routines of his retirement. If only he could re-establish them quickly perhaps the incident would have no lasting effect on his wife. Now he'd recovered from the shock of seeing that bone sticking up at him like an accusing finger, he had no squeamishness at all about any of it. If he'd known the outcome he'd have kept his mouth shut about his unfortunate discovery. No, no, he thought, it wouldn't have been possible; too heavy a burden to bear, the knowledge that the thing was still out there. At least they'd got rid of it speedily enough, which was one small mercy.

Look at that crowd milling around. Trippers in their hundreds, come to gawp from the rope-line. If it wasn't for those duty policemen they'd be all over the place, tramping his garden in to quagmire without a second thought. What pleasure could they find in gaping at a bunch of men digging? Staring like so many sheep. Photographers too, professional and amateur, poking and prying, waiting – waiting for what? Did they imagine that the man, the murderer, would still be lurking out there after twenty months, waiting to give himself up to their lenses? The idea wedged in Lang's mind. Glowering, he scanned the distant faces more intently. Perhaps he *was* there, their killer, right in the midst of the crowd, chuckling up his sleeve in evil glee, quite safe, with nothing to fear. Quickly Lang dropped the curtain and pushed back into the lounge.

'Jenny.'

She did not reply, not even glancing up when he placed himself directly in front of her.

'Jenny,' he snapped, 'stop this nonsense at once, d'you hear.'

Still no response. He tried a softer tone, almost tender. 'I know it's upsetting but don't let it get you down.'

'I can't help it,' she said in a surprisingly firm voice. 'When will they go away?'

'Soon I expect.'

'She was really only a child.'

'She was sixteen,' said Lang.

'I keep thinking about her.'

'You mustn't just sit here brooding.'

'What must her poor mother be feeling right now.'

'Jenny,' said Lang shortly, 'I'm hungry. Make my tea.'

'What?' the woman asked, blinking.

'It's tea time.'

She sighed loudly and closed her eyes. Lang shook her tentatively as if afraid that parts would fall off. With a long indrawn breath she pushed herself to her feet. 'Yes, it's tea time again.'

'Eggs will do,' said Lang.

The woman nodded and made her way slowly into the kitchen. Lang remained in the lounge, following her apprehensively with his eyes. He was afraid of her again, as he had been before in Glasgow. She was holding her hands in the odd manner she'd adopted three or four years ago when things were building up to the first crisis. Yes, he knew that grotesque pose all too well; palms cupping elbows, wrists knuckled in against her ribs as if she had a cramp. From the centre of the room he watched her light the stove, set out the frying pan and scoop lard from a packet into it, then she passed out of sight. He knew she'd gone to the larder for the eggs. He grunted and took a seat in the armchair, easing back in it, lifting the unopened copy of the morning paper from the top of the T.V. set. Doreen English simpered at him. He crumpled the front page, ripped it off and tossed it into the waste box. Without much interest he set himself to read the trivial social gossip on page three. By its style it almost cheated him into believing that there was more real substance in its columns than anywhere else in the paper. He had absorbed no more than a paragraph, when a crash brought him to his feet. He dashed into the kitchen. The smashed eggs, albumen and shell mingled in shapeless pools, all over the tiles lay flecks of orange yolk splattered across Jenny's feet and legs. Her head went forward, her body doubled over his arm. She was wailing silently again, keening in her throat and nose. Lang said nothing, pursing his lips. He held her down for a minute, pressing, waiting for her to be sick, but her retching yielded nothing. He lifted her with the ache in his spine, and carried her through the hall to the bedroom at the rear of the house. He lowered her and rolled her awkwardly into the centre of the bed. She lay there prone and rigid, brown shoes sticking up, hair square on the knoll of the pillow, her stomach rising and falling rapidly. She covered her face with her hands.

Lang picked two tablets from the box in the table. He pried his wife's fingers away from her cheeks and with his thumb lifted her lips. Finally he got her mouth open and the tablets inside, but when he lifted her shoulders to give her water from the glass she went limp on him. He glimpsed the white of the tablets on her tongue, flattened her lower lip with the rim and tipped the glass back until water flooded her mouth and dribbled over her chin. When he looked again the tablets were gone. Gingerly he let her flop back on the bed.

'Will I get the doctor?'

After a long pause she managed to shake her head.

'Can I bring you anything?'

She shook her head again, this time with emphasis. Her arms were straight by her sides and her lids down. Lang felt her forehead, in obedience to the diagnostic instructions of old home nursing manuals. She was as cold as death, but dry, not clammy. He thought that was a good sign.

'What can I do?' he asked.

'I'll be ... all ... right, Norman,' she whispered huskily. 'Leave me alone.'

'No, I'll sit here, just here.'

'Leave me, Norman,' she said. 'Get your tea.'

'Well, all right,' he said. 'You're sure now?'

'Yes.'

'Call me if you want anything.'

'Yes, Norman,' she said. 'I will.'

Thankfully he slipped out of the room. If she wasn't much improved by bedtime, he would sleep on the couch. She was right; it was better for her to be left alone.

*   *   *

55

By nature Ryan was not a lethargic man, and on waking his brain instantly took command of his body, so that he was standing in front of the bathroom mirror with his open razor in his hand almost before he had come unsheathed from sleep. His eyes were crusted, his throat ached a little – was he coming down with a virus again – and his tongue thick in his mouth. But, as he scraped away at the stubble, his mind ticked over at an alarming rate and he hardly noticed the discomfort with which late duty and middle-age had saddled him. Like many another in his trade the pattern of the week made no impression on him. He lacked the in-built clocking mechanism which gives clerk, factoryhand and shopkeeper an individual slant on each day. It never occurred to Ryan that it was Tuesday, the city half holiday, the day the travelling bank came to the hamlets in the country, or that his wife would later do the weekly wash on the Bendix he'd bought her last year. He was thinking about Doreen English, and Chief Superintendent McCaig. Outside he could hear the soft step of Jean's bedroom slippers as she shuffled about making his breakfast. The kids were just waking. He carved the long ground blade across the lather and tugged his chin tight to throw his bristles into relief.

Just what was McCaig up to? Did he hope – no, not even McCaig would hope for that – did he *suspect* that the county might be on the verge of another sensational case like the Moors Murders of three years ago? Every man on the force had followed the progress of that horrifying crime with appalled interest, for it had thrown up problems, administrative problems too, which nobody in or out of uniform could ignore. He remembered how McCaig had talked, coldly subjecting each layer of repulsive detail to theory and analysis. The total lack of compassion in the Chief's conversations came back to him now. The press would be playing up that angle for all they were worth : even evil incarnate can be reduced in time to a convenient, popular symbol. Killing for the joy of it. Death as a fine art.

He notched the skin on the point of his jaw and groaned, jabbing his thumb on the instant start of blood.

Evil for its own sake. What a lousy empty life that must be. Or was it? Perhaps it wasn't. He had no right to take the standpoint that devotion to a black cause was any less fulfilling than devotion to no cause at all. Only he personally couldn't understand it. Sellars, a Sergeant at the time, dewy from the college, had rattled off all sorts of phychiatric jargon, but for Harry Ryan, and most of the lads too, it was at root a crime just as incomprehensible to them as to any average citizen. Was Doreen the victim of a man like Brady, drawn innocently into a cult of murder and outrage? He played about with the idea, wondering if that was behind McCaig's assertion that Anna Ewart, and maybe some others, had gone the same road. No, this killing bore the hallmarks of a simpler motive – if any motive which drives a man or woman to the ultimate sin can be considered uncomplicated.

He fastened the tab of toilet paper to his skin and stuck it down with the pinpoint of blood which he had released, then he cleaned his shaving tools and went in for breakfast.

Resting his chin on his hand, elbow on the table, he tried to sort out a few main issues. What the hell *were* they looking for? What manner of killer, what kind of lover? There was something so guileless in the way Doreen had guarded her relationship with the stranger that it didn't match at all with the craftiness which she'd exployed to be with him : this mixture of innocence and cunning was puzzling – or is that really what little girls are made of, not sugar and spice at all. Ryan had few illusions left about the human animal, male or female.

Long since accustomed to her husband's ways, Jean slid toast, tea and fried eggs under his nose, then crept off into the back rooms of the bungalow to rouse her children.

Ryan ate automatically. Probably a straight case of passion, he decided, spilled-over lust. Yet, whoever had throttled Doreen English had been mature enough, cool enough, to make a bloody good job of hiding her. Even the stealth and deadly secrecy, in which the girl herself had co-operated, spoke of some sort of calculation. There it was again, that strange sinister collusion between the victim and killer. It was almost as if death had been their ultimate design all along, as if she had connived to make it easy for him to do her in and escape society's revenge. She must have loved him a lot to be blinded or uncaring in her passion for him. Passion! God, passion and marmalade!

He pushed the toast into his mouth and finished dressing at

the little mirror on the back of the cupboard door. He wandered through the house into the bedrooms where his son and daughter should have been. Empty, the beds askew. Sounds of protest from the bathroom: phase two of the schoolday ritual – washing. He went in, squeezing himself past the bath. His daughter Jean, young Jean, had commandeered the sink, her right as an *almost* adult person. Burbling through toothpaste she was delivering her usual haughty remarks about the total lack of privacy in 'this house'. Seeds of rebellion, but not serious.

'If you got up half an hour earlier ...' Ryan said, an ancient argument the logic of which did not appeal to his offspring.

'Why should I?' Toothpaste spluttering.

'If you want the bathroom to yourself.'

'If you got *him*,' a flash of the brush at her brother, 'up early then he'd be finished, wouldn't he?'

From under the wet facecloth wee Gordon protested the injustice of all his sister's systems, and pushed at his mother's wrist as soap suds invaded his eyes. Ryan handed him a towel, saying, 'Anyway, it's time I wasn't here.'

Then the children were facing him, obediently waiting to be kissed. He knew they didn't really appreciate the warmth of that demonstration of paternal affection but they submitted to it with admirable patience.

'You off today?' Gordon, aged five, asked.

'Does it look it?' said young Jean witheringly.

'Now, now,' Jean said. Ryan kissed her too.

'When're you going to be off again then?' Gordon demanded. He was dressing himself, awkwardly, from the pile of clothes on the side of the bath.

'The weekend, perhaps.'

'The *weekend*,' Gordon said shrilly, 'that's a long time.'

'It's only three days,' Jean said.

'After today,' young Jean added smugly. 'Today's only started.'

Ryan nodded, grinning, and went out into the hall. He said nothing to his wife about when he would be home again and she did not ask. She knew what the case involved. He opened the door, went down on to the path and turned left towards the garage at the side of the house. Then he saw the Hillman turn into the avenue. He stood for a moment, waiting. Blair drew the car up at the kerb and, even though Ryan was already coming down to the gate, touched the horn disc twice.

Ryan reached the side of the car and pulled open the door. He glanced back at the house where Jean stood in the doorway. He waved to her; she waved back. Blair had not spoken yet, nor started the engine. He sat with his hands on the steering wheel, looking out at the stand of firs at the end of the wide avenue of new bungalows.

'What are you doing here?' said Ryan.

'I thought I might just catch you,' said Blair.

'It was quicker than phoning really.'

'What's up?'

Blair switched on the engine and glancing over his shoulder through the rear window, put the Hillman into reverse. He pulled it back and made the first leg of the turnabout, then paused long enough to look at Ryan.

'They found another one,' he said.

He fisted the wheel vigorously and shot the car round fast, pulling it in toward the left and away up the incline in the direction of the Galtway crossing and the main Balnesmoor road.

'So,' said Ryan, expelling his breath. 'McCaig was right.'

'Ay,' said Blair. 'It looks like it's Anna Ewart.'

SEVEN

Less than twenty-four hours after the remains of Anna Ewart were carefully unearthed from the banking, eight hundred yards from Lang's back gate, identification was positively confirmed. With the finding of a second body the village of Balnesmoor, the town of Lannerburn and County Police Headquarters at Thane were awash with reporters and cameramen. Rumour was rife that a string of sensational discoveries was about to be made, and, conditioned by recent crimes on both sides of the Atlantic, every major newspaper in the world was determined to have a man in on the ground floor. McCaig was an old hand at controlling the press; in his daily conferences he gave the impression of being brutally

59

frank. But his frankness did not extend to handing out confidences, and only in the privacy of the chiefs meeting did he express his considered opinion that Balnesmoor had given up the last of its dead. He did not, however, call off the search. He might be wrong : every possibility, however vague, had to be explored and the diggers on the moorland's edge were supplemented with handpicked voluntary workers culled from three counties. McCaig divulged to no one his reasons for supposing that there were no more secrets under the heather, but the officers who knew him well enough to ask were shrewd enough to provide their own answer – pattern. For an ordered mind like McCaig's, pattern was all. Except for a handful of minor details it might have been the same crime twice.

Two sixteen year old girls from the same district of the same city, both pretty, both bored and disgruntled with the trials of adolescence, both careful with their secrets. Anna Ewart, too, had a loyal, lying friend willing to cover for her 'lost' hours, while she created opportunities for . . . for what then? For love, or sex, or romance, or a dish whipped up from all three. Both girls had been found in well-dug, spade-dug, holes in a half mile stretch of overgrown banking in Balnesmoor, County of Thane. Anna Ewart, like Doreen, had gone missing on a Saturday, but in her case the whole weekend – she was allegedly youth hostelling with the misguided girl chum – passed, before her disappearance was noted, and an investigation got under way. She never turned up at the youth hostel. Later the chum confessed that Anna never intended to turn up. It was all part of a plot, a giggly game, to free Anna to go off with her 'boyfriend,' for forty-eight delicious, enviable hours of sin.

Like Doreen's, Anna Ewart's body was fully clothed when found. The only items missing were contained in a small week-end rucksack which she had taken with her when she left home. The rucksack and its contents were never discovered. Glasgow had all the details to hand ready to ship out to Thane. The file gave the picture of a girl, ordinary in every way – save one : she had carried fancies into reality, the seeds of discontent had flourished into promiscuous sex. Had she been picked, as it were, by hand, soothed and tamed by hand, just as she had been done to death by hand? McCaig thought so. Though he was careful never to put it into so many words his direction of the case bore out his opinions. But where did the killer come from? That massive question mark hovered over all.

Did he come from Craigiemill, Glasgow, or from Balnesmoor, Thane, or from some other corner of Scotland; a real unknown?

Motive; opportunity; disposal. Motive; indeterminate, to say the least of it. Opportunity; carefully plotted to give complete freedom of action over a minimum period of ten hours, longer in Anna's case. Disposal; predetermined, second time around anyway, to allow easy access by car, quiet, and good camouflage for the sites. The chances of being spotted on that track during the early hours of the morning were very remote indeed. The only house nearby was Lang's, and the occupants were used to seeing cars in the dark. It wasn't Lang's house then, of course, for Anna had been buried in March, fourteen months ago. The graves were concealed beneath bushes which, even without leaves, provided a dense screen of branches over the raw earth oblongs. A piece of twine, corroded by weather, was found tied to the trunk of a hawthorn bush. It was sixteen inches long including the loop and had been cut. Was the killer so prepared and so thorough that he even thought to carry twine with him to tie back the undergrowth while he marked off and excavated. The holes were each five feet deep, five and a half feet long, three feet wide, regular and well-defined. Ryan could imagine the method, but not the iron nerve of the man who had the patience to be thorough: the root-infested ground, crash of the bushes on the backswing, hack of the spade, shudder of metal as the blade struck rocks, furtive glances upward at the sky above in case an early dawn caught him out. A blacked-out car, or van, would be dark against the banking. But what of Lang's house over there, pasted pale on a background of trees? How often did the man look at it over his shoulder in a welter of sweat wondering if there were eyes peering at him out of those blank window frames? Of course, being normal folk, the Herrons slept at night. But someone knew him, this man, and perhaps someone had seen him at some stage. Behind the deaths lay reasons, and those reasons were as valid as any other item in the case. Questions, answers, reports: did you know either of these two girls, have you seen anything, any stranger, any car? Do you go up on to the

61

moor? Administration, hoofwork and the slow, dreary sifting of an awful lot of moorland. The net was spread in all directions, but the closest meshes fitted over Balnesmoor, Lannerburn and the Craigiemill suburb in Glasgow. A little wider perhaps, it covered all the towns and villages in the county – Kilcraig, where Ryan lived, Galtway, where Sellar's brothers farmed, Thane itself, stuffed with policemen, McCaig, Ashe, McDonald, Blair. Ryan also had a book, and in the book were the names of fifty-three strangers, any of whom *might* have information which *might* lead to something, which *might* be shaped and buffed into a key which *might*, with luck, unlock doors which the killer had closed after him. Then again it might not.

After the hectic activity of Tuesday, while most of the detective squad toured hotels and motels, cafés and restaurants, garages and even private homes with their questionnaires, Ryan and Blair set off on their odyssey to track down Cooper's friends.

Into County Headquarters flowed a large number of false reports, each to be followed to its disappointing end regardless of its source. The public were swift, but not accurate, in their response to the appeals for information : twenty months was a long, long, time. The week slipped from Tuesday into Saturday and young Gordon Ryan did not have his father to play with, in fact he hardly saw him at all. As far as Ryan's family were concerned the head of the house might have been a ghost, or a gnome, who raided the larder and used the bed, but was never seen in daylight. A new week began.

For practical purposes the Coopers' book proved useless. On Monday Ryan co-ordinated reports from stations outside Central Scotland, reports from as far away as Cornwall, Belfast and Rhyll. He filed these with his own sheets and added them up : the total came to naught. Only one name remained unaccounted for, for he had gone off to Canada, married there and settled to a job – so it turned out. It took Cooper to run him down and write him and receive the reply 'Sorry, I saw nothing. I was drunk most of that weekend. But I remembered it, Jack, and what a hell of a time we had.' It seemed nobody ever forgot a Cooper party, only its details. Ryan returned the book to Cooper personally, asked him about the missing name, and a few more desultory questions, thanked them for their co-operation and went back to Thane. One week of grinding labour, and he had come up with nothing. The whole force, Glasgow and Thane, had come up with nothing; not a single concrete lead. Still, the reporters hung around and until the last of them drifted off there was always hope of a break. Journalists had noses for that sort of thing. But even after the last thin drop of news had been extracted from the deaths of Doreen and Anna, the last curt paragraph buried deep in the centre columns, would it be over then? No. While the killer was still free there was always the chance he might kill again. Next time perhaps there would be no daft little pensioner to stumble across the bones, and the girl would remain missing, locked in the limbo of that world, for ever. That was the horror of it really, Harry Ryan thought, not what had happened in the past, but what might happen to some poor bewildered kid tomorrow. He might have thought of his daughter, but even Detective Inspectors have the knack of mental censorship which helps, at times, to keep them sane. Always someone else's daughter, never your own.

Another bitch : she wasn't innocent at all, Lang told himself. They couldn't pull the wool over his eyes and drown him in a welter of maudlin sympathy. They as good as said she wasn't innocent, came right out and said it, and plastered that photograph of her in a scrap of a bathing suit all over the front page to make sure the message was clear. Any girl who flaunted herself before a camera in that indecent pose had no one but herself to blame for what happened to her. She was just like those bitches in the night-time cars down at the bottom of his garden, giving themselves up, sweating and squeaking in the throes of their sin. No escaping these days from the taint of their dirty capers; society was too permissive and death and bloody violence were hardly more than just forms of recompense. But why here, in Balnesmoor of all places, where the air was clean and the sky big overhead, and he had bought property outright?

With Jenny bedridden, Lang was forced to employ one of the less particular women from the village to come every morning and clean up the house. It had cost him a pretty penny already and when she charged him an extra pound just to lug a few groceries with her, hardly even a shopper full, he had almost got rid of her on the spot. But he couldn't bring himself to face the village. He thought of them down there, greasy smiling faces behind their counters or hovering casually behind piles of tins, waiting to slide out for a 'few words' with him – to pump him, to wring him out like a washcloth, gathering drops of gossip as if they were drops of gold. He paid the cleaner to bring the provisions, and locked himself in the house.

The local doctor, who came under the National Health scheme, and therefore did not have to be paid, was an elderly man, older than Lang even, and not well versed in 'upsets' of the mind. He was sympathetic, but not anxious about Jenny's nervous condition and recommended as a cure the good old reliable Scottish medicines of patience, fortitude and time. If they had lived in a city, Lang thought bitterly, he would surely have prescribed a change of air too. On Lang's insistence the doctor finally parted with two prescriptions, one a strong sleeping draught to overcome her nightmares and the other for iron tablets to stave off her tendency to anaemia. One evening when he could get no word out of her at all, not even the graciousness of a nod, Lang was worried enough to consider bringing in a specialist from Glasgow, but, even more worried about his financial state which he knew at all times down to the last penny. He decided that he could not afford the expense, and held the decision back as a final desperate resort. Only he, he felt, could really help her weather the storm. He elected to do so by locking the front and rear entrances and refusing to come out for anyone. If they'd a family, or even friends, they could have escaped from Balnesmoor until the hub-bub died down, but, childless and friendless, there was just nowhere for them to go. This house was their home, bought and paid for in hard cash, and Lang's stubborn streak enjoined him to sit tight no matter how hard the world battered at his walls and upset Jenny.

The police interviewed him again and he was sensible enough to open up for them. A Sergeant, unknown to Lang, put a few simple questions, all to do with the new girl, Anna Ewart, and somehow he managed to get through the inquisition without his anger erupting. Of the dead girls he thought little or nothing, and the purpose of the army out there on the moor became daily more obscure. He gave up buying newspapers, for the pictures of the house, his house, which appeared frequently made the place look so seedy and drab, side by side with grainy shots of the moor searchers and blown-up portraits of the dead girls. The house was made sinister and dirty by the association, as if it was actually the site of the murders or the sanctuary of the murderer himself. After stills of the place appeared on the news, Lang even disconnected the T.V. set, but the activity outside was dying off slowly : they no longer worked at night. Reporters crawled back to drink in the local hotels and discuss tactics in the never-ending battle to win fresh information for their rags. The moor lay almost deserted, slumbering again. The sounds of nocturnal creatures rose up from it as they gradually repossessed their territory. Only after dusk did Lang deign to open the windows of the kitchen and let cool air flood in. The heat of the days, a false artificial stuffiness, drained away like water seeping from a stagnant pool. Moths appeared softly, spiralling around the light, knocking their heads in daft frustration against the shades. Owls, of which there were many in the vicinity, shook off their lethargy and returned to their hunting grounds, puncturing the darkness with their hollow calls.

Alone in the lounge, the lamp behind him, Lang let time filter away like the bad, overused air of the sealed rooms. In the bedroom Jenny seemed remote. The T.V. was dead; he had no news to read, no news worth reading. He was thrown back on endless accounting, doing it automatically, progressively at first, all in his head. Arms over the sides of the chair, short legs planted in worn slippers, collar lying on the carpet like a dog's dish, counting, he lost himself. The silence did not frighten him but encased his calculations like the steel body of a computer, hiding slots and bars and fuses. He checked his tiny income against estimates of expenditure, snatching at the comfort of the margin he had prudently allowed for error. The security of house ownership balanced against his capital, portions of interest and pension rate. His thoughts opened outwards into broader considerations which he felt compelled to account for too. Inflation, devaluation of the pound, possibility of war, a slump to bring prices to rock bottom, the business of Britain and International finance all affected him : arithmetic progression cheated, up and down the columns, bringing him back at length to personal issues – the cost of one cigarette, say, the high price of the unhealthy, self-destructive pleasure of five minutes' smoke in the mouth.

He did not hear her until she spoke. He swivelled round, terror clawing at his bowels, and flung himself out of the chair. Even after recognition he was too shaken and too angry to be considerate.

'God, woman,' he cried, 'you nearly killed me there.' He slumped into the chair again. 'Could you not knock first? I thought you were in bed.'

With her hair up, her haggard face was even starker than it had been that afternoon. The dressing-gown fell around her as heavy and still as papier-mâché.

'I want out, Norman.'

He was still trembling, and bunched his fists together to stop it. 'At this hour?'

Her sudden composure and lucidity struck him as a trick. Had she been leading him on to this contrast by feigning illness? He saw her schemes and the possibilities behind them, and, irrational himself, immediately set up his guard.

'I want to leave this house,' she said.

'We've nowhere to go.'

'I don't care,' she said. 'I want out.'

'I suppose we could afford a week in Largs, or Dunoon, if you want,' he said. 'At a boarding house. You like . . .'

'I mean for good.'

'Don't talk rubbish, Jenny,' he said. 'We can't leave here.'

'Norman, I can't stand it.'

'Rubbish. When they clear out everything'll get back to normal quick enough.'

'It's not them,' said Jenny with excessive patience. 'I told you, it's what happened. I'll never be able to go out of that door again without thinking about it.'

'You're overtired. We'll talk about it tomorrow.'

'I want to leave tomorrow.'

Lang jumped to his feet. 'I suppose I just walk up to the first person I meet and get him to buy my house. What'll we live on, Mrs Lang? What'll we live on?'

'You *must* sell it.'

Lang laughed hoarsely. 'And who's going to buy it, d'you think? Jenny, I couldn't give this damned place away. Perhaps in a year or two, when . . .'

Though her voice was still calm it had dropped so low that he had to strain to hear her at all. 'If I have to stay here much longer, I'll die.'

'*Rubbish!*'

'*Please,* Norman, sell it.'

'No,' he said, then relenting added, 'not for a while anyway.'

If he had been looking at her directly he would have detected the beginnings of the twitch, high above the mouth. But he went on to explain to her, in terms of finance, just why he could not sell his house, and, brooding over the phrases, stared at the carpet. The tic, which started subtly under the surface flesh soon found the big cords of muscle at her jaw and jerked them. Her head shook and the stem of her neck turned taut as wood. The outlandish spasm rattled down her body, flicking her arms, bunching her fists, making her claw the air as in a wrathful prayer for vengeance. The first scream reawakened him. In dismal ineptitude he threw himself upright, hands fastened on the chair-back to observe her torment. He did not rush towards her until she sank down like a wax candle melting in a furnace, and only caught her the instant before her skull struck the base of the lamp. Her body was utterly limp, the dregs of tension whipping through her calves like the passing off of a demon from the soul. She was totally unconscious when he rolled her back into bed and covered her up.

He was shaking himself now, horrified by the grossness of the fit. The doorbell rang, frightening him again. He flew to it and opened it and peered out over the sagging chain.

'Something wrong, Mr Lang?' the young constable asked.

'My wife,' said Lang, 'a bad dream, that's all.'

The constable nodded sympathetically. 'Ay, it's a rum time you've been having. Anything I can do?'

'She'll be all right, thanks,' said Lang. 'Goodnight.'

'Goodnight, sir.'

The policeman stayed on the doorstep, watching Lang with a touch of curiosity. Hastily Lang closed the door and worked the bolt. He pressed against the wood, listening and waiting until he heard the heavy tread on the concrete, softening on the grass, and knew that the boy had gone back to his post. He pulled out a chair and dropped into it, groaning with indulgent self-pity, and found relief in the sound, almost pleasure. After

67

some minutes he tentatively resumed the reckoning of his affairs. For the sake of sanity, he must at least appear to do what she asked of him. If she had any memory of her demand come the morning, he would call on Galbraith and then assess the chances of disposing of the house some time in the very near future. That settled, he let his brow go down and, head cradled on his arm on the table, fell asleep.

Part Two

ONE

'You must be joking.' Galbraith said. 'Stick it up for sale now and all you'll get for it's a mass of bad publicity. Take my advice, sit on the place for a couple of years then, perhaps, you'll be able to recoup some of your money.'

'I can't wait,' said Lang.

'Your wife, hm!' said Galbraith. 'Of course I appreciate how she must feel, but I think you should have a serious chat with her. I'm sure she'll see reason.'

'She won't see reason,' said Lang. 'I've got to get her out of Balnesmoor.'

The sunlight made the woodwork in the offices dark and rich, casting a rippling shadow across the grain, shadow and grain interleaved so that against it Galbraith's head, in a beam of sunlight too, was oddly noble. The agent's clothes helped, the rugged well-tailored tweed: how much, Lang thought, had that suit cost? It was twice as good as anything he'd ever had on his back, including the one he was married in – and the shirt too, and the hand-lasted shoes. Stinking of money, was Galbraith. If only he'd half, even a quarter, of Galbraith's assets he wouldn't be in the pickle he was in now. No, he could expect no real understanding from this man, so wide was the gap between their situations.

'Take a holiday,' said the agent. 'Go off to the seaside for a while. By the time you come back this murder business may have blown over, *then* we can re-assess the possibilities.'

'I want you to sell the property,' said Lang, dogmatically, 'Right now.'

'Hopeless,' said Galbraith. 'Only an idiot, or a ghoul, would buy it at the moment. I mean, we just don't know how many

69

more mouldering corpses the police are going to howk out of your front lawn, do we?'

'They weren't actually on my land,' Lang reminded him.

'Sure, sure,' said Galbraith, 'But, I ask you, if you saw an ad. for a house currently featuring as a star attraction in a really disgusting murder case would you buy it?'

'I'm willing to take a loss for a quick sale.'

'A *loss*! Hell's bells, Lang, I doubt if I could *give* the bloody place away.' Galbraith sighed and leaned over the desk, tapping his pencil on the blotter. 'Look, if you're hoping some nut, some queer will pop up and grab the place, forget it. Unfortunately, most of today's perverts tend to be rather money-conscious.'

'You could try.'

'Can't you *afford* to go off for a couple of months 'til the air clears?' asked Galbraith.

'No.'

'But there are dozens of ways of raising cash. Possibly you could even use the house for that; you know, as collateral on a loan. I could put you on to somebody.'

'I'm not going to borrow,' said Lang. 'I won't put myself into debt.'

'It's not debt,' said Galbraith. 'It's just a business transaction. I doubt if you'll get much but it might be enough to tide you over.'

'No,' said Lang. 'Anyway, if the house is worthless who's going to take it as collateral. Would you give me a loan?'

Galbraith did not fluster easily. He smiled and after a tiny hesitation confessed, 'No.' Lang made a dubious sound in his throat. 'All right, Mr Lang, I'll be frank with you. It's a nice house, a lovely house, in a perfect situation, but after the... events of the last two weeks – well, it's of little or no value. It might even be as much as five years before it cools off, and in five years the property will have depreciated physically, though with the inflationary spiral still climbing, it's possible you might ...'

'Sell it for me.'

'I *can* try,' Galbraith said, 'but I'll have to charge you a fee in excess of the percentage, if it doesn't go. And I don't think it will.'

'How much?'

'Cost of advertising,' said Galbraith generously. 'That's all.'
'All right.'
'You seriously want me to set the wheels in motion?'
'Yes.'
'Well, sure,' said Galbraith. 'If that's what you want.'
'It's not what I want,' Lang said, 'but it's what has to be. It's either the house or my wife's health.'
'Honestly?' said Galbraith. 'I'd no idea things were quite so serious.'
'They are,' said Lang. 'They're very serious. I'd just like to get my hands on the man who did it, killed those girls and buried them on my place.'
'*Near* your place,' said Galbraith. 'If it's any consolation, which I don't suppose it is, yours isn't the only property to have the edge taken off its value. At the minute, Balnesmoor is a dirty word, and if any more mouldering dollies come to light I'll wind up bankrupt.'
Lang sneered inwardly at Galbraith's hyperbole : nothing would ever bankrupt Galbraith. He was too smart to put all his eggs in one basket. He would never know what it was to shape up to ruin, and penury. His sort were indestructible.
'When will you make a start?' Lang asked.
'Hey-ho,' said Galbraith. He ruffled the pages of his desk calendar. Since you're determined to go through with it, we may as well get on with it right away.'
'Fine,' said Lang, sourly.

McCaig swung the garage door shut and walked away without bothering to fix the padlock. He was bone-weary and anyhow nobody in Thane was stupid enough to try to pinch his car; if they did, he'd plaster the bastard against the wall and teach him a lesson he'd never forget. He had violence on his mind a lot just now, mentally burning off his frustration at how badly affairs at headquarters were going. Even the bloody neds from the newspapers were getting critical with their wisecracks. Involuntarily he darted a glance down the road past the wall of the coopers' yard just to make sure none of the press had had the brass neck to follow him right to his doorstep. The lamp at the end of the street was out again; he stopped and walked out a couple of paces from the house to count the number of burned-out mantels. Five : Christ, what

71

was the Master of Works playing at, five out of eleven. Another month and it would be like the blackout again. The pipes were rotten anyway and in places the reek of the leaking gas was almost overpowering. This short sedate-looking road with its solid, red sandstone early-part-of-the-century bungalows, must be about the stinkiest place in the county: Coal gas, and the harsh, sour, fecund stench of the mound of old barrels in the lanes between the sheds, mixed with sickly perfume of pensioners' roses from the gardens along the row. He put the tattered briefcase under his arm, fumbled with the key-chain, unlocked the front door and went in. The house was pitch dark, musty, he detected a niff of stale bedding in the side room, and rank, cheesy aroma from the kitchen. He'd forgotten to put the dish back in the fridge. Flies droned in the gloom when he entered, resentful of his intrusion into their feasting grounds. He swatted about him with his hat and switched on the light. Cheese uncovered, crescents of rind, butter too, the half pint bottle of milk a funny colour though it was supposed to be fresh and whole from the cow that morning. He brushed the loop of the cardboard flowerbasket which was taped to the shade and a tiny insect, not even a big fat bluebottle, dropped off, a testimonial to the lethal powers of D.D.T. Dumping the briefcase on the table, he ran through his chores swiftly, not appearing to move fast, but doing out of habit several different things at once, still flapping occasionally at the drones around him with his hat: windows wide open, cold tap running loud, stove on, kettle filled from the running tap, plugged in, rancid remains of last night's supper scooped into a plastic bag and dumped in the can; two shirts, one vest and socks up from the floor and into the laundry bag, milk out, bottle rinsed, briefcase open; he deposited the tins and packets on the cloth, opening the wrappings to sniff the bacon and read the stamp on the butter pat. He was so utterly buggered that he had no hunger left, but he went on stoically preparing food because he had to eat. This was the earliest he had been home in eleven days: not that it mattered much whether he came home or not. There was nobody now to bother whether he kept some semblance of regularity, or ate, or did not eat, or stayed out all night, slept half an afternoon. He hadn't needed her, after all, not with a fast cooker, a reliable alarm, plenty of grocers near headquarters and a laundry at the end of the road. For years before she finally blew up he had known it was inevitable. What the hell did she expect him to do when she challenged him; tell her some smarmy lie just to make her feel better for half a day or so?

'*You don't need me, do you?*' she'd shouted.

'No.'

He sunk the opener into the tin of steak and kidney pie and worked it round the rim, stripped off the lid and slid the pie into the oven. He opened a tin of green peas next, then one of pears, tipping the peas into a pot and the pears into a dish. He dug into the papers in the side of the case and brought out the latest issue of *Time* magazine. He turned over the pages to the international section and standing in the middle of the floor under the light, pear tin in one hand, magazine in the other, read through the telegraphic account of the crime which had briefly put Balnesmoor on the map. It even mentioned his name, but that gave him no thrill at all. In spite of what Ryan and some of those other backbiting jokers might think he didn't give a fart about fame. He had no pride left, only the burning desire to cling on to what he had gained, jealously guard the position which had cost him so bloody much. He sipped the pear syrup slowly, eyes on the page.

'Save some for me.'

To McCaig's credit he had control of himself in an instant, holding down his first impulse to back away from the voice.

'What the hell're you doing here?' he asked.

'Char–ming,' the young man said. 'Charming indeed.'

'All right, all right,' said McCaig, putting the tin and magazine on the table. Derek came over and lifted both, drinking and reading exactly as his father had done. 'I thought you were still at college.'

'Vacation time is here again,' said Derek. He waved the copy of *Time*. 'In all the best places, aren't you?'

'Vacation. I thought you'd got a job or something,' said McCaig.

'That's summer,' said Derek. 'This is still Easter. I go back tomorrow.'

'You've been away?'

'Went camping up North,' said Derek, 'but it pissed the whole time. Come to think of it, I was pretty pissed the whole time myself.'

73

'You need money?'

'Father, fath–er,' said Derek maliciously, 'I do not come only when I am in need.'

'All right,' said McCaig. 'D'you want something to eat?'

'I wouldn't say no to that.'

'How did you get in?'

'Through the front door. You left it unlocked,' said the young man. 'I've been strolling up and down for hours. You looked right past me a minute ago. I was down at Auld Nick's gate.'

'Were you?' said McCaig drily. 'What do you want to eat?'

'I'm not fussy,' Derek said. 'Some of that pie'll do.'

McCaig nodded and took off his jacket, looked around then tossed it carelessly on a chair.

'You need to get yourself a woman,' said Derek.

McCaig did not answer and the young man went on, a taunting quality, insolently apparent in his tone. 'Not necessarily to cuddle up with,' he said. 'I mean some old biddy who'll keep the joint in shape for you. Jesus, you must be able to afford it, getting your name in *Time* an' all.'

'How are the studies?'

'That's right, change the subject,' said Derek. 'The "studies" are fine.'

'How long have you to do?'

'You'll have me off your neck for good and all in one year and one month,' said Derek. 'As if you didn't know.'

'Set the table.'

'Okay.'

McCaig observed his son out of the corner of his eye as he stirred the peas in the pot on the stove Derek and he were as like as two peas, Muriel used to say. She certainly had not intended it as a compliment, but looking at the boy now, at twenty-one, it was complimentary enough to sadden McCaig. If he had ever been like that, all whipcord muscle and sunburn, with cloudy dark eyes like a lazy rakehell's then he couldn't recall it. He certainly wasn't now, with the fat on him and the abrasions of twenty years of bad living showing all too clearly. Maybe a stranger would have picked up the family resemblance in the shape of the nose or the sulky, stubborn she called it, pulled-down mouth. Probably the boy had lots of girls chasing after him. He'd had his chances too when he was that age but the war had got in the way – the white belt and the stick, the gloves, cap brim like a visor on the nose, the duties and the separateness and the code of behaviour of the M.P. – then it was back to the beat again. He'd had his chances even then, but he'd just never any time to give a woman what she wanted : never any time to think of them, to build up the sweat which starts the action. Being wanted, desired, was what made a woman open her legs, that or money. The truth was that he never really did want them that badly, and hadn't the gift to feign it. Muriel was the exception. It wasn't just want with her, but *need*. She was the first girl he'd ever met that he could not brush out of his thoughts. He had to have her : unfortunately he still had enough charm left to make her realise it. It would have been better for both of them, Derek too, if she'd gathered her wits long enough during their courtship to imagine what life with him would really be like. It took her too long to learn to read the sad facts of his character, find out that he could do only one thing well. Even Muriel put it down to pride; stiffnecked, self-centred pride. But it wasn't, at least not after he'd got into his thirties. No, the very facts of the job cancelled out his interest in the promotion ladder. He couldn't stomach all that T.V. shit about vocation and devotion to duty or the fine feelings incurred by serving the public. After a couple of knifings, the sight of a man being whipped to a pulp by flailing motorbike chains, the sound of a woman's screams over the railings of the riverbank as the body of her kid came up out of the muddy water, the hysterical bewilderment of a nine year old raped by her half brother, breathless voices of informers on phones telling scared greedy little tales – after all these things and a couple of thousand more like them, he had no heart left for games, for golf, or bowls or bagpipes, or chess or flowerpots – no heart left to put into minor passions. He didn't need them, not with the wedges that had been driven into him still swelling with the obsession that was the job. Even Derek had only been a nuisance, crying when he wanted to sleep, needing time and attention, trying to draw him out of himself and away from the job on hand. He even pretended to Muriel it was simple ambition. But she should have seen through him to the brawling, dirty microcosm behind his insulation against self. Muriel just wasn't bright enough; her lack of understanding and his decision never to put her

75

through the hell of striving for comprehension had slowly poisoned whatever they had when they started. But he would not fight with her. He'd witnessed too many fights, screaming, clawing, man-woman cat-fights ever to allow himself to be dragged into one. He knew that Muriel would have welcomed occasional bloody great rows as a substitute for communication, but he didn't care enough to make the effort. Derek could always say he had never seen his parents fight, never heard a cross word come out of his old man – but then he had never heard many words come out of his old man. During the year after Derek had passed up from the Academy to Strathclyde University to Study Engineering, the domestic situation had grown distractingly worse. She didn't like county life – though they lived in Thane for fifteen years before she discovered it – she didn't like his new job, didn't like anything. Even the high salary which gave her money to play with only emphasised her discontent. He put up no struggle, but neither did he yield to her pleas for a new house, a new car, a continental holiday, etc. etc. He chose that year to force her to realise that what she hated was not any of the things she complained of, but only him, her husband of twenty years. He knew change would only serve to throw the true source of her unhappiness into high relief, and, never placing faith in panaceas, quietly agreed to her leaving him. No question of a divorce; just a 'visit' – suddenly she was shy, determined but shy, protecting him, just as if he'd understood nothing of what had been happening to them day by day for two decades : a long visit then to her younger sister down in Lytham St. Anne's. On the morning he drove her into Glasgow to catch the train south he knew she would never come back. In his way, he was glad. With Derek installed in a students' hostel in Glasgow, with his own rabble of friends, there was no one to whom he owed a debt – save the officers and men of Thane County Police Headquarters.

'Heard from your mother lately?' McCaig asked as he bisected the pie and tipped it, not as hot as it should be, on to two plates.

'Had a letter end of April. She wants me to go down for a couple of weeks in summer.'

'You should go.'

'I went last year, remember.'

'Didn't you like it?'

'With Auntie Betty and Uncle Willie and that bloody cousin hanging round me. Jesus!'

'You used to like it,' said McCaig.

'I was younger then,' said Derek. 'Anyhow, I'd no option but to like the lousy place, considering we never went anywhere else.'

'True,' McCaig admitted. 'What's your cousin Caroline like now?'

'Caroline,' said Derek swinging himself on to a chair at the table, 'wouldn't make a good poke for a blind hunchback.'

McCaig made breath drift audibly through his nostrils and let the boy wonder whether the sound meant disapproval, or amusement. He wasn't even sure himself. Finding that he had an appetite after all, he began to eat.

'You'll stay the night?' he said at length.

'Okay. But I'll have to get back first thing.'

'I'll give you a run in,' said McCaig.

'Can you spare the time,' said Derek.

'If you're early enough up,' said McCaig. 'Anyway, I've got business in Glasgow.'

'The big case,' Derek said. 'Really got you going this one, by the sound of it.'

McCaig only nodded, not wishing to give his son the opportunity to annoy him by asking questions and, what was worse, preach his adolescent opinions about crime and society. He had just begun to feel comfortable with the boy again, almost to enjoy himself, and he would rather by far have sought out some other common ground – found out how the lad lived, what he got up to and how he was faring at Strathclyde. Perhaps Derek sensed the direction the conversation would take, for he resented these sudden forays into his privacy. He considered himself an adult now – he was too, McCaig supposed – and consequently entitled to lead his own life without explanation to anyone, least of all his father. Anyhow, the McCaig tendency to reticence was probably well established in the genes.

'Tell me, Dad,' said Derek, 'are you on to anyone?'

'You read the papers,' said McCaig gently. 'They get everything we have.'

'Aw, come on,' said Derek 'I know better than that. You're stuck, aren't you? According to the *Herald* you are. Don't tell me the combined forces of Glasgow and Thane can't get anywhere at all.'

'I'm afraid we can't.'

'You'll have done the old megaphone round the town, and the door-to-door routine?'

'Of course, of course,' said McCaig impatiently, his reply tinged with annoyance at having to answer such a stupid question.

Derek took a packet of French cigarettes from his pocket and shook it at his father. 'Want one? They're pretty harsh.'

'Not in your life,' said McCaig, remembering his experiment with Derek's Continental fags last December. Derek chuckled indulgently and lit one of the loose pungent tubes, coughing on the first draw. McCaig lit a BENSON & HEDGES filter, and pulled smoke through the taste of tea. Derek settled back. Something in his son's expression made McCaig uneasy. Was it another manifestation of their apartness that Derek could disturb him just by his manner?

'About the Balnesmoor business,' said Derek, 'I might ...'

'Look, son,' said McCaig as warmly as he could. 'Look, I've been up to the ears in it for nearly a fortnight, and I'm sick to death of the bloody thing. I've discussed it, talked about it and thought about it morning, noon and night. I'm at home now and I've no wish to discuss it here. All right?'

Derek did not appear aggrieved. 'I appreciate that,' he said. 'Besides, you won't want me at your throat with all my cocky notions : okay?'

McCaig grinned; the lad was learning the kind of common-sense which comes with maturity, the ability to see himself and his actions objectively. 'More or less,' McCaig admitted.

Derek brushed his hair back with his fingers, kneading his scalp. 'Well, okay,' he said. 'But I've got some information I thought you might be able to use.'

'How the bloody hell can you have information?' said McCaig. 'You haven't been in the bloody county since Christmas.'

'If you ask me nicely,' said Derek, 'I'll tell you what it is.'

'All right,' said McCaig indulgently. 'What's this valuable piece of information you think you've got your hands on?'

'I didn't say it was valuable,' Derek said calmly. 'I don't

know if it means anything at all, but it might. You might even have dug it up on your own.'

'What?'

'There's a bird in Lannerburn called Syme, May Syme. She holes out in a trailer parked in a field just beyond The Place.'

'I know it,' said McCaig. 'What about her?'

'She's a semi-pro actually,' Derek said, without so much as a blush. 'She works in a garage or some place during the day, but at night she ... entertains.'

'How d'you know about the local whore?'

'Anyway,' Derek went on, ignoring his father's question. 'Round about Christmas last year somebody laid into her.'

'That's a hazard of the trade.'

'Maybe so, but vice out here in the country tends to be pretty uncomplicated.'

'Now just what the hell d'you know about vice?'

'Wait, wait; the point is – some charming character laid into this old bag with a whip.'

'Where?'

'In her trailer.'

'Who was he?'

'Search me,' said Derek, 'But, Jesus, he really flayed her.'

'I expect she got well paid for it.'

Derek shook his head. In the cloudy eyes was a glint of distress even at the memory. McCaig shifted his buttocks on the chair, put his elbows down. His tone was firm, controlled, but the indulgent note had gone out of it now. 'Maybe,' he said, 'you'd better tell me how you got this information.'

'Take my word for it,' said Derek. 'It's the truth.'

'Were you with her?'

'Well, yes,' said Derek. 'I was. Not when it happened, of course.'

'This was last December, when you came home here for the weekend, right?'

'Yeah!'

'And that's what you did with the money I gave you for Christmas, right?'

'Okay, okay,' said Derek, raising his palms in a gesture of placation. 'Don't read me a sermon.'

McCaig sat back, suddenly grim. 'Whoring around's a dangerous entertainment,' he said. 'You can wreck yourself in a week at that game.'

'Please,' said Derek. 'I didn't *have* to tell you. Anyway, I don't go that way much, not often, I mean. I wouldn't want to, even if I could afford it.'

'One good dose of the clap at this stage in your career ...'

'Don't give me the heavy father stuff,' said Derek, 'just tell me if the data's any use.'

'It might be,' said McCaig. 'Did you see the marks?'

'Did I see the marks! Jesus, you couldn't miss them. She looked as if she'd been minced. It took her all her time to open the door. In fact she wouldn't open the door at all until I told her who I was and she took a long squint at me out of the window.'

'You weren't daft enough to tell her your real name?' said McCaig.

Derek looked surprised. 'Yeah!'

'Oh, Christ,' said McCaig. 'Didn't you realise I'm well-known in these parts.'

'Frankly,' Derek said, honest enough to redden at the realisation of his stupidity, 'I didn't think.'

'If you must get up to mischief with whores,' said McCaig, 'I'd be obliged if you used a false name in future. And make sure you don't carry too much money, and if you ...'

'No more lectures,' said Derek, 'or I'll walk out right now.'

Sulkily McCaig kept his mouth shut, and his son continued, 'She only let me in because I told her I had a bottle with me, which I had. She hadn't been out of the trailer for three days 'cause she was ashamed to be seen.'

'Face marked?'

'Not her face so much, but all around her throat and neck and down over her tits.'

'Don't tell me you ...'

'No, no,' said Derek, screwing up his face in disgust at the suggestion. 'I wasn't that desperate. But her robe-thing was open and she had cream all over the welts. I asked her about it and I think she was so glad that I wasn't going to ... you know, or anyway just glad to see a human face again, she told me a man had done it to her. She didn't give me too many details, but I got the impression she'd brought him back to the

80

trailer and he'd offered her a lot of lolly to let him give her a couple of strokes with this whip he had. Silly old bag should've known better. Anyway she agreed, reluctantly I suppose, because she didn't strike me as being the hard-bitten type, and he gave a couple of hard strokes : then, when she told him to quit it, he lost the wool and really let her have it.'

'Didn't she bawl?'

'Search me,' said Derek. 'I was interested enough, but... well, the inside of that place was reeking, and she wasn't much use to me in the state she was in, so I got out pretty fast.'

'Give her anything?'

'Hm!' Derek admitted.

'How much?'

'Couple of quid, and the bottle I had with me. It was only vino anyway.'

'I see.'

'Any use to you?'

'It might be,' said McCaig, thinking that it might be. He brooded about it for several minutes, then glared up at his son. 'But listen, it's time I told you a few facts of life, Derek.'

Quickly the boy slipped off the chair. 'In that case I'm off to bed. Still keep my old room up, Pop, do you?'

'Don't be funny,' said McCaig.

'Teddybear an' all.'

As Derek went towards the door, McCaig called, 'Hey!'

'What?'

'I'm not finished.'

'If you're going to preach, you are,' said Derek.

'No,' said McCaig. 'I won't preach, I promise. Just answer me two questions.'

'Okay!'

'Did she know who you were; connect you with me, I mean? '

'I doubt it.'

'And who told you where to find her in the first place?'

'That is my secret.'

'Who told you?'

'How about a game of cribbage?' the boy suggested.

McCaig tried to fix him with his most threatening stare, but either he was too tired, or ... no, he couldn't bully the lad. He got up slowly, pulled a dish-towel from the rack and threw it across the kitchen. 'All right then,' he said ruefully. 'But only after we wash up.'

TWO

With the tray across her knees she sat propped in bed, watching the corn-coloured rectangle of light which the sun printed on the wall shift slowly into a new shape. She cupped both hands around the soup bowl as if taking nourishment from contact with its heat. Not until after he had begun his account of the meeting with Galbraith did she begin to eat. This was no time, Lang realised, to embark on any kind of argument with her, or to parade his hopelessness on the off-chance that she would see reason and change her mind. When she was back on her feet, however, physically and mentally stronger, then he would have no compunction about playing on her reluctance to face up to the chore of starting life in a new place. He still could not believe that her hatred of Balnesmoor was more than a temporary emotion. But there was no sense in telling her of Galbraith's mocking assurance that the property, under the present circumstances, was practically worthless just yet. He invented small cheerful lies, and, to her grave questions, gave quick answers, overlaying one small deceit with another until he almost found himself believing them. The picture he drew of buyers rushing at them with fistfuls of money was so convincing that he came dangerously close to admitting into his thinking the notion that he too wanted to get away from Balnesmoor. Money: he clenched his teeth in his closed mouth. If one had enough money, and the patience of course, it would be possible to find another house as quiet and as comfortable as this one. The damned county was probably littered with them, but money was the big stumbling block. He'd always lived in cramped dull rooms in rented properties, and he would not go back to that. He had earned the right to live how he wished but to leave her would mean leaving broke, financially set back fifteen or twenty years, worse than he was before in fact. Now he had no monthly pay cheque to count on. Even if some hard-headed, unsentimental person did turn up

82

they would be as aware of the situation as he was and quick to seize advantage of it. The most he could hope for from the sale of the house would be five or six thousand pounds, half its real value. To count on more was stupid : to count on making a sale at any price was stupid, as Galbraith had so emphatically pointed out.

'How much does Galbraith think we'll get?' Jenny asked.

'About what we paid for it,' Lang lied glibly.

'I thought it would have been less.'

'Well, we may drop a bit, but good properties in this part of the county are always at a premium.'

'How anyone can live here now, I don't know,' Jenny said.

'There's no sentiment in business,' Lang told her.

'You don't understand at all, Norman, do you?'

'It'll be a week or two, maybe longer before we hear anything,' he said.

Jenny frowned and shook the cooling broth as if the diced vegetables in it held some prophetic message. 'I know,' she said, 'so I want to go back to Glasgow.'

'Yes, we both will,' said Lang abstractedly.

'Tomorrow,' she said.

She sought his eyes, but he looked away from her, shifting his thighs on the bed, her erect body rolling in response to the movement of the springs, like the mast of a small vessel keeled about by lapping waves. 'I must,' she said.

'Where'll we stay then?' snapped Lang. 'Tell me that.'

'A hotel, just a cheap one would do.'

'I can't afford even a cheap hotel for more than a night or two, and it might be months before we get shot of this place.'

'It would save money if I went and you stayed behind,' the woman said.

'You can't live in Glasgow in a hotel on your own, you're not fit for it.'

'I'll be all right once I get out of here,' Jenny said. 'Listen, Norman, you can't understand what it's like for me. Every time I go near those windows and look out I think I see them, standing there, looking at me.'

'Who?'

'Them, those girls. I feel them coming across the lawn to knock on my door, to ... I can't shake them off, Norman. I'll never be able to open the kitchen door again without imagining

83

they'll be there on the step, just standing, all ... all dirty and soiled, staring at me, pleading for me to help them.'

'Jenny ...'

'I'm frightened. I want people near me.'

'*I'm* here.'

'I want a lot of people all the time.'

'You never told me any of this before,' said Lang.

'I never felt it strong enough – before.'

'You'll get over it,' he said lamely.

'No,' she cried. 'I'll never get over it.'

She shivered, soup spilling on to the tray's glass top, a cube of white potato in a puddle of golden-green water.

'You won't like living in Glasgow on your own,' said Lang.

'Yes, I will. I know I'll be all right there.'

He walked across the room, sunlight gilding his cheeks and silvering his hair and moustache, adding an alien dignity to his features. He stopped at the window and shading his hand over his eyes, peered out at the burgeoning mass of foliage on the trees. 'Summer,' he murmured. 'It's summer.'

'Well, Norman?' she said. He did not reply. She said, 'I'm not asking you to leave, not until you sell it.'

'What about your clothes?'

'I'll just take a suitcase.'

'I'd have to come with you.'

'I'll be all right, Norman, really I will. Once you sell the house and we get the money you can come.'

'Once we sell the house,' he said quietly. Rooks infested the uppermost branches of the trees. Sheened glossy black, they cawed and craked complainingly at each other. The scuttle of a rabbit at the fence caught Lang's attention. He watched the creature, until something startled it and it laid back its ears, glided beneath the wire and scurried off into the undergrowth.

'Supposing we took a month at the seaside,' he said.

'Then what would we do?'

'Come back here.'

'No, Norman.'

He spun round to face her, the dusky colour under his skin not health, but the pumping blood of temper. 'All right,' he said loudly. 'I'll tell you the truth – Galbraith says there's no hope of selling this place, not for years anyway.'

'You told me ...'

'I told you a lie,' said Lang.

'I don't care what Galbraith says, I must get out of here.'

'It'll be the ruin of me,' said Lang without a trace of melodrama. He turned again to the window. The rabbit was back, travelling in fits and starts downhill by the fence towards the moor.

'You don't care what happens to me, do you Norman?' Jenny said.

'It's for your good I'm doing it at all,' he said. He waited for her retort but when it didn't come, he returned from the window and stood, almost contritely at the foot of her bed. He plucked a minute fleck of swansdown from a corner of the coverlet.

'I think you'd rather I went into that hospital – for good this time,' she said.

'Jenny, for God sake don't say these things.'

'If I have to go in,' she said, 'I won't come out. I'll be inside until I die.'

He held the weightless fragment of feather in his palm and breathed upon it, not intentionally. It soared upward, then floated gently to the floor. He watched it with the same degree of concentration and the same numbness as he had watched the nibbling rabbit. 'We'll go into Glasgow tomorrow,' he heard himself say, 'and find a hotel. But once you've settled in, I'll come back here and do . . . whatever I can about selling up.'

'Norman,' Jenny said. 'I'm sorry.'

He said nothing to this and after a moment Jenny lifted her spoon and began to sup daintily from the bowl. Lang sighed.

'It'll be cold now,' he said.

'No,' the woman said with a fragile smile. 'It's just right.'

Ryan's innate caution caused him to glance around the shed to make sure that Johnstone was not lurking unseen in any of the stalls. Birnie, his left hand flat on the sleek haunch of the nearest beast, said, 'It's all right, in y'come.'

'You're Birnie?' said Ryan.

'That's me.'

'You phoned my house and asked me to come out to see you this morning?'

'Ay.'

85

'All right,' said Ryan. 'Here I am; what's all the secrecy for?'

'I never really thought you'd come,' Birnie admitted. 'But I thought I'd chance it. It had t'be you, Mr Ryan.'

'Why?'

'I don't want it t'get back through any of the Sellars lads that I've been givin' information t'the police.'

'They wouldn't hold it against you, surely?' said Ryan.

'Y'never know,' said Birnie. 'Any roads there's those as might get t'hear of it as shouldn't; that's why I asked you t'come personally.'

The byre smelled clean and sweet, the metal of the milking machines gleaming and the rubber red and soft. Even Birnie had the trim appearance of a young suburban commuter on his weekend off, tweed hipsters tucked into a pair of sawn-off green gum boots, a Norwegian sweater as white as pure milk, a blue reindeer knitted into the back. He was around thirty, Ryan judged. The senator-style haircut was probably designed to hide premature balding. His skin was bronzed by outdoor work, but a blonde stubble did not hide the ugliness of the acne pits which littered his chin.

'Johnstone's not here?' said Ryan.

'Gone in to Lannerburn for the morning. That's why I asked you t'come today,' Birnie explained.

'What's on your mind?'

'See Johnstone,' said Birnie. 'Y'should keep an eye on him.'

'Yes.'

'He's worth the watching,' Birnie went on.

'In any special connection?'

'Women,' said Birnie, with a sinister wink.

Ryan wondered who out of the dozens of Sergeants and Constables had been the one who originally questioned Birnie. He must have been questioned, of course, because his, Ryan's, directive had indicated that there were three farmhands none of whom he had met. He cursed himself now for galloping off to Galbraith's without ... finishing? ... finishing the job at Johnstone's. It probably wasn't serious though, for he didn't trust Birnie. There wasn't yet the slightest gripe in his innards to indicate the intuitive excitement which generally, though not always, precluded a find.

'How long have you worked here?' Ryan asked.

'Six year.'

'Like it?'

'It's okay.'

'You don't live in Balnesmoor, Birnie, do you?'

'Marland,' said Birnie. 'Lived there all m'life.'

'Married?'

'Naw.'

'You live with your parents? Are they both still alive?'

'Well, they were this mornin',' said Birnie. 'Hey, who're you supposed t'be interested in, me or Johnstone?'

'Neither of you,' said Ryan. 'At least not yet.'

'Another thing about him . . .' Birnie started to say.

'I take it you mean Mr Johnstone?'

'Ay, another thing about him, he batters lumps out her from time t'time.'

'Does he?' said Ryan. 'Batters his wife about? How d'you know all this, Birnie?'

'Keep m'eyes an' ears open.' The man shifted away as a cow at the rear end of the shed made water noisily. Birnie's voice came slightly muffled from behind another animal, and cautiously, for he was wary of the beasts' back legs, Ryan strolled up the centre avenue, until he could look along the flanks, past the big barrel belly, at the young man. Birnie appeared to be consulting a gauge which, like a small alarm, was fixed at eye-level to the stainless pipe. 'Knocks hell out'r he does. Bastard.' He wheeled round again and the suddenness of the movement startled the cow, making it drag its head against the ring, lowing plaintively and clattering its hooves on the concrete. Birnie patted it and soothed it fondly. 'He nips in for a whack at'r occasionally. I've heard her bawlin' fit to bust.'

'How often?' said Ryan.

'Often,' said Birnie. 'An' there's others an' all. He's got women all over the county, Johnstone has.'

'Can you name any of them?' said Ryan.

'I thought you'd be interested,' said Birnie. 'Well, I can't name many, but there's one anyway I know about.'

'Who?'

'She lives down in Thane, an' her name's Denholm, Allison Denholm. She's not been in the county very long.'

'Is that the only one?'

'There's dozens, I'm tellin' you,' said Birnie. 'But he's

87

carryin' on with the Denholm girl. He's a terrible man for the women.'

'How about you, Birnie?' said Ryan innocently. 'I'll bet you've quite a harem yourself.'

'A harem?' said Birnie. 'Och ay, I've had m'share.'

'Then what makes it different with Johnstone?'

'He's married.'

'That's not a police matter,' said Ryan. 'A divorce agency's maybe, but not the bloody county police.'

'An' he beats up Edna.'

'Edna?' said Ryan as if he did not know the name.

'Ay, Mrs Johnstone.'

'You always call her Edna?'

'Not t'her face,' said Birnie.

'Does he mark her up badly then?' asked Ryan. 'Black eyes, that sort of thing?'

'Sure, batters lumps out her.'

'On the body too?'

Birnie hesitated, then smiled. 'Aw naw,' he said, slyly. 'You're not catchin' me that way, sir. About her body I know nothin'.'

'Thanks,' said Ryan.

'Here,' said Birnie. 'Are y'goin' to'do somethin' about it?'

'About what?'

'About Johnstone.'

'I ... doubt it,' said Ryan, turning. 'But thanks for the information.' He walked out of the byre, leaving the young hand staring after him with a worried expression on his face. Now, Birnie was up to something, but just what Ryan could not at that moment decide. He strolled around the gable end of the building and set out slowly towards the place where he had parked the car discreetly out of the sight of the farm house. Then he stopped, lit a cigarette, and admired the view of the moor. From here he couldn't see the workers, and it made a peaceful scene. Birnie certainly had something in mind beyond the call of duty as a righteous citizen when he called him. Perhaps he simply wanted to make trouble for his boss; cut his own throat too if Johnstone ever found out. Was Johnstone a lecher, a bit of a sadist? If he was ... This, Ryan thought, is getting more like a bloody American private eye story every minute – who's been sleeping in my bed stuff. God, if it went on this way maybe he'd wind up being rubbed down by two Swedish blonde twins at last. He hesitated, took an undecided pace towards the car, then turned around and made his way back towards the farmhouse again.

Fifteen minutes later he was washing down his third griddle scone with a second mug of sweet milky Nescafé. The woman watched him eat. She was smiling as if the sight of his hunger amused her. Breakfast dishes still lay on the table and a night-dress was tossed over the back of a chair. She wore a stained cotton shirt in a tartan pattern and shiny denim jeans. She was easy to talk to, Ryan discovered, and now that her husband wasn't around seemed much more able to relax. She was still sexy but somehow she didn't seem to thrust it at him as she had done the last time he'd been here with Blair. Still, she was attractive, with that narrow waist and the rise of the belly out of it stretching the uncompromising material of the jeans, making firm, suggestive creases just at the nip of the thighs.

'More coffee, Inspector?'

'No thanks.'

They had talked about the case, but she had been tactful enough not to probe beyond the skimming of information which the papers had given. Was it tact, or just disinterest? He had gently questioned her about Birnie, and had got just the kind of answers he might have expected – a good dairyman, but moody, argued with the boss, and went on week-long sulks when he would talk to no one, not even her.

'Not even you?' said Ryan.

'Yes,' Edna Johnstone said. 'He's normally very chatty t'me.'

'Perhaps,' said Ryan, making a joke of it, 'he fancies you.'

'Maybe,' said the woman.

'I doubt if your husband would like that.'

'No.'

'Is he ... is your husband the jealous type then?'

She looked at him with amusement, leaning forward with her elbows on her knees and the cigarette between her knuckles streaming smoke back across her face. She jerked her head shaking her hair away from her eyes. 'Was it wee Birnie brought you up here today?'

'No, I was in the area and as Birnie had apparently slipped through the net...'

'I thought it might've been him. He's a born troublemaker.'

89

'Is he?' said Ryan. 'In what way?'

'Just is, a natural born troublemaker.'

She rose and put her coffee mug on the table, then stretched, the cigarette dangling loosely from her lips. 'Will you wait for Phil to come back?'

'How long will he be?'

'When he gets into town there's no tellin' how long it'll take him,' the woman said. Ryan watched her tuck in her shirt tails, glimpsing a band of naked flesh. 'Was there something special you had t'ask him?'

'No,' said Ryan. 'No, nothing special.' He grinned at her. 'To tell you the truth, Mrs Johnstone, I just fancied a cup of coffee on the sly.'

'Like another?'

'Oh, no,' he said, ostentatiously inspecting his wristwatch. 'I've taken up enough of your time.'

She shrugged, 'Don't worry about me,' she said. 'I've got all day to kill.'

Ryan reluctantly picked up his hat, and, thanking her for her hospitality, got out of the farmhouse into the cool fresh air. Well, he decided as he walked swiftly to the car, if Johnstone had to go outside for his pleasure he must either be badly oversexed, or a raving nut – either way, the habits of farmer Phil might just be worth investigating. He got into the Hillman, slammed the door, and pulled out, up the bumping incline to the roadend, reversed on to the macadam surface and headed over the back route to Lannerburn in search of Allison Denholm.

THREE

A month or so after his father's fatal stroke, Galbraith quietly relinquished his membership of Radleigh golf club, using his new-found influence to skip the waiting list into the county's premier club, Heathwood Park. His motive for the change was not sentimental, but based on the realisation that if he stayed on at Radleigh his recreation would be spoiled for years to come by the shadow of his father's achievements as both golfer and committee-man. Anyway, Heathwood Park, though more

90

expensive and less convenient to the office in Lannerburn, numbered many young businessmen among its members and Galbraith conducted a number of satisfactory transactions in the locker-room and bar. He had one inflexible rule, however – never discuss business on the course. Consequently, he seldom lacked company at any hour of the day or the week. Out in the sunshine on the peninsula of fairway behind the eleventh green at eleven-ten on a Wednesday morning, he shaped up an iron to loft his overshoot back towards the pin. His partner and opponents were out of sight; over the steep sandy maw of the bunker he could barely discern the top of the pin. He addressed the ball, wriggled his hips, settled his feet into the grass, and checked off his grip. His control of the irons was very poor and even as he began the back swing he could almost hear his father's histrionic groan of dismay, a maddening sound held perfect in his mind down to the last scathing inflection. He connected cleanly with the tilt of the blade, squeezed his eyes shut, opening them again in time to watch the ball loop high, thud softly on to the crown of the bunker rim, hover for an instant, then drop back skittering down the fine raked sand to the bottom. He swore horribly under his breath then heard, and not mentally, the slow mocking handclap which his father had used as a means of castigation. He whipped round, looking this way and that, half afraid that the old man's spectre had dawdled over the miles from Radleigh to have some sport at his expense here in the June sun. The sun made the figure above him at the edge of the tee of the seventh blurred and indistinct. Galbraith shaded his eyes.

'Tyler?' he cried.

He listened to his step-brother's laughter, and watched him, still clapping, come down the incline. Galbraith swung his club lightly, trimming the grass, and laughed too, a highly artificial laugh to signify his highly artificial pleasure at the surprise meeting. 'I didn't know you were back.'

They moved together and shook hands like old friends. Tyler Ballentine was a tall gangling man, with thick dark brown hair, peppered now in a distinguished fashion with grey. His complexion was nut-brown, shiny with exposure to a stronger sun than ever shone in Scotland, his arms, too, up to the hems of the short-sleeved shirt. He had a low affable voice which accented the rich Scottish r rather than disguising it in an

91

attempt at the metropolitan English which Galbraith affected. In spite of the four years they had lived together in pretence of kinship Galbraith always felt the distance between them. The unapproachability of the elder man undermined his confidence and took him back to the period when he doubted his own identity so badly that he made a real damned fool of himself sometimes trying to prove himself the equal of his new brother. He had succeeded too, in the long run, but the bitterness of that odd triumph was his. If Ballentine remembered the incident, he gave no sign, never had, of suffering from it or harbouring a grudge. It had happened a long time ago anyway, and afterwards they had gone their separate ways – as they had come together – unrelated by ties of blood. Even his father, Galbraith thought, for all his domineering manner and commanding personality, had never been able to link the four of them, the new wife too, into a family unit. There were some things you just could not order up, and domestic harmony was one of them. The old goat should have realised it when he fell in love with a bloody widow, complete with a teenage son. It was just sex anyway, and nothing that a couple of fast pokes wouldn't have cured : but no, Robert McQuarrie Galbraith was an honourable swine, even if he wasn't exactly upper crust or aristocracy, and he wouldn't simply allow himself to grapple with the plump protuberances of Inez Ballentine and be done with it. He had to go and marry her and even sonny, himself, aged seventeen, had known that the gilt would be off the gingerbread before a year was up. And so it was; there they all were stuck in the mansion at Marland – which he'd later sold – trying to pretend that all was sweetness and light. If Ballentine had not had some sort of affection for the old bird he would have shipped out and lived in Glasgow; if he, Galbraith, had gone up to Oxford, as was the plan, instead of sneaking in the back door of the firm brandishing his acumen like a torch in the dark, the marriage might have survived. Well, it did survive, but the deaths, coming as they did within a six month of each other, had been really a blessed relief – first the woman of a cerebral haemorrhage, then his father. It meant that he and Ballentine could stop squaring off over their parents' welfare, and a few other things as well, and start growing up. They were still, to all intents and purposes, friends of course, a pretence which, with absolutely nothing in common except a somewhat tragic – or farcical, depending on how you looked at it – interlude in their pasts, was not too difficult to maintain. He grinned warmly and pumped away at Ballentine's fist.

'How was the trip?' he asked. 'Profitable?'

'Not bad.'

'You got the sun anyway.'

'Golfing,' said Ballentine, 'I did a lot of it over there, especially in California.'

'Kept the end up for Britain, I hope?'

'Of course,' said Ballentine. 'I only lost when it was politic, business-wise.'

'You were always hot at that,' said Galbraith. 'What brings you way out here though, on a weekday morning?'

'I'm with friends,' Ballentine explained, nodding back at three men on the tee behind him.

'Yes,' said Galbraith, unable to keep the excuse out of his tone. 'So am I.'

'Your irons haven't improved.'

'Well, I don't get much practice,' said Galbraith. 'Busy, you know.'

Ballentine glanced pointedly over his shoulder.

'I'd better not keep you,' Galbraith said quickly, 'Looks like they're waiting.'

'Yes,' said Ballentine. They shook hands again.

'I may see you at lunch,' said Galbraith. 'If not, we must have dinner together soon.'

'Call me next time you're in the city.'

'I will,' Galbraith promised.

He watched Ballentine mount the incline on to the tee and saw the three men there look down at him casually, probably as Ballentine explained who he was. There was no need for that: two of them were members, and knew him slightly. He tried to tie the faces to an occupation, but could not; something to do with whisky, no doubt. One thing about Tyler, he had no scruples about doing business all around and over the ball. Still, he had the manner for it, so subtle and discreet and charming that not even the most ardent golfer could take offence : a game to match, a game to command respect. As he watched his step-brother select a club a tiny idea entered his mind, far back. It had no chance to develop for his partner was

93

calling at him to get on with it. He turned and waved, then gripped the iron and stepped gingerly on to the sand. His concentration was gone; he wasn't even thinking about the stroke as he drew the clubhead back. He was trying to grip the idea again, encapsulate it in practical method, but it was too elusive. The moment of impact snapped him back to the matter on hand. The ball soared up out of the bunker with a minimum of hissing sand; the strike felt so good, though he hadn't even tried, that it was no surprise at all when his partner appeared at the edge of the green and said, 'Good God, Galbraith, what happened? You're pin-high.'

He winked smugly and stuck up his thumb.

'Always at my best in a tight corner,' he said. 'Didn't you know?'

The wall of the town police station was a positive mural of warnings against warble fly, foot and mouth disease, potato blight, sheep-worrying, and the dangers of fire in woodlands. The desk sergeant's name was Cruikshank. He was four years off retiral age and played the bagpipes in the Lannerburn and District Pipe Band. He was known not only as a good piper but as a character who, when he grew old enough, would be elevated to the rank of local worthy. Contrary to public myth, most policemen weren't 'characters' at all, the word annoyed Ryan – not even the high-ranking detectives, perhaps them least of all; but he did not grudge Cruikshank his popular, colourful personality – Every trade had one somewhere. The station was deserted; Ryan went through the small hall and softly let himself through the counter flap. From a tall stool against the window Cruikshank watched him, then with a theatrical flourish took out his pocket watch and consulted it, frowning.

'I don't believe it,' he said.

'But it's true,' said Ryan.

'My God, Inspector, have y'not been told?'

'Told what?'

'About the proper conduct for C.I.D. officers,' said Cruikshank solemnly. 'I mean, this early-bird stuff'll be gettin' the whole force a bad name.'

'Sorry,' said Ryan. 'I'll try to mend my ways.'

'See's you do then,' said Cruikshank. He tucked the watch away. 'Now, what can I do for you?'

'I need the benefit of your vast experience and acute powers of observation,' said Ryan.

'Of course, of course,' said Cruikshank modestly. 'What is it this time; somebody growin' half an acre of cannabis up in Thane? I'm hot stuff on cannabis.'

'Phillip Johnstone?' said Ryan.

Cruikshank pressed his gaunt forefinger against his gaunt nose. 'A cow man, has a farm in Balnesmoor and a bonnie bit of stuff for a wife.'

'That's him,' said Ryan. 'Is he in town often?'

'Often enough,' said Cruikshank. 'What's on then? Is it the moor girls?'

'It might be,' said Ryan. 'I don't know. But I'm told Johnstone's quite a lad for the women.'

'Ay,' said Cruikshank. 'He's all that.'

'Allison Denholm, do you know her?'

'Denholm,' said Cruikshank, still caressing his nose. 'Denholm. Ay, I've got her. But I didn't know she an' Johnstone were ...'

'Neither do I for sure,' said Ryan. 'Are there others?'

'One anyway,' said Cruikshank, grinning now. 'But she's anythin' but exclusive. May Syme, big May. Works in Hogg's garage – pardon me, filling station out at the crossroads. Afternoons and weekends.'

'In a bikini?' asked Ryan.

'Eh?'

'In England the filling stations have their girls all done out in bikinis now.'

'D'you tell me,' said Cruikshank. 'Ay, a very progressive race, the English. No, you'll not find May in a bikini. She's a bit past that, never mindin' the weather.' Cruikshank came over to the desk and, moving the polished shell-case ashtray, hoisted his haunch on to it. 'Is this a break, Mr Ryan?'

'I doubt it,' said Ryan. 'But you never know.'

'It's a bad business,' Cruikshank said. 'It was like Bedlam here last week, but it's cooled down now. I haven't a man on the premises, though. They're all out workin' for your lot.'

'What about May Syme,' said Ryan, 'and Allison Denholm?'

'May's accommodatin',' said Cruikshank. 'She's at it all right, but she's discreet about it, and never makes a nuisance of herself. She lives in a trailer in the half-acre field between *The*

95

Place and the boneyard. Like as not you'll get her at home now, if you're interested.'

'Who ... uses her services?' asked Ryan. 'Any idea?'

'Not in detail,' said Cruikshank. 'If she was a highland dancer, I might be better informed, but as it is ... Ay, well, there's a few of the locals, this Johnstone joker, and another dairyman from Marland – no wait, that's funny, he's one of Johnstone's lads ...'

'Birnie?'

'Ay, Birnie, that's right,' said Cruikshank. 'I used t'know his father.'

'What about Birnie?'

'He's down in town a lot, right enough,' said Cruikshank. 'He's a sleekit sort, I believe, but I've never had any occasion t'tangle with him officially. I'll tell y'another secret, though, Galbraith's been out there at the caravan more than once.'

'Galbraith,' said Ryan in surprise. 'I though he'd be able to do better than some old pro.'

Cruikshank shrugged. 'Maybe he prefers it. It's probably cheaper than butterin' up one of the horsey crowd, or some wee deb from the tennis club.'

'And Allison Denholm?'

'She's only been here about a year. She works in the county offices, secretary t' McGillivray the supplies officer. Keeps herself to herself, I'm told. She rents a couple of rooms in Mammy Irvine's building, the one in Moorburn Street, by the Gospel Hall.'

'I know it,' said Ryan. 'Who else does Johnstone consort with?'

Cruikshank shook his head slowly. 'No more that I know of at the moment, but he's had a wheen in the past. Mind you, I think he's a looney. If I had a ...'

'Wife like that,' said Ryan, 'you'd never leave home.'

'Not even,' said Cruikshank, 'for the bloody pipe band.'

Ryan left his car by the yard gate and walked into *The Place*. The railway line broke off at Lannerburn. Tracks curved under the span of the bridge which brought the main high road into town, then split into a dozen disused sidings plugged with antique rolling stock long since out of service. Coal rees leaked their dregs from rotting canvas stands, and a disused signal-box, smashed to a shell by the village boys, towered over the area like the dwelling of a witch. The place was a bloody eyesore, a thorn in the Council's flesh. Plans had been afoot for years to dig it up and convert the acreage into a bus station, but they never seemed to come to fruition, much to the satisfaction of the squatters who had taken possession of the ancient caravans, wheelless buses and carriages all over the railway ground. Wrecked cars cluttered the fringes, burned out vans, decrepit Fords and Austins, many of them stripped and cannibalised to feed the ancient transport of the families in the vicinity. They were the ragged hem of society, not tinkers, not gipsies – who would have scorned the place – but drifters lacking the ambition to be comfortable, or the energy to be itinerant. The men put in time as casual workers on the farms around, potato-howking, berry-picking in season, and the women begged rags around the doors of the town. The ramshackle dwellings were ugly and unpainted, no redeeming flowerpots or vegetable gardens here, just odd ropes of half-washed clothing hung out to dry in the sun. Though welfare and health authorities complained from time to time and the police kept a weather eye on the inhabitants, the community was neither large nor active enough to be troublesome. When Ryan walked up the wide, muddy central aisle he received no more than a few mildly curious glances from the women in the doorways, and a broadside of stares from the children who fluttered like sparrows in the dust. He soon reached the fence at the limit of the railway property and climbed over it into the field. With *The Place* behind him the view was quite pictur-esque, the overgrown walls of the town's old graveyard with the dainty steeple of the original parish church rising out of it. Part of the wall, he noticed, had collapsed under the tree roots' pressure and lay in a broad mound like the grave of an unknown giant. The ground was sour, weeds prolific, the grass too sparse even to make good grazing. One of the massive power pylons which filed across the county was planted at the far end of the field and in its shadow sat May Syme's trailer. It was a large one, not old. Ryan reckoned the woman had probably picked it up cheap, one side being badly scraped and dented; even through a fresh coating of pale-blue paint, rust-scum showed. The ladder leading to the door was bright yellow, the curtains, drawn now over the windows, red, giving

97

the trailer a garishly cheerful appearance. Ryan knocked on the door. Morning sunlight fell full upon it and it gave out that unique smell of warm varnish which reminded him of his father's garden shed. He knocked again loudly, then, receiving no answer, pushed. The lock clicked and he went in.

He faced another narrow door with a large notice hand-written on cardboard pinned to it – *Sweet Pees*. Stepping over the threshold, he squeezed himself into the long main interior. The table carried an empty ale bottle, an almost empty wine bottle, empty bottle of milk, empty bottle of Coca-Cola and two empty cups, a plate with the heel of a lettuce sandwich and the crust of a mutton pie, a second plate decorated with fragments of mustard pickle and a whole uncooked coil of pork sausages, two tinfoiled segments of Swiss cheese and a packet of oatcakes. A can-opener, a corkscrew and three Bank of Scotland pound notes lay beside the litter. A woman's clothing spilled over a canvas camp chair, and on a small armchair sat a red plastic basin full of freshly washed but unironed laundry. Ryan moved into the room. Under the end window a bed took up the width of the trailer. A plastic curtain tucked into a strap prevented daylight from penetrating and disturbing the slumber of the woman below. She lay on her back, half buried in a quilt, one arm dangling over the bunk-edge. The fingers of the hand were open, short nails almost brushing the matting on the floor. She was completely naked. Her breasts were gargantuan, huge umber aureoles around the nipples, tufts of brown hair beneath the armpits. Yet her face was almost angelic, like the faces of women in the Italian paintings Ryan had seen in Glasgow Museum, big-jawed, small-mouthed, long lids to the eyes.

'Miss Syme,' he said quietly.

When she did not respond, he went forward, peering in the gloom around the table. The scars on her upper arms were quite discernible and not, as he'd first thought, just a trick of shadow. They were old scars but some of them, the broad band across the upper left breast, for instance, would probably never fade. 'May.'

She stirred. Ryan shifted discreetly back towards the door. Brown hair dropping across her face, she rolled over on to her elbow and blinked at him. Her breasts drooped pendulously, ugly, and as she dragged up her hips the quilt slipped, giving Ryan an unwelcome glimpse of naked flanks.

98

'Who're you, for God sake?' she growled drowsily.

'I'm a police officer.'

'Eh?'

'Inspector Ryan.'

She stared at her nakedness, then fumbled with the quilt and rolled back with it, punching up the pillow. She propped herself up, modestly covering herself to the throat.

'What time is it?'

'Almost eleven.'

'Better come in then,' she said. 'You'll have had a good swatch at me b'this time anyhow.'

Ryan grinned and put the washing basin on the floor. Seating himself he offered her a cigarette from his packet, but she shook her head. 'I'd like to ask you some questions.'

'How d'I know you're the law?' she said.

Obediently Ryan opened the curtain a little and reached into his pocket for his credentials. She folded her arms patiently on top of the bedclothes, then said, 'Never mind. I'll take your word for it.'

Ryan stroked the tip of his chin with the edge of his identification card. Now that he could see her more clearly he judged her to be well into her thirties. She really was big, very passive at the moment. He must be careful not to rile her, he told himself; she looked like the kind of woman who might have an ungovernable temper and he did not relish the idea of brawling with a huge naked whore in such an enclosed space – not before lunch anyway. He took his time formulating his first question, but even then it was too direct.

'Do you know a farmer called Phillip Johnstone?'

'Ay.'

'Does he . . . visit you here?'

'Ay.'

'Often?'

'Naw, not that often.'

'Did he put those marks on your arm, by any chance?'

'What marks?'

'Come off it,' said Ryan. 'I saw them. I couldn't help it. Who beat you up?'

'None of your bloody business, mister,' she said. 'What rank did y'say y'were?'

'An Inspector.'

99

'It's the Balnesmoor murders, is it! What's Johnstone got t'do with them?'

'Not a bloody thing,' said Ryan. 'How about the scars?'

'I got them accidental-like.'

'Look,' said Ryan, 'I'm not here to arrest you for ... well, anything. I just want some information about your boyfriends.'

'I've got no boyfriends.'

'All right,' said Ryan. 'About the men you bring back here. Now, look, May, you can co-operate, tell me a few answers, or you can go all stubborn and play dumb, but I think, in your circumstances it'd be a hell of a sight better to tell me what I want to know and save yourself trouble.'

'Is that a threat?'

'Yes.'

She thought it over, nodding her massive head, then she laughed, making the sheet tremble and slide down her bosom until Ryan was again treated to the sight of the dark flabby nipples.

'Phil Johnstone, eh?' she said. 'Naw, he never marked me. Johnstone's not like that.'

'Who was it then?' said Ryan. He had a feeling of excitement, those telltale marks had stimulated him, professionally of course, and he had every intention of finding out who had put them there.

'I don't know his name. It was a while ago, anyway.'

'It wasn't ... Birnie?'

'Birnie!' she said. 'My, my, Inspector, but you've been busy. Did wee Birnie tell you about me?'

'Was it Birnie?'

'Hardly,' she said.

'Are you going to tell me, or not?'

'He was a stranger.'

'You really are making this bloody hard for me,' said Ryan. 'It wasn't Bobby Galbraith by any chance?'

She glanced at him quickly, then drew her knees up and hugged them; her girth made it difficult. She succeeded in knitting her fingers around her shins and held herself in balance, rocking slightly, sullenly. 'I rent m'home, here, this trailer, from Mr Galbraith,' she said quietly. 'And that's an end of it.'

'So he just comes here to collect the rent – in person.'

'What're you after, copper?'

'I know what those marks mean,' said Ryan. 'I'm not some stupid p.c., y'know. Somebody took a whip to you. Or do you go in for that sort of thing so regularly you can't remember who it was. How much did he pay you?'

'You dirty-minded bugger,' she said. 'I'm not like that.'

'I could have this trailer removed, if . . .'

'Naw, y'couldn't,' she said. 'It's owned legal by Galbraith. You've no case t'close it.'

'I could have it watched then,' said Ryan. 'And that wouldn't half put a damper on your trade.'

'It really was a stranger,' she said. 'He came in a car t'the garage. I work in a garage, Hogg's garage.'

'What kind of car?'

'A Rover, a 2000.'

'What did you call him?' Ryan asked.

'I never called him anything,' she said.

'Did you bring him back here?'

'Ay.'

'What for?'

'What the hell d'you think,' she blurted out, then corrected herself. 'For a drink'r two.'

'Why not to a pub?'

'Ach, cut it out.'

'You didn't get the registration number of the car, by any chance.'

'What d'y'think I'm are,' she said. 'It was dark. It was near Christmas. He picked me up in the garage . . .'

'How?'

'Asked me where he could get a drink in private.'

'Is that how you always do it?'

'I knew what he meant.'

'All right,' said Ryan. 'What did he look like?'

'He was tall, dark, quite good-lookin', maybe about thirty-five'r forty. I never got a real close look at him.'

She stopped, sulking, and Ryan prompted her. 'Go on.'

'Anyway he . . . we had a drink'r two out my bottle. He seemed like a nice bloke, y'know. An' . . . well, he admired me, an' he . . .'

She paused again, sinking back against the pillows, the small

101

rosy lips plump with temper and her brows drawn in a pucker
that might, Ryan thought, presage a storm.

'He offered you money to let him ...?' Ryan said quietly.

'Ay, but it was just two strokes. He made it sound like a
game, but I knew he wanted it. I've never done that sort of
thing before, y'understand, but he wanted it an' he seemed like
a nice bloke.'

'How much?'

'Ach, look ... twenty quid.'

'For two strokes!' Ryan exclaimed.

'Ay, but I still would never've done it if I hadn't liked him,'
she said. 'Anyway, it's common in London, so I'm told.'

'It looks like he got his money's worth?' said Ryan.

'Ay,' said the woman sadly. 'I was wrong about him. He ...
he got carried away; lost the place. I did everythin' t'get him
t'stop, but ... he couldn't. He had the whip with him, a dirty
thin black thing it was, and he went at me with it. Put his fist
in my mouth. I couldn't get up. He ... I blacked out
eventually. I wouldn't've thought it of him though.'

'Was he gone when you came round?'

'Ay.'

'Without ... paying?'

She hesitated once more. 'He left me fifty quid,' she said.

'New notes?'

She shook her head. 'Bits an' pieces, old paper.'

Ryan sighed. 'At least he did that.'

'It wasn't worth it,' said May Syme. 'Take m'word for it.'

'And you never saw him again?'

'Not really,' she said. 'And I don't want to, either.'

'What do you mean, not really?' asked Ryan.

'I thought I saw him in Lannerburn High Street, but maybe
I was wrong.'

'Where?'

'Outside Henderson's shop. Y'know it.'

'Was he walking, or in a car, or what?' asked Ryan.

'It was the end of January, I think: ay, about then, an' he
was just comin' out of the shop. That's right. He had a blue
suit on,' said the woman. 'But it might not've been him.'

'What was he wearing the night you brought him here?'
Ryan asked.

'Sports-jacket and trousers and a white shirt. It wasn't cheap

102

rubbish though, and the watch he had must've cost him a fortune.'

'Right,' said Ryan. 'I think that's about all, Miss Syme.'

'I hope it's of use t'you,' said the woman. 'Here, is it in your mind that he done in them two girls?'

'No,' said Ryan. 'I'm just making enquiries.'

'He might have,' she said. 'Y'can never tell with the nice ones.'

Ryan put on his hat, and pushed a tin ashtray across at her. She held the cigarette between finger and thumb, a long column of ash on it now. She cleverly transferred it to the tray without spilling a crumb, working the end out, screwing against the tin in Ryan's palm.

'Tell me,' the Inspector said. 'What did your other ... friends think when they saw the marks? Did it give them ideas?'

'Not them,' May Syme said. 'I'm choosey.'

'Didn't they, Galbraith for instance, ask for explanations?'

'Some of them did.'

'What did you tell them?'

'To mind their own bloody business.'

'Fair enough,' said Ryan. He had another question on the tip of his tongue, but before he could formulate it to draw the most effective answer, there was a quiet knock at the outer door. Both the policeman and the woman stared down the length of the trailer, then exchanged a glance.

'Who is it?' May Syme called.

The door opened wider and round the narrow aperture between it and the bathroom, stepped McCaig. If he was surprised to see Ryan he gave no sign of it, merely tipping back his hat from his brow, and smiling at the sight of the woman in the bed and the startled expression, guilty too almost, of the Inspector. 'Don't let me interrupt,' McCaig said.

'Who's he?' said May Syme.

'That,' said McCaig perhaps a little too quickly, 'isn't important. Go on, Ryan, pretend I'm not here.'

'Now who the bloody hell does he think he is, orderin' you around like that,' the woman exploded. Ryan, warmed a little at her defence of his rights, told her that this was his boss, then to McCaig said, 'I'm just finished anyway.'

'I'll walk you over to the car,' said McCaig. 'Where is it?'

Ryan told him, then, without so much as another glance at the woman in the bed, the Chief led him out of the trailer on to the grass. As soon as they were out of earshot, Ryan asked the question which had been nagging him since the moment McCaig had stepped into view. 'What's up, sir, has something cracked?'

'Cracked!' said McCaig. 'No, no, nothing's cracked.'

'Then what ...?'

'I wasn't looking for you,' McCaig said. 'I came to have a word with her in there. Christ, she really is a blowsy old bag, isn't she! What did she tell you?'

They were strolling across the field now towards the fence, and as Ryan outlined the story of the whipping-Johnnie in the Rover 2000, McCaig listened without a sound, both men quite oblivious to the stares of the squatters when they passed down the centre of *The Place*. He finished his account, standing by the Hillman, and only then realised that McCaig had either come on foot or parked his car elsewhere.

He opened the passenger door. 'My car's round at the parish church,' McCaig said. 'You'd better drop me off. I suppose you're going round to see this other girl of Johnstone's, Allison Denholm.'

'I thought I'd do that, yes.'

'I don't know,' said McCaig, after Ryan had taken the wheel. 'It's not the kind of lead that seems to be going anywhere, at least not in a straight line. What about this character Birnie?'

'I don't know about him yet.'

'Anything there for us, do you think?'

'Might be,' said Ryan. 'Or it might just be spite.'

'Let me know, Inspector,' said McCaig. 'I've an interest in this oddball line of yours.'

'Yes,' said Ryan. 'I'll give you the report as soon as it's through.'

'I thought,' said McCaig, 'I was being pretty smart tacking on to the tart, but it seems you beat me to it.'

'I'd like to talk to this joker with the whip,' said Ryan.

'So would I,' McCaig said sibilantly.

Ryan toyed with the idea of saying nothing but the question was too important to ignore. 'How did you find out about her?' he asked.

The Chief grinned. 'I knew you'd ask,' he said. 'I had a private source.'

'A wee linty, hm,' said Ryan, perfectly satisfied with the answer. 'One of her "specials"?'

'Almost,' said McCaig. 'Almost.'

FOUR

The breeze caught grit up from the street and flung it in a whirling eddy against Lang's legs. He angled his body against it, gripping the suitcase tighter. Lang fumbled the guide book from his pocket. Folded to one particular page the book had a dozen blue ink ticks marked marginally against the names of hotels. Eleven were deleted by a neat cross-stroke; only one remained – *Gilfillan's Private Hotel*.

'Well?'

'Oh, I don't know,' said Jenny.

'At least the terms aren't crippling.'

Set ten yards back from the pavement behind a rusty iron railing, the hotel was protected by a moat of sparse grass into which the brickwork sank as if, over the years, earth and masonry had become mingled and inseparable. Curtained with faded lace, the window had a coating of grey grime just sufficiently opaque to justify the term *Private* in the guide advertisement. A concrete path bisected the grass and led to a tall single door, panelled in corrugated glass. An old coconut mat lay dead on the step, presided over by a wake of empty milk bottles. The only double window on the frontage allowed a glimpse of a table set with sauce and vinegar bottles and a cut-glass vase of plastic flowers. A notice taped to the inside of this window stated – *Open to Non-Residents: Bar: Meals*.

'Come on,' said Lang. 'We'll see what it's like inside.' He led the way through the gate, any protest which Jenny may have made lost in the tumble of passing traffic. Lugging the case he turned the door-handle and passed into the hall. Jenny followed him.

She knew that this was the one he would choose for her, the last on the list – and the cheapest. The entire tour had been leading up to the inevitability of *Gilfillan's*; time was now

105

running out, though it was not too late for him to catch the last bus back to Balnesmoor. He had not told her he would return that evening but she would suggest it, he would argue for a while then agree. She didn't mind : there was a feeling of life here. The hall supported a coat rack, a grandfather clock with a motionless pendulum, and an empty desk placed across a doorway with a key-board behind it. A corridor ran to the left and a carpeted staircase went up, cutting out of sight on a half landing. There were heavy doors around her, big worn knobs and signs – *Lounge: Dining Room: Gentlemen: Bar.* She heard the strains of a radio and perhaps the murmur of human voices from behind the lounge door. Though the building was dark and old and gloomy, like the inside of her skull, she could feel people all around her. It fitted, comforting her; only Norman standing by the desk seemed out of place. Yes, he was part of the memory of Balnesmoor, a figment of all she was trying to reject. The rush and roar of the city outside soothed her and drew her thoughts away from silence; the silence terrified her, external silence, silence like the deadening of kapok. She craved only to be left alone in the middle of the city, the uncongenial drabness fitting for her kind of retreat.

The woman at the back of the desk was a spare, pared down, leathery ex-chorus girl, with a button nose and eyes like small brass hooks. 'Yeah?' she asked.

'I . . .' said Lang. 'We'd like a room. For my wife.'

The woman lifted a pen moored to a short length of hairy twine. She gave it a little shake, disentangling the string from four rings which glittered on her fingers, then offered it and the open register to Lang. 'How long?'

'I don't exactly know.'

'We're awful busy,' the woman said.

'Would three weeks . . .' Lang said.

The woman tried hard not to grin. 'Three weeks !' she said deferentially. 'Ay, I can give y'a nice room for three weeks, sir, at the back, nice an' quiet. Bed and breakfast?'

'Don't you serve meals?'

'Uh-huh, all meals, dinner an' tea.'

'What are your terms?' said Lang.

'Double room you'll want?'

'I . . .' Lang looked round questioningly at his wife. Jenny shook her head. 'There's no sense in it, Norman.'

106

'Are you sure, tonight anyway?' said Lang. 'I'll stay if . . .'

'No,' said Jenny. 'You'd better get back to the house.'

Lang turned to the desk again. 'Just a single room, thank you.'

'Room an' breakfast, five guineas the week,' said the woman.

'What!' He fumbled the accommodation guide from his pocket but as soon as the woman saw it and before he could begin to remonstrate, she said, 'That's long out of date, sir. Naw, five guineas's the best I can do : supper's included.'

Lang gaped round at Jenny, not for advice or even approval but in frustrated rage, as if he blamed her for the position into which his own cunning had forced him. Jenny said, 'If it's all the same I'd rather have a room at the front.'

'It's pretty loud at the front,' the woman said.

'That's all right.'

'Well, it's up to you, dear. I do have a nice single at the front, as it happens.'

'Thank you,' said Jenny. 'I'll take it.'

Lang stepped back from the desk and, shielding his face, murmured to his wife, 'Listen, it's not worth it. We'll try . . .'

'It's getting late,' Jenny said. 'Besides this is the cheapest so far.'

'Ay, you'll be fine an' comfortable here,' the woman remarked. 'Not find any place's reasonable anywhere around.'

Lang put down the suitcase slowly. 'All right.'

Brushing past him, Jenny quickly lifted the pen and fashioned her signature. She smiled softly as she did so, winning an almost kindly grin of response from the woman behind the desk. The key was offered. Jenny took it into her hand and closed her fist over it possessively.

'You'll need to hurry, Norman,' she said. 'If you want to catch the bus.'

Since the moment she admitted him to the tiny flat, Allison Denholm hadn't stopped moving. She paced like a caged animal, bored and irritated by confinement. There was an innocence in her expression which seemed to give the lie to the tale she told Ryan. According to her version, which, so vehement was her style of telling, the Inspector believed, she had been kicked out of her parents' home in Helensburgh after bringing disgrace to the family by having an affair with a

107

piano-teacher. Ryan found no humour at all in the lover's profession. Allison's statement was unrepentant, factual and chillingly cynical. 'The bastard wasn't even worth it,' she said.

She had been seventeen then and during the next three years had worked first as a typist in a Glasgow advertising agency, before wangling a job in the same trade in London. The capital gloss still showed in her manner and dress, all of it probably wasted on the office boys down in the County Offices. The flat was neat and spotlessly clean : a bed in an alcove – the 'other' room probably – and a tiny kitchenette behind a curtain. An Adler typewriter and a copy-stand filled with script rested on an old table under the window. Ryan had deliberately waited until the evening to catch her at home, and had apparently disturbed her in some additional work. When he came to question her on a personal level, he felt uncomfortable, for her attitude changed from cynical co-operation to outright hostility. When he tentatively mentioned 'boyfriends' she had an outburst of cold rage.

'Boyfriends!' she cried. 'I don't have any use for them.'

'No-one at all?'

'Not one.'

She made five strides between table and kitchenette, swivelled on her heel and came back. Her long slender legs punched out the hem of the skirt.

'So, you've no friends in Thane or Lannerburn?'

'Who needs them! I came here for peace and quiet and I was getting it nicely thank you until you came along.'

'I'm sorry, Miss Denholm,' said Ryan firmly. 'I wouldn't be here if it wasn't important.'

'Now you sound like a salesman, not a cop,' she said.

'I'm seeking information about two men,' said Ryan formally. 'And I have reason to believe ...'

'Who are they?'

'Phillip Johnstone ...' He knew instantly that the name meant nothing to her. 'He has a farm in Balnesmoor.'

'Ah!' she said. 'I'll bet this has something to do with the killings.'

'Do you know a man called Phillip Johnstone?'

'Never heard of him : and just for your information I've never been in Balnesmoor in my life,' the girl said.

'You may have known him under another name, perhaps,' said Ryan with patience. 'He's a tall chap, with dark . . .'

'Look,' she said, 'I know the names of my . . . of the staff down in the office. Beyond that, I don't know anybody. Understand me, *nobody*!'

'How about the name Birnie?' He knew he had struck oil. But it puzzled him that after her emphatic denials she made no attempt to cover up. He was sure this girl had cool enough nerves to pass off the lie.

'I know Birnie,' she said. 'Is he the reason you're bothering me?'

'How well do you know him?'

'He'd like to poke me,' she said brutally, 'but he isn't going to get the chance. Did he tell you I knew something about your murders?'

'How did you meet him?'

'He tried to pick me up. I went out for a walk – last year, September, just after I got here, on a Sunday, and I drifted into the new hotel in Kilcraig, I don't know it's name, for a drink. Birnie was in the lounge bar and he tried to pick me up.'

'But you . . .'

'I told the little bastard to drop dead.'

'He persisted?'

'Are you kidding, he practically dragged me out to his van. Nobody bothered, they just stood around laughing. But I fixed him. I got him with my knee right where it hurts; he let me go then all right.'

'Didn't you complain to anyone?'

'Who for instance?' Allison said. 'No, I went back and had another drink; when I came out he'd gone.'

'Weren't you . . . frightened?'

'Why should I be frightened?' the girl said. 'It happens all the time.'

'But you've seen him since?'

'Unfortunately. He's a persistent little louse, follows me around, into restaurants and bars where I am, and makes a damned nuisance of himself. He really wants me badly.'

'I gathered that,' said Ryan.

'It's pathetic really. Fancies himself a great lover, I suppose.'

Ryan could understand why the girl appealed to Birnie; she

109

had a sophistication – and a surface innocence – which Birnie had probably not encountered before. She was sexually attractive too. Not Ryan's type though, a bit like one or two of the young French film stars he'd seen in the *Palace* in Lannerburn, slender and pert and boyish but with that vicious, almost sadistic streak coming through, the blue eyes and soft mouth notwithstanding. In high heeled shoes she was probably taller than Birnie.

'If he's making a real nuisance of himself,' said Ryan, 'we, the police, could have a word with him, give him a warning.'

'Don't worry,' the girl said. 'I'll only let it go so far.'

'All right,' said Ryan. 'You've been very frank, Miss Denholm. I wonder if you'd answer me one more ... frank question.'

'Oh boy, I can sense something really obscene coming up,' the girl said. 'When you actually apologise in advance. What?'

'Have you been ... out with *any* man since you came to Thane?'

She stopped pacing and stared at Ryan, and for a moment he thought she was going to spit in his face. Then she smiled, her lips tense, and teeth small and cruelly white.

'Listen,' she said softly, 'I've answered that already, but just for the record, I've finished with men for good an' all. I've had two abortions already, two dirty, lousy, illegal abortions – don't worry they weren't done in your bailiwick – but the second almost killed me. It was an expensive little lesson in what men can do for you, so I've kicked the habit. I don't need men now. Is that clear? I just do what I want to do and I'm happy to do it alone. I only came to your town to lick my wounds. That's not against the law, is it?'

'I see.'

'I doubt it,' she said. 'They snuffle around my skirts like dogs, like Birnie, but I know how to deal with them all now. Your killer hasn't been here.'

Ryan was on the point of asking another question but the answer came into his mind and he closed his mouth and got to his feet. The girl opened the door for him. She was attractive, neat and clean like the flat, but cold too, icy. He felt some pity for her, mingled with dislike.

'Why did you pick Lannerburn to ... lick your wounds?' he heard himself ask.

'I did it with a pin,' she replied. 'A big map and a small pin : satisfied?'

Ryan nodded, and she closed the door on him.

As he went down, a huge marmalade cat, startled out of its nap, leapt across the narrow landing and vanished down the twisting stone steps. Slowly Ryan followed it out into the warm, red, evening street.

McCaig was alone in his office, jacket off and sleeves rolled up, his shirt very pale against the dark window. He listened patiently as Ryan told him about Allison Denholm and Birnie. 'Do you believe her?' he asked, as soon as Ryan had finished.

'Yes,' said Ryan. 'I think so.'

'Then how come Birnie put you on to her? He must be thick to cause trouble for himself.'

'It was just a way of getting back at her for ignoring him,' said Ryan. 'Not very bright of him, but maybe he hoped we'd take his word against hers.'

'Well, he was right about Johnstone whoring around anyway,' said McCaig. 'I wonder what he's got against his boss?'

'Maliciousness again,' Ryan said. 'Perhaps he has a shine on Mrs Johnstone, too.'

McCaig snorted. 'Bloody backwoods Casanovas,' he said. 'And what about this yarn of Johnstone beating up his wife. Not that it matters to us, wife beaters are ten-a-penny; so long's she doesn't complain officially it's none of our business. Mind you, if he was hacking lumps out of women all across the county, then maybe it would mean something relevant.'

'But he's not,' said Ryan. 'Though this joker in the Rover seems inclined that way.'

'So maybe wee Birnie did us a favour after all,' said McCaig. 'I'll leave it to you to find out more about the man with the whip. Here, Galbraith doesn't rent the Denholm girl her room, does he?'

'No, I thought of that,' said Ryan. 'And he doesn't.'

'Right,' said McCaig. 'You'd better get home, I suppose. By the way, the Langs are moving out. He's put the bloody house up for sale.' The Chief chuckled at the stupidity of it, but Ryan only frowned.

111

'Have they gone?' he asked.

'They baled out this morning,' said McCaig, 'according to my report. But I've a strange feeling Lang will be back for a while. He'll never get rid of it now, of course. I wish he would.'

'Why?'

'I'm curious about that place; I'd like to have a sniff around it, a real proper sniff, without attracting too much attention.'

'Search warrant,' Ryan suggested.

'Christ, no,' said McCaig. 'Even if I could wangle one, I'm not so confident we'd find anything to want to make a noise about it.'

'Is that all?' asked Ryan.

'Yes,' said McCaig. 'Except that I want you to bring young friend Birnie in fairly soon. Make him sweat a bit. He needs a lesson. I'll teach him to mess around with The Force just for his own petty ends.'

'And Johnstone?'

'Nothing there,' said McCaig. 'Let him stew.'

FIVE

The night of the day he deposited Jenny in *Gilfillan's* hotel Lang broke open a half bottle of Standfast and lay awake in bed for hours, sipping the expensive stuff while counting the cost of every swallow. Soon he was calculating items other than the whisky, and performing his small miracles of budgeting. The first thing to go would be the cleaning woman, right away in the morning. He had no occupation now and was still healthy enough, in spite of the back, to buckle down with Hoover and duster, provided there was nobody to witness his loss of dignity.

This he did, paying the woman and telling her not to come again. His headache made him even more gloomy than before. He could only counter it with anger, and activity. After tea and toast, which settled his queasy stomach a little, he walked down to the village. He was mad enough now to brazen out their questions. Though there were hardly any policemen on the moor – even the press men seemed to have gone – he was still a sure target for gossips. But his manner was gruff enough to deter them, and after a few tentative questions even the assistants in the Co-op took the hint and served out his order mutely. He bought enough tinned food and cigarettes, at eight per day, to last him a full week, then lugging the laden shopper, set out along the main street for the house again.

The car drew up alongside him. Though he was aware of its presence, he ignored it. It crawled along by the kerb, keeping abreast of him. He walked faster, dragging the load. The car growled on a few yards and the door opened.

Ryan said, 'In you get, Mr Lang. I'm going your way.'

Lang scowled, but because the sun was hot and his feet had not recovered from pounding Glasgow pavements, and the bag was a ton and his spine hurt, he crossed around the bonnet of the Hillman and climbed in. He sat there in the passenger seat, stiffly, the bag on his knee, his cap square on his head and his moustache limp with sweat. Ryan slammed the door and moved the car carefully into the empty street. As they left the village, travelling slowly, Ryan said, 'I heard Mrs Lang wasn't too well.'

'She wasn't.'

'And how is she now?'

'Better.'

'Up and about again.'

'Yes.'

'At home, is she?'

'She's in Glasgow.'

'Ah well, best to get out of here for a while, I suppose,' said Ryan. He shifted the car slowly into the mouth of the track. 'Don't you fancy a break from Balnesmoor yourself?'

'No.'

'I thought . . . you might have considered leaving permanently,' said Ryan.

'Who told you that?'

'Nobody told me,' said Ryan. 'It was just a thought.'

'Ay,' said Lang. 'It'd be Galbraith. Well, it's no secret. You'll all be able to read it in the papers come next week.'

'I hope you're lucky,' said Ryan.

'So do I.'

'Would you ... let us know before you move out?'

'Why?'

'No real reason,' said Ryan. 'But it might be of interest to us to see who buys the place.'

'I'm not running away, you understand,' said Lang suddenly.

'Of course not,' said Ryan. 'I think it's a wise policy, considering.'

'You lot just want a chance to dig up my lawn,' said Lang.

'No, no,' said Ryan mildly. 'Nothing like that.'

'Well, you won't get the chance while I'm here,' said Lang. 'Not without a search warrant, and if you get one of those, by God, I'll want to know on what grounds. I'll write to my M.P.'

'I told you ...'

The Hillman came to a halt and Lang said, 'I've work to do.' He opened the door and, pulling the grocery-bag after him, got out.

'Good luck with the sale,' Ryan called as the small man crossed the windscreen towards the gate. Lang did not look back but stumped over the lawn and let himself into the house with his key. The blinds were all drawn and some of the curtains, to keep the sun from fading the carpets. It looked as if the house was in mourning, or already uninhabited. He slammed the kitchen door and locked it with all the bolts. By God, they wouldn't get laying a finger on his property, not while he was there. By God, they wouldn't. He peeped out of the side window through a fingerful of curtain, and watched the damned police car drive sedately away. Then he sank back against the wall, worn out with fury. What, he wondered, just what the devil did they hope to find anyway under his fine lawn, or, and the thought made him flinch forward as if the paint had turned hot, behind these very walls? It took will-power and the rest of the Standfast to drown out his fear. By that time half a day was over and he could begin preparing for the next.

Blair brought Birnie to Headquarters late that evening. When Ryan entered the interview room he was surprised to find the farm hand calm and composed, one knee crossed over

114

the other, reading a copy of the local paper. As Ryan closed the
door, Birnie looked up at him and grinned, 'Nice night,
Inspector,' he said conversationally.

'Birnie,' said Ryan, 'what's the game?'

'Eh?'

'I saw Allison Denholm. She told me she'd never heard of
Johnstone, but she told me all about you.'

'Lyin' bitch,' said Birnie casually.

'I saw May Syme as well,' Ryan said.

'Who?'

'Now don't fart about, Birnie, or I'll get angry,' Ryan told
him. 'For two bloody pins I'd have you inside.'

'For what charge?'

'I'd find one,' said Ryan.

'Listen,' said Birnie, 'I know m'rights an' you're not supposed
t'bully voluntary witnesses.'

'Why did you bother to drag the police into it?'

'Doin' m'duty.'

'This had nothing whatever to do with the murder case,' said
Ryan. 'This is only some damn' nonsense of your own.'

Birnie was silent, picking at the top of an acne scab on the
point of his chin. His knees were still crossed but there was
tension in him now, very apparent. Ryan said, 'I think the
general idea was for me to bounce up to Edna Johnstone and tell her that her husband was whoring around the
country ...'

'She knows that.'

'You didn't want to spread the poison yourself, Birnie,
because you wanted in there with a shout when they split up.
It was a ridiculous notion in the first place, and shows just how
little you know about either human nature or the workings of
the police force.'

'He hits her,' said Birnie.

'That's beside the point,' said Ryan. 'As it happens you *have*
helped us, and by God you'd better co-operate now and no
mucking around or I'll turn you over to the Chief's tender
mercies.'

'Co-operate : how?' said Birnie, but not eagerly.

'You know May Syme?'

'What of it?'

'How about her ... other friends, know any of them?'

115

'Naw.'

'You're sure.'

'Certain!'

'Why do you hang around Allison Denholm?'

'She's . . . different,' Birnie admitted.

'Of course she's different,' said Ryan. 'You can't have her for a couple of quid.'

'Look,' said Birnie, 'Galbraith has Syme occasionally when he wants her. He's the priority man.'

'That's not news, son,' said Ryan. 'I want news.'

'That's all I can tell you.'

'You'd plenty to say the last time, so just wrack that wee brain of yours for a minute, and see what else comes to the surface,' said Ryan. 'I mean, do you expect a pat on the head for screwing up a lead in a murder investigation, just to appease your own bloody vanity?'

Birnie jumped to his feet. 'Wasn't vanity. She's a nice woman.'

'Which woman do you mean?'

'Edna, Edna Johnstone.'

'Dear God!' said Ryan in exasperation.

'I thought . . . I thought somebody should know about how he treats her.'

'A nosy wee vigilante,' said Ryan. 'But why did you drag Allison Denholm into it?'

Birnie sat down again, his hands in his lap, his head hung. 'Don't rightly know,' he admitted. 'She wouldn't have nothin' t'do with me, and I got t'thinkin' maybe it was really Johnstone. He's in Lannerburn often enough for it.'

'I don't get the connection,' said Ryan.

'Christ, I don't know if there is one,' said Birnie. 'I was just hopin'.'

'Birnie, how many girls have you had in your tender life?'

'Hundreds.'

'Is May Syme the only one?'

'I told you I've had hundreds; dozens anyway,' Birnie cried.

'But not Edna Johnstone and not Allison Denholm?'

'Not yet,' said Birnie with a flash of defiance.

'Supposing you had a choice, Edna or Allison, which would you pick?'

116

'Fat chance of that,' said Birnie. 'With one marrit an' the other such a snotty snob.'

'And that just leaves you with old May Syme.'

'Bloody old cow.'

'Do you talk to many girls, try to pick them up the way you did Allison Denholm?'

'Sometimes I chat up a bird or two,' said Birnie. Ryan could see that the farm hand was now torn between the desire to deny everything and get clear of the whole mess and the innate protective urge to build himself up as a popular lad with the ladies.

'Farm girls, shop girls, that sort of thing?' Ryan said.

'Ay.'

'And visitors, trippers, hikers, schoolgirls . . .'

'Naw!' Birnie shouted. 'Naw, naw. I never had nothin' to do with strangers.'

'Except Allison Denholm.'

'I told you, she's different.'

'You tried to pick her up in a bar, thinking she was another one like May.'

'I knew she was different.' Birnie said. 'I thought she looked . . .'

'Go on, Birnie.'

'I thought she looked *lonely* too,' Birnie blurted out.

For a moment Ryan did not speak, then he leaned on the desk and took a quarto memo pad from the desk drawer and a pen from his pocket. His voice, when next he spoke, was gentle, smooth and soothing. 'All right, Birnie,' he said. 'I'd just like to get a few facts for the report, then you can go.'

'What report?'

'I've got to make a report,' said Ryan.

'About me an' . . .'

'Just you, Birnie,' Ryan said. Then he began to question him about his schooling and his home life, recording all the trivial details which made up the man. When the answers came at him and went down on paper, he was gratified to learn that his theory had been right – Birnie was just a daft, lonely idiot who didn't know what to do about girls. Whatever else he might be, Ryan thought, he wasn't the stuff that killers are made of : he just didn't have the brains to kill and hide. Not like the man in the Rover, or the lover of Anna and Doreen. He finished the

117

report and let Birnie go, hoping that he had enough on paper to convince McCaig that no more need be done in that direction.

SIX

Alone in the hotel lounge Jenny waited for her husband until late on Saturday afternoon. The feelings she had were of excitement soured by a vague and indefinable emotion, and pleasure in the recollection of the events of the week gone by. She had accompanied two elderly sisters, permanent residents at *Gilfillan's*, to the cinema on three evenings, and the lavish Technicolor musicals had blown away the webs of depression which lingered in the corners of her mind. Those nights she had the gay tunes for company in the difficult hour before sleep. Norman would have to come : her money was all gone. She told him so, peevishly, by telephone on Friday afternoon. Yet he had made no promises. Indeed, he'd said almost nothing; as the afternoon ticked slowly by, her nervousness increased. It wasn't only the lack of ready cash which made her anxious, but the thought that he may have devised some method of forcing her to return with him to Balnesmoor. At half past four he finally showed up, startling her by the abruptness of his appearance in the door of the lounge. He was like a stranger to her : no, not a stranger but a dead relative, a figment of the past which she had thought to be beyond recall. She dropped her magazine to the carpet and jumped to her feet, taking a backward pace as he advanced. Already the street was in shadow, the lounge dull and darkening as if the five or six hours between evening and night had been telescoped into minutes. A freakish silence marked his progress across the wide room, no sound of traffic, or children or passing feet on the pavement. Involuntarily she put her hand to her throat, then his fist closed on her arm and he drew her inexorably towards him and dutifully kissed her forehead. 'How are you, Jenny?'

Drained, she eased herself back into the sagging armchair. 'Quite well thanks, Norman.'

The cheap ornaments in a corner display cabinet rattled as a heavy truck roared past the window to signal the restoration of

118

sounds and vibrations, in the dust-filled room. Norman stood before her with his hands behind his back. He had changed; it was not just her fanciful imagination, he really was different. For a second she could not decide just how he had altered then the evidence pieced itself together and she realised he had stopped caring for himself. His flannels were baggy, his tie creased, shirt collar grimy and stained, his brown shoes unpolished and ingrained with a week's dirt. Even his moustache was untrimmed and straggled over his lips to merge with the stubble on his jowls. Unkempt, soiled, uncared for – still she could rouse no pity for him, not a whit of guilt or a fleeting twinge of self-recrimination at her desertion. Her concerns were totally egotistical and egotism made her strong.

'Sit down,' she said.

And he did so, facing the armchair, his back to the window.

'They've gone,' he said. 'The police have all gone. The moor's as quiet as the gr . . .'

'I've met some nice ladies here,' Jenny said. 'They're very good company.'

'The garden's coming up now,' Lang said, 'Flowers and everything.'

'Have you been working at it?'

'Not really.'

'I went to the pictures this week,' Jenny said. 'I haven't been to the pictures for years.' She waited, but he did not, as she expected, ask the price of admission. 'I need more money.'

'Yes, I brought some,' Lang said.

'How much?'

'Same as last Saturday.'

'I'll need more than that, Norman.'

'What for?'

'Things,' she replied vaguely.

'We'll need to be careful,' said Lang, but his heart was not in the protest.

'Has the house been advertised?' Jenny asked.

'Just there on Thursday.'

'No time for replies yet, I suppose,' Jenny said.

'There won't be any.'

'Well,' said Jenny, 'we'll just have to wait and see.'

'I think you should come back with me,' Lang said. 'It's costing too much, having you here and me there.'

119

'I'm not going back to Balnesmoor.'

'Don't you want us to be together?' Lang said.

'If you want to be with me,' said Jenny, 'come to Glasgow.'

'I have to look after the property,' said Lang. 'It'll fall to rack and ruin if I don't.'

'Do they know who did it yet?' Jenny asked.

'What?'

'Who killed the girls.'

'If they do, they've said nothing, and arrested nobody,' Lang said. 'If only I hadn't gone into that damn' bush and burnt it.'

'I wonder if he killed them there in front of the house.'

'I doubt it,' said Lang, frowning. 'He'd bring them there by car.'

'Don't you ever think about them, Norman?'

'Why should I?' Lang said. 'They're dead.'

'I suppose so,' said Jenny. 'They didn't have much of a life, did they, either of them, being snuffed out at seventeen like that. Still, maybe they had the best of it.'

'If I hadn't gone into that bush,' Lang said, more to himself than to his wife, 'we might've been able to get rid of the place before they were discovered. In a year or two there'd have been nothing to find anyway, just some clothing and a few small bones.'

'It's the acids in the ground that do it,' Jenny told him. 'They were just children too.'

'They knew what they were doing, those two,' said Lang. 'Why did he have to pick on Balnesmoor, near my house?'

'What time's your bus back, Norman?'

'Are you coming with me?'

'No.'

'All right,' he said. 'You'll rue it when we've no money left.'

That was all he would say.

Afterwards when he had gone off to catch his bus, Jenny stood in the upstairs front single room and watched the busy movement of the Saturday night street below. If only he'd told her a lie, told her that he really needed her and could not live without her, then she would have allowed herself to be persuaded, even knowing that it was a lie. But he said nothing, and she, with long dormant unsuspected pride rising in her, would not deign to prompt him. All he'd had to say was that he wanted her back because he needed her, and she would have

120

risked the agonising fantasies which haunted her in Balnesmoor; no, she would have acted to do his bidding out of an
ingrained submissiveness, itself a kind of strength. She would
have gone, would have obeyed, all for the cost of one small
falsehood. Yet he didn't even think it necessary to pretend that
he cared for her, missed her, and once more she was left alone
without the consolation of his stated longings. She shifted
suddenly from the curtain and placed her forehead against the
coppery glass of the old wardrobe mirror. Then she let the tears
come, not for Doreen English or Anna Ewart, not even for
Norman Lang, but wholly, unashamedly, for herself.

'God, you're going to seed,' said Galbraith, critically inspecting the finger which he had just swept across the surface of
the coffee table. 'What happened to the woman?'
'She's in Glasgow,' said Lang.
'I mean the cleaner, the char?'
'I couldn't afford to keep her on,' said Lang. 'Now will you
answer my question – have you had any replies yet?'
'Had a few phone calls,' Galbraith admitted. He pulled the
curtain from the window and contemplated the rain. Even
while he was talking the idea was stirring again, like the tendril
of a fern muscling its way up to light and air. He observed the
rain veiling the moorland and making the heads of the flowers
in the strip by the terrace nod vigorously and frequently with
bigger drops. The bloody house itself seemed to be fertilising
whatever it was that he had to think about. The idea was
interred so deep that he couldn't coax it up voluntarily, and
needed the artificial stimulae of places and phrases to do it for
him. It had been a day just like this when he knew he was
going to have the guts to sell Muirfauld, the family mansion
which had belonged to the Galbraith's for four decades. That
was hardly even history, but his father who had inherited the
land his grandfather had bought, and the tradition of slinging
up dwellings on it, would have gone quite ape. It had torn him
only slightly to part with it; it was really a bit of a hole, a
crumbling mock-baronial memorial to the aristocratic aspirations of a money-grubbing Victorian peasant who, by travel
and graft, had coined enough loot in America to come back to
his native village like a lord. Even as a boy Galbraith had
never felt that the place was home. When his mother died – he

121

was nine then – the last grain of sentiment had trickled away. In the years between nine and twenty-five he believed he hated Muirfauld, but cold-bloodedly putting it up for sale was quite another matter; only then did he realise he did not quite want the house to pass out of his possession. But, steeled by greed and the determination to prosper, he'd got shot of it to *The Society of Jesus,* which for Galbraith was roughly equivalent to blowing it sky-high. They had turned it into a sort of spartan hotel for conferences, retreats and weekend Bible frolics. What the hell was he trying to sort out? He lit a cigarette and drew on it fiercely, frowning.

'What phone calls?' said Lang, for the second or possibly the third time.

'Hm!' said Galbraith. 'Oh, sure I had calls, the usual bunch of cranks. Actually, I've been trying to tamp down on publicity. The kind of thing some of those bastards had in mind to print would've made your hair curl.'

'What?' said Lang.

'Feature stories about this "haunted" house. God, I tell you, haunted houses are the bane of an estate-agent's life. Have you ever tried to sell a house that had even the whiff of a poltergeist about it? I did once, the old mill-keeper's place over in Kilcraig. Couldn't get rid of it, for . . '

'Nobody wanted to buy?'

'You must be joking,' said Galbraith. 'I'd only one offer.'

Lang stared at him, pointing like a retriever at distant game.

'I didn't think you'd want to take what they offered,' Galbraith said.

'What was that?' said Lang, trying to keep the whining greed out of his voice.

'Two hundred quid,' said Galbraith. 'Now, you're not *that* desperate.'

Lang sat back, pressed against the chair like a man under the stress of massive acceleration, his flesh flared, and his eyes bulging.

'You don't look well,' Galbraith remarked.

'I'm all right,' said Lang. He struggled upright and lit the cigarette he'd been saving for after tea. 'Will you keep trying?'

'Sure,' said Galbraith. 'But I warned you it would be next to impossible.'

'You're not really interested.'

'I'll admit my heart's not in it,' said Galbraith, 'but I am doing my best, you know. What more do you want, a slot on T.V. Personally I wouldn't buy the place and not just for technical reasons. I'm notoriously hard-headed, but even so I wouldn't want to have to look out at that moorland reach every time I passed the window. Brrr; no. It's not for me.'

'There's nothing wrong with this house. It's comfortable and quiet, and a perfect . . . retreat,' said Lang.

'If I were you,' said Galbraith, 'I'd go back to Glasgow, and take a little part-time job to tide you over. The situation's not quite hopeless. I'm sure I'll get rid of it for you – in time.'

'I can't wait,' said Lang. 'I'm not a youngster. I don't have time to play with.'

'Point taken,' said Galbraith.

Lang shoved his hands in his pockets, and his shoulders slumped forward. The firm old cheeks were hollow now, anxiety eating him up from within like a cancer. Feeling a sudden chill, Galbraith turned up his macintosh collar. Time to play with! That struck a tiny chord somewhere in his memory, like the ripple of a child's finger over harp strings. Pretty soon he wouldn't have time to play with either. Then he remembered.

The scene was with him as clearly as if it had been projected on the wall in vivid Technicolor with hi-fi stereophonic sound and full orchestra and chorus – Clare and Tyler and he in the shell of this very house, standing on the raw floorboards watching dusk creep over the hills. That must have been, that *must* have been just a couple of weeks before the end. He could see Clare's round childish eyes on him, and the blush of the fading sun on her cheeks, and the innocent mouth. And he was talking about *time*, of all things, telling Clare they had time to play with, but only backtracking and delaying, not wanting to admit that, beautiful though she was, he expected more than just the satisfaction of her body. He was a pompous twit then, but the disease, which he must have had, he *must* have been harbouring that same summer evening, was to take the wind out of him. And the rest of it following, the deaths and the departures and the brawling and bawling. It was just as well he was resilient, or had been young enough to grow out of the

123

scars, or had a tough enough hide not to be destroyed by it all. That was it. The idea broke the crust of deliberate amnesia and wriggled up, growing like the beanstalk in the fairytale. He heard himself sigh with relief : and Clare vanished.

'Listen,' he said excitedly. 'I ... might have some news for you in a day or two.'

'Good news?'

Then caution, the reflex of the experienced agent, came to his rescue. He played down his enthusiasm. 'Well, news anyway,' he said, travelling towards the door. 'I mean, when we've had time to get in more replies.'

'I thought ...'

'In the meantime,' said Galbraith, 'I wouldn't let the dwelling run to absolute seed. All right?'

'Are you going?' Lang asked, bewildered by the sudden briskness.

'Yes,' said Galbraith. 'I have to. I'm pretty busy these days. You're not the only client on the books, you know.'

He got out of the kitchen door before Lang had time to open it for him and with a reassuring wave, picked his way across the pools standing on the lawn and down the slope towards the track where he had, foolishly, parked his Vauxhall. Funny, nobody ever used the front yard of the house for its proper purpose, with the gravel approach and all. His old man had built the place facing the wrong way, for the view, the panorama, was the magnet which seemed to draw everyone to the back – front? – of the building. He hesitated, made a balletic leap over a particularly large puddle, and stopped, letting his eyes shift from east to west across the landscape. The blackened cavern and raw remains of the police diggings were already sprouting the new green spring growths which would very soon erase them – quicker than memory. He saw the hills and the moor gate by the farm, and the faint, grey stem of smoke held static between the rainy sky and the chimney pot over the kitchen. A chug of lust sounded down in him, deep and echoing, when he thought of Edna, or was it the *memory* of the memory of Clare Hughes. Better to think of Edna. She was still available, and had nothing to do with the plan he had in mind. She would bring her big swarming body to him whenever it was safe and drain him out without ever intruding into the private garden – jungle – of associations. He

124

would think of Edna, try to wangle a safe forenoon with her soon, just keep himself from thinking about Clare, and the part she had unwittingly prepared for herself all those years ago, in the plan he had just devised. To go through with it, even to make a beginning, with Clare Hughes in mind, was too callous even for him. He would not allow himself to really think of her again, not until it was all over, one way or the other, and Tyler had taken the bait.

On a warm Sunday afternoon, Ryan, after almost a week of rain, was not thinking about the case. He was concentrating all his energies on amusing his children. The plastic ball bounced high and rolled across the lawn. Ryan pursued it, roaring threateningly, cocking out his elbows, with care of course, to fend off his son's wild attack on his person. Wee Jean lifted her head from the colour-supplement, and tutted as the knotted bodies of her father and brother tumbled past her. 'Don't make so much noise,' she said haughtily. 'I'm trying to read.' Gordon hacked the ball against her shins and in an instant, as if the mischief was all the invitation she needed, she flung aside the magazine and leapt out of the garden bench on to her father's back. Ryan gripped her tightly, strapping his left arm back and around her legs, then grunting, for she was no light-weight now, shambled ape-like after Gordon.
'What'll I do with her?' he shouted. 'What'll I do with this sister of yours?'
'Drown'r,' Gordon cried. 'Throw'r'n the loch.'
'Too far, son,' panted Ryan, already starting to crumble.
'Spank'r then,' Gordon suggested maliciously; he had never seen his sister spanked.
'Okay,' said Ryan. With the last of his strength he swung the girl wide from him, her hair streaming and her legs, for she knew the rules of rough-house too, straight and loose and graceful. He went down on one knee and pulled her to him, dropping her across his lap. Pinning her with one hand he lifted the other high and held it there.
'Father,' Jean shrieked. 'Don't you dare.'
'How many?' Ryan asked. Gordon, who was almost inclined to believe that his father was serious, indulged his wish-fulfilment to the hilt. 'Five hundred,' he yelled gleefully. Ryan's hand swished through the air, and paused an inch above the

125

small round seat of the girl's denims, padding down with feather softness. 'One,' he said, lifting the hand again. 'And . . .'

'Harry.'

He held the hand up where it was, and glanced across towards the kitchen door.

'Telephone,' his wife told him.

'Who is it?'

'It's the shop.'

'Damn!'

With an air of resignation his daughter disengaged herself and got up, preening her hair and sweater to make good the damage her father had done to her beauty.

'You're not going?' Gordon complained.

Ryan shrugged. As he made his way across the patch of grass to the door, he heard wee Jean tell the boy, 'If it's the shop he'll have to, silly.'

He passed through an appetising smell of pot-roast and cauliflower in the kitchen, into the small hallway, and lifted the receiver from the table. 'Ryan.'

'Cruickshank,' the voice said. 'I'm sure you remember me?'

'Who could ever forget,' said Ryan. 'What's in the wind?'

'I've a wee piece of information,' Cruikshank said, 'guaranteed to ruin your dinner.'

'Let's have it.'

'Remember the lady you called on?'

'Which one,' said Ryan, 'May Syme?'

'That's her,' Cruikshank said. 'Well, she's done a bunk.'

'What?' Ryan gripped the receiver more tightly and brought it closer to his ear. 'How do you mean, done a bunk?'

'Gone, vanished, disappeared.'

'Are you sure?'

'Fairly,' Cruikshank said. 'She hasn't been at the garage for three days an' she was supposed to be on all day today, so Hogg, the boss y'know, sent a lad up there t'see what was keeping her. And she wasn't there.'

'How come he notified you?'

'Well,' said Cruikshank, 'he thought maybe we had her in clink, for . . . some reason'r other.'

'Anyone see her leave?'

126

'I'm working on it,' Cruikshank said, 'But by the looks of it she just slipped away in the night ... or ... something.'

'Right,' Ryan said, tucking his shirt into his belt as he spoke. 'I'll be right over.'

SEVEN

The price of the view from the dining room of the *Caledonian Highland Hotel* was added to every dish and bottle on the menu. Americans and visiting English probably considered it worth it, for the spread of the loch, pine-shrouded slopes and rock-sculptured peaks were not only incredibly beautiful but had that 'real' Scottish quality which reminded them of Scott and Burns and Rob Roy McGregor. It was all laid on by the management, of course, and could be observed, right down to the shaggy golden-brown longhorned cattle at the water's edge, in warmth and comfort from behind a tablecloth full of traditional fare. Galbraith had come hot from two rounds of golf at Heathwood Park; a lost ball on the thirteenth fairway had cost him so much time that he had no moment to spare to quench his thirst at the club. Now, after two glasses of ice-cold lager – all he would allow himself, since he was working – he felt considerably better and confidence began to come up in him again like brewer's bubbles. The soup and trout and peppermint ice lay snug inside him, but he was wary of the expansive feeling which came with physical satisfaction and jogged the conversation along most casually until he was on to his second cup of coffee. Usually he had a little difficulty in making talk with his step-brother, for there were many dangerous areas wired off, normal source of contact for two men who had shared a helping of their youth. Tonight, however, he found Ballentine uncommonly helpful, not at all morose. Since he wasn't going to be mocked with subtle wit, Galbraith permitted golf to be the subject and, with tales of the American courses to keep the pot boiling, the dinner was pleasantly prolonged. Ballentine was smiling as he lit his first cigarette, and settled back. 'All right now, Robert,' he said, still with a friendly smile. 'What's it all for?'

'I beg your pardon?' said Galbraith.

127

'Don't pretend it was only for the pleasure of my company.'

'Didn't you enjoy it?' said Galbraith.

'Of course I did,' said Ballentine. 'I often come here with friends. I always enjoy the food, and the wine, and the view, but that's not the point. I'm curious now as to your reason for asking me to dinner in the first place.'

'If you can't accept a friendly . . .'

'Please,' said Ballentine. 'I know you better than that: anyway, we don't have enough in common to make a whooping social occasion of it, so perhaps you'd better stop pretending and get on with what you have to say.'

Galbraith licked his lips. Then he grinned. 'Sure, Tyler,' he said. 'You're right, as usual, and I thought I was being so clever-clever about it. No wonder you make a fortune fleecing all those poor distillers.'

'Flattery,' said Ballentine, 'will have no effect. What is it, Robert, money? Are you in trouble financially?'

'God no,' said Galbraith, bridling at the very suggestion. 'Business couldn't be better.'

'What then?'

'You won't believe this . . .'

'Probably not.'

'. . . but I thought I might do you a favour.'

'How kind!'

'Stop being sarcastic just for two minutes, Tyler, and listen, will you?' said Galbraith. 'You recall the house, the Balnesmoor place.'

'Yes.'

'Well, it's up for sale again.'

'Yes.'

'And I think I can get it for next to nothing.'

'Why don't you buy it then, Robert?'

'I don't need it,' said Galbraith. 'I mean, I've just spent . . . well, let's say a considerable sum on my place, doing it all up, and I don't need another.'

'Buy it for resale, if you want to do it privately.'

'I could do,' Galbraith lied, 'but I thought I'd give you the chance. You always did like it, and it would give you a foot in the county, near the golf club.'

'Not near my club,' said Ballentine. 'But it's true, I used to . . . like the place.'

128

'Yes,' said Galbraith. 'I've been feeling a shade guilty lately –
put it down to old age – at not letting you have it at the time.
Are you interested now?'

'How much?'

'Not much,' said Galbraith. 'I think the owner could
be persuaded to part with it for around eight or nine
thousand.'

'It used only to cost half that.'

'Ah, but times have changed,' said Galbraith. 'Prices are
soaring. It would probably value at around twelve.'

'So, Robert, you're going to do me a favour, and let me have
it for eight or nine.'

'It's a snip, Tyler,' said Galbraith. 'Are you interested?'

Ballentine laughed softly. 'Really,' he said, 'you must
imagine I live with my head in the sand. Just because I was
touring in the U.S.A. doesn't mean to say I stopped reading
The Scotsman and the *Glasgow Herald.*'

'Oh!'

'So I know about the house and what happened, and I know
you can't give the place away.'

'Six thousand then,' said Galbraith. 'I can get that for it. I've
even had an offer.'

'Who from – the black museum?'

'Oh, now look,' protested Galbraith. 'You're exaggerating
things terribly, Tyler. Nothing happened in the house itself.
Just those things on the moor, quite far away actually. It's not
as if the place had been turned into a slaughter-house or the
repository of umpteen mangled corpses. Frankly, I can't
understand why people adopt this attitude.'

'What attitude?'

'Shunning it, wanting rid of it, wrinkling their noses at a
perfectly good piece of property. It's not as if those girls even
came from Balnesmoor. I mean, they were strangers.'

'And this chap who wants out,' said Ballentine, 'what's his
name ...?'

'Lang.'

'Yes, Lang, is Lang just a sentimentalist?'

'He's old,' said Galbraith, 'and his wife's the nervy type,
highly imaginative, not like you and me.'

'But I thought you were using sentiment, my sentimental
attraction to the place, as a selling point,' said Ballentine.

129

'God,' said Galbraith, 'you always twist around my good intentions, don't you. Do you want it, or not?'

'Thank you,' said Ballentine, 'but it doesn't mean that much to me.'

'It's a bloody good buy, believe me. Old Lang's desperate to get rid of it. In three or four years you could turn a good profit, make four or five thousand on it easily.'

'No, no, Robert,' said Ballentine. 'I don't want it. I wouldn't have it as a gift.'

'But if I threw in Clare Hughes to go with it . . .' Galbraith exploded angrily. He bit off the sentence. 'I didn't mean that. Sorry.'

For almost a minute Ballentine said nothing, the smile still on his face but icy now, like the rictus of Novocain. At length he said, 'If you want to keep the house in the family, why don't you buy it yourself.' He paused again. 'If not for sentiment, Robert, why not for gain?'

'And leave it empty for three years, not earning?'

Ballentine dropped his napkin and got slowly to his feet. 'You could turn it into a shrine,' he said.

'That's a lousy . . .' Galbraith began, then he too stopped. 'Perhaps I will,' he said looking up at the man viciously. 'Perhaps I'll just do that.'

'Romantic,' said Ballentine, as the waiter came forward with the bill.

'For profit,' said Galbraith. 'For simple profit.'

'Naturally,' said Ballentine. 'Here, you get this. It was your show after all.' Dropping the bill by Galbraith's plate, he walked quickly out of the dining-room.

Before Galbraith could settle the bill and get out after him to make his peace, Ballentine had gone. Galbraith sighed and crossed the park to the Vauxhall, and got in. He sat there for a while staring out at the dense green pines, but seeing nothing. All that rancour; old wounds which he'd been stupid enough to open up again. Ballentine was a hopeless case, nursing the hurt of what was after all just an accident. How did he know he was ill – a curse on the bloody old whore. He couldn't even recall her name or her face now, just some of her erotic techniques which had seemed magnificently depraved, sensational, to a lad of twenty-one. He had no intention of hurting Clare. If he regretted anything it was the pain he had brought

130

to her. Damn Ballentine though, he only got what he deserved, waiting sullenly apart from them yet near enough to step in and take what was left, like a bloody jackal. Nobody told him : Clare didn't, and Ballentine, that secretive bastard, wouldn't. Clare, with the innocence and the eagerness making that high-octane combination which was quite unlike anything he had ever known, must have known that Ballentine was nuts about her. But innocence, like the peel of a fruit, must be stripped away to get at the juice. Anyway, she was *too* innocent; eager to be loved but not to sweat out the exercises which a man needs to make him completely happy. After the nightmare month he had sworn off virgins forever – and had, almost, kept his vow.

For his father's benefit he had been tearfully contrite. In spite of the scandal and recriminations he had always felt that his father pitied him, but yet had used the incident ever after as another instrument in his armoury for subduing his son. The Balnesmoor house was more closely linked to his life in some ways than Muirfauld had ever been. But he had never lived in it, never even spent a night in it. But it was linked to him, built for him. Maybe dinner with Ballentine had been useful after all. Why shouldn't he buy the place, and keep it – not as a shrine, but as an investment? In a couple of years folk would have forgotten what happened, and a five roomed, stone-built ranch-house with luxury fittings would always hold its value. Besides, it was near Johnstone's farm and Edna ... Too near perhaps, too dangerously near. Still, he would think about it very seriously over the next few days. If Lang would accept an economical sum, perhaps he would after all just take the plunge, and shove the notion that he was desecrating the shrine right in his beloved step-brother's moaning face.

'Was the door not locked?' Ryan asked.

Cruikshank shook his head. 'Apparently not. You can talk to the boy later if you like. I expect you'll want to take it further.'

'That depends on McCaig,' said Ryan.

The interior of the trailer was not as it had been the last time he had visited it, but spotlessly tidy, the table folded back in its place and the air, musty and warm, holding the artificial fragrance of a freshener. A starving bluebottle buzzed along the bottom of one of the window frames. Ryan stooped, and with the nail of his index finger pulled open a small cupboard. It was quite empty. He moved to another and opened it in the same manner : empty too.

'It looks,' he said carefully, 'like you're right. She's done a bunk. There don't seem to be any clothes or shoes in the place.'

'Or grub,' said Cruikshank. He was standing in the centre of the room, bent a little, compactly holding in his elbows to prevent them brushing any surface which might hold a print. 'Just like she'd redd the place up before going on holiday.'

'And not locked the door.'

'Does it lock?' asked Cruikshank.

'I don't know yet,' said Ryan.

'Strikes me it was the prototype of "the ever open" variety,' said Cruikshank.

'Who did she know in the town that she might've told her plans to?' said Ryan. 'Presumably she said nothing about it at the garage?'

'Not a cheep,' said Cruikshank. 'She left off at eight on Wednesday and that's the last they saw of her.'

'Did she draw her wages?'

'Nope, they were due on Saturday, but she never turned up for them. Hogg would probably not've bothered with her except that he was bloody short of staff and she usually phoned him if she was . . . ill?'

'Was she ill often then?'

'Occasionally,' said Cruikshank. He raised a brow. 'Maybe three or four times a year.'

Ryan sniffed. 'Air freshener,' he said. 'May didn't strike me as the type to use air freshener.'

'Y'never know with women.'

'Well, it's bloody funny,' said Ryan. 'Less than a week after she tells us about this character with the whip, and we have her up for a run through the gallery of queers and kinks, she takes off without a word to a soul.'

'Did she recognise anyone in the picturebook?'

'Unfortunately not,' said Ryan. 'Not even a hesitation.'

'That was only the county record, of course,' said Cruik-shank. 'Her . . . friend might've come from outside.'

'Like Glasgow,' said Ryan. 'Like Craigiemill in Glasgow.'

'My lips're sealed,' said Cruikshank. 'I never give opinions on Sundays.'

132

'Something doesn't chime right about all this,' said Ryan, frowning down at the neatly made bed. 'One tiny lead from this woman, and not a very hopeful one at that really, and then she vanishes. Gives certain wild theories a modicum of weight.'

'Might be nothin' in it,' said Cruikshank. 'But, to break my golden rule, I'm like you, I smell a smell about it.'

'Air freshener,' said Ryan. 'A cleaned-out home, but an unlocked door and money still lying unclaimed for her at the garage. Not like a woman to trot off an' leave money lying.'

'Want the boys in with the fingerprint equipment?'

'Yes,' Ryan said slowly. 'Yes, I think so, and the forensic crew and the rest of it. Meanwhile I think I'll root out Sandy Blair and make a few calls.'

'Johnstone, Birnie and Galbraith?'

'For a start,' said Ryan.

'Mind if I come along.' said Cruikshank.

'Bucking for C.I.D.?' asked Ryan.

'Me, at my age,' said Cruikshank. 'Don't be daft, man. In fact when I take off this bloody uniform there's nothin' left of me. I even have blue pyjamas, complete with stripes.'

'Come on,' said Ryan. 'Let's make some calls.'

Galbraith pulled the Vauxhall recklessly around the majestic gateposts of the villa and heard it crunch over the gravel. Just as the white-painted door flared up in the headlamps he killed the lights and applied the brakes. The car stopped, chips spraying out from the tyres and pattering on the pathway which curved through the rhododendrons to the side entrance. He only did crazy things when he was slightly drunk – not when he was sober and certainly not when he was reeling. Having stopped off at the *Lannerburn Hotel* for a few friendly whiskies, he was feeling the effect now. Bed : a huge glass of milk spiked with a nip, then bed. It was the perfect solution to his current problem, the best place to forget all the worries that the dinner had imparted. He got out of the car, rounded it to the boot and fished out a leather satchel full of dirty socks and damp towels brought from the locker at the club. Just as he came up from locking the boot, the beams reached out of the darkness between the shrubs and pinned him, startled and temporarily paralysed, like a rabbit. He could not see beyond

133

them, blinded, and the first inkling of what was going on only came to him when the three men walked out of the source of the light. Panic cleft him like a bolt of lightning. He hefted the bag up to protect himself, his shoes sliding back into the gravel for the necessary purchase to break and run.

'It's all right, Mr Galbraith,' Ryan said. 'It's only the police.'

'Yes, yes,' said Galbraith, quivering with relief, determined not to show his foolishness. 'Yes, yes, I know.'

'We'd like you to answer a few questions please.'

'Can't you quit working even on a Sunday, like normal people?' said Galbraith. He kept his mouth back from Ryan, in case they nabbed him for being drunker than he ought to be in charge of a vehicle. The manner of their approach, the fact that they had been lurking in wait for him, all balled together to make him feel guilty, and the new guilt mingled with the old guilts already churned up from the bottom of his mind, until panic came back to him in a fresh and solid form.

'Could we come into the house?' Ryan suggested.

'Yes,' said Galbraith. 'But you'd better have a damn' good reason, I can tell you for ... Oh, never mind, I suppose you're only doing your job.'

He opened the front door of the villa with his key and ushered the three silent policemen, even one in uniform, inside. The study was his pride and joy and he could not resist showing it off, even to policemen. They probably hadn't seen anything like it and he left them to admire it for several minutes while he took himself into the kitchen and swallowed a half pint of cold milk from the fridge. Gasping, he wiped his mouth and then went into the lounge to see what the hell was up. By the looks on their faces they weren't particularly impressed with the décor or furnishings. Hell of a time he'd had too, to pick up quality African timber to panel with : no appreciation, these plebeian cops. He burped into his cupped hand, enthroning himself casually in the Eames armchair.

'Did you know a woman by the name of Syme, May Syme?' asked Ryan, as soon as he was settled.

'May ... Syme,' said Galbraith. 'Yes, I believe she has a trailer on part of my land. Useless little acre or so behind the graveyard.'

'How well do you know her?'

134

'Hardly at all.'

'Have you ever been in her trailer?' Ryan was putting all the questions, the other two, tall men, just sat and stared hard at him. If they thought they could intimidate him, they were far wrong. His brain was still a little cloudy with alcohol and it took him just an instant too long to grasp the point of each question. He forced himself to sit back, and fumbled his cigarette case from his pocket. Without offering them around he took a cigarette and lit it. 'In her trailer. Good God, no. Why should I be in some old bag's trailer?'

'Is the trailer actually yours?' asked Ryan.

'Not exactly,' said Galbraith. He had to be careful. If they caught him out in a few little lies no saying what big truths they would refuse to believe. What the devil had the old bitch been up to anyhow. 'What's this woman been up to?'

'Not exactly?' said Ryan. 'Could you explain that a bit better, Mr Galbraith, please?' God, they were being polite tonight, chillingly courteous. They'd ignored his question; that put him on his guard. If May bloody Syme had used his name, got him into some of her hot water . . .

'Well, I advanced her a portion of the original cost of the caravan, and I add a small sum with accrued interest on to each of her monthly payments of ground rental. Like a mortgage, only not so involved.' It was legal; he had a couple of shoddy documents to prove it, signed by the Syme woman, himself and his typist as witness. It was an agreement, just a plain simple agreement which he'd thoughtfully drafted to cover just such an eventuality as this.

'I see,' said Ryan. 'Now, Mr Galbraith, when did you last visit Miss Syme?'

'Visit!' he said. Somebody had blabbed: it could only have been the old cow herself. Christ, he'd roast her next time he saw her. That's what came of giving people a chance. He had too soft a heart, but she'd reminded him a bit of one of the women of his youth, the first one maybe, or the second, and the freedom . . . 'Yes, I have visited her, now I come to think of it.'

'For what purpose?'

'Just to . . .' Tell no lies yet: their expressions were grave, glinting grave. He didn't want to get into anything he couldn't get out of. 'What's been said?'

'You know, Mr Galbraith, what May Syme is?' said Ryan.

'All right,' he said. 'Sure, she *used* to be a pro., but she promised me when I let her have the trailer ...'

'What did she promise you?'

Galbraith made a grimace, being too tense to fashion the masonic smile of a man of the world to other men of the world. 'That too,' he said. 'Occasionally.'

'You paid her?'

'Of course I didn't pay her!'

'She did it ...' said Ryan, '... just out of the goodness of her heart?'

'I suppose she liked me,' said Galbraith. 'What's all this about anyway?'

'When did you see her last?' Ryan asked, a gentle demand.

'About a fortnight ago. Wait a minute – sure, it was fully two weeks ago, on a Friday, I think, late evening, night.'

'Did she say anything to you about moving away from the district?'

'Moving away ... No, why, has she?'

'It looks like it,' said Ryan. 'Do you have a key for the trailer?'

'No,' said Galbraith. 'I don't. There is only one, unless, of course, she had others made.'

'But there is a key?'

'Well, there was last time I recall. I certainly remember one three years ago when she showed me the trailer.'

'Did you know May Syme before she ... rented the trailer?'

'No,' he said. 'Never saw her before. I really don't know where she came from either. It never seemed to crop up in ... conversation. She wasn't county though, of that I'm sure. She sounded like a Glaswegian by her accent.'

'Where were you tonight, Mr Galbraith?'

'I don't see what that has to do with it,' said Galbraith. 'As a matter of fact, I was dining in the *Caledonian Highland*.'

'Alone?'

'With my step-brother.'

'Did you come directly here?'

'Now, look ... No, I had a drink, one quick drink, in Lannerburn on the way home.'

He waited for the recriminations, warnings about what can happen to men who drink and drive, but no one said a word.

'Listen,' he said, 'I'm puzzled about this sudden flush of

136

interest in old May. Is she connected with ... certain recent events?'

'Probably not,' said Ryan.

'Then what are three cops doing in my house at ten o'clock on Sunday night, grilling me about her?'

'If you hear from her, or see her again, Mr Galbraith,' said Ryan, rising, 'I'd be obliged if you'd let us know.'

'I don't know what you're fussing for,' said Galbraith. 'She's most likely gone off with some man.'

'Oh,' Ryan said. 'Anyone in particular?'

'No, but if the chance came along to hook up with a meal-ticket, I doubt if she'd think twice about it.'

'At her age?' said Cruikshank.

'Sure, especially at her age,' said Galbraith.

After he had seen them out and watched the Hillman pull away down the side avenue, he warmed up a pan of milk, undressed, bathed quickly and got into bed. Sipping the bland liquid slowly to kill his heartburn, he pondered his position now in regard to the Lang house. Twist it how he would he could see no way in which May Syme's departure radically affected him. Frowning into the glass he cursed himself for forgetting to ask what would happen to the trailer now that she had gone. It was the kind of question that anyone with a clear conscience would be quite entitled to ask, and that Ryan, for all his suspicions, would be obliged to answer to the best of his ability.

EIGHT

A tall young man with a straggling blond moustache and eyes of the palest blue McCaig had ever seen answered the door. He allowed it to fall open, one arm raised to rest his hand on the lintel, his body slack as an unstuffed doll. He looked down on McCaig and said, 'Yah?' Scandinavian accent, McCaig thought, or a very fair imitation.

'Derek McCaig in this flat?'

'Yah.'

'Can I see him for a minute?'

The blond giant contemplated McCaig blandly, then swung

the door shut a little, so that McCaig could only see the profile as he announced, 'Deck, is somebody for yew.'

McCaig heard his son's voice shouting cheerfully from another room, 'Bloke or bird?'

The giant peered at McCaig before answering, 'Gent'man.'

McCaig said, 'I'm his father.'

'Fadder,' the doorkeeper relayed, and admitted McCaig to the room.

His son was in a spacious bedroom adjacent to a main room littered with clothing, tennis rackets, golf clubs and books. Through the bedroom door McCaig studied the scene, a round wooden table littered with cards and piles of silver and notes, five young men, including Derek, seated round it. A pall of cigarette smoke hung below the ceiling down to the level of the cartwheel-sized tasselled shade on its yard of brass chain. Derek pushed back his chair and came out quickly.

'Is yor fadder?' the Scandanavian asked anxiously.

'Yeah, of course it is,' said Derek. 'Sit in for me, sport, will you?'

'Okay,' said the blond, and went into the bedroom closing the door behind him.

'I thought you'd be hard at work,' McCaig said, 'studying.'

'I was,' said Derek.

'It didn't look much like it.'

'Mathematics,' said Derek. 'All those percentage plays, you know.' He dug a hole in the junk on the couch, tossing a track-suit and a pair of Keds, two odd long soccer stockings and a pyjama jacket in dark-blue silk on to the floor. 'Have a pew.' Even before McCaig could settle himself, he asked, 'What brings you to the underworld this summer's night?'

'Just passing,' said McCaig. 'I thought I'd drop in.'

'You've had a letter from mother?'

'No. Why?'

'I thought she'd write and ask you to "have a word with me" about going down there this summer.'

'Nothing to do with me,' said McCaig. 'You're working anyway, aren't you?'

'You're dead right I'm working,' said Derek. 'I need the money.'

'Hm!' said McCaig, a noncommittal sound. 'Could you use a pound or two right now?'

'*Could* I !'

'Are you in debt, son?' the Chief asked.

'No, no,' said Derek quickly. 'I win when I play cards – well, nearly always. But I can always find a use for money. There's this anorak ...'

'You know,' said McCaig sitting back and folding his arms. 'I shouldn't have offered you money.'

Derek's eyebrows went up quickly. 'Don't tell me you've changed your mind.'

'No,' said McCaig, 'but now you'll think I'm bribing you.'

'For what?' Derek said. 'Not that I have any objection to being bribed, mark you.'

'The money has nothing to do with it,' said McCaig. 'Put it down as a present. But the question I want to ask you is important.'

'You coming to me,' said Derek, puzzled, 'is certainly a turn up for the book. All right, what?'

'You ... told me about a woman called May Syme.'

'Ach, that again!' Derek said. 'I thought you'd let me off too easy.'

'I must know who told you about her.'

'Why now, all of a sudden?'

McCaig hesitated. 'She's gone missing.'

'Has she now!'

'It's just possible she went of her own volition, but on the other hand ...'

'I get you,' said Derek. 'She came up with something when you went to see her – as you obviously did – and now you're running down all her contacts.'

'Who told you about her?' said McCaig. 'She wasn't that well known.'

'Now you've got to make me a promise,' said Derek soberly. 'I don't want to get him ... this person into hot water, because he did me a favour ...'

'Some bloody favour,' murmured McCaig.

'He did me a favour at the time; anyway it was a very casual question on my part. I really wheedled the information out of him.'

'Who?'

'Your Inspector Sellars, actually.'

'Sellars,' said McCaig, nodding, his expression betraying nothing. 'So it was Sellars, was it?'

'It was dead casual, Dad,' said Derek. 'I met him in Lannerburn and we got to talking and ... well, you know, I led him round to the bit about vice in the county, and what was there for a poor lad to do. He went on about the pubs and the new bingo hall, then told me about May Syme – just as part of the local scene, you understand. I don't suppose he'd have told me, not McCaig's lad, if he'd thought I was going to horse out there myself. That's all there was to it, honestly.'

McCaig showed his disappointment, drumming his fingers on the arm of the couch. 'Sellars would know about her, of course,' he said, half to himself. 'So that's no bloody use.'

'You think she's got something for you on the moor girls?' said Derek. 'How does that come about?'

'It just does,' said McCaig.

'If it's only because she vanished then I don't see why you're hot and bothered. Life goes on, you know. I remember you telling me ...'

'I told you a lot of things,' said McCaig. 'One of them being that I was a secretive devil.'

'Ah!' said Derek, grinning. 'I'm seeing it clearly now. She had a contact. Some bit of information : maybe she saw someone, and you think he got rid of her to stop her identifying him.'

'Just like the telly,' said McCaig.

'Well, I wouldn't go that far,' said Derek. 'But maybe she went missing for fear of him. And maybe he'll come looking for her. You've a guard on the trailer, have you?'

McCaig said nothing. This was his son; the way he talked sometimes reminded him of his own age of innocence, when he had been able to sit back in his chair and theorise like a bloody Victorian detective. Half the appeal of a murder was being able to do one's own deducing from the facts printed in the papers, twist the facts to suit favourite theory. He'd put up with a lot of that in his life, and hell of a lot of shit about 'Inspector, don't you think ...' and, 'Chief, my wife says ...' It might be all right for a constable to natter on about his job in a pub but the man with his hands up to the shoulders in all the dirt of mankind had no urge to talk about it afterwards. Not even to his son. Look at him, McCaig thought, stuffed full of

140

pet theories, praying I'll sit up and take notice of him. He had taken notice of him once already and it had proved of value. Perhaps just being listened to was all the lad wanted, just to have his father take him seriously for a while. It was a kindly pretence. 'Are you keen to get back to your cards, son?'

'Not particularly, why?'

'Like to go out and have a bite somewhere, and maybe a pint to wash it down?'

Derek smiled, trying to hide his astonishment. 'I'd love to.'

McCaig heaved himself up. 'Come on then, get your tie on. You can tell me what you think while we're eating.'

'Fine,' said Derek, suave now. 'But tell me, have you a guard on the trailer in case the man comes back?'

'No,' said McCaig, matching the mood with a serious answer. 'You see, we tend to think that this man already knows where she's gone.'

'Really,' said Derek. 'Now that's interesting. Know what I think?'

'What?' said McCaig, with no trace of indulgence.

'I think you're on to something there, Dad. I really do.'

'By the way,' McCaig said, 'I don't want any of this in the papers.'

'Naturally,' Derek said. 'My lips are sealed.'

If McCaig was 'on to something' as Derek had prophesied then the trail ran exceedingly cold. No one could recall the strange man in the Rover. No one had seen May Syme after she'd left work on Thursday evening, and Hogg, the Garage Manager's, statement cast another gloomy shadow on the woman's disappearance. She had been cheerful on Thursday, showing no sign of desperation, despair or even stealth. Hogg said he had always liked old May. She was good at her job, trotting out with the pump, always with a joke for the regular customers. The regular customers were questioned too, but came up with no useful information. Ryan tackled Birnie and Johnstone separately, but neither man could throw any apparent light on the enquiry. By now the gossip was filtering out through the county and all the staff of the C.I.D. were warned to fend off reporters' questions. If May had gone of her own accord, she might turn up again and make a laughing-stock out of the police. McCaig dreaded that, as much as

141

McCaig dreaded anything. The connection, he kept reminding himself, between the prostitute and the bodies of the two dead girls was very tenuous anyway. He promoted investigation circumspectly.

In the meantime Robert Galbraith was busily brainwashing Lang. Having decided to purchase the house for himself, he baited the trap carefully. For all his desperation, Lang, at first, would not bite, but then, as the days passed and no redeeming miracle occurred, he began to sniff at the carrot, to nudge Galbraith into repeating his offer, and finally clopped into motion. From that moment Galbraith had no difficulty in leading him to an agreement. At the tail end of July, Galbraith heard the words he had wanted from the little man : 'I'll take it.' For the price of six thousand three hundred pounds the property was almost his.

The business of sale and purchase was easy meat for Galbraith. For the sake of expediency he promoted the transaction and all attendant manoeuvres himself, taking on the chores ostensibly out of the goodness of his heart. Though he never met the wife, Galbraith heard from her often. Lang relayed the message gloomily; Jenny would be happy to settle for something as unelaborate as a rented flat in a quiet district of Glasgow, a two or three roomed box in one of the more secluded blocks. Galbraith, who had hardly to exert himself to locate such a residence, set up a viewing for Lang and his wife and, upon their decision to accept it, went through the formalities of signature and agreement. Anything to get rid of him. The closer Galbraith came to ownership of the Balnesmoor house the more he wanted it. Though his greed became demanding, it did not smother his caution.

The removal, as most removals do, spread over the course of a week. Some of the furniture was put in store – Lang would not agree to sell it – and small personal items were taken by mini-van to the new flat where Jenny Lang, suffused with new-found energy, assimilated them into the framework of a home. Carpets, curtains, blinds, furniture all went on one afternoon : the house was left bare. Only Lang lingered in the barren rooms like a poltergeist, or a bad smell, long after the pantechnicon had carted away the stuff of his life. Galbraith found him in the early evening, seated on the top step, the open door of the kitchen at his back and two suitcases by his side. The garden and the moor were lush with summer, the sky was flushed like pink icing washed through with an excess of cochineal. Galbraith held his ire well, smiling. Legally the old man was entitled to squat on the place for another four days; but he had good reason to want the place to himself that night. It had an inexplicable hold over him : he wanted it to be physically his property. Like a child with a new toy wrapped in its box between his knees he could no longer contain his impatience. Lang looked at him blankly, the eyes not troubled, not even sad but as blank as clay marbles. Perhaps he was waiting for forty press photographers to troop over the moor to record the momentous occasion for the edification of the breakfast-table public, to have the melancholy of his moment set on a par with the tragedy which had originated it, the private grief : it was grief, real and sturdy, confused with the ceremonies of violent death. Somewhat to Galbraith's surprise, however, the handing over of the property had attracted no attention from the reporters. Galbraith had been careful to inform Ryan of the transaction and had even promised the police freedom of the house and garden for a short period. They were only clutching at straws at this stage in the case, making final despairing gestures before admitting that they did not know who had killed Doreen English and Anna Ewart and probably never would. If they dug up from the lawn, or from under the flooring another ... No, the idea was unthinkable. They weren't going to be that thorough; besides he had to take the risk if he ever wanted peace again. The house might turn out to be a white elephant, a damned handsome, expensive white elephant. Perhaps his judgment was wrong; the market might slump. But he'd made his decision, committed himself to the risk and he could not back out. He didn't *want* to back out. He really wanted the house. Somehow the last few months had opened his eyes to the value of having it – an intricate value admittedly, tied in with sentiment and spite as well as greed. Tonight after he got Lang well out of the way he would celebrate.

The vision of Lang hunched on the stoop like a weazened gnome crept out from under the hill was almost too much for him.

'I really thought you'd be off with the van?'

'No,' Lang replied.

143

'Can't tear yourself away?' said Galbraith. 'Don't you think it's all for the best?'

'Maybe it is.'

'Never mind, you'll be united with your good lady, and you'll soon settle down. There's more to do in Glasgow.'

Lang lobbed a pebble on to the lawn.

'What time's your bus?' asked Galbraith.

'Time yet,' said Lang.

'I'll drive you to the stop, if you like.'

'Did you tell the police?' said Lang, 'that I'm out.'

'Sure.'

'They'll be up with their spades in the morning?'

'Spades?' said Galbraith innocently. 'What the hell for?'

'Looking for more.'

'God, I hope they don't find them,' said Galbraith, as if the idea was fresh to him. 'I'd have no chance of a sale then.'

Lang grinned maliciously. 'Be funny if they did find something though.'

'Not for me,' said Galbraith. He studied the old man carefully. 'I think you'd like that to happen, just to see me lose money.'

'Oh, no,' said Lang in a voice which indicated quite the opposite.

Galbraith glanced ostentatiously at his watch. 'Well, I don't want to rush you ...'

Lang pushed himself to his feet, put his hands to the small of his back and arched out his pot belly. His eyes were creased as he peered out over the lawn and the moorland to the line of distant hills, lavender and almost translucent like a water colour wash. Galbraith hoisted up the suitcases and turned towards his car. 'Coming?'

Lang reached behind him and slammed the door, locked it and tucked the key down into Galbraith's breast pocket. The agent nodded solemnly, then walked off down the slope.

Lang followed : he did not look back.

Half an hour later, Galbraith heaved a sigh of relief as the bus pulled away from the stop at the head of Main Street. He waved to Lang who, stiff and unsmiling in the rear seat, gave no sign of response. The old man was staring straight into the back of the driver, or perhaps through the windscreen at the

144

road to Glasgow. Galbraith waited until the bus was out of sight, then scampered back to his Vauxhall. He climbed in and set off for the ranch-house again to keep his clandestine appointment with Edna Johnstone with whose help he planned to baptise his latest acquisition in a most appropriate way.

Part Three

ONE

The play was a boring, pre-London run, with an all-star cast shaken out of mothballs for the occasion. It was all Galbraith could do to stay awake. He did not enjoy comedy much at the best of times and the August evening, displaying itself down the side curtains of the aisle, drew his eyes away from the stage. He kept awake by plucking chocolates from the box on the knees of the girl by his side. He had met her in a bar only three weeks ago. She was too intense for him really but her body appealed to him. He intended to let the relationship ripen for a while in the hope that her concern with the arts extended to sex too – though he had his doubts. She was an infant teacher in a Glasgow school and Galbraith suspected, secretly obsessed with the desire to snare a wealthy husband. He put his hand on her knee, gently but not gingerly. She did not remove it, but bending over murmured in his ear, 'I'd rather you didn't, Robert.'

God, he hated polite rebuffs. Removing his hand slowly, he watched the strutting, stiffly-posed figures in the deep rectangle before him for a minute or two, then closed his eyes and thought longingly of the first interval and the shiny bottles behind the bar. Gin : sure, gin and tonic water, maybe even two to help him survive the second act. If only he could nap without snoring. Applause rattled round him, the curtain jerked and began to slide down. He hitched himself forward in the seat, and asked the girl if she'd like a drink. She told him she'd like an orange juice : would he bring it to her, as she wanted to study the programme notes. He patted her knee, muttered a few charming phrases then set out for the circle bar at the double.

147

He dropped the first glassful over his throat until ice and lemon rind knocked on his teeth. He ordered another, and a carton of orange juice, left the latter on the counter and lifted his gin.

'Going at it a bit, Robert, aren't you?'

He pulled back, and turned. 'It's that bloody awful play, Tyler,' he said.

'It's not that bad,' said Ballentine. 'Are you alone?'

'Nope, I've a young lady with me.' He clinked the rim of his glass against the carton. 'The kind who drinks this stuff and reads her programme in the interval. How about you?'

'I'm on my own.'

'What're you drinking?'

'Whisky, thanks; but I've got one over here.'

'Oh, right,' said Galbraith, edging away from the crowd to a small table in a corner. He took a swallow of gin then casually remarked. 'I bought that house, you know.'

'Which house?'

'The Balnesmoor place : took your advice and bought it for myself.'

'Good for you,' said Ballentine. 'The corpses don't bother you then?'

'Not me,' said Galbraith. 'But I'm willing to hold it.'

'You'll probably have to,' said Ballentine. 'Still, it would make a nice little love-nest for someone.'

'I don't quite follow.'

'For you perhaps, Robert.'

'Me!' said Galbraith. 'God, I don't need a love-nest. I've got one already.'

'I just thought it might be convenient to have one in Balnes-moor,' said Tyler. 'A ... different seat of operations. In any case it's quite fitting you should have the place for yourself.'

'I really *don't* dig you, you know.'

'I'm pulling your leg,' said Ballentine. 'You're jumpy and over-sensitive, Robert. What's wrong?'

'Nothing's wrong at all,' said Galbraith.

'Dad built it specifically for you. I'm sure he'd be pleased you finally have it for yourself. Spent a night there yet?'

'What the hell for?' said Galbraith. Even above the buzz of conversation, his voice was strident enough to make a few heads turn. 'I mean, it's just another property to me. I deal with hundreds of them in the year. It's just another bloody property.'

'Of course it is,' said Ballentine. 'I remember you telling Dad that – a long time ago. You said then it was yours though.'

'Well, it was,' said Galbraith sulkily. 'But I didn't care enough for it then to want to keep it.'

'You needed the capital.'

'True.'

'But you don't need the capital now, surely?'

'Cash is always useful, Tyler,' said Galbraith. 'But an investment's almost as good.'

'I think,' said Ballentine from behind his glass, 'you wanted me to convince you that you should grab the place for yourself. I don't imagine you really expected me to buy it – or anyone else for that matter.'

'Don't drivel, Tyler,' said Galbraith, trying to grin. Temper was boiling in him, the headache which had begun almost as soon as he heard his step-brother's voice pulsed painfully behind his temples. He envied Ballentine his calm unruffled bearing, and hated him for his condescending manner. Why did he have to condescend? He was a bloody mental sadist, Ballentine was. When he walked away, left, it would be all right again, but in his presence Galbraith was always troubled by odd fragments of emotion and mis-matched sensations. He supped the gin, biting the firm bitter flesh of the lemon with his front teeth until he experienced the ache of the acid in the gums and spat the rind back into the empty glass. The sonorous undulating hum of bar-room conversation was suddenly urgently amplified and he was conscious of sweat on his brow.

'You drink that stuff as if it was water,' said Ballentine.

'Most of it is,' said Galbraith. He wiped his forehead with his handkerchief. 'Bloody hot in here.'

'Tell me about the house,' said Ballentine. 'Was the old chap happy with your offer?'

'Why do you want to keep on about that place?' snapped Galbraith. 'I'm sorry I ever mentioned it.'

'If you hadn't,' said Ballentine, 'I'd probably have asked.'

'Ah!' Galbraith let his breath out in a burst from the diaphragm. 'You *are* interested, aren't you?'

'Only in you,' said Ballentine. 'Only in a purely fraternal

149

way. I'm quite fascinated by your personal censorship system, Robert, which allows you to possess a property which has seen so much . . . grief, shall we say? What did the police have to say about the change of ownership?'

'Not a word,' said Galbraith. 'I let them have a go at the grounds and the house just in case, but naturally they found nothing. In fact, Tyler, the only person who seems madly interested in the transaction is you.'

'And your murderer, of course,' said Ballentine. 'He must be keeping a fairly wary eye on the deal; it's so close to his midden.'

'I never thought about him,' said Galbraith. 'Funny, somehow I just can't associate him with anything that's happened.'

'I admire your ability to forget,' said Ballentine. 'I couldn't.'

Glancing across at the bar Galbraith considered the effect another gin would have on him, but the buzzer for the second act put paid to his deliberations. Plucking up the orange juice he gave Ballentine a curt good night and returned to his companion in the circle.

He gave her the drink, and settled down into his seat just as the curtain rose. During the rest of the play he had no inclination to sleep : too much on his mind now, whipped up by all that Ballentine had said. Perhaps it had been wrong of him to take on the burden of the ranch-house and capitalise on tragedy. Still, he hadn't planned it. It was an act of God more or less; for centuries acts of God had been fair game commercially for those not openly involved. Ballentine wanted him to feel bad about it. Ballentine would gloat over any misfortune which happened to him, particularly if it was connected with that bloody house. He almost wished he could get rid of it again; it brought the past too close for comfort. If only he could find a buyer straight away all his problems would be solved. If only!

Tuesday morning, and Galbraith was still depressed. The brief, unfortunately unconsummated affair with the primary school teacher fizzled out over a few passes in his car in the lane at the back of her flat. His mind had not really been on the exercise but instead of making him less demanding, more tactful, his indifference killed his natural caution and he had been left alone nursing the sting of her palm across his cheek. Luckily for her the Vauxhall door opened promptly and she'd been half-way out before she struck, otherwise ... Well, the tussle so focused his ire that he might well have retaliated. God, he'd have to be careful : he didn't want his name splashed across the *News of the World* some bleak Sunday morning. He shuffled the travel brochures listlessly and dealt them out like playing cards. He needed a holiday, yet the thought of passports and flight schedules and involved currency wearied him. Last autumn's sortie to the sunny shores of the Med. had been a total wash-out. What with bad weather, poor food and totally unco-operative girls, he could have done better probably in Oban or Anstruther. He looked down at the folder in his hand, studied the bust-line of the girl who lay on the beach. Promises! The glowing account of the hotel and the beauties of Majorca did not titivate his enthusiasm. But he had to go somewhere, clear out of Thane for a while; the summer was wearing thin. Perhaps he should hang on and arrange a winter vacation at an Austrian ski-ing resort; bright days, the healing night cold, crisp snow, logwood fires, air like chilled wine – a far cry from Thane with its abrasive wind scouring the Lannerburn streets, harsh with dust, chaff, and the stink of exhaust. He was drinking too much. Automatically he shook up the residue of Alka Seltzer water and swallowed it down, immediately lighting a cigarette to kill the flat taste of the stuff. Would he go now, or wait for the ski-ing season? Business was chugging along quite merrily; increased rates recently announced by Glasgow Corporation would undoubtedly drive quite a few new residents into the county, folks who could afford the price of the move and who would be after decent houses. He looked up at the wall-board photographs of the best of his properties, the ranch-house included. He owned two six-acre plots to the west of Lannerburn, but building on them had been stayed by dispute over access rights. If only that bit of litigation would miraculously unravel itself, he would have something to occupy his mind. He badly needed a flurry of activity or a fresh exciting woman, to lift him out of depression. Edna Johnstone's demands only made things worse. Perhaps he was losing his nerve but he could hardly function with her now, smothered by fear of discovery. Her hubby was just the kind to seek an old-fashioned revenge, like plugging him on the spot

151

with a 12-bore shotgun. The ranch-house was too convenient, and Edna too greedy. He would have to do something about Mrs Johnstone; not that she hadn't a lot of erotic talent – she could give a corpse an erection if she set her mind to it – but she was demanding and scheming and Galbraith had sufficient experience to read the signs. If only he'd thought of the implications before he'd hustled Lang into selling : maybe he was getting old! Lethargically he stubbed out his cigarette and shook another tablet from the tube. Still that damned caravan to think about too, lying empty at the mercy of the scavengers from *The Place.* He wished Ryan would make up his mind, about its fate. He hauled himself up from the desk and carrying the glass with the tablet in it, walked over to the toilet door. The inter-com. phone sawed urgently. He hesitated, put the glass on the ledge of the sink, went back into the office and lifted the receiver.

'Yes, Sandra.'

'Somebody to see you.'

'Who is it?'

'Lady,' came the secretary's stringent voice.

'Do I know her?'

'Search me. She's interested in renting a house. Have we anything suitable?'

'Give her the books,' said Galbraith.

'Hm,' said Sandra. 'It's you she wants to see.'

'All right,' said Galbraith, automatically adjusting his tie. 'I'm free just now. Just send her in.'

He got behind the desk, swept the Alka Seltzers into a drawer and assumed a casual executive pose. An irrepressible sensation of anticipation stirred in him in the few moments before the lady's entrance. He half expected to be astonished; it might be Clare Hughes. Impossible! He yelled silently to himself. Impossible! The door opened, the girl came past Sandra : it wasn't Clare Hughes. Galbraith got up, smiling, and shook her hand.

'I'm Robert Galbraith, what can I do for you, Mrs ...'

'Denholm,' the girl told him. 'Miss Denholm.'

Galbraith pulled out a chair for her. He understood why Sandra had called her a lady. It wasn't just a temporary lapse into courtesy on his secretary's part, but the whole bit – the chic clothes, manners and mannerisms, poise and assurance, all

152

magazine perfect : not gorgeous, something too icy about her, a surliness rather than aloofness, bold eyes not flirtatious but threatening. Probably in her early twenties, maybe a little younger; he found it hard to tell. He watched as she removed her gloves – no rings on the third finger. So she wasn't just a blushing bride on the track of an ideal villa. She crossed her long slender legs and drew the hem of her skirt over her knees. 'I'm looking for a house to rent,' she said.

'For yourself?' asked Galbraith. He lowered himself into his chair and lifted the Parker pen to play with.

'Yes, just for myself.'

'Some place not too large, I assume,' said Galbraith, thinking of the caravan lying vacant there and wondering frivolously if she was the kind of girl who would ... No, he decided. 'Furnished or unfurnished?'

'Preferably furnished,' the girl said. She was Scots after all : somehow he'd got the impression she was English. 'I have one of your properties in mind.'

Galbraith said, 'One of my properties?'

'In Balnesmoor.'

He felt his stomach tighten, a stab of excitement going into his bowels, but he remained outwardly quite composed. 'In Balnesmoor,' he murmured. 'Now just which house is that?'

'A ranch-house,' the girl said. 'I'm sure you know the one I mean.'

'Oh, the ranch-house,' said Galbraith. 'I'm afraid it's not furnished. And, of course, it's pretty luxurious – five rooms and all the usual offices.'

'I know,' said the girl, 'but it shouldn't be terribly expensive.'

'In any case,' said Galbraith cautiously, 'I ... am trying to sell it.'

She lifted her gloves, and slapped the edge of the desk lightly with them, staring at him. 'Now Mr Galbraith,' she said, 'you and I both know you're having difficulty selling that house, and probably won't, at least not in the near future. I'm perfectly willing to rent it from you for a reasonable sum, and move in immediately. Wouldn't that solve a problem for you?'

'I don't quite see ...'

'I need a place to work,' the girl explained. 'I'm chucking my job in the County building – that's where I heard the gossip ...'

153

'What gossip?'

'About you buying the ranch-house and closing it up for a while. I thought it would suit my purpose perfectly, if we can agree on an economic rental.'

Galbraith chewed his upper lip thoughtfully. Had May Syme somehow told the dolly about his last charitable gesture? This one was quite a different kettle of fish. Sure, he could have old May on tap for a trailer in a half acre of useless ground but this girl apparently valued herself as worth a ranch-house. 'You're giving up your job?' he asked.

'I'm taking in typing,' the girl said. 'I've been doing it in my spare time – theses and scripts, that sort of thing.'

'Oh!' said Galbraith, 'and can you make it pay?'

'Yes,' said the girl, 'if I really work at it. I'm a pretty efficient typist.'

'And you want somewhere quiet?'

'Exactly.'

'But why do you need five rooms?'

'I don't,' said Allison Denholm. 'I'd only use two, perhaps three at most.'

'But what about furnishings?'

'I thought you might be willing to put some in. I don't require much, and I know where I can pick up some office equipment at a reasonable rate.'

'I can see you've given things a lot of thought before coming here,' said Galbraith. 'What if I say no?'

The girl shrugged. 'I'll look elsewhere.'

Galbraith rolled the Parker round in his fingertips, thinking of Edna Johnstone's reaction when he told her he was leasing out the house and to whom. It was Edna who held him back. otherwise the arrangement was ideal. He liked the idea of having a good-looking girl in the house, a girl who wanted peace and quiet. It wouldn't do the property much harm, in fact it might even be beneficial. He could ensure that the lease was renewable six-monthly with a three months notice clause on cessation of tenure; then when the heat went off, he could clear her out and sell it. In the meantime it would be earning. He looked at the long slim legs swinging a little as she nervously, or impatiently, awaited his reply. Furnishing presented no real problem : he still had odd bits and pieces from Muirfauld in store, and could always buy a few extras at bargain prices in the saleroom. She had fine hands too, long like her legs, with short pink unpainted nails, very restless like a pianist's, or ... sure, like an expert typist's. He could probably put some work in her way too – for which she might be grateful.

'What,' he said, 'do you consider an economic rental?'

'What's your price, Mr. Galbraith?'

'Fourteen pounds per week,' the agent suggested.

'I can't manage that.'

'Well what can you manage?'

'I was thinking in terms of nine.'

'Ten,' said Galbraith, 'if you meet your own heating bill.'

'Not fabric repairs!'

He grinned at her shrewdness. 'No, I'll guarantee to keep the property wind and water-proof. Is ten satisfactory? You can probably claim tax relief if you're working from the house.'

Grudgingly she gave him the glimmer of a smile. 'Very well.'

'All right,' said Galbraith. 'I can have it furnished, after a fashion – it won't be terribly grand, of course, – in a couple of weeks or so.'

'I'd like to move in as soon as possible,' said the girl.

'Two weeks yesterday,' said Galbraith. 'I'll draw up the missive, and have it ready for signature.'

She rose and stood before him. He could not be sure that she was not, under cover of pulling on her gloves, merely giving him time to admire the line of her body, tilted provocatively forward like a model's. 'Miss Denholm,' he said, 'Tell me, if you don't mind me asking, don't the ... circumstances which have brought the house up for rental worry you?'

'Not in the slightest,' the girl said.

'There might be a ... little ... ah, publicity when you move in,' Galbraith warned her. 'I'm not sure I can stop it leaking out. Girl alone in murder house, that sort of thing.'

'I'm not afraid of the dark, Mr. Galbraith,' the girl told him defiantly. 'There are worse things in this life than murder.'

'Hm,' said Galbraith, putting his hand lightly on her elbow to escort her to the door. 'Yes, I suppose there are.'

'Believe me,' the girl said as she went out, 'I know there are.'

Allison Denholm crossed the black tarmac forecourt outside Galbraith's building, rounded the corner of the Royal Bank and, looking quickly left and right, hurried over the main street into a public call box outside the post office. She removed her gloves, draped them on the book, opened her handbag and took out a slip of paper with a number typed upon it, then her purse. She laid the shillings and sixpenny pieces in a row across the top of the directory, and dialled a number. It rang faintly in the depths of the earphone.

A voice answered, 'Allison?'

'It's me,' she said, examining her mouth and chin in the square of mirror. 'I got it for ten, and what's more he'll furnish it!'

'Did he offer to take you round there?'

'No.'

'Didn't you ask to see it?'

'No. It wasn't really necessary, was it?'

'Not really,' the voice said. 'When do you move in?'

'Two weeks from now.'

'Good,' the voice said. 'I'm very grateful to you, Allison.'

'No need to be,' the girl said. 'The arrangement suits me perfectly. I wouldn't have agreed otherwise.'

'Good,' said the voice once more. 'Thanks again.'

Allison looked down at the mouthpiece, then pulled it closer. 'Will you ... come when I'm in?'

'Not if you don't want me to?'

'Oh, yes,' the girl said, her tone deliberately diffident. 'I don't mind. If you can be bothered.'

'All right,' the voice said. 'Then I will.'

In the mirror the mouth smiled at itself, quite expansively, showing small white teeth. 'I'll look forward to it,' she said, and hung up.

TWO

English visitors thronged the promenade at Largs; the Ayrshire resort was a natural target for the Bank Holiday cars which streamed over the Border in search of quieter highways and cheaper prices than could be found in the south. The sun drew sounds upward into the bracing air, the ghostly music of hand-held transistors, the timpany of the amusement arcade, the tame sea crunching rhythmically against the shingle. Boat hirers worked down at their huge-wheeled jetties as frantically as Cuban gun-runners, the fathers of the thigh-booted waders displaying cruises and prices along the tarmac, salty stained and brown, smelling of mussel-bait and petrol. Besieged by legions of children, kiosks and candy stalls stood like white forts along the front. Aloofly cleaving the water of the bay, the steamers came and went, set in splendid silhouette against the Cumbrae's placid grazing land across the narrow firth. Kintyre and Bute and the spine of Arran were visible too along the horizon, somnolent and content, lulled by the warmth. Jenny Lang slanted the cone away from her coat and licked off the soft dribble of ice-cream which trickled from the tip. Her tongue probed and scooped and she swallowed slowly. Milky white drops fell to the dusty concrete at her feet. Beside her a fat man in a fair-isle pullover slumped, head dropped back against the rim of the litter basket which was riveted to the rear of the bench. He snored slightly, vast stomach heaving against thick freckled, folded arms. Arm-in-arm a herd of teenage girls trooped along the prom. squealing and giggling at every passing lad. From beneath the bench an aged cairn terrier clicked out to dab at the spillings with its faded pink tongue, looking up with a startled frown, like an old Presbyterian minister smitten by obscenity, as a macaw high in its cage over the arch of the miniature zoo shrieked and craked raucously for attention.

Jenny finished the cone, chewed the nub of wafer and wiped her sticky mouth on her handkerchief. Norman lit his second cigarette since tea in the boarding-house, and inhaled contentedly. Jenny glanced at him from the corner of her eye. He was staring out over the water, the newspaper on his lap pinned down by his elbow, a tiny smile sewn on under his moustache. His cheeks were ruddy, polished by a week's good weather. Jenny was glad she had forced him to come back to dear old Largs where, forty-odd years ago, they had spent their honeymoon, though she had not used sentiment as one of her arguments. He was all for sulking in the flat in Glasgow, but she had nagged on about the need for a holiday. She was now sure that when they returned to the city he would settle down and quit his moaning about the lost peace of Balnesmoor. In spite of his surly pessimism, she had managed to ferret enough information out of him to take stock of their financial situation.

To her surprise, she discovered that it wasn't nearly as bad as Norman made out. Their pensions would provide them with food and clothing; Galbraith's money would cover the rent and rates and provide a few wee luxuries – quite enough to see them through. She did not argue with Norman when he blethered on about finding another place in the country, but she felt no need to agree with him now, preferring silence to a lie. She knew they were finally settled for life, and could pass the rest of it contentedly – if only he would give them the chance. She truly preferred the unpretentious flat in the depths of Glasgow to the ranch-house. Norman would never know that it wasn't the fierce pace of city life which had dragged her to the verge of a breakdown three years ago, but his carping meanness and overwhelming ambition to mark his existence with a country house. It hadn't only been ambition, but obsession. Still, that time was no more than the vague memory of a nightmare, harmlessly tucked away in the past. The scrimping, isolated winter in Balnesmoor had been rather like a bad dream too, rising up stridently to the spring's horrifying climax. Now that was all behind her too, she began to see in the discovery of those poor girls' bodies an accident not wholly without blessing. From her own selfish viewpoint, the rare coincidence, by driving her again to the brink of despair, had finally forced her to grab control not just of her sanity but of her life, compelling her to choose between buckling or surviving, between meekly complying with Norman as she had always done or clashing with him. Picking the latter course got her her own way in the long run. Now she saw that it was best not only for her but for him too, and the fiftness of their release drained off the dregs of her guilt. There he was smiling to himself, enjoying life, and for once not counting up the cost.

'Penny for your thoughts, dear,' she said. He stirred and looked round as if surprised to find her by his side. 'What are you thinking about?'

'Nothing,' he said. 'It's a lovely night.'

'Will you be sorry to go home tomorrow?' Jenny said. 'I will.'

Lang uttered a non-committal grunt which she took as an affirmative.

'I'd like to walk for a bit,' she said, 'round to the Broomfields.'

'All right,' Lang agreed, 'But wait 'til I finish this.' He held up his cigarette. Jenny nodded.

The fat man emitted a shuddering groan and tugged his elbows as if to draw an invisible sheet snugly about his paunch. Jenny winked gaily at her husband. Lang put the cigarette in the corner of his lips and settled back against the bench, carefully folding his newspaper. Opening her handbag Jenny dug into the corner and discovered a green packet of mints. She popped one into her mouth and offered the packet to Norman. He ignored her. The paper was poised in his hand, held out like a chorister's score, his fingers behind it pushing the page up to his incredulous eyes.

'Sweet?' Jenny said, her voice trailing off in bewilderment. Lang leapt to his feet and Jenny started back, digging her handbag into the fat man's side and waking him grumbling from his slumber.

'Norman, what is it?' She reached for his arm but he yanked himself away from her, slapping the paper with his fist. Under the ruddy skin the blood had risen giving a contused and empurpled swelling to his jowls. 'Norman, are you ill?'

He smashed his hand into the newspaper again. 'He got rid of it. The bastard got rid of it.' Then he shouted, 'The miserable bastard.'

Crowds passing on the promenade hesitated, staring over at him with a mixture of amused curiosity and embarrassment. Jenny heard the faint puzzled mutter of voices asking each other the same question as she was asking herself. The macaw joined in too, clawing up its cage, splitting its malevolent beak in a demanding scream. Jenny stood up and pulled the paper from Lang's fist. 'Where : where is it?'

'There.' His finger stabbed down into the page. She caught the tiny heading close to the bottom of the column, *'Girl Rents Murder House.'* Faintness wavered over her like steam, spectators, shingle, cars, kiosks, all spinning around. She lifted her arms and Norman caught them, pulling her upright. She put her head down and it cleared and she was in control again.

'What has it to do with us?'

'Galbraith knew,' Lang said. 'See, he had a girl lined up t'put in. One of his fancy women, his cheap tarts, his whores. That's why he bought me out.'

'You don't know for sure, Norman,' Jenny said.

'Ay, but I do know,' Lang told her. 'I know the way his mind works. He cheated me out of my house, and I'll get him for it.'

'Norman, there's nothing you can do.'

'Isn't there,' Lang cried. He flung the paper away and the knots of spectators stepped swiftly back from it as if it held the contamination of a disease. 'Isn't there : just you wait and see.'

Suddenly conscious of the attention he had attracted, he drew his wife to her feet again and clamping her arm through his, marched off across the car park in the direction of the boarding house, trailing Jenny behind him.

Galbraith's forearms were braced flat on the carpet, naked but for the watch. He used the swift constant rotation of the second-hand as a focal point to distract his mind from his loins, holding back against her greed, prolonging the moment of release for her satisfaction and his own vanity. She whimpered huskily, her head switching from side to side, eyepits sallow and lips parted. Her tongue lolled out and he could see the metal fillings in her big back teeth. He inspected them for a while then glanced slyly at the watch again, working automatically with his hips. Sweat sucked obscenely in the hollows of their bodies. Her breasts, flattened and spread, high-tipped nipples slanting outwards, were heavy enough even in gravity to retain a swollen avenue down the parting. He nuzzled it with his chin, the softness pressing against his jaws. Then he raised himself up to plunge his mouth over hers, delving with his tongue, but even then through the spray of black hair on the scatter cushion he was conscious of the dial of the Rolex and its warning. Why did she do it? Why did *he* do it for that matter? Running the terrible risk of discovery. In spite of the soothing lies she told him, she had no real notion where her beloved Phil was, and she didn't give a damn. He could be sitting on the step with his shotgun trained for all she knew or cared. It wasn't her Johnstone would plug. Galbraith felt the slackening and closed his eyes, bucking more strongly until the upheaval of her belly threatened to dislodge him. When she had called him at the house something in her tone had impressed him – an ultimatum, a riot about the news item? Apparently she hadn't seen it at all. Still, he would have to

160

break the bad news to her today, and his technique, the lack of selfishness, deliberate calculation and pandering to her appetite were merely leads to the verbal battle which would surely follow. Unlike most women, she was always jolly and replete after a good-going session on the flat of her back, none of the old post-coital *tristesse* which had been the bane of his love life. She might take the news reasonably enough : God, he hoped so! She hadn't even asked him about the furniture. Couldn't wait to get started on the main event. Edna, for all her hunger and debauch, just never took time to savour the full excitement of the act. Where *was* Johnstone – in Glasgow, like she said, or just out for a pint? The Rolex said the pubs would be closing in ten minutes. Panic shivered him. He concentrated fiercely, shifting his chest over her and ramming his hand across her mouth. The noises she made sometimes could be heard a mile away. He felt the spasm in her and locked her buttocks with his arm, the big watch squeezing into her flesh. At the final instant her eyes flared open, the glaucous pupils spun back into her head. With intense relief, Galbraith experienced the shudder of departing energy flicker up from his heels. For a few wild seconds he switched off the reasoning mechanism and snatched what pleasure he could from the afternoon's performance.

Under her lids her eyes were alive again, burning dark. She dabbed sweat from her bosom with her underskirt, the cardigan around her shoulders and the bar of the electric fire grooving the flesh of her thighs and belly with a radiant pink, making the black hairs dry and spring up again. Galbraith pulled on his undervest and shirt, kneeling to tuck them down into his pants.

'You're in a hurry,' Edna Johnstone said. 'I'm not surprised you're not tired though.'

'What's that supposed to mean?'

'Nothing,' she said. 'Just that you were fast.'

'It's your fault,' said Galbraith. 'You've too stimulating an effect on me.'

'I'm not going to fall for your flattery,' the woman said. She flicked the underskirt at him making the hem sting his knees. He struggled into his trousers. 'What's the panic for?' she said. 'I told you he's in Glasgow, and won't be back for hours. Don't get dressed, Bob.'

'Edna,' Galbraith said – he zipped up his fly – 'I'd like to make a long afternoon of it, but I've got some business which must be attended to.'

'On Sunday afternoon?' she said. 'Ay, the golf club, I suppose.'

'Not the damn' golf club at all,' Galbraith said, keeping his voice low and reasonable. 'It just happens that people looking for houses usually ...'

'I know, I know,' Edna said. 'You've told me often enough already. When'll I see you again?'

'I don't know. It depends.'

'Don't you like it?'

'Yes, of course I like it,' said Galbraith, 'but it's not going to be so easy for us to meet in future.'

'Is it not – how?'

Galbraith gently put the lighted cigarette between her lips. She leaned back naked and large, the posture jutting out her breasts, arching her stomach lewdly. She put her head on one side, hair cascading over her shoulder, like a picture in a sophisticated all-male magazine, as if she'd studied up the pose. No magazine ever had one like that, not sold over the counter anyway, and she was real; the warm sexual scent and the hair and the glistening dew of perspiration which still dappled her skin made her real. For all that Galbraith was tired of her. In two years he'd had enough. The largeness of her had begun to cloy – just as the willingness, the bovine passivity of Syme had palled too. He kept smiling though, beginning to crinkle his brows in apology. 'I've sold this place,' he said. 'I'm sorry, Edna, but economically ...'

'You what?' She darted her eyes this way and that as if seeing the furniture for the first time. 'You sold it! I thought this stuff was for our comfort?'

'I told you ...'

'Who bought it?'

'A woman,' said Galbraith. It would have to come out. 'A woman bought ... Well, she's renting it actually. I'm making a damned good thing out of it, too good to turn down.'

'A woman,' said Edna. She ripped the bobbing cigarette from her lips and thrust it at his nose as if to brand him. He pulled away sharply and stood up. 'A young woman, I'll bet.'

'She's not exactly old,' Galbraith admitted. He sat on the

162

small p.v.c.-covered armchair out of sight of the lounge window and tugged on his stockings.

'I suppose she'll see you right now, an' I'll get the heave.'

'Don't be ridiculous, Edna,' said Galbraith. 'It just means we'll have to go back to being careful, like we were before.'

'Careful!' the woman sneered. 'You mean going back t'seeing each other once in a blue moon and only when it suits you. I thought you bought this place t'keep it empty.'

'No, Edna,' Galbraith explained patiently. 'I bought it to make money, and I never led you to believe otherwise, did I?'

'Selling it furnished?' Edna said. 'I mean *renting* it: furnishing it for your young piece. How will she pay you, eh?'

'Edna, please get dressed.'

'Giving me the heave, Galbraith?'

He stamped his foot into the shoe. 'Edna, for God's sake.'

She ran her hands down her body, the cigarette angled in the fingers trailing smoke across the rich plump flesh, clingingly. 'She better than me, Bob? Is that why you're installing her?'

'Look, Edna,' Galbraith said sternly, 'I'm sorry you're upset about it, but I've never made you promises. Even that night I gave you the lift, it was you that started it so you can't blame me now for "casting you aside". Anyway, I'm not casting you aside. I'm just making profit out of the house: that's my job, how I make my money.'

'She must be some girl, if she'll come to live here, even for free.'

'She is *not* living here free. She's paying a substantial rent. In any case, what's wrong with living here?'

'Is she coming alone then?'

'Yes.'

'She must be a right tramp.'

'What's wrong with living here?' Galbraith demanded again, loudly this time. 'It's a pretty good house.'

'With two kids dead outside.'

'Don't give me any of that balls,' Galbraith said. 'It doesn't worry you when you're lying here with your legs open.'

'That's different.'

'Sure,' said Galbraith sarcastically. 'It's a good enough place to get yourself screwed in but anybody who can bear to live here must be . . . Oh, I don't know, nuts or something.'

163

'That's not fair!' said Edna. 'I thought you and I were ...'

'Then you thought wrong.'

'When's she coming?'

'Tuesday,' said Galbraith. 'Look, Edna ...'

The door bell rang.

They stared at each other for almost a minute until the sound of the chimes from the box on the back of the kitchen door struck again. 'Jesus!' said Galbraith, whipping round to the window and then swinging out of the chair. 'It's him.'

'No, no. It can't be him. He's in Glasgow.'

'He's back. It's him.'

The woman was crawling on all fours across the carpet collecting pieces of her clothing into her arms as she went. 'Who is it?'

'It's him. It can only be him.' He plucked her shoes from beneath the armchair and pushed them into her arms as she stood up. 'Keep calm. Keep calm,' Galbraith hissed.

'What'll we do?' Edna said. 'Face him out?'

'Christ, no!' Galbraith cried. 'Listen, get into the hall at the front of the house, dress yourself and when you hear me talking to him in here get out across the path into the bushes.'

'I can't ...' The bell rang once more and Galbraith pushed her, hard enough to leave a bruise on her shoulder. She staggered, saying. 'Listen, Bob, what'll I ...'

'Do's I say. *Move.*'

She went, Galbraith after her to pull the connecting door tight shut. If Johnstone rampaged in, storming through the house like a whirlwind searching for her, then he was sunk. But Johnstone could hardly know for sure. Stall him, hold him off, act calm and reasonable. He lifted the cobbler's hammer from the corner where the fitters had left it, closed his eyes and rapped hard on the carpet. For the fourth time the bell vibrated, prolonged and insistent. Galbraith banged furiously on the floor. He was still in his shirt, and rolled up the sleeves tightly, like a handyman, as he went into the kitchen. Through a bone-dry mouth he got out the words, 'I'm coming. I'm coming.' Whistling with almost no volume and no tune at all, he opened the door. There was no one on the step. Galbraith sagged, swinging the hammer against his side, staring. Nothing, no one interrupted his view of lawn and moor. Not even a dwarf could have slithered out of sight on the sloping grass. He

sucked in a huge breath and stepped out into the daylight. He
shifted his eyes, only his eyes, to the left. Lang was caught in
the act pressing himself against the lounge window.

'*You!*' Galbraith bellowed. 'What the *hell* are you doing,
Lang?'

'Looking for you.'

'What for? Our business is finished.'

'You're a bastard, Galbraith.'

'I beg your pardon.'

'You had somebody up your sleeve for this house all along.'

Galbraith rubbed his brow. Lang lumbered back along the
path, his arms cocked out at the elbows like a wrestler in search
of a hold. 'You've no right to be here,' shouted Galbraith.
'Clear off.'

'How much profit're you making off my house?'

'Now see here,' said Galbraith. He lifted the hammer across
his body. Lang stopped, legs spread, and they confronted each
other with a yard of concrete between them.

'This girl . . .' said Lang.

'She wants the house.'

'You had her lined up, Galbraith. You shoved me out to get
her in, didn't you now?'

'Don't be so bloody ridiculous. I didn't shove you out.'

'*Liar.*'

'That's slander, Lang. It's a good thing for you I don't have
witnesses.'

'She's in there, isn't she?'

'Christ Almighty!' said Galbraith. 'Of course she's not in
there.'

'Then who is? Another of your fancy-women?'

'*Now look*, Lang . . .'

'You said it would lie empty.'

'Yes, but I didn't know then that somebody would want to
rent it,' said Galbraith. 'It happens to suit the lady. She's not
squeamish. God, Lang, what do you want me to do – turn her
down. Anyway it's got bugger-all to do with you now. It's *my*
house. I bought it quite legally, so why don't you just buzz off.'

'Does she know what she's doing?' said Lang. 'Living here
and the murderer not caught yet.'

'He's not going to be in the least interested in her. In fact,
he's probably half-way across the globe by now, lying very low.'

'How d'you know?' Lang demanded. 'He might just be waiting for a chance like this, to get a girl alone in a house.'

'Well, that's her problem, not mine,' said Galbraith. 'She's got her head screwed on the right way, and if there is any risk, then she knows about it.'

'There's no saying what's buried here still,' said Lang.

'The police have been all over the ground and found nothing,' said Galbraith. 'The investigation's as good as closed.'

'But they might be wrong.'

'Look, Lang,' said Galbraith with ponderous patience. 'Things just don't stop because a couple of silly girls got knocked off and buried here. The police have other things to do, and so have I. I've got a business to run, and that's just what I'm bloody-well doing. I mean, this was just the fringe of the affair anyway. To us, to you and me, the matter of the house was the important thing.'

'I worked for years ...'

'Think yourself lucky,' said Galbraith thinly, 'that you didn't raise a daughter. I'd say we're damned fortunate just to have a house to worry us.'

'Who is this girl?'

'Just a girl,' said Galbraith, 'who happens to want a quiet, private place for a while to work in.'

'What is she, a trollop?'

'Don't dare say that again,' said Galbraith, 'or I really will lose my temper.'

'No *nice* girl would want to live here,' said Lang.

'You'd be surprised what nice girls'll do when it suits them,' said Galbraith. He brandished the hammer. 'Now, if you don't mind, I'm busy.'

Lang hesitated. His anger had cooled, but he was not yet ashamed of it or of the other strange urges which had brought him back to Balnesmoor. 'Have you no men who'll work here then? Do you have to do the job yourself?'

'It just so happens ...' Galbraith began, then shook his head. 'No, why the hell should I explain. It's none of your business.'

'When'll she move in?'

'Again that's none of your business.'

'All right,' said Lang. 'All right then, Galbraith.'

'Good-bye.'

Abruptly Lang swung away and trudged along the path and

down the slope to the fence. Galbraith watched him negotiate the fence and turn left – a last long ferocious glance seeming to glance off the wall like a shell – and pass out of sight. Then the agent went back into the house. He closed the door and leaned against it and lit a cigarette, took one drag and dived for the bottle of vodka he had stashed in the pocket of his jacket. Only as the liquid went back over his throat did he remember Edna. He hurried through to the hall. She was gone. He looked around, mystified, for the chains and bolts on the back of the door were all securely in place.

'Edna.'

The cupboard door opened an inch and he saw the dark eye there and the pale glint of her cheek. She was fully clothed.

'It's all right,' he said. 'Come on out.'

'Was it Phil?'

'No. It was Lang.'

'Lang! What did he want?'

Galbraith said, 'He didn't like my renting the house.'

'Neither do I.'

'Yes, but he thought it was morally wrong.'

'He didn't spot me through the window, did he?' Edna asked.

'Christ, I hope not,' said Galbraith. 'Listen, you'd better go. I've had enough excitement for one day.'

'There's no hurry.'

'*Please*, Edna.' He put his arm around her and steered her gradually to the door. 'I thought you'd have gone already.'

'Huh!' the woman said. 'I couldn't get the door open.'

'Oh,' said Galbraith, 'I forgot about that. It's never used, this door.'

'Maybe your new tenant'll want it,' said Edna Johnstone. 'You'd better find her a key.'

'Edna, darling,' Galbraith said, 'I'm the last one to rush you but ...'

'All right,' the woman said, going into the kitchen. 'I don't suppose you'll be happy 'til I've gone.'

Sure, he thought, as he opened the door and made a quick scrutiny of the track; sure, I want rid of you. I'm not keen on your game now. He eased her past him and allowed her to turn, pushing her mouth up to his, crushing her body against him. He still had the bottle of vodka in his fist and held it out,

167

not to spill it. She went along the back of the house and, while he searched the middle distance, rounded the gable into the safety of the road. Galbraith continued to stand at the door, slugging occasionally from the bottle, the cold fire of the spirits easing his nerves. Lang's appearance had rattled him badly; he hoped the little bugger wasn't going to cause more bother. He would have to warn Allison : no, perhaps not. In spite of her apparent indifference, perhaps she would change her mind if she thought there was going to be trouble connected with the house. He wanted her to take it, to live here. Not just for the income; he wanted her to live here because in some ways she reminded him of Clare Hughes.

Far off between the high dusty hedges he saw Edna Johnstone making her way up towards the farm-house. He lifted his arm and shook the bottle. She waved back at him, to signal that all was well. He returned to the kitchen, poured vodka into a cup and sat up on the table to drink it. Clare Hughes and Edna Johnstone and Allison Denholm – past, present and possibly future. The dozens of other girls who had studded his bachelor dreams on cold nights didn't count at all, they were only faceless, nameless entities drained of their juices now. Clare and Allison : the gap which separated them, and the connection which stretched taut as a nylon cord between Galbraith the boy and Galbraith the man, made a stimulating subject for speculation. He looked at his hands and found that they were trembling. He put down the cup, lifted the hammer and battered the wall with it viciously until all his pent-up frustration was spent.

THREE

McCaig poured tea from the pot which the constable had brought in. Ryan reckoned the set-up was supposed to be friendly, but it chimed odd; the Chief with the pot in his hand saying to each of them in turn 'Sugar : milk?' and their obediently solemn replies. The tea ritual was probably designed to put them all at their ease. Other men would have taken a discreet jug with them in the pub round the corner but McCaig's sense of formality, conditioned by his loneliness, would not allow a relaxation of the mores of headquarters. It was tea without sympathy, for sure. Ryan felt uncomfortable. He could see from the look on Sellars' face that he too was disturbed by the inherent grotesqueness of the situation : police college was never like this, never like the tutor's study in the good old Cambridge days. Only Sergeant Blair seemed to be able to accept the props of the *ex-officio* conference with equanimity. Perhaps this was how it was done before the war.

McCaig was sporting a new suit too, a smart bespoke garment in grey, white shirt and silk tie to match. Ryan wondered if the Boss was about to make some personal announcement, thawing out under the influence of – of what? promotion, or engagement, or just success. Success was the last thing McCaig had to celebrate. Perhaps his wife was making one of her very, very infrequent trips north, and the new suit and the tea-party were quite unrelated. Or had the son, Derek, got a First Class Honours or whatever they got in Engineering at Strathclyde? Another covert study of the Chief's countenance and Ryan put all speculation aside. McCaig was only softening the blow – no more, no less; it must be business. He had been spending a lot of time in Glasgow of late, without aides, not even a staff driver to gossip about ports of call. Ryan could imagine the dog fights in the dingy C.I.D. offices as the top brass pulled the Ewart-English case back and forth among them. And May Syme; had McCaig flung her in to keep the pot boiling? Ryan was not about to become a martyr to curiosity by asking out of turn. Whatever McCaig chose to tell them about the liaison with the C.I.D. in the city would be information gratefully received, the rest they would have to whistle for. But whatever was coming it could not be good : nothing was good these days, with the straggling ends of two murders and one disappearance spilled across the ordinary duties of the force. As Sellars had said, another couple of weeks and they'd all be back checking dog licences. Ryan balanced the tea-cup on his lap and lifted a Blue Riband from the plate. None of the three detectives spoke but each followed the Chief's progress from cup to cup intently, warily, as if watching a bee pollinating flowers. Finally McCaig replaced the pot on the nickel tray and lowered himself into his chair. He stirred, sipped and set down his own cup, and looked up at the men. The unexpectedly amateurish exhibition of melodrama

169

suddenly struck Ryan as irrepressibly funny, and he hastened his cup to his mouth before laughter could break out.

'Right,' said McCaig. 'Have a quiet mouthful of tea, and while you're at it, think up a subject for conversation. Just casual conversation, you understand, gentlemen, without any politics or official reports involved.'

'I don't suppose you mean the weather, sir?' said Blair.

'No, I don't mean the weather.'

'How about Anna Ewart and Doreen English?' said Sellars. 'Should we . . . talk about that?'

'If you like,' said McCaig.

'I'd rather talk about May Syme,' said Ryan. 'I liked her.'

'Here, here,' said Sellars, 'you'll be getting yourself a bad name, with admissions like that. You don't drive a Rover by any chance?'

'Not this year,' said Ryan. 'I traded it in.'

'Somebody may have done just that,' said McCaig. 'Somebody who lost his head and then regretted it. If the county is his stamping ground he certainly covered his tracks efficiently, even with a population of a hundred-and-fifty thousand to help him.'

'And half of them women,' said Sellars with a sigh.

'We traced all the Rovers extant,' said Ryan, 'and it got us no-where.'

'Glasgow's just too bloody near,' said Blair. The three men waited for the Chief to make some comment about Glasgow but he did not, merely nodding.

'He may still be shoving around in his Rover,' said Ryan. 'In Cornwall, or someplace. It's where May Syme went that's the puzzle.'

'I think we tackled the problem wrongly,' said Sellars. He took tea demurely, ignoring McCaig's quick glance. 'Glasgow obviously thinks the girls were killed there and brought here. Now, we've sieved out the whole village and half the county without turning up the slightest connection between the girls and Balnesmoor. Neither friends, nor relatives, no picnics, no Sunday jaunts. As far as we can tell they never crossed the county line alive. It's not really our business to track down every kink who's flitted through the county in the last three years. We can't anyway. Somebody's bound to slip through unaccounted for, and the chances are that . . .'

170

'Wait, wait,' said Ryan. 'The girls *are* tied to the county. They were found here, close together in a perfect spot. So we know he was here at least twice. We *know* he was here twice, but we *don't* know for sure that he was here oftener. We can only assume that he has some, albeit remote, connection with Balnesmoor, or Thane itself, because he picked the same, not obvious location to bury his girls in.'

'And May Syme?' said McCaig.

'She's dead,' said Ryan. 'I'm sure of it.'

'Itchy thumbs, Inspector?' said McCaig gently.

'Yes, just a feeling if you like, sir, but the total absence of evidence regarding the killer of English and Ewart and the ... well, the stranger who removed – we'll say removed – May Syme means that he was ... pardon, *they* were both very certain not to be identified, or even seen. They're both blanks, crosses, totally anonymous, and the very fact of their anonymity, the care each took not to be identified, makes me certain that they were one and the same person.'

'I ... I heard a theory not so long ago,' said McCaig. 'That May was taken off the scene because somebody, the joker with the whip we'll assume, was frightened she'd identify him. Now not even the most rabid flagellationist, is that the word, Sellars?'

'It'll do, sir.'

'Even the most rabid sadist isn't going to risk the murder, or abduction of a full grown woman who hasn't any intention of making formal complaint just for the sake of keeping her quiet. He was frightened of identification; suddenly frightened of it, after five or six months, and if he was frightened he had very good reason.'

'Because the old bag might tie him in with the other two killings,' said Sellars. 'We've chewed that over before.'

'And I decided it was a probability,' said McCaig. 'Even though some people didn't wholly agree with me.'

'If she's dead,' said Blair mildly.

'If he took her,' said Ryan emphatically, 'he killed her.'

'Yes, he's a dab hand at disposing of bodies,' said McCaig.

'With thousands of acres of moorland out there, it wouldn't be difficult, not if he's an organiser,' said Sellars.

'And killed to a plan,' said Ryan.

171

'Even psychopaths, loonies, make plans these days,' said McCaig. 'We're organisation daft. Anyway if he did for old May, he got rid of the remains well enough. That ties him tighter to the county, moves him right into our bailiwick.' The Chief paused, swinging the chair a little from side to side, making it creak, the sound loud in the silence. At length he said, 'I assume you know Galbraith's rented out the house.'

'We can't stop him,' said Sellars. 'He was bloody lucky though.'

'He's renting it on the cheap to a single girl who'll live and work there alone,' said McCaig.

'Quite the philanthropist, Mr Galbraith,' said Blair. 'First it's May Syme and her trailer and now the ranch-house.'

'You interviewed this girl Denholm,' said McCaig, 'didn't you Ryan?'

'She's ... all right,' said Ryan. 'Had a hard life, though most of her difficulties seem to have been her own fault.'

'Like Birnie?' said McCaig.

'Birnie's what might be termed an act of God,' said Ryan. 'No, I think this girl can really take care of herself. It's just as Galbraith said – she wants the house because she knows she'll get it cheap.'

'When does she move in?' said Blair.

'Tomorrow,' Ryan told him.

'I gather you've been keeping an eye on the situation, Inspector?' said McCaig.

'Yes.'

'Any special reason?'

'Not ... a logical one,' said Ryan. 'I mean, if we could be sure the killer was reasonably sane then we could stop looking in the county, but if this character's bent then he won't operate by logical patterns. He might not be concerned with escape. He may think he *has* escaped, that we can't track him down much less build a case against him.'

'And he'd be bloody right,' said Sellars.

'Go on Ryan,' McCaig said.

'Well, here's Allison Denholm, roughly the same calibre as Doreen and Anna, though older and more experienced. She's alone in the world and she's sitting in a house miles from anywhere with acres of moorland on the doorstep, a house with an aura about it, a place ...'

172

'God, Ryan,' said Sellars, 'you'll have Dutch mindreaders on the job next.'

'She's a victim,' said Ryan quickly. 'Allison Denholm's a victim born and bred.'

'Victimology, the new science,' said Sellars. 'I suppose you think this fiend's so cocky he picks them out, sets them up, tells them to keep their mouths shut about him, and when he's good and ready, he does them in. And it doesn't even cross his mind that Balnesmoor's no longer safe. I don't buy that.'

'Lightning doesn't strike the same place twice,' said Ryan.

'Well, that's balls for a start,' said Sellars.

'Ay, but you'd be surprised how many people believe it,' said the Sergeant.

'What do you propose we do, Ryan?' said Sellars. 'Ask this Allison Denholm to be sure to let us know who kills her? I'll bet the killer doesn't even know she exists.'

'If he reads the papers he knows she exists,' said McCaig. 'You may be right Ryan, he might be the kind of man to be excited by the idea of a pretty girl in a lonely house right on his "beat"; a rare chance to settle the urge in him again.'

'It may not be chance at all,' said Ryan. 'He could have planned it.'

'Galbraith?' said McCaig. 'You think Galbraith knows about it?'

'I think Galbraith knows more than he's willing to admit.'

'About May Syme?' asked Sellars.

'About a lot of things,' said Ryan. He met McCaig's eye and to his surprise saw a grin spread over the Chief's face.

'It crossed my mind too,' said McCaig.

'God, the audacity of it,' said Sellars, but the jocular sneer in his tone was made rigid by doubt. He frowned. 'Shouldn't we have a word with the girl?'

'No, no,' said McCaig. 'That's the last thing we want to do, at the moment.'

'We've nothing to tell her anyway,' Ryan said defensively. 'It's only guess-work.'

'I think however,' said McCaig, 'you should do a wee bit of discreet nudging in a certain direction. It's a last resort.'

'Of course,' said Ryan. 'I've never been very keen on our friend Galbraith.'

'He's a type you can't help but resent,' said McCaig.

173

'Sir,' said Sellars, 'is all this just . . . casual conversation?'

The Chief's brows went up. 'I told you it was. We're just passing the time of day, idly you might say.'

'Uh-huh!' said Sellars. 'That's what I thought.'

'Fine,' said McCaig with a paternal smile. 'More tea, gentlemen?'

When she stooped to look into the oven of the cooker Galbraith had acquired for her, her skirt pulled across her buttocks. They were small, firm and tight under the material, perfectly proportioned like the long finely-moulded legs. From under her jacket the same downward movement of her body pushed out her breasts, firm too, though not large, conical, in the white sweater.

'Quite suitable?' said Galbraith.

'Yes.'

'And the rest of the place?'

'It's all right,' she said. 'My desk and cabinets will be delivered tomorrow. They'll fill up the lounge. I'll work in the lounge.'

'I . . . brought in some provisions this morning,' said Galbraith. 'Courtesy of the landlord. They're in the cupboard – coffee, tea, sugar, milk, that sort of thing.'

'Thank you.'

'I can't imagine how you'll manage without a car.'

'It's not far to the village.'

'I suppose not,' said Galbraith. 'But on a pouring wet day it's far enough.'

'I like walking,' said Allison.

'I . . . wouldn't venture too far on to the moor though,' said Galbraith.

'Why not?'

'It's easy to get lost there, especially in misty weather,' Galbraith told her. 'You can work in the garden if the weather's good. I had the lawns cut. I'll send somebody with a power-mower from time to time. I don't suppose you're passionately interested in gardening?'

'If you tend the grass,' the girl said, 'I'll look after the flowers.'

'Perfect,' said Galbraith. 'They're lovely, aren't they?'

'Did Lang plant them?'

174

'I suppose so,' said Galbraith. 'He was terribly keen on gardening, of course.'

'What do I do about milk? There's a farm ...'

' I... wouldn't bother with the farm if I were you,' said Galbraith hastily. 'I believe the couple there tend to be rather standoffish, don't like strangers, you know.'

'That's Johnstone's farm, isn't it?'

'Yes, as a matter of fact,' Galbraith admitted. 'Do you ... know Johnstone?'

'No,' said Allison. 'If they're standoffish, I probably won't go there. I can have the van deliver from the village.'

'Of course,' said Galbraith. 'How did you know it was Johnstone's farm?'

'I read it in the newspapers.'

'Ah, yes, I see,' said Galbraith. 'I wouldn't go there,' he added again, lamely.

'Well, thank you, Mr Galbraith,' said the girl. 'It was very kind of you to ferry me down here.'

'All part of the service,' said Galbraith. 'I hope you'll be comfortable.'

'I'm sure I will.'

She folded her arms and stared at him with disconcerting frankness. He knew he was being dismissed but somehow he could not bring himself to take the broad hint. Just to watch her in the context of the kitchen gave him pleasure, a strange, indefinable pleasure, warm and sentimental – was it sexual really? – and he was reluctant to give it up. He felt gawky and tongue-tied, like a sixteen-year-old, but the silly grin would not come off his face or his voice take on suaveness. Really he should go; not rush things yet, just play along with her and leave, but he didn't want the feeling to end. It was like that brief period in the creation of a monumental hang-over when the alcohol in the bloodstream is neutralised and the organs are calm and cold, like shapes of marble, when any cessation of intake will drop the brain back to sobriety and any increase will project it forward into total drunkenness. He hovered, buttoning his jacket and unbuttoning it again, while she stood before him with arms folded waiting for him to leave.

'Have you see around the garden?' he asked. 'There's a tap out there for a hose.'

'Is there?'

175

He whinnied nervously. 'Yes, folks who first had this place used to have bathing parties on the grass.'

'Did they?'

'Quite mad they were,' he said. 'Perhaps you'd like to look round the estate while the rain's off.'

'No thanks,' said the girl. 'I'd like to unpack.'

'Oh, well,' said Galbraith, 'I'd better push off then, and let you get on with it.' But still he did not move to the door, giving her a last chance to ask him to stay. 'There's a hut too, in the garden, for tools and deckchairs. Do you have a deckchair?'

'No, Mr Galbraith.'

'Oh, well, I've a couple of spare ones at home I can let you have. I'll bring them down sometime,' he said. 'Sunday perhaps?'

'If you like,' she said. Galbraith experienced the same kind of thudding in his left side which, so he believed, preceded cardiac occlusion. His breathing was high and rapid and his skull as light as a helium balloon. 'If I'm out,' Allison went on, 'you can leave them in the hut, can't you?'

'Oh, you might be out?'

'Yes.'

'Well ... when ... I mean when will you be at home?'

'Sunday,' she said. 'Perhaps.'

'Sure,' said Galbraith, 'I'll chance it on Sunday then. See how you like the house, and all that.'

Allison turned the handle on the kitchen door. 'You're very kind,' she said drily, standing back to let him sniff daylight and clearly view the garden.

'I suppose I must go,' said Galbraith. He bowed to her, hesitated, offered his hand. She took it, gave one perfunctory pump and released it. He brought it back slowly, and let it hang limply by his side, shoving the other hand into his trouser pocket. 'Well, goodbye then, Miss Denholm.'

'Good-bye, Mr Galbraith.'

'If you want anything ...'

'I'm sure I shan't.'

'If you ...'

With a final polite smile and an inclination of the head, she firmly closed the door on him. But Galbraith didn't mind: he was too steeped in boyish rapture to be put off by such a little

176

thing. Sunday, he would be back, with deckchairs, fruit perhaps and a bottle of sweet wine; votive offerings. He sailed across the lawn and, whistling, popped into the Vauxhall for the drive back to the office.

FOUR

The first trace of autumnal sheepsgold was washed up in the leaves by a week of torrential rain, the moorland dunned by continuous downpour into a dull senility which even brilliant Sabbath sunshine could not revitalise. Greens faded, burnt-paper browns would not smoulder readily into crimson; a light early-morning frost starched the flags on the pin of the golf-course stiff as cardboard and in the fields of the south county the harvest was teased up sadly from the wet earth. In *The Drovers*, a pub adjacent to police headquarters in Thane, Ryan talked farming with casual Sunday drinkers for half an hour before returning to his duty. With a glass of ale and a ham sandwich inside him, he felt a little less depressed than he had done earlier that morning. He paused in the doorway, lit a cigarette and looked up and down the side street. Out of the doorway of the antique shop, Birnie moved forward. Ryan watched him approach, the rolling gait almost clown comic. He came directly up to the Inspector.

'Can I have a word with you?' Birnie said.

'What is it?'

'I ... want help,' said Birnie, plaintively. 'Real, this time.'

'What?' said Ryan.

'Saw a man yesterday,' said Birnie. 'Honest, Mr Ryan. He was up'n the moor near ... near the place where they found the ... near the house.'

'Birnie!' said Ryan warningly.

'Naw, honest, I swear it's the truth.'

'You know who's living in the ranch-house now, I suppose?'

'Ay, but that's got nothin' t'do with it.'

'What about this man?'

'I never got a real close look't him,' explained Birnie.

177

'I was busy with the coos, an' I couldn't get up there but he was about for a bloody long while.'

'It's a long way to the ranch-house, Birnie,' said Ryan. 'How did you manage to see him so clearly?'

'I never said I saw him clear,' protested Birnie. 'I just said I saw him. He was skulkin' round along the edge, crouchin' up an' down the hedges, sometimes lyin' down. I never thought much about it when I saw him first...'

'What time?'

'About the back'f three,' Birnie replied. 'But he was in the area till five anyway. I ... I got the impression he was watchin' the ranch-house.'

'It could've been a bird-watcher,' said Ryan.

'Ay, maybe,' said Birnie. 'But he didn't look it t'me.'

'Why didn't you phone the police?'

'I never thought't the time; then last night ... Ach, I got worrit about it.'

'About Allison Denholm?'

'If y'like,' said Birnie. 'Mind you, Mr Ryan, I've never been near her since...'

'All right,' said Ryan. 'You were right to tell me; thanks.'

'What'll y'do?'

'I'll look into it,' Ryan promised.

'I wouldn't like nothin' t'happen t'her.'

'I said I'd look into it, Birnie,' Ryan said. 'You can leave it to us. If you're thinking of toddlin' over to protect Miss Denholm. I wouldn't bother. I doubt if she'd appreciate your concern.'

'Ay, okay,' said Birnie. 'I've got you.'

'But,' said Ryan, 'if you see him again, anyone, just let us know.'

'I will,' said Birnie. 'Right away.'

Ryan strolled down the street, turning once at the corner to see the farmhand still hovering at the doorway of the pub. Once more Birnie nodded encouragingly, as if to impress finally on the Inspector that he was telling the truth.

So, Ryan thought, somebody's interested in Allison Denholm – perhaps. It was always *Maybe*, or *Perhaps*, yet the further he progressed in time from the girls' killings – how faint and insubstantial they seemed now – the narrower the limitations of space became. Small details accumulated' : the disap-

178

pearance of May Syme, the renting of the ranch-house, and now a stranger on the moor. But the technique was quite different from filling a box with clues; physical evidence was nil. The many questionnaires, Glasgow's too, had proved only so much waste paper. All the man power, brain power, power of organisation poured into the case so far had yielded naught. The few – *perhaps* – important finds which had fallen his way, had all gravitated from the half-acre of moorland, spreading out like rings across a pool. Was somebody sizing-up the ranch-house, or was Birnie just up to his tricks again? For days now, since the tea-pot discussion with McCaig in fact, Ryan had been feeling let down. Other work intervened; he was surprised how these trivial cases, none of them involving death or violence, had assumed almost as much importance to him as the murders. If it hadn't been for May Syme's disappearance – all right, Ryan, call it murder – he would have asked McCaig to take him off the case completely. There would still be activity in Glasgow, unsung dog-labour involving a couple of Detective Sergeants, perhaps an Inspector, gripped by the circumstances of the killings. Like Marchbanks, moody, passionate and a poor loser; an officer like Marchbanks would never really give up. Sometimes Ryan wished he'd been cast in that mould; but he could not sustain the intensity of first anger for five months.

He entered headquarters by the side door, collected his hat from the rack in the office and went out again by the front. Even if it was wasted effort he would continue to plug away. The man on the moor might be the stranger who battered May Syme, might have wheedled the Glasgow girls into his car, might have killed them and buried them on Balnesmoor. This *might* be his first error : then again it might not. Ryan got into the Hillman and set out for Balnesmoor.

'Damn,' said Galbraith as soon as he recognised the figure climbing from the car. He sat forward, resting his elbow on his knees and gestured in Ryan's direction.

'Police,' he explained to the girl in the chair beside him.

She opened one eye. 'I know,' she said.

'Oh,' said Galbraith, 'I didn't realise you were familiar with our local bobbies.'

'He asked me some questions once.'

179

'They ask everyone questions,' said Galbraith.

'I'd a hellish time with them. Even now they won't let me alone. It's ... well, it's because of the house, Allison, it's so close to the site.'

The girl stretched her legs, and pulled her feet back. Her sandals slipped off and she dug her toes under the straps to lift them again. Though Galbraith persisted in his lie that he had unearthed them from his shed at home, the two garden chairs were brand new. Allison accepted his gifts more readily today than last Sunday; he felt he was making progress. He'd even persuaded her to call him Robert. If only this was happening in spring instead of autumn he could be sure of sustaining a kind of open air relationship for months. But with cold weather ahead the casual garden parties would end. He was not confident enough yet to suppose that she would establish their friendship on a more familiar basis – Sunday lunches, long afternoons by the fire splitting the papers among them, dinners at the *Caledonian Highland,* or car trips to Glasgow. If every weekend held such promises he would be a happy man indeed. But Allison, though he imagined her less ... 'reserved' than when they first met, made no promise at all. There were depths to this girl which her youthfulness hid well. He pondered on how soon, if ever, he could expect her to trust him enough to let him touch her.

The sun was brilliant, almost blinding. He pushed the dark glasses down from his brow and in the momentary dark lost all definition. He got up, stretched casually and, his eyes growing quickly accustomed to the coloured glass, held out his hand to Ryan.

'Afternoon, Inspector,' he said. 'You've met Miss Denholm already?'

'I have,' said Ryan.

Oddly, Galbraith felt more at ease in the presence of a third person. 'Glass of wine, or a lager?' he offered, cocking a thumb at the tray on the grass.

'No thanks,' said Ryan.

'What can we do for you then?' Galbraith asked. He was still standing, one hand on the back of Allison's chair, as if master of the household. Her hair brushed against his fingers as she inclined her head. Solicitously, while awaiting an answer, he tucked a cushion behind her neck. Ryan's expression was as uninformative as an uncarved gravestone.

'Miss Denholm,' said Ryan, 'did you see anyone on the moor yesterday afternoon?'

Galbraith looked down at the girl. He could see the line of the brassiere and the small cleft between her breasts lying tenderly behind the rim of her blouse. She kept a smile on her face but her eyes were suddenly alert. 'No,' she said.

'Were you at home?' asked Ryan.

'Yes.'

'All day?'

'Yes, all day. I was typing in the lounge till well after seven. Then I made a meal in the kitchen, washed my hair, then I watched T.V. for a while.'

'Were you ... alone?' asked Ryan.

'Of course.'

'I only dropped in this afternoon,' said Galbraith, the explanation coming out before he could think to censor it. 'I mean, I'm not ... I wasn't here yesterday.'

'Who was it on the moor?' Allison asked.

'We don't know,' said Ryan. 'We had a report that a man was seen acting ... suspiciously up there.'

Galbraith clenched his teeth, frowning, scrutinising Allison to ascertain how the news affected her. More bloody trouble probably, some crank peeping in on her, on them. He glanced up at the moorland; the hills supported bruised clouds of a vivid purplish-blue colour, like a stain of bramble juice across the neutral land. The expanse of wilderness had a hostile, almost malignant quality full of secrets, a porridge of history, enduring practically unchanged a home to no man, but with a life all its own. Verdure was stealing across the track again, seeping up through the fences into the lawn. Seeds of thistledown drifted silently across the sky, invidiously seeking to claim every cultivated inch by innate patience and strength of numbers. For Galbraith the thistle epitomised a whole curriculum of natural law. He batted at the fluffy parachutes around him as if they were hornets, shaking his head lest they lodge in his hair.

'Who made the report?' Allison was saying.

'A farmer in the vicinity,' said Ryan.

'Johnstone?'

'No.'

181

The girl laughed coldly. 'Lord, don't tell me it was Birnie again – and you *believed* him!'

'Has he been bothering you?' asked Ryan.

'Not in the slightest. I haven't set eyes on him since last we met,' Allison said. Galbraith had lost the thread of the interrogation : who was Birnie? The girl went on, 'You must've frightened him off Inspector. Was it Birnie?'

'Is it likely you'd notice any strangers in the vicinity?' asked Ryan, ignoring her question.

'I doubt it,' the girl answered.

'Look here,' Galbraith said, 'do you really think there's a prowler loose on the moor?'

'There's no need to be alarmed,' said Ryan.

'Allison,' said Galbraith, placing his hand firmly across the crown of her shoulder, 'be careful. Lock your doors and don't go out after dark. I'll have a telephone installed as quickly as ...'

'I'm *all right,*' the girl declared, shaking off the agent's hand. 'I can look after myself.'

'Oh, I don't think you're necessarily in any danger,' said Galbraith, 'but ...' He turned to Ryan, and said sternly, 'Can't you put a constable on guard?'

'Robert, for Heaven's sake stop it,' said the girl. She got up and slipped her feet into her sandals. 'It's nothing.'

'If you see anyone near the house,' said Ryan, 'Don't hesitate to call us.'

'I'll make sure the phone's put in by Monday,' said Galbraith grimly. 'I'll pull a few strings at the Manager's office.'

'Will you?' Ryan said to the girl. 'Let us know?'

'Of course,' Allison said. 'But it was probably just a hiker or someone who lost his way.'

'Maybe,' said Ryan, 'but your co-operation would be appreciated.'

He tipped his hat and shifted as if to leave, then, changing his mind, waved to Galbraith; the gesture unusually imperative for such a mild-mannered man as Ryan. 'Walk down to the car with me, Mr Galbraith.'

Galbraith felt his facial muscles stiffen – guilt again, guilt over nothing. Probably Ryan was only going to lecture him on the need for caution, or perhaps ask him to make sure that

182

Allison was protected – a good excuse to call often. He could not tell from her expression what she was feeling, but if there was even a grain of fear behind her poised, cynical indifference then he would play on it, turn it to his own advantage. He strolled after the Inspector and side by side they crossed the lawn towards the gate in the fence.

'Listen, Galbraith,' said Ryan, 'what possessed you to set the young lady up in that particular house?'

'Sure,' said Galbraith, 'I appreciate how it looks but actually she came to me with the proposal. I'm glad to have her there though.'

'You seem to have a penchant for lonely girls,' said Ryan.

'I don't think I like your implication,' said Galbraith.

'You did set her up, didn't you?' said Ryan.

'I ... helped her a little,' Galbraith admitted. 'I like her, sure. She's an attractive girl, and I'm susceptible to attractive girls. It's a normal reaction.'

'But it's not natural to install them in trailers and houses all over the county,' said Ryan.

'Please don't be petty, Inspector, and don't exaggerate. I suppose you're narked because May Syme went off without a word. What you really want is a police state.'

'You've forgotten what was found just over there in that thicket,' said Ryan.

'I haven't forgotten,' said Galbraith. 'But like any normal person, I am doing my damnedest to forget. Listen, are you worried about this character on the moor? Is there something you didn't tell Allison? If he's known to be dangerous or something, perhaps you should let me in on it.'

'I've told you all I know,' said Ryan. 'I'm still checking on it.'

'Who's this person, Birnie, anyway?' Galbraith asked. They stopped outside the gate, by the front fender of the Hillman.

Ryan shrugged. 'A dairyman for Phil Johnstone.'

'What does he have to do with Allison?'

'You sound ... jealous, Galbraith,' Ryan said quietly.

'She didn't tell me she knew any farmers.'

'Tells you everything, does she?' said Ryan.

'Not necessarily,' said Galbraith. 'But she knows she can trust me.'

183

'That's more than I do. You've never been straight with me Galbraith,' said Ryan with abrupt vehemence.

'I suppose you've reached the stage of looking for a scapegoat,' said Galbraith. 'Well I've no intention of filling the bill. I've always co-operated to the fullest. I let you into the house with your science kit, didn't I – *and* you found nothing.'

'What do you want from this girl?' said Ryan. 'She's not like the Syme woman. Even you must be able to see that.'

'It's none of your business,' snapped Galbraith. 'I'm sick and tired of people telling me what to do. First it was my old man and then my bloody brother, and now it's you lot. What d'you take me for, some teenage yobbo. I'm genuinely sorry about what happened here, but I've got nothing to do with it. I don't resent authority, but I'm rapidly coming to the conclusion that authority resents me. Now, how about cutting out all this nonsense and leaving me in peace.'

'That young lady,' said Ryan, jerking his head in the direction of the garden, 'has had enough grief packed into her life already, Galbraith. I don't know if she told you about any of it but if she hasn't, I won't betray her confidence.'

'So you think I'll do her harm,' said Galbraith, in genuine astonishment. 'I wouldn't harm her for worlds. I like her, I tell you. And I don't just mean I want to pull her into bed. Have all cops got dirty minds like yours?'

'We're paid to have dirty minds,' said Ryan.

'Well, this time you've got hold of the wrong end of the stick. Just because I had a little innocent fun with old Syme, doesn't mean to say I'm a louse. I *like* Allison Denholm.'

Ryan put his foot on the hub-cap of the Hillman. He pushed back his hat from his brow. Cloud was frothing up over the moorland though there was no wind to drive it, only the speed of the turning earth running the west land into downpour and night.

'You liked Clare Hughes too, didn't you, Galbraith?' Ryan said.

'Clare ... Hughes?'

'Don't tell me you've forgotten the name.'

'What do you know about Clare?'

'I know that she's dead,' said Ryan.

'It was an accident,' said Galbraith. He pulled off his glasses, thrusting his face forward. The flanges of each nostril contracted, depressed, then flared again, so that the whole shape of

184

his face seemed to alter and change with each second. 'I had nothing to do with it. I was a hundred miles away.'

'I know it was an accident,' said Ryan. 'I dug up the Fiscal's report.'

'She fell.'

'And drowned,' said Ryan. 'Accidental death. Those Galloway cliffs can be very dangerous.'

'She never did have a head for heights.'

'Pity she was alone at the time,' said Ryan. 'It would have saved so much time at the enquiry if there'd been a witness.'

'I don't see . . .'

'You liked Clare Hughes too, didn't you?' Ryan said. 'You must have, you were engaged to her.'

'Who told you this, my bloody brother?'

'Nobody told me,' said Ryan. 'I found it in the files of the *Gazette,* tucked away in wee paragraphs and odd columns.'

'What's your point, Ryan?'

'My point, Galbraith, is that most of the women you've *liked* don't reach middle age.'

'Why've you been checking up on me? You don't seriously think I'd anything to do with those girls,' Galbraith said. 'Christ, you do, Ryan? You've picked me out and now you're going to hound me. Well, I bloody-well won't have it, d'you hear. I'll take action. I'll complain. It's persecution that's what it is : unwarranted intrusion . . .'

'Calm down,' said Ryan. 'Your girl-friend'll hear you if you shout like that.'

'Why are you interested in Clare Hughes?'

'Tell me about her.' Ryan said.

'She was . . . engaged to me. It wasn't wholly my idea. My father wanted it. I told you before, he built the ranch-house for me, to try and win me round to the idea of marriage. Only I got fed up being bullied. I broke the engagement. That's all.'

'And Clare Hughes left the county.'

'Yes, I believe so.'

'Don't you know?'

'Sure,' replied Galbraith. 'She left. I don't know where she went.'

'She went to Dumfries,' said Ryan slowly. 'To stay with an aunt. And eight months later she . . . died.'

'Not my fault.'

'No,' said Ryan. 'Just an accident. It as good as killed her mother too.'

'They all left the county,' said Galbraith. 'For all I know they all went to Dumfries. It's the past now anyway, long time ago, dead and ...'

'What age was she?'

'Stop it.'

'She was eighteen, wasn't she?'

'About that,' said Galbraith. 'Now, for God's sake stop asking these pointless questions. I've done nothing to be ashamed of – then or now.'

'Was she a virgin when you knew her?'

'Christ, shut up, Ryan. *Shut up.*'

Ryan paused, took his foot from the awkward angle on the wheel. 'All right,' he said at length. 'I'll stop.' He walked around the back of the Hillman and let himself into the driver's seat, lit a cigarette from the packet in the glove compartment. When he cocked his head and peered up through the open window, Galbraith was still standing there, arms by his sides the glasses hanging from his fingertips. 'You're a bastard, Ryan,' he said.

'Yes,' Ryan said. 'I have to be sometimes.'

'You won't stop me,' said Galbraith.

'Stop you?'

'I've nothing to be ashamed of,' said Galbraith. 'You won't stop me seeing her.'

'How can I?' Ryan said. He reversed the car gradually up the track, backing it over his own tread marks in the soft black mud. With his fist still on the wheel, he put his face out of the window and called, 'It's your house she's in, after all.'

'Bastard,' Galbraith shouted, as Ryan screwed up the window and sealed himself in.

The Hillman swung backing out of the dead end and shot forward into the lane, gathering speed as it climbed the incline into the aisle of trees. Numb with rage, Galbraith leaned back against the fence. He stood there for ten minutes, totally motionless, sagging wire cutting painfully into the small thick clots of fat at each side of his spine. Then, without even glancing at the girl in the chair in the garden, he walked straight forward into the tangle of soaking shrubs across the track. Slashing left and right, he fought his way through them

186

to the lip of the moor, and drew himself up over the crumbling black dirt. His shirt was plastered with mud, his flannels flecked and torn by gorse and bramble thorns, but once on the bleak open plateau he stumbled forward again in a dead straight line, heading for the distant hills.

Rain drove him round eventually and lashed him back to the oblong of warm light which clung to the rain-blurred dusk. The window tugged him out of madness and anguish, long-overdue guilt bubbling up to the surface at last, carrying him back faster than he could run, like a house or a village, like a whole land spinning backward into the static blackness of storm. By the time he reached the ranch-house he had no pride left, no vanity, no will even to think of another refuge, only the chilling, sodden weariness of exhaustion. She took him in, sat him down, dried his hair and arms and face, cooked for him, gave him drink, and let him sleep in the armchair by the fire until he was ready at last to face the journey home. She did all those things and never once asked where he had been or what kind of emotion had driven him out across the moor. Not that night nor any other night did she question him, and for her comfort and her tact Galbraith loved her all the more.

Ryan no long dwelt in anticipation of his evening T.V. programmes. He thought of them, and of Jean, only in passing, the decision apparently already made somewhere in the back of his mind. He deliberately shifted other thoughts into the fore-front, much as he pushed the Hillman's gear-leaver into higher revolutions. When he reached the roundabout he automatically turned the wheel for Thane. He had work to do, but no time to bother with explanations. He would toil along, dovetailing some facts and a lot of fancies, shifting them around, tapping them together into some solid shape.

His speculations narrowed suddenly like the close beam of a torch. He'd always assumed that May Syme's disappearance was connected with the man in the Rover, the man with the whip – what if there was no such man! What if the old cow had been lying to him, lying to protect her meal-ticket, to cover up for Galbraith. What if Galbraith himself had marked her? Ryan was sure that the agent was capable of it; he had sensed instability there. Under Galbraith's plausible manner were the churching emotions of a volatile character, the kind of mixture usually associated with an adolescent in the throes of puberty. He had to find out more about Galbraith – about his past, his girls, and whether he had an opportunity to ... Steady, Ryan, he told himself, one inch at a time, no hundred yards dash for a solution yet. He must creep slowly towards the reckoning that Galbraith *might* be capable of killing. The hunter out of the country, *not* out of the town? Possibly! The Inspector formulated a mental picture of Robert Galbraith at the moorland track, poking and prodding, crumbling earth between his hands, considering, struck with the seclusion of the thickets and their suitability as cover for a corpse. Not a rare game, lots of people played it, tucking away the notion secretly, a bit ashamed of their grisly pastime. Deep river mud, narrow hidden cave, well-shaft in a deserted farmyard, rotting heap of manure in the corner of a field – how easy to bury an enemy there. An inward giggle at their audacity and the conception was lost *for ever*? But what if the conception had not been lost on Galbraith, had lingered dormant, ready for the time when urgent need would arouse it. Why shouldn't Galbraith pick up girls in Glasgow? He was personable, charming and well off. He had mobility in all senses of the word; a Vauxhall and no family to answer to, his own home and his own business, he could come and go as he wished. He liked women – liked or hated, Ryan could not quite determine the exact nature of the passion yet – and women probably liked him. He was not old enough yet to sound the warning light in the mind of a teenage girl nor so young that he was brash and gauche. Would a schoolgirl be susceptible to his apparent sophistication? As soon as Ryan reached headquarters he hurried to his office and dug out the files of the case. He set the photographs in a line across his desk, propped against the wall. Faces, bodies, gestures encapsulated in the false immobility of the camera lens : he studied them undisturbed, chin in hands, for ten or fifteen minutes then looked away out of the window. It was raining; the transition from fine weather to foul had happened without his noticing it. The drops on the pane cast a fretwork of shadows over the desktop and the surface of the prints. He switched on the lamp, and slowly reached for the telephone.

FIVE

Glasgow was gloomy. The blazing neon beacon directly below the living-room window only served to make the approaching darkness colder, like freezing moon-frost filling the air. Inside the flat was cosy; the gas fire purred, the red-shaded lamp on top of the T.V. set reflected on crockery and picture-frames until the whole room was warmed by miniature echoes of its glow. Lang ate like an automaton, neatly dicing the omelette and buttered bread, forking the cubes alternately into his mouth. Jenny came out of the kitchenette with the teapot under its yellow foam-plastic cover. She stood by his side, talking, and poured tea into his cup.

'I'll never understand what makes you do it,' she whined. 'I mean, you've no proof that he cheated you. Even if he did, we got a nice convenient home in exchange. If they catch you, you'll be for it. I don't want you to go there again, Norman.' She turned up the volume. 'Norman, do you hear me?'

'Yes.'

'I'm sick of you trotting back and forth, never telling me where you're going, or how long you'll be. I know where you go all right. I'm not as daft as you think. Haven't we had enough bother? I hope you're not still thinking of taking him to court.' Sharply, she called across the room. 'Norman, have you given up ...'

'Yes.'

'Well, I'm glad to hear that at any rate,' said Jenny. 'He was quite generous with us really. I mean, we'd never have found this place if it hadn't been for him. Even if he did want this girl ...'

'Yes.'

'I'm just thankful we got out when we did. It was far too much for me.'

'You'd have got over it,' said Lang.

'I couldn't be expected to run a five-roomed house on nothing,' she said.

'I didn't ask you to.'

'I got tired of counting every penny, Norman.'

'You think this is better?'

'Much, much better,' said Jenny. 'Food's cheaper in super-

189

markets, I get out when I want, and we've a nice lot of neighbours.'

'They know about us, don't they?' said Lang.

'What does that matter?' the woman said. 'They don't blame *us*. They're sorry for us in fact, very sympathetic.'

'I don't like people being sorry for me.' said Lang.

'You do go there, don't you?' she said.

Lang clinked down his fork and supped tea noisily.

'If you don't go to Balnesmoor, where do you go?' Jenny said.

'Have you forgotten all about the girls then?' he said.

That stopped her : the voice cut off. His back to her, he went on, drinking slowly in little sips, dampening his moustache with the scalding liquid.

'No, I haven't forgotten,' she said after a blessed pause. 'But . . .'

'You used them to get what you wanted.' Lang said.

'That's not true.'

'Not one of you cared any more than I did about those "poor" girls. You just pretended to be sorry, to get your own way.'

'I hope you don't mean me?'

'I do mean you; and Galbraith and all the rest of them,' said Lang firmly.

'What put this notion into your head?'

'It's been there for a while.'

'That's why you're mad about the house being rented?'

I was too gullible,' said Lang. 'I should never have listened to any of you. You all cheated me.'

'Me included?'

'You most of all.'

She did not react meekly, dissolving into the act of self-immolation as she would have three months ago. She placed her hand to the base of her throat and fingered the pearls on her necklace thoughtfully, then nodded. 'Yes Norman, I can see how you'd think that.'

He swivelled round in the chair, kicking his feet from under the gate-legged table. 'And what about the girl that's living there now?'

'What about her?'

'She must be either stupid or an insensitive bitch to rent the place.'

'If she'd come to us to buy the house,' Jenny pointed out, 'you wouldn't have thought ill of her.'

'It's all right for you to put it all behind you,' Lang snapped. 'Ay, I hear you talking all the time, and humming away to yourself in the kitchenette. You're glad it happened. You're happy.'

'Would you rather I was miserable?'

'You're happy at my expense.'

'If it would bring those two girls back to life,' said Jenny, 'then I'd go on suffering for them. I'd even go back to live in Balnesmoor. But it won't.'

'It's not them I'm thinking about,' Lang declared. 'It's him.'

'Galbraith didn't ...'

'I don't mean Galbraith,' Lang interrupted. 'I mean the man who started it all.'

'What man?'

'Him; the killer. He's still out there somewhere, you know, having a right good laugh at you and me. I'll bet he's watched every move we've made, just like the police did.'

Jenny edged forward in her chair. 'Are you feeling all right, Norman?'

'I feel fine.'

'You've been under a strain,' Jenny said.

Lang closed his eyes, then opened them again quickly as if there were figures on the inside lids which he could not bear to see. 'If I hadn't gone into that bloody bush ...'

'Did you ever think how many other lives you saved?' said Jenny. 'If you hadn't found ... what you did, he might have killed others and buried them there on the track, while we were actually in the house too.'

'Yes. I've thought,' Lang admitted.

'Then it was worth it,' said Jenny. 'For all we lost in the process.'

'Was it!' said Lang savagely.

He got up from the table and planted himself in the narrow armchair by the hearth, dogmatically placing slippers on the tiles of the imitation grate, sliding his knees close to the wire-screen of the mantel. His arms hung slack over the chair sides, his eyes riveted to the blue-green cones of burning gas. 'The only thing to stop him is to catch him.'

191

'Would that put your mind at rest?' Jenny asked. 'If they caught him?'

After a period of brooding silence Lang answered, 'If it was the right man, it would. If it was Galbraith.'

'Norman . . .'

He jumped out of the chair, stumped through the hallway and locked himself in the lavatory. The atmosphere of the tiny room was tainted with the stale seep of concrete and new distemper. But he stayed there, shivering, for over an hour. He preferred the chill discomforts of solitude to her persistent questions, and the answers he could not help but give.

On the top floor of one of the better-preserved blocks in the city centre, the office admitted a magnificent view of the river and the hills of Renfrewshire. It seemed to Ryan that the whole city of Glasgow nestled at Ballentine's elbow. He waited several minutes in an outer chamber before a middle-aged secretary admitted him to the inner sanctum. Ballentine climbed quickly from behind the welter of paperwork on his desk. He shook Ryan's hand and motioned him to an armchair, then took up an attentive stance with one haunch resting on a wooden ledge against the window.

'Sorry I couldn't make it earlier in the week,' he said. 'But I've been up north. One of those unexpected flurries of activity, you know.'

'It's good of you to spare me the time,' said Ryan politely. 'I won't take up too much of it, I hope.'

'No hurry,' said Ballentine courteously. 'How can I help you?'

'Your brother lives near Lannerburn,' Ryan said. 'Do you visit him much?'

'Hardly ever,' said Ballentine. 'We're not close.'

'Are you in the county often?'

'I play golf there occasionally,' said Ballentine, 'but it's usually in and out again. Wait though, I did have dinner with Robert in the *Caledonian Highland* – when, oh, a couple of months ago.'

'You don't own any property in Thane I take it?'

'That's Robert's line, not mine,' said Ballentine. 'You Thane people haven't ventured into whisky distilling yet so I've no excuse to haunt your territory. I was a . . . resident, of course,

192

for a while, but you probably know about that from Robert. May I ask your purpose Inspector?'

'I believe,' said Ryan carefully, 'you and your brother ...'

'Step-brother,' Ballentine corrected.

'Step-brother,' Ryan said. 'I believe you both knew a young woman called Hughes; Clare Hughes.'

'Of course, we both knew Clare,' said Ballentine. He frowned. 'Robert was engaged to her for a while.'

'Would you know where Clare Hughes is now?'

'She's dead,' Ballentine replied. 'She killed herself.'

'Really!' said Ryan.

Ballentine pursed his lips, studied Ryan in silence for a second, then said, 'You knew she was dead, Inspector, didn't you?'

Ryan bowed slightly.

'Then why ask me?'

'I ... need details about Miss Hughes' death,' said Ryan, 'and I wasn't sure if you'd be willing to talk about it.'

'Why not?' said Ballentine. 'I only knew her through Robert. Look, I'd prefer you to put your cards on the table, Inspector. If I know what you're after I might be able to answer you more fully. Besides, I rather resent being treated like a hostile witness.'

Ryan nodded. 'Very well, Mr Ballentine.'

'It concerns Robert, doesn't it?' said Ballentine. 'And the Balnesmoor house too, unless I'm much mistaken.'

'What makes you think it concerns the house?'

'Come now,' said Ballentine. 'The house was built for Clare and Robert. Everyone with fourpence for a newspaper knows what happened there. Robert tried to talk me into buying it, you know.'

'I didn't know,' said Ryan.

'Naturally I wasn't interested.'

'Why did he think you might be?'

'I liked the place,' said Ballentine, 'when it was first built, but that was years ago. Robert sometimes tends to forget how things and people change. Anyway, I see he's found a tenant after all.'

'Mr Ballentine,' Ryan said, 'you told me Clare Hughes killed herself, that's not what it says in the Fiscal's report.'

'No, it says *accident*, but authorities are always reluctant to record a verdict of suicide without concrete proof, aren't they? Everyone knows she killed herself, threw herself over that cliff.' Ballentine wrinkled his nose. 'A bloody decisive way to go.'

'Why does ... everyone think she killed herself if there's no corroborative evidence?'

'Popular opinion has it that she broke her heart because Robert jilted her.'

'What do you think?' Ryan enquired.

'I don't think that was more than a small contributory factor,' Ballentine replied. 'Clare never struck me as being a terribly ... stable person.'

'Did her death affect your brother much?'

'He was cut up about it, of course, but Robert ...'

'Yes.'

'Robert's resilient,' said Ballentine. 'Egotistical too, which helps. He was young enough to ... well, shrug it off. I hope that doesn't make him sound callous.'

'Your step-father knew about it?'

'You couldn't keep anything from him,' said Ballentine. 'Everyone in Lannerburn knew about it. It was quite a hot little scandal at the time. I'm surprised you don't remember.'

'That was before I came to Thane,' said Ryan. 'How did your step-father take it?'

'He was furious,' said Ballentine. 'He had a vile temper when roused. Frankly I don't think he really believed all the gossip. What cut him up was being crossed by Robert. He loved having his own way in all things. Quite a remarkable specimen I suppose.'

'Did you get on well with him?'

'Quite well,' said Ballentine. 'I was almost an adult before my mother married him. I never ... asked anything of him really: nor did I ever interfere in his dealings with Robert. I suppose we got on fairly well on the whole.'

'Did he know that Clare Hughes was being treated for a venereal disease?' asked Ryan.

'God, you have been thorough,' said Ballentine. 'Not many people know about that. Old Galbraith didn't, that's quite certain. There was some talk about pregnancy and abortion, but the real reason for her moving out was even nastier. As you say – a disease.'

'How did you find out?'

194

'He told me – Robert, I mean,' said Ballentine, without hesitation.

'I thought . . .'

'He asked my advice. He didn't like me much but he trusted me not to tell his father. Robert was confused. He was only about twenty then, and frightened he would die of it or something.'

'You mean Galbraith contracted it from Clare Hughes?'

Ballentine shook his head. 'I don't know. Robert claimed she infected him.' He raised his hands in gesture of hopelessness. 'No one was bright enough to connect his illness with the broken engagement. He didn't have it badly, a few weeks discreet treatment in Glasgow soon got rid of it. But by that time Clare had gone and Old Galbraith was breathing fire and smoke. Robert . . . changed quite a bit after the incident, started standing up to his father more. It was all very messy, and I was very much a spectator. I didn't want to get involved.'

'Funny,' said Ryan, 'I had the impression that the Hughes girl was . . . not the kind to mess around with more than one man. She was only eighteen – though I don't suppose that it makes any difference.'

'It's ancient history now, almost everyone mixed up in it is dead,' said Ballentine. 'Is old man Hughes dead? I think he is.'

'Last year,' Ryan answered absently.

'Then why this sudden police interest?'

'Your step-brother rented a trailer to a woman by the name of Syme; do you know her, Mr Ballentine?'

'Syme? No, I can't say I do. What trailer? I didn't know Robert dabbled in small stuff.'

'And the young woman who's rented the ranch-house, do you know her?'

'No, I don't think so. What's her name?'

'Allison Denholm.'

'Never heard of her either,' said Ballentine. 'You seem interested in the girls Robert does business with. Is he up to something he shouldn't be?'

'Would you say your brother has lots of women?'

Ballentine grinned. 'He's very popular with the ladies certainly. I've never concerned myself with his private life though. Don't tell me this girl's making trouble for him?'

195

'Is he like his father?' Ryan asked suddenly.

'He has his father's temper, though he controls it better,' Ballentine replied. 'I remember once, the only time we came to blows – over a stupid card game or some such thing – he practically killed me. A real tiger he was on that occasion, quite took me by surprise. I had to run away eventually or he would have done me serious injury. As it was he broke one of my fingers.' Ballentine held up his left hand. 'See, it's still a little bit bent.' The broker studied his finger for a moment, then slowly lowered his hand. 'You really must tell me where your questions are leading, Inspector. I hope I haven't been talking Robert into hot water. What's he been up to?'

'He hasn't been up to anything,' said Ryan, getting to his feet. 'I . . . I'm just checking out a report.'

'Concerning Robert?'

'About the new tenant of the house,' Ryan lied.

'Good God, what's he hooked this time?' said Ballentine. 'Don't tell me he assaulted her, or something.'

'Is he capable of it?' asked Ryan.

'No, that's why I'm surprised. Is that what it is?'

Ryan smiled. 'Nothing like that, Mr Ballentine. Just a routine check to clarify some points. You've been very generous with your time : thank you.'

'I thought . . . I had the suspicion that it might have some-thing to do with those murders,' said Ballentine.

'Oh!' said Ryan. 'Why?'

'You were on that case, Inspector, weren't you? And then Robert bought the house? Your questions make me think you might imagine Robert's tangled up in it.'

'We have to suspect everyone,' said Ryan smoothly. 'A large part of my job's eliminating innocent parties.'

'Naturally,' said Ballentine. 'Well, I hope I've helped elimin-ate Robert. He's such an idiot in some things. I'm sure he'd never think to protect himself.'

'Against the police?'

'Against suspicion,' said Ballentine. 'If I happen to see him in the near future, may I tell him you questioned me?'

'By all means,' said Ryan. 'It's just routine.'

'He'll probably laugh about it,' said Ballentine.

I doubt it, Ryan thought, I doubt if he'll find it all that funny.

'Thank you Mr Ballentine,' he said. 'I don't think I'll have to bother you again.'

SIX

Galbraith held the travelling clock at arms-length and focused on it, disbelievingly : seven bloody fifteen on a Saturday morning, and the telephone ringing fit to waken the dead. He put the clock on the bedside table and rolled over, pulling the clothes round his head. The taste in his mouth was filthy. He rubbed his tongue over his teeth, like props sticking up from an oast-house floor. Sensation had not yet reached his legs; they were as lifeless as rolls of dough. He wriggled his hips to flop them over, but the action drummed pain up into his skull. Left shoulder first he wallowed on to his back again, nose and eyes over the edge of the blanket. His heart was thudding against his armpit; this is how he would die one day, just like this, all alone in bed, suddenly and without much warning, a brief agonising prelude, then the total loneliness of death. The telephone was still ringing, just as it had rung that early morning donkey's years ago – it seemed like yesterday sometimes – and he had jumped out of sleep in the big barren bedroom in Muirfauld, lifted it from where he lay and Ballentine had said quietly into his half-awake ear, 'Clare killed herself last night.'

The telephone went on and on and on and on; he could not bring himself to answer it now. He slid his hands over his ears, pressed them against the flesh, the stubble over his jawbones making a dry rasping sound on his palms. He would lie here for ever before he would answer it. Mrs Baxter, the cleaning woman, could answer it when she arrived at eight. He had no doubt it would still be ringing then, for the tone had the suggestion of persistence. Saturday – no Mrs Baxter on Saturday : it would ring on for ever, then. He'd be buggered if he'd answer it. No one in the world could make him answer it and there was no one in the world he wanted to speak to anyway at seven-fifteen in the morning. No one, nobody? Except Allison Denholm! Allison Denholm wouldn't call him – or would she? He shifted his hands behind his head and

197

propped himself up a little, straining foolishly to define the precise timbre of the bell now, as if some special quality in its monotonous jarring would tell him whether it was the girl or not. The more he thought of her the more convinced he became that it could be no one else. It couldn't be business; Sandra knew better than to disturb him at such an ungodly hour on a weekend. It might be Edna Johnstone. He chewed over that possibility, then in a sudden lather of curiosity, swept aside the blankets and stumbled out into the kitchen where the nearest extension lay. He switched on the light, for daylight did not penetrate the venetian blinds, and grabbed up the receiver.

'Galbraith,' he said breathlessly, one hand over his heart as if swearing to the honesty of the name.

'Robert, what took you so long?'

'Who is that?'

'It's me, Tyler.'

'God, what do you want at this time in the morning?'

'Did I drag you out of bed? I'm sorry.'

'I nearly didn't answer.'

Galbraith stretched his leg, which had recently come into his possession again, and worked over the breakfast stool. He sat on it, shivering in the loose silk pyjamas, his feet naked. He looked along the shelf above him with its rows of unused jars, herbs mostly, but could not find the packet of Perfectos he generally kept there.

'Still with me?' asked Ballentine.

'Yes.'

'Looking for a cigarette?' said Ballentine.

'Hang on until I fetch one, will you? said Galbraith.

He hurried through to the bedroom and returned to the telephone a few minutes later, snug in his dressing gown and slippers, a cigarette burning in his lips. He coughed into his fist several times then lifted the receiver again. On the brief trip he'd had sufficient time for his mind to creep to the borders of panic, but he refused to let his imagination haul him over. Still, he could not help but recall the last occasion Ballentine had called him before dawn, and listened to the voice now with trepidation. 'I'm back,' he said. 'What's your problem?'

'Did you know,' Ballentine said casually, 'that the police are making enquiries into your background?'

'Come off it, Tyler,' Galbraith said. 'Of course I know. I've been questioned.'

'Ah, but I don't mean quite that,' said Ballentine. 'They're interested in *you*, Robert T. G. Galbraith. They sent an Inspector along to ask me some questions about you.'

'What sort of questions?'

'Oh, pretty general things,' said Ballentine. 'About your boyhood and your sex life, that sort of stuff.'

'Christ!' said Galbraith. 'The bloody cheek of them. Who was this Inspector : wasn't Ryan by any chance?'

'Yes, that's him,' said Ballentine. 'Do you know him?'

'I know him all right,' said Galbraith. 'Listen, Tyler, what was the *exact* nature of his questions, can you remember?'

'Not accurately, of course,' said Ballentine. 'It was rather staccato and I was so busy being ... well, guarded, that I didn't have enough concentration ...'

'*Think.*'

'You sound worried, Robert,' said Ballentine. 'Don't tell me you've got something to be worried about?'

'Don't be bloody ridiculous, Tyler,' said Galbraith. 'I'm just ... puzzled and naturally annoyed. How would you like a bunch of sneaky cops probing into your life, giving your friends the impression that you'd done something to be ashamed of?'

'You ... haven't, have you?' asked Ballentine.

'Oh, my God!' said Galbraith despairingly.

'Perhaps I shouldn't have told you,' said Ballentine.

'I'm glad you did,' said Galbraith quickly. 'I appreciate it no end. I mean, at least I know where I stand. Now what sort of things did Ryan want to know about me – my sex life? What the hell d'you mean by that?'

'About ... look, I don't quite know how to put this,' Ballentine said.

'Don't try to spare my feelings,' said Galbraith. 'Just put it in words of one syllable.'

'About some woman you rented a trailer to – Syme? Would it be Syme?' said Ballentine. 'I didn't know you owned trailers too.'

Galbraith let his breath out, and coughed again as his lungs deflated. 'May bloody Syme,' he said, half to himself. 'So that's what the song and dance is for. I might've known they let that one slip too quietly.'

'Who is this woman?'

'Never mind, Tyler,' said Galbraith. 'I'll explain it all next time I see you. Now what else?'

'About the girl in the ranch-house. I'd the feeling you'd run to grief over that place. The stigma, and . . .'

'Allison!' Galbraith exploded. 'Don't tell me they're creating trouble for her.'

'I don't quite know,' said Ballentine. 'Ryan was very interested in your relationship with her, and your reasons for "installing", that's the word he used, installing her in the house in the first place. Are you sleeping with her, Robert?'

'Of course I'm not sleeping with her : she's a thoroughly nice and respectable girl.'

'Just the kind you like.'

'Now, look here . . .'

'I'm sorry. That was a bit below the belt,' said Ballentine. 'Ryan asked about Clare Hughes too, though.'

'About Clare Hughes.' Galbraith slipped to his feet, pushing the stool back with his buttocks. It caught on the edge of the matting, toppled and fell with a crash which shook the dishes and jars all around the kitchen.

'What on earth was that?' asked Ballentine, startled.

'Nothing, nothing,' murmured Galbraith. 'What did he want to know about Clare? What did you tell him?'

'I really didn't get the point of the questions,' said Ballentine. 'He seems to have amassed quite a startling collection of facts about that period in your life. I was careful not to tell him much.'

Quietly Galbraith asked, 'How much?'

'Not about . . . that,' said Ballentine. 'I didn't think it was any of his business.' He paused, then added doubtfully, 'Actually, if he had an inquest report he might already know about . . . you know. I'm not sure if that sort of thing leaves scars or not.'

'All right, all right,' said Galbraith. 'What else?'

'That's about all,' said Ballentine. 'I don't think you've any need to worry, but I thought I should let you know.'

'Yes,' said Galbraith. 'Thanks. Wait, just . . .'

'I've told you everything,' said Ballentine pleasantly. 'And I really must go now. I'm off to Islay in ten minutes. Look after yourself, Robert.'

Abruptly the line went dead. Galbraith opened his mouth but hearing only the growl of static thumped down the receiver. He lifted his cigarette from the ledge. It had burned a bullet-shaped groove on the woodwork and tasted of varnish, acrid smoke scalding his throat and lungs. Coughing in short racking sobs, he groped his way to the sink and hung over it spitting phlegm on to the stainless steel. The spasm passed. He wiped his eyes and mouth, cleaned perspiration from his face, only to find it wet again a moment later, damp and cold with the sweat of anger and anonymous fear. They were after him at last.

Lang took the raincoat from the peg in the hall cupboard, folded it and stuffed it into the plastic shopping bag over the thick rubber gumboots. Jenny watched him, leaning against the jamb of the living-room door, her hands deep in her apron pocket. Lang ignored her. From the flat below, the sound of the radio drifted up, the volume turned high so that the children in bed could listen to their weekly record programme. Outside the wind played with the open landing window, slamming and clicking it against the frame as it had done all night long.

'Is it the weekend this time, Norman?' Jenny said.

Lang pulled on his cap, sullenly.

'I hope you've got your key?' she said.

He looked quickly up at her, and she explained, 'I might just decide to be out when you get back.'

'Where?'

'I don't know yet – the pictures perhaps,' she said. 'I'll leave something for you in the oven, don't worry.'

He hoisted up the bag and shifted towards the hall door. Jenny didn't follow him, and he went out of the house without a word. She did not go to the window to watch his eager dogged run to the bus stop, but lingered in the hall, her cheek against the wood, then, after some time, returned to the living-room. She lifted her handbag from the chair, took out her purse and slipped it into the apron pocket. In the kitchenette she carefully cleared the breakfast dishes from the sink, then did her chores in the bedroom. At length she went back into the living-room and consulted the clock on the sideboard. She pulled on her winter coat, and a plastic mac, her gloves and shoes then left the flat, locking it behind her. Five minutes later

201

she was in the call-box at the corner, dialling a number. A minute passed, voices rose and fell like the whispering of distant ghosts. She prodded coins into the slot, and received the rich bass voice in her ear. She moistened her lips, then said, 'I'd like to talk to Inspector Ryan. Tell him it's Mrs Lang.'

They picked up Lang as soon as he stepped from the bus, not, as Ryan had been shrewd enough to guess, at the Main Street halt but out at the edge of the village. Blair and a constable brought him to Headquarters and marched him, not even protesting yet, into the Inspector's office. Ryan was waiting.

'I've done nothing wrong,' said Lang, as soon as he saw Ryan.

'I'm not accusing you of anything, 'said Ryan placidly. 'I just want to ask you a question or two.'

'Bringing me here like that, in a police car,' Lang said.

'May I ask what you're doing in Balnesmoor?' said Ryan.

'Private business.'

'The same kind of private business you had up on the moor last Saturday?'

'What about last Saturday?'

'Where were you last Saturday, Mr. Lang?' Ryan asked.

Lang glanced from Ryan to Blair to Sellars. He could sense the youngest man's suppressed laughter, not far beneath the surface, but the Inspector and the Sergeant were treating him with a weary sort of indulgence. He did not know which attitude he found most distasteful. 'Nowhere.'

'In Glasgow?' asked Ryan.

'Yes.'

'You weren't, Mr Lang,' said Ryan. 'I have it on good authority that you were up on the moor near the ranch-house.'

'It's a damn' lie,' said Lang. 'Who told you anyway?'

'You were identified,' said Ryan. 'You've been there more than once this week, too. It's an offence to do that sort of thing.'

'The moor's not private ground,' said Lang. 'I wasn't trespassing.'

'So you *have* been on the moor,' said Ryan. 'I thought so.'

'I can do what I like.'

'You can't,' said Ryan. 'At least you can't hang about

202

looking in folks' windows. I know, the house was yours, but you sold it, and that's the end of it. Now please, Mr Lang, just toddle back home and stay there.'

'You can't make me.'

'No, I can't make you,' said Ryan. 'I can only advise you, but if the tenant of the ranch-house makes a complaint then I can bring a charge against you, and I'm sure you don't want that.'

'Boy, I can see that story in the Sundays,' Sellars remarked.

'What's the attraction in the house now, anyway?' Ryan asked.

'I can go where I like.'

'Is it the girl?' said Ryan. 'If you're curious to see what the ... tenant of your old home's like, then I'm sure I could introduce you. I don't think she'd mind.'

'Ask Galbraith.'

Ryan paused. 'What have I to ask Galbraith?'

'He cheated me out of my house to put in one of his fancy-women,' Lang blurted out. 'I know she's a fancy-woman.'

'Have you seen her?'

'No,' said Lang. 'She never comes out. But she has men in there.'

Again Ryan paused. 'Men?'

'Yes, men. Galbraith ...'

'You said men,' Ryan interrupted. 'Who other than Galbraith?'

'I've seen them,' said Lang darkly. He knew they were giving him all their attention now; unintentionally he had struck a nerve. He handled the thought gingerly. They were obviously interested in the girl too. He *had* seen a man, a stranger, but not actually at the house, on the track though, hurrying not west but east, breaking through the bracken on to the narrow peninsula of the moor behind the trees. When was that – Thursday morning. In the window he had glimpsed the figure of the woman, holding the curtain aside. Yes, she'd been watching the man too, watching him depart. He recalled his indecision whether to risk going closer and perhaps being spotted, or keep back deep in the hedge, too far off really to observe detail. There *was* something going on, perhaps something sinful and sinister, and he wanted to see, to be shocked, to be involved. Odd that she never came out, not while he was there anyway. In a week she hadn't crossed her doorstep during the hours of the late morning and the afternoon. Even the vans did not call. He would have doubted that she was there at all but for the occasional stirrings of the curtains, like on Thursday, when she seemed to be peeping out at the moor and the track in anticipation. Waiting for her men? What happened at night he dared not think; what stews of sin she lived in there in the pretty house that was his once, not so long ago, before it had drawn the stink of death and wickedness to it like a whirlpool. 'Yes, I've seen them,' he declared.

'How many?'

'A lot,' he lied.

'Can you describe them?' asked Ryan.

'All sorts of men,' said Lang. He heard Sellars cough behind him, a signal, and could imagine the young whelp making a derisive gesture, screwing his forefinger into the side of his head. He tried to bring to mind the anonymous figure he had seen that Thursday on the track, scratching his memory for details. 'One of them was quite tall, and wore a black overcoat.'

'Marvellous,' said Sellars softly.

'Now just how many do you mean, Mr Lang?' Ryan persisted. 'Five, ten, twenty?'

'Four or five.'

'Any of them in cars?'

'Not that I saw,' said Lang. 'They come creeping up the track.'

'I see,' said Ryan. 'And you're up on the moor, hidden?'

'I can go ...'

'All right,' said Ryan. 'We've had enough of that. I think you'd better go home now.'

'It's a free country,' said Lang.

'Do you want to spend a night in the cells? They're not very comfortable,' said Ryan. 'But, believe me, if the young lady down in Balnesmoor gets an inkling you're spying on her, she's just the type to call the police and make a charge. I don't think you'd get much sympathy from her somehow. Do you, Inspector?'

'Sympathy? Nape, I doubt if she knows the meaning of the word,' said Sellars.

'Do I make myself clear?' asked Ryan.

Lang sucked a corner of his moustache. 'Yes,' he said.

'So just be sensible,' said Ryan. 'Sandy, run him to the bus.'

As the Sergeant ushered him out, he heard Sellars' hissing chuckle, and the words, 'I always thought he was a bit touched, but this just ...' The door closed, and he was going down the corridor with the Sergeant's hand on his arm and the heavy shopping bag hanging from his elbow. They hadn't thought to look in it, which was one thing he had to be thankful for. What had they meant about the girl 'not having any sympathy'? Why were they so interested in the occupant of the house?

He was still thinking out feasible answers when Blair deposited him on the one o'clock bus from Thane to Glasgow, and stood resolutely in front of the station watching him out of sight. Lang turned, scowling at the tall patient figure until the bus cut down off the main street on the Glasgow road.

'Fares.'

He looked up blankly at the heavy-set conductress who peered down at him as if he was some strange repugnant insect.

'Is it Glasgow you're wantin'?' she demanded.

'No,' said Lang. 'Balnesmoor.'

He held up the coin.

'You don't mind my waiting here?' Ballentine said.

'Not at all,' the girl said. 'You're paying for it.'

'You're not curious?'

'Do you want me to be curious?' she said. 'If I asked you, would you tell me?'

'That would rather depend on the question.'

'All right,' the girl said. 'Why are you waiting? Do you expect him to turn up?'

'I think so.'

'He'll come around tomorrow for sure,' she said. 'Are you prepared to wait ... overnight?'

'If necessary,' Ballentine said.

'This isn't a practical joke,' the girl said. 'You're actually out to hurt him, aren't you?'

'Yes.'

'Why?'

'I knew you'd ask, eventually,' said Ballentine.

205

'It's the secrecy,' the girl said. 'And the expense. You wouldn't go to all this trouble just for a joke.'

'You haven't told anyone, have you?' Ballentine asked.

'That was part of the agreement,' she said. 'I've kept my word.'

'Good.'

'Where did you leave your car?' she said.

'In Kilcraig.'

'That's miles away.'

'I walked over by the back road,' Ballentine replied.

The girl laughed. 'Like a spy.'

'If I was a spy,' said Ballentine, 'I'd have come by helicopter.'

'Will I make coffee?'

'I don't mind if you want to carry on with your work, you don't have to talk.'

'It can wait,' she said. 'It's not every day I have a man to entertain.'

'Why *do* you think I'm here?' Ballentine said.

The girl smiled. 'I'm not sure.'

'You don't like him much, do you?' Ballentine said.

'Who? Your brother . . .'

'Step-brother.'

'Your step-brother then: no, I can't stand him. He gives me the creeps. I've met too many like him to be enthralled by the type.'

'He likes you?' said Ballentine.

'I think so.'

'Don't you know?' Ballentine said. 'I thought you would be able to tell.'

'He likes me,' the girl admitted.

'Is he in love with you?'

'I should ask for a definition of the word,' said the girl.

'I'm sure you know what I mean,' said Ballentine.

'Yes, he's in love with me,' she said. 'He'd do anything to get me on my back, but he's not going to.' Her voice rose a little. 'That's not part of the bargain, I hope – to open my legs for him?'

'Quite the contrary,' said Ballentine.

'I just wanted to make sure,' she said. 'I know I told you I'd do almost anything for money, but . . .'

206

'I promise you won't have to put up with his attentions
much longer,' said Ballentine.

'Does he know you're here?'

'No : nor will he,' said Ballentine. 'No one must know. That's
the best part of it.'

'You were lucky, weren't you?'

'Sorry?'

'To meet me when you did. I thought you were just another
wolf at first, but there's something about you ... you're quite
different, not that sort at all, are you?' the girl said. 'Even
when you first got out of the car I could tell. Funny!'

'I only stopped because you reminded me of someone. I
don't make a habit of accosting girls in country lanes.'

'You're lucky you didn't get kneed in the balls,' the girl said.

'You're not sorry, are you?'

'No. I'm glad.'

'Good.'

'Tell me about this girl I remind you of.'

'She's dead now,' said Ballentine.

'Did he know her too, your brother I mean?'

'Yes.'

'Ah!'

'I think I'd like some coffee now, please,' Ballentine said.

'Of course,' she said. 'Are you *sure* he'll come today?'

'Yes, he'll come.'

'But if he doesn't, you'll stay the night.'

'If you don't mind.'

'No,' Allison said slowly. 'I don't mind.'

'Good,' said Ballentine. 'You're a good girl.'

SEVEN

Lang came to the site by lanes and footpaths, skirting
meadows, scuttling under the shelter of windbreaks and dikes,
out of the village in a wide circle, over the moor at the back of
the Johnstone place. It was after three before he reached his
beat along the back line of the track above the ranch-house; he
was exhausted. He unpacked the shopper, spread a raincoat in
a hollow just under the edge of the moor, well protected by

207

brown clumps of undergrowth and fading fern, then he lay down. He ate a bar of chocolate and smoked a cigarette, cupping it furtively in his palm and dispersing the smoke carefully so that it would not be seen. Two hikers startled him, passing behind him going east, but they were intent upon their route and preoccupied with the weight of the swollen rucksacks on their backs and did not notice him. After their voices had trailed off, the silence seemed all the more intense. A cow lowed in the far distance, plaintive and lonely; a hoodie crow cleared its throat in a far-off tree. The air was misty damp and, as time passed, his skin grew cold and sodden like the bark of the branches around him. Though his back began to ache and twinge as if a giant pin was sticking through him, he kept watching the house. He changed position more and more frequently – lying like a sniper on his belly, kneeling like a penitent, supporting himself on knee and hand like a scout at spoor. He sat back with his legs straight out over the edge of the raincoat, the dampness coming up from the ground into his calves. He stared at the house, trying to sustain his excitement, hatred and anticipation by imagining the meaning of the small movements which he could discern inside – a hand against the curtains, the opening of the blinds in the kitchen, the vague shape of a figure. His discomfort made him vigilant and strengthened his determination to sit tight until dusk robbed him of his view. Even then ... some night he would risk all, creep up over the lawn and look in on her : perhaps even tonight. He felt sure it would be a revelation, confirmation of his sanity. Lately he had begun to doubt not just the prudence or wisdom of his actions but the very springs of his reason. There was a reason, a whole series of tiny linked reasons like wooden beads on a wire. Had to be! A reason for the man killing and the girls being killed and him stumbling across them, and all the rest that had happened to him since. There in the grass hollow, planted between foliage and earth, he felt himself close to hidden sources of life, roots and stones around him, minute seepings of water feeding all. Where the fire had raged the growths were strong and green; only the tarry stains on some of the trunks to remind him of the spot. In some locked vault of his brain, he hoped, perhaps, that the man would come again, kill again, bury again; that he would be privileged to watch, a silent spectator at the unimaginable rite.

Perhaps he was desperate enough for that knowledge and the purity of feeling that it would bring to squat for ever amid the chilling mist of Balnesmoor – for ever, until he died.

At a quarter to five exactly Galbraith's Vauxhall drew in to the track, stopped, and the agent got out. A hand moved the lounge curtain again, a girl's hand, and dropped it. Galbraith hurried across the grass, and rapped on the back door. It opened. Lang, his mouth open, wriggled forward, parted the leaves with his elbow and watched, breathless with expectation.

Galbraith had been drinking. In the morning, seated in his pyjamas and bathrobe in the kitchen with the percolator and the sugar dish by his elbow and the cup in front of him, it had been coffee. Then his mouth, like his thoughts, turned sour and thick and he tried to get rid of the taste with vodka; when the vodka failed he shaved and dressed, drove out to *The Lodge House* and started out with a long lager to flush his stomach and kidneys, followed by a double whisky to kill heartburn. About one-thirty he ate smoked salmon and sandwiches and potato chips, all salty, then more lager and the whisky. But it was pointless : he could not rid himself of the fear. All the liquor did was melt rage down into maudlin self-pity. Who could he turn to now? Who could he go to? If only he had a wife or a decent understanding mistress. All corridors of his life were empty, rooms and chambers filled only with clay figures with no feelings, no ears to listen or mouths to comfort, not even eyes with which to see him. If May Syme had still been around she would have steamed the misery out of him and left him relaxed. But May was no longer available.

Clare would have been twenty-nine, young still. Why did they want to persecute him by unearthing all that again : God knows it had taken all his will to bury it. Poor Clare : Poor Robbie! The fine smooth neat pale body marred. Clare was vain about her body, but innocent enough to be ashamed of the vanity. He had taught her about her body, the sweet power of it, and the pliant usefulness of every part, passing on lessons he had learned from women not fit to lick her shoes. He had joined her to them not knowing ... How could he have known that he was doing her ill – *not evil, ill*. And when she came to him, he discarded her, pushed her aside.

Where he drove he could not later remember, when it

209

became important that he should remember every second, every yard. His eyes had transmitted to his brain and his brain to his hands and feet, but without recording. The core of the afternoon was a total blank, a half-drunk total blank.

When he fetched up in the track at Balnesmoor, he was almost surprised to find himself there. Yet not so really, for the fusion of Clare and Allison Denholm had accomplished itself not during the course of that single tipsy afternoon but over the weeks since he had met her. The events of the previous Sunday had acted as a catalyst, giving him a retrospective glimpse of what he had cold-bloodedly sacrificed, and a preview of what he might even now gain. If Allison had helped him once, then she might do so again. He had nowhere else to go. He stopped long enough to comb his hair and straighten his collar and tie, brush cigarette ash from his jacket, then push himself out of the car. The mist was low over the moorland; the silence had a sepulchral quality, heightened by the cawing of an unseen rook. He shivered, buttoned his coat and hurried over the lawn towards the haven of the house. He rapped quickly on the kitchen door. Shifting nervously from one foot to the other, he glanced back over his shoulder at the plastered countryside. He chapped his knuckles again upon the door, and also pressed the bell. Inside the kitchen he could hear the bell sounding and . . . yes, movement. She was at home, not out wandering, or shopping. God, she was at home. The door opened four inches; he saw her face, aloof and cold.

'It's me, Allison,' he said. 'Can I come in?'

'What do you want?'

'I want to come in – just for ten minutes.'

'I'm busy.'

'Five minutes then,' he pleaded. 'I'm frozen.'

'No.'

'Well, will you come out with me? We could go for a drink.'

'You've had one too many already, Mr Galbraith,' the girl said.

'No, no,' he said. 'Look, Allison, *please* let me in.' He put his palm flat against the wood.

'Get off, Galbraith,' the girl said. He felt her lean against him. 'Go on, clear off. You don't own me, you know.'

'I just want to talk to you.'

'Well, I don't want to talk to you, so that's that,' the girl said. 'Now will you clear off and leave me in peace.'

'What's wrong?'

'I don't like you,' she said. 'In fact, I despise you, Galbraith. You're a louse.'

'Allison!'

She pushed the door until only an inch of space remained. Through it he could see her lips move, shaping out the name perfectly, but he heard no sound. 'Clare Hughes: Clare Hughes: Clare ...'

He sprang at the door, but she was too swift for him. He heard the bolt click, just as he struck with his fists.

'Let me in,' he cried. 'Please let me in.' He smote the door frame petulantly. 'Allison, you *must* let me in.'

She did not answer. He continued to beat upon the door for a while, then rushed along the path to the window, and tapped on that, crying, 'Allison, what's wrong? What is it? Why won't you let me in?' The glass shuddered under his fingers, vibrating like a skin. He stopped. 'Allison,' he called. 'Can I come back tomorrow? Will you let me in tomorrow?'

She gave him no answer, not even the satisfaction of a rebuff. If only she would come out again, tell him how much she hated him – she couldn't hate him, not after what he had done for her and what there was between them. *She could not hate him.* He would sort out her confusion, make her see she was fighting spectres from the past, not him, not hating him, not Robbie.

'Allison?'

He leaned forward and cupped his hand over his eyes, peering through the drawn curtains, trying to penetrate her secrets. It came to him that she had someone with her, another man. He jerked back, then forward again.

'Allison, who's with you?' he called, his cheek cold upon the glass.

All that greeted him was the flattened echo of his question. He drew away from the window, backing away from it, over the concrete slabs, his heels groping behind him, over the verge on to the grass. He walked backwards down the slope, his eyes fixed on the expressionless façade of the building, his body swaying. Then finally he turned and ran for the Vauxhall. He knew that they were watching him, revelling over his misery.

*   *   *

211

'Is that what you wanted?' Allison Denholm said.

'Yes.'

'Did it do your heart good to hear him beg?'

'Slightly,' said Ballentine. 'You didn't pity him, did you?'

The girl grinned, and her eyes became slits. 'I enjoyed it,' she said. 'I enjoyed his pathetic little performance. He's been drinking. I expect he'll go and have another bucketful now to drown his sorrows.'

'Then he'll come back.'

'Oh, will he?'

'Of course,' said Ballentine. 'But we'll be ready for him.'

'What's the next step in your systematic destruction of Robert Galbraith?'

'You seem ... eager to help me,' said Ballentine. 'Do you hate us all, or just my step-brother?'

'I hate all men – almost all. I like to make them suffer, if I can,' the girl said. 'I think you understand.'

'Indeed I do,' said Ballentine. 'Perhaps that's why we're here at all, because we are so akin. Perhaps that's why you let me talk long enough in the lane that afternoon to interest you.'

'You interested me from the moment you stopped the car.'

'Why?'

'I'm not sure,' the girl said.

'By the way, I told you a lie, you're not the first girl I've ever picked up,' said Ballentine.

'I didn't think I was somehow. Did you use the others to get back at him, too?'

'Oh, no,' said Ballentine. 'They were different; not suitable.'

'Was this girl Clare one of them?'

'No,' said Ballentine. 'She's dead too, though.'

'What?'

'Clare Hughes is dead.'

'Yes, but ...'

'You asked me about the next step,' said Ballentine. 'It may be a little more complicated.'

'Why do you look at me like that?' Allison said.

'Like what? I'm sorry if it embarrasses you.'

'It doesn't embarrass me, no : it ... I wish you'd stop it.'

'I thought we understood each other?' Ballentine said.

'I'm ... not so sure now.'

'You know what hate is, don't you?' Ballentine said. 'You

212

told me you hated all men, so you must know what hate is. We're teaching poor old Robert a very valuable lesson, and your part in it is by far the most important.'

'How long do you want me to .. ?'

'Not much longer,' said Ballentine softly.

'I'm not sure ...'

'You can't back out now. You told me you wanted – peace. I've given you a down payment. Do you remember what you shouted at me when I opened the car door – you shouted "Go away, leave me in peace". Didn't you?'

'I thought you were another one.'

'Another man come to "sniff up your skirt",' said Ballentine. 'But I don't want you. That's the true beauty of it – I don't want you at all.'

'I've heard this line,' the girl said. 'If you do want me ...'

'Yes.'

'... I think you would be gentle.'

'Very gentle,' Ballentine said. 'I will be.'

'I'm not ... dried up, or deformed,' she said. 'I still have feelings there. If you ...'

'I wouldn't dream of it.'

'You're just using me to make him feel bad.'

'More than that,' said Ballentine. 'Let me tell you. I think you've a right to know.'

'What if I don't like the idea?'

'But you must,' said Ballentine. 'You really must. It's too late to back out now. Imagine it's happening not to my step-brother but to the man who paid for your cut-price abortion, then walked out and left you lying on the floor. Do I have the story right?'

'Yes,' the girl said, hardly moving her lips.

'Imagine it's him we're having our revenge on, not my brother at all. He means nothing to you. Bring to mind the face of your Canadian; think of the pain. There was pain, wasn't there?'

'There was pain all right. God, there was pain.'

'You won't ever have a child now, will you?' said Ballentine. 'He's stopped you from having a child.'

'Yes.'

'Then you should be glad to help me. You should enjoy it. It's a valuable function you'll be performing,' Ballentine said.

'Why are you touching me?'

'I'm just comforting you,' said Ballentine. 'I will be gentle.'

'I don't . . .'

'My brother's not innocent either, you know,' Ballentine said.

'Please don't touch me like that.'

'Not at all innocent. Oh, he's very successful, and gives every appearance of enjoying life. He has his business and his golf and . . . and his girls. I wonder how many girls Robert's had. He's funny really : he likes two sorts of girls – innocent ones and raddled old whores, the filth of the streets, whom he can treat with contempt. But he knows they're steeped worse than he is in vileness; they can teach him vileness. I wonder how many nice young girls my brother's spoiled. But not all young girls are nice, are they, Allison?'

'I don't want you to . . .'

'I imagine Robert's found that out too, been surprised more than once. It's so easy to surprise a person like Robert.'

'You're hurting,' the girl said. 'You're hurting me.'

'You *look* innocent, Allison; you look so innocent. But you're not innocent at all, are you? You've already accumulated a lifetime of experience in lust and passion, and pain – we mustn't forget the pain. Pain is a very important part of it.'

'Let me go. I can't . . .' Her lips moved against his palm. Under his fingers her words were only a series of vibrations, impulses in the sinews and muscles of her throat.

'Let me tell you what sort of a man Robert is. I'll tell you about Robert, shall I? And about Clare Hughes. Clare was like you, only her innocence was real. I suppose she loved Robert. Yes, I suppose she did, at first that is, until he'd taken and done what he wanted with her. But it wasn't enough for him just to drop her, to allow me to . . . allow me to love her, try to make her love me in spite of him. I couldn't make her believe I wasn't like him. She wouldn't allow me. The disease did it, the disease he gave her, and the pain and the misery, and the shame he caused her. No, she would have none of me. I only wanted to help her get well, forget what Robert had done to her. But no . . . no, she couldn't separate us in her mind. Perhaps she still loved him, even after he'd shot his filth and contamination into her and spoiled her, burned her body out with his dabblings just as he burned out her mind. Can you hear me, Allison? Nod your head if you can hear me. Good.

214

'No, don't move. I want you to be calm. I can't be gentle with you, if you're not calm. Is *your* body scarred? Do you have scars on you? Let me see if you have scars, love-scars. Let me see.'

He clenched his hand into a fist driving her tongue back upon itself, holding her teeth apart over the area where she had just drawn blood, shifting his arm across her, pinning her back, while he worked. 'I must see if you have scars. The last one had scars, but she deserved them. I put the outward marks of her vileness on her. No, don't kick, Allison. I don't want to cause you pain. You're not like the last one at all. You're more like Anna or Doreen, or most of all, like Clare. I would never have hurt Clare.

'Yes, I see them; I see them. But you're still like Clare. They didn't have scars on them but they were like Clare too, only so easy to find and to have; they wanted me. Not at all like Clare. They found what they wanted. I gave them what they wanted. I think it's what you want, too. Think how nice it will be to have it. Think how nice to pay him back. You said you would help me.'

He shifted his grip again, the prow of bone spanned between finger and thumb, flesh sliding over it as she twisted and lashed helplessly against him.

'You will help me. You'll help me to take it all from him, won't you Allison? *You must now,* you have no alternative. We'll take it all from him, you and I, all his success and all his pleasure, the happiness he never deserved, we'll pay him back for all those girls. There will be no girls where he's going. Thirty, forty years of solitude to think about his crimes, to fathom out whom he offended, and who dug up his guilt. Yes, Allison, we'll make Robbie pay, you and I. No one will know it was us, will they? No one will know it was us.'

He stared down at her, smiling softly, eyes on her eyes. He wondered if she was smiling too, smiling at the perfection of it all, smiling with that wistful happiness Clare had had when they stood in the shell of this same house, under a tender blue sky sliced into segments by the clean timber beams. Smiling Clare, nurturing in her thighs the corruption of Galbraith.

'You won't be cold,' he said. The words rode his breath like tiny weightless flecks of foam. 'You won't be under ground like the other three, just a thing, a dead thing. I need you here

215

where they'll find you and look after you and bury you nicely with no marks. Not like they will bury Robert when his time comes. He'll be old, and thin and harried when they put him down.

'It's Robert they'll want. It's Robert they want now. They can smell guilt off him. You'll give them Robert, won't you? It's you that'll give them Robert now, out of this house.'

She made no reply. He plucked his hand away, and touched her cheek. Her head flopped down, dropping limp. He did not need her answer. She would perform her function without complaint.

EIGHT

The Lodge House was hardly the most respectable pub in the county, though the aspirations of the landlord to cleanse the lounge bar of hard-drinking ruddy-faced farmers and woo motorists in search of the picturesque had encouraged a recent painting. Galbraith could taste the paint in his beer; or was it that he could no longer distinguish between the taint of thinners and whisky. The draught bitter was beginning to take him keenly and aerate the bellicose regions of his character. He had passed through the numbness of shock and rejection, via a phase of maudlin remembrance full of regret for roads not trodden, into the vague erotic spell of coveting the bed-partners of every married man he knew. He was on his fourth half-and-half pint when Phil Johnstone arrived. The short step from sexual envy to point blank aggression was prompted by Johnstone's authoritative demand for 'Four pints over here then, dear.'

Occupying a long table in the corner in solitary state, Galbraith looked up. His brows drew down like sharpened flints. Three other rustics were with Johnstone, older men, stolid and thick-waisted in their Saturday night suits and watch-chains, cartoon farmers. Johnstone had a sharp style of dressing, natty, a little vulgar, his dark hair sleeked with pomade, his jowls smooth and oily. To Galbraith he appeared insolently vigorous and young still; his voice boomed out in the almost deserted pub. Galbraith could imagine the sort of

216

cheerful night the farmer had ahead of him. The barmaid
came around from behind her counter bearing a tray of beer
and set it down on the table at the far end of the lounge. One
old worthy, like an umpire, occupied the centre of the room,
the rest was space, an insulting distance placed deliberately
between Galbraith and the farmers. Edna Johnstone would be
alone down in Balnesmoor, hot-thighed maybe, her nipples
burning a hole in her blouse. It would serve Allison right if he
broke his new-made vow, drove post-haste to Balnesmoor and
stretched Edna Johnstone right there and then over her kitchen
table. The thought of the farmyard odour tickled the tissues of
his imagination : sluggishly his body obeyed the summons. He
grinned a warped grin, and chuckled audibly to himself. The
whisky glass and half pint of ale looked very fresh and inviting
on the wiped formica top; the thirst he had would not abate.
He reached out, took the glass, drank off half the beer, poured
the whisky into the tumbler and shook up the head again. He
glowered at Johnstone, eyes savage with hatred, his twisted
smile betraying a cunning enjoyment of the situation. The
smug, secure bastard'd be out for a night on the town. There
was a dance in the Masonic halls – with young girls, and beefy,
randy-arsed wives crying out for a length. Johnstone would be
popular with them, handsome, arrogant bastard. Muirfauld
and education, money and success stood between him and those
women : he could not go bulling among them, had to take it
sly like a creeping fox in a hen run. But he'd had one anyway,
who preferred him to the farmer. One up, one better. He
thought of Edna, fixing the image of her big grasping naked
body to stir himself to decision. Yet other images kept merging
with it – Allison's litheness and coolness, her touch, controlled
and academic, a typist's touch, light and quick : not the
shoving, shovelling hunger of a country wife. Allison's fingers
would be tentative and endearing, with an innocent explorative
quality – like Clare's. Dead Clare's – murdered Clare's. As
surely as if he'd been with her on the cliff-top and had pushed
her body into the frail wind, he had murdered her – murdered
her from a hundred miles away.

Johnstone was staring at him. He became aware of the
silence, aware of his own mumbling, introverted conversation.
Even the wet rag of the barmaid, scooping out glasses behind
the bar, made no sound, her chop-fallen apprehensive fat face

averted so she could peep at him surreptitiously. The wizened old man at the round middle table held his mouth an inch from the surface of his beer, shifting his glance first to Johnstone then to Galbraith. The elderly farmers who flanked Johnstone were as uniform and characterless as earthenware pots.

Galbraith growled. The warning came up through the tubes of his throat like the rumble of a train in a tunnel. 'What the hell're y'lookin't,' he murmured; then shouted, *'Well, what's wrong with me?'*

He caught a vague impression of the barmaid's fatuous smile blooming out of the bar lights on his left as he staggered to his feet, her towel-shrouded paw held out as if to wipe him away. He put his knee under the table and tilted it over, glasses and tray in a tinkling symphony until the table top crushed them with wooden thunder. He stepped carefully over the debris using the upturned leg as a crutch. The barmaid vanished from the edge of his sight, leaving a swinging plane of light where she had been, the diminishing wail of her voice summoning the Landlord. He moved forward up the planks of the lounge floor, feeling for each step with the sole of his shoe like a man crossing an icy pond in the dark. Johnstone patted his oily black hair, and inched out from behind the table. His friends watched with mute expectancy.

'What's wrong with me, Johnstone?' Galbraith cried. He stopped, spread-legged, adjacent to the old man who unfocused his pupils and, by not seeing tried, not to be seen. 'I'm good enough for the likes of you.'

Johnstone cocked his head, the dour mouth hardly opening. 'I know you,' he said. 'Ay, you're Galbraith.'

'Bloody right, I'm Galbraith. I'm not 'nyone else,' said Galbraith, jerking his neck with emphasis. 'But I'm good 'nough. You ask'r, Johnstone, you just ask'r. I'm a bloody better man'n you.'

'Listen, Galbraith,' said Johnstone, lifting his fist, the forefinger, stained with nicotine, extended. 'Better belt up.'

'You've heard 'bout me then,' yelled Galbraith happily. 'I'll bet you've heard 'bout me. I'm good 'nough. I'm bloody good 'nough.' He took another pace towards the crouching figure of the farmer. 'She not tell you 'bout me Johnstone?'

'Who; just who?'

'Don't y'know who?' slurred Galbraith. 'You should know who. Y' can have all your bloody big fat cow-girls, Johnstone, but I've got *her* when I want'r. She never turns m'down.'

'Christ,' said Johnstone. 'Y'mean Edna.'

'Edna,' Galbraith said. He grinned and stuck out two fingers, obscenely crooked. 'Sure, your bloody Edna. Me she comes t'for'r ...'

'You heard him then,' said Johnstone, flinging the phrase out behind him like the jacket of a man who cannot wait to fight. 'Right, Galbraith.' He slid forward, his lean hips as gracefully controlled as a ballroom dancer's, brushed aside Galbraith's outstretched arms, and punched him twice with the left hand, disdainfully.

Galbraith whipped back. The knuckles struck him again on the mouth and pain spread like warm oil across his cheek and into the cavities of his nose. He shook his head, his vision clearing. The farmer's wrist snapped out again. The blow connected just above the ear, crushing the flesh scaldingly. Galbraith blinked, rushed forward into a furious rain of punches, and rammed his nails into Johnstone's eyepits. The farmer's scream of rage was cut off, and he was gouging, every muscle in his body spurting power to his hands, Johnstone's forearms beating him, clubbing his lowered skull. He bore down harder and felt himself sinking. They flailed backwards on to the planking with a crash which made the glasses rattle and bottles leap on their shelves behind the bar. The farmers and the pensioner drew back their feet and leaned over the tables to watch. He thrust deeply into Johnstone's eye sockets, the shrieking in his ears like singing, an anthem of pain, which in his drunken delusion he imagined couched in his step-brother's tones. A shoe came up under his chest and he was ripped away, sailing, free of all contact, fingers still hooked inward like reaper spikes, slippery with blood. He landed on his shoulders, buttocks following hard. All feeling went out of his legs : they folded before him shrouded in the skirts of his overcoat, like gigantic tents. In the hammock between, he saw Johnstone's foreshortened figure swell up, the brown hand across the white face, swaying head flicking little droplets of bright red blood from the crevices between the knuckles. Johnstone lowed and bellowed, swinging his head, thrusting like a great blind monster sniffing for its prey; then he lumbered forward and the leg rose. Galbraith

219

strove to roll away but his nerves would not react. During the time it took the heel of the shoe to haul back, cant, and the leg to begin its slow piston-like descent he knew he could not evade it. He was shouting, spewing out words like vomit from gaping lips. Then the heel breached the sagging wall of coat cloth between his thighs, rose and fell again with lightning speed, and lifted, all before he experienced the first agony. When it reached his brain, running up through his guts and chest like a river of molten steel, he blacked out. He did not feel the third blow follow through with all Johnstone's fearful energy behind it, like a man grinding out a venomous striking snake.

Two yards from the writhing figure on the floor, the old man winced in sympathy and with a lifetime of methodical stoicism behind him, automatically pulled out his pocket watch to check the exact time of the murder. It was, as he later stated, exactly ten past six.

She turned Galbraith away : Lang warmed with the recollection, and congratulated himself for the rashness which had brought him out to this God-forsaken spot in defiance of the policeman's dire warnings. Even if they nabbed him now, stuck him in a cell and disgraced him, he would have the memory of Galbraith stripped of his wealthy arrogance snuffling round the house, whining and snivelling like a whipped cur. She had kicked him out. The lowest scum of the gutter considered herself too good for Galbraith. Yes, even harlots had his number. What had Sellars said – 'She doesn't know the meaning of sympathy'. Lang could well believe it. She had put one over on Galbraith all right, so certain of the attraction of her body that she could deny him entry when she liked, knowing that he would not have the power, the will to shove her out. If only he, Lang, had possessed a similar kind of strength he would have discovered the weakness in Galbraith himself and acted on it. For over an hour after Galbraith's undignified departure, Lang hugged himself with glee, then, with the September night drifting down like soot upon the tiny particles of rain, he began to hunger for more. His appetite for information, and the urge to see for himself the lineaments of the woman in the house increased. Slowly he smoked down a cigarette, his gaze fastened on the lounge window. Did she only come out at night, this girl-woman, appear with the fall of dark like a witch, or a vampire? There was no sign of a light yet in any of the panes.

He thrust the butt into the wet earth off the island of the raincoat, pushed it down until it vanished, save for a tiny wisp of blue smoke stealing up through the grass pad. It was almost too dark to see the house clearly now. He must go, creep down on to the track back to Balnesmoor and the bus. But he would be back. Galbraith would be back. Yes, he was almost certain that Galbraith would return to plead for ... The house was dark and still. Was she sitting alone in the dark? Perhaps she was not alone : the realisation made Lang's breath catch in his throat. Another man – several men! And the girl, the witch, the vampire, the demonic bitch, thrusting Galbraith away because he did not fit in with the evils she had planned. They were all evil under the skin, selfish women. He had glimpsed it before, the wickedness there, in office girls who jutted their bums and breasts at men, giggled and stuck out their tongues. But society did its best to hold it down. What if here in Balnesmoor, close against the hairy belly of the wilderness, one woman let it boil to the surface? Incarnate evil, linked with the awfulness of the place, like the witches of olden times haunting gibbets and boneyards, supping wickedness from the air, matching evil done with evil yet to do. The thoughts raged through him, devouring his reason, making him avid to see exposed that which he could only imagine through a veil of respectability. Would she enact the mysterious sins he had glimpsed in the eyes of the girls in the photographs, the dead girls? He swung his head sharply, nervously to the left, and groped with his eyes into the blind grey dusk, peopled with trunks and gnarled upraised branches. Suddenly the stench of the rotting leaves and boughs and stiff fern fronds took on the nauseating effluvia of evil. His pupils contracted, probing the still curtain in search of movement, hoping in fear for the rise of some ... some *thing* to convince him of his folly and drive him in terror from the place. Frantically he grabbed up his belongings, stuffed them into the shopping bag, and lowered himself into the dense soaking tangle which overhung the track. Whatever evil there was, he did not want to see it after all; he was not entitled to see it. Regardless of noise, he crashed and stumbled through the thickets hauling the shopper behind him. His boots slithered, his old shanks could not control the weight;

221

the handle of the shopper snagged on a twig which snapped loudly and released the tension which held him spread-eagled against the banking. He dived forward, covering his face and fell full length across the muddy track.

With all the breath knocked out of him, he lay still, head hung against his hands, and let the fire in his lungs burn itself out. He took clean breaths up from mouth and nostrils close to the cold smooth mud. Wetness was seeping through the cloth over his elbow, his knees felt as if they might be bleeding, but in his back he felt no pain at all. For a brief spell he experienced a kind of tranquillity, then, with a revival of the panic which had spurred his flight, propped himself on to his knees and peered cautiously around. Outlined against the house wall up on the crest of the hillock of the lawn, stood the tall figure of a man.

Lang could see him quite distinctly, black garbed and, in his stance above, seemingly massive. Squatting, Lang was completely motionless, holding back his fright. The figure came forward, over the slope of the lawn, legs vanishing into the shadowy mist as if into water. He was heading directly for the track. Fright, not cunning, held Lang immobile. Even when the man veered to the right and descended to the gate, Lang could not make his muscles work. He heard the faint swishing sound of feet in the long weeds, not fifty yards from where he sat. The shape passed out of sight. The hinge of the iron gate shrieked rustily. Lang crept forward on his belly to the fence, lifted the bottom strand of wire and wriggled under it. The snicker of buttons on the metal strand was as loud as hooves on cobbles in the waterlogged silence. Crawling flat, he eased his boots through; then paused, face down. From far away round the curve of the track came the rushing of shaken leaves. The dark figure was searching for him, wanted him, would patrol the whole length of the track, spot him, pursue him, run him to earth. On his elbows and knees he walked himself across the lower regions of the lawn towards the tall sea of weeds. If the man would only stay by the gate, Lang thought, perhaps he could steal through the weeds, round the gable of the house and away. This quarter of the garden was hidden from the lounge; the girl would not be able to spot him, and direct her lover to his hiding place. *He must not be seen.* Yet he was coming out above the ground mist and low-lying cover, coming out into clear view, on the wrong side of the house to escape with ease.

Over to the east where the trees were dense, he could have risked a run for it, but here the wire and the track lay open, and the man might find him if he broached the lane. No, through the high dripping weeds, belly and thighs dragging on the earth, hands like the claws of a mole pushing back the stalks, parting them, head and shoulders into the gap, all with the muted reined-in haste of a panic now controlled. Curving away from the dangerously exposed line of the fence, he brought himself closer and closer to the ranch-house path and the blind gable wall of the lounge. The rise of the ground told him where he was. He did not dare lift his head and he lay still, judging himself not more than ten feet from the concrete path which flanked the wall to the kitchen door. On the other side of that path was the garden shed, the tree-line and freedom.

He listened for what seemed an eternity, his heart jarring noisily in the cavity under his ribs, stuffed and full like a haggis simmering in brine. He heard no other sound, and cautiously raised his face over the level of the weeds. The house windows showed nothing. He scanned the garden – no sign of the man. He crouched, then on impulse scuttled over to the wall and stopped there, hands against the roughcast brick, panting, waiting for the shout. Nothing. If he went around the house and past the front door, he could forge a path through the bushes and avoid the road. He edged down the side of the wall stealthily into the gloom of the dense tree mass. At the corner he paused, stuck his head round the corner and tucked it back again hastily. The man was tramping determinedly along the yard walk towards him. Lang cast a despairing glance at the weeds; the short run was still too much for him. He shot back round the gable and pressed himself on the open façade, listening. From inside the house came no sounds and no light. He distinctly heard the crunch of a shoe around the corner, and set off past the long window, heading for the square shape of the shed fifty yards away. He never reached it. Acoustics had tricked him; as he hurtled past the yawning door of the kitchen, he saw the man ahead moving away from him downhill towards the little building. Exposed and desperate, Lang lunged to the right. Just as the figure stopped and turned, Lang vanished through the open kitchen door. Somehow he had entered the house.

It was not calculation, or even sense which carried him there, only the impulsive reaction of his legs. Initially he was shocked to find himself standing in the darkened room, strung-up in readiness for the girl's shrill screams; but anything was preferable to the hunt in the garden, a dank and sinister capture outdoors. At least here there would be light, he would see the man and this witch woman, and perhaps. ... He remembered the front door. He could be through the house, out the other side and jinking off down the roadway in a matter of a minute. And the girl? Was she lurking in the black recesses of the lounge, or out in the hall, aware of him, waiting to fell him with a hammer or a candlestick? He had no time to work out rational aspects of the decision, acting on it as it came to him, instantly.

The lounge door was firmly closed. He opened it, and entered the room, shoulders hunched in expectation of a blow. He closed the door behind him, tip-toed down the length of the room, familiar in shape if not in furnishings, and stepped into the L-shaped hall. Still no one challenged him. He hesitated, feeling out into the limited darkness, groping across it into the second leg and finally to the back of the main door. As soon as his fingertips touched the chains, he was aghast at his own stupidity. It was locked like a keep, of course, locked and barred and chained and bolted just as he'd left it. He fumbled over it, accounting for each fastening in turn : Galbraith had left the whole collection intact. He whirled and waded back into the gloom, just as someone entered the kitchen. The slamming of the door paralysed him, leg raised, hand against the wall. He stopped breathing, slid his palm slowly down the wall until it bumped the handle of the deep cupboard which cleft half the house's length. He jerked at the handle and felt the ball sink back in the lock and, with a faint clicking, yield. A moment later he was inside. Stripping off his tie, he looped it through the plastic handle and eased the door after him, drawing back until the steel bearing connected and shut fast. Releasing one end of the tie, he inched it through the narrow crack, which, even as the tail came to him, was delineated by a hairline strip of light. Lang cowered into the utter darkness, shifting his feet delicately. He encountered a broom handle, gripped it and guided himself down until he was squatting on the floor. He felt behind him, touched a length of material, fibrous and coarse, wound round upon itself – carpet in an untidy bundle – and sank slowly back against it.

The faint fragrance of perfume, a scented floor polish perhaps, came to him, mingled with the musty odour of the carpet. Straining his ears, he detected small noises through the wall of the lounge. He fixed his eyes on the splinter of light, cowering, knees drawn up, ready to spring out on whoever should open that door. Lang knew there was someone there, close by, listening as he was. Long minutes went by, an age of nervous waiting, tension, but the door did not open. After a while even the wafer-thin ribbon of light went out, and Lang was left in darkness, the faint sweet dusty smell in his nostrils and the nagging worry of what next to do pressing on his brain like an ingot of crude pig iron. There was nothing to do but wait. To submit himself to their mercy from the ignominious depths of a cupboard would be more than he could stand. Sooner or later the man outside and the girl too, wherever she was, must sleep; then, perhaps, he could escape. Vowing adamantly to himself that, if he did win free of this cursed house, he would never again return, he sank back and closed his eyes.

NINE

The phosphorescent hands were still, pointing at six exactly. He put the watch to his ear and listened; stopped. Had he dozed for long? He had been thinking longingly of Jenny, wondering what she would do if he did not return. The last bus to Glasgow passed the bottom of the lane at nine-seventeen: how soon was that? Jenny would have his meal waiting and the room bright as a new pin. In spite of her threats, she would be there to serve him as she always was. He had never really thought of Jenny as a good wife. When they had been parted at the time of trouble she had appeared as a traitor, a threat to his hard-won security. Now he saw in her the essence of his

225

security; her breakdowns part of the penalty of his reliance on her. If only she would come and lead him out of here now.

No sounds now, no lights. His stomach rumbled with emptiness and tension. He put his hand in his pocket and toyed with his cigarette packet, took it out, opened it and extracted the last cigarette. He placed it in his mouth – a crumb of loose tobacco on the tip of his tongue stinging him when he bit on it.

More time passed. The end of the cigarette was soggy with saliva. He took out a match-box, held it tightly to prevent it rattling, and pushed it open. For what seemed hours he sat quite motionless, the match in one hand, the box in the other and the cigarette drooping from his lips. His appreciation of danger had waned; the deep perfumed dark of the closet was comforting, and familiar to him, and offered no threat. Eyeing the bottom of the door and listening intently, he placed the head of the match against the sandpaper and with a hasty impulsive stroke scraped it down. Flame bloomed, cupped in his palm. Lowering his head, the tube probed and ignited and the satisfaction of tobacco smoke poured back into his throat. He sighed and cocked his wrist. With the leap of light on the point of being extinguished, he saw the pale stockinged foot sticking from the carpeting a yard in front of him. He hauled his knees back from it as the burnt wood of the match-stick split and fell. His lungs sobbed, throttling the abject terror in his throat. The pitch blackness was suddenly hostile, the sweet odour no longer harmless, but stitched to the memory of that cloying stench which had swarmed over him in the thicket. He pressed his shoulders against the wall, shaking. The match-box tumbled over his knees, spattering its contents across the floor. He fumbled around by his boots, picked up a match and struck it, holding it forwards in the direction of the carpeting. The foot hung awkwardly, neat naked toes encased in nylon, the material pressed up by the prominent twisted ankle bone. Even with so little light he could discern a few wisps of hair under the fabric where the calf began to swell. The match went out; he scrabbled between his knees for another, found it, cracked it. There was no help for him now, no pulling back from the ultimate realisation that he was sitting with death, sharing its stillness and darkness, like a man entombed in a grave. Flame scorched his fingers and relieved him. He held on to his lip with his teeth, trembling, until he could find another and draw

226

it against the box. He gave no thought to discovery or to the man outside. Only with light could he live, as if the light was air and the glow of it against his flesh was the manifestation of the breath which distinguished him from the creature under the rug. He had no doubt that she was dead. But the remnants of sanity and compassion prompted him to lift back the carpet slowly, and, in the space of time it took to burn out a single match, reveal the body, limbs and features of the corpse.

The open eyes in the lolling head were fixed on him – full of a gentle recrimination for being too late. The short hair still retained its golden lustre, and the pale long-fingered hands had a voluptuous quality which was yet despairing, the body offered in expectation of rebuff. Darkness descended once more, but he did not reach for another match, kneeling motionless, sweat dripping from his brows like the passing out of a fever. The stranger had killed her, had killed her and escaped, had killed her while he, Lang, was sprawled on the moor praying for it to happen in his sight, to share the humiliation and indignity of murder – without its guilt.

His head reeled. The taint of wax and sulphur mingled with the perfume of the dead girl, and the over-ripe fecundity of a body already beginning to decompose in a million subtle ways was like a whiff from the gap of hell. The house was smothering him. He crawled to the cupboard door and pulled himself up. Even if the man was lurking there, waiting to kill him too, he could not remain hidden. He pushed against the catch and the door swung open. The damp air of the hallway flooded over his skin. He listened. The tread of a foot on the floor of the lounge brought him back to his senses, filling him swiftly with the desire to avenge the gross deceit which had been forced upon him. He drew the broom from the closet, and slid into the pitch-black shadow at the angle of the hall behind the door of the lounge, gripping the handle tight.

Ballentine worked assiduously through his list of chores. He had not been caught unprepared, but with so much hanging on the success of the venture, he was compelled to be even more careful than last time. The strange sound outside still worried him. Perhaps, had his nerves not been keyed up with the excitement of the afternoon, he would have ignored it. He held the cloth in his gloved hand and polished the coffee cup. Stored with care in his memory were visual reproductions of each and every item he had set his naked hands upon. He shifted lightly about the lounge and kitchen, feeling his way from one to the other in the dark. The Rover, taken from the private lock-up in Craigieburn, Glasgow, just for the day, was parked in the car park at the back of the *Adderly Hotel* in Kilcraig; before he went to fetch it he would risk switching on the lights for a moment. In the meantime, however, he had to wreak havoc on the household, creating signs of struggle consistent with the pattern which the police would devise to fit the character of their prisoner. He did not doubt that his plan would work. Save for his rash pursuit of the noise outside, he had made no error.

The girl had been so perfect, he'd been almost sorry to kill her. But her perfection lay in her attributes as a victim. She had died quietly, not like Syme who, when he wakened her in the bunk in the trailer, had fought him desperately with the strength of a devil. She would fight no one now, ever again, or lead men to corruption. To the young girls, oddly, life seemed less sweet than to the prostitute; they slithered to an easy death under his hands, a death they almost appeared to welcome. The Ewart girl's smile was touchingly serene, until her cells hardened and rictus stretched her features into a grotesque leer, still apparent when he buried her. He burnished the tiles at the side of the armchair, then set to work on the chair itself. His senses still inflamed, he would not relax until he had got himself to the Rover and out to a quiet stretch of the roadway. There he would change all his clothing and bury it in the peat bog beyond the forestry bridge. Unlikely risks, eventualities, he had thought through, too. They might confront him at any given moment, but none had cropped up yet. Perhaps none would. But he was prepared for Robert to arrive outside thumping, shouting, pleading for admission. If someone reported the Rover, it could not be connected with him; false plates would curtail identification, and the locker in Glasgow was safe as a bank. He was so convinced that the police would concentrate their attentions on Robert, he had no fear of being associated with the crime at all, and could rely on the simplest alibi.

From his jacket pocket, Ballentine produced the hip flask which he had stolen from Galbraith over two years ago, in preparation for the circumstantial ritual of this night. He flicked off the lid, swallowed a mouthful of whisky, lit a cigarette, Benson & Hedges; same brand as Robert smoked, pinched the tip into an oval, one of Robert's habits too, then flung the flask down upon the rug. He watched the liquid leak out on to the rug, golden in the glow of the fire, then seated himself on the arm of the chair and massaged his aching feet. The size eight, plain pattern shoes which he had worn all day, were too small for him of course, being Robert's fit, and the leather had strangled the blood supply : his toes were quite numb. Discomfort and exhaustion were the price he had to pay : triumph would come later, the private triumph of seeing Robert locked behind bars for the rest of his life. He put the cigarette to his lips and inhaled. Every nerve-end in his body was tinglingly alive and the tobacco tasted harsh and bitter on his tongue. Suddenly his eyes widened. He turned his head towards the curtained window. The sound was not identical and seemed nearer this time; a stealthy creaking, faint and faltering, there then gone. He experienced the texture of air against his cheek, as if some large object had stirred it, the ripple travelling through it as through a liquid of low density. For minutes he strained his ears, but did not hear the noise again. But he was concerned enough to put his cigarette on the rim of the ashtray on the edge of the grate and creep to the lounge door. He peered out : only the inky blackness of the hallway, chopped by angles and corners, greeted him. He made himself listen, pushed fear down into him, burying it deep; could not allow himself to believe that the sound came from the cupboard. Allison was dead, must be dead, could not be anything but dead. As he drew down her stockings and panties and stretched her on the length of old carpeting, he had felt the first unwieldiness in the limbs. Her legs were beginning to go firm when he bent her into the position in which she would be found. *She could not be alive:* he refused to submit to the unthinkable, yet found himself in mortal terror of the cupboard. He could not go near it, stepped back from it, out of the hall and slammed the lounge door. Turning, he kicked over the plastic magazine rack, spilling its contents across the carpet, pushed up the rug and scattered sheaves of manuscript from her typing table across the room. He stopped again, ensnared. The shuffling sound came from the hall. The lounge door hung

229

ajar. Was that, too, only part of his fancy, an error of recollection? Had he left it that way? The whining, like that of a defenceless animal, was weakness : he clamped his jaws together to stop it then forced himself away from the patch of light by the fire. He willed his hand to the side of the door, and slowly drew it open, penetrated the darkness, treading with dreamlike weightlessness until he reached the cupboard. The door of the cupboard was open too, yawning wide like the entrance to a pit. He touched the inside of the wood, brushing it with the leather glove, took another pace and laid his hand on the light. Crawling up, his thumb came to rest on the switch. He pressed it, blinking. She lay unwrapped, sprawled out, the folds of the carpet around her like the leaves of a great plant. Her lips were parted, her legs jutted apart, her hair spilled wantonly on the hessian. Her eyes, wide open, stared at him.

He felt his jaw go down, then pain darting into his skull from the base of his neck, clouding his mind. He staggered forward, already sinking. The pain came again, duller this time. He pitched forward and fell into the cupboard, his face crushed down upon the dead girl's thighs. The resonant darkness closed in upon him.

The anguish of the last hour swelled in Lang's belly like a yeasty growth and, as the stranger went down, he vented it all with a howl of rage, smiting the skull three or four times with the head of the broom. Then he pitched the broom away, slammed the cupboard door, ran blindly through the house and out on to the lawn. He dithered for a second, swaying and spinning drunkenly in indecision, then rushed to the fence and scrambled over it in to the lane. His small bent legs pumped furiously, the misty air clogging into his lungs like clay. He did not dare look back. All he could think of was the highway, cars, lights of the village, people – people who would spirit him away from here, far away, back to the city and to Jenny, back to where he belonged; people who would know what to do about the horror he had left behind in that house; the police. He no longer cared who the girl was, or the man either, or what strange destiny had bound them together.

He staggered on to the roadway, wheeled wide into the centre, shuffling, his feet hardly consuming the ground, head

230

hanging, pointed at the faint glow of the village in the distance. A small green van swerved to avoid him and drew up with its front offside tyre in the ditch. Lang was unaware of it. If he saw it at all, he regarded its passage as unconnected with him, just another preoccupied tenant of the world hurtling past towards his own small corner. He dragged on towards the first house. When the van reversed and drew abreast of him, still he paid it no heed. Only when the door yawned and the young voice bawled at him did he emerge from his dogged dream, and, stopping, lost volition, reeled and dropped to his knees on the tarmac. Hands on his shoulders, anxious voices consulting, asking if he was drunk. He gathered the last of his strength, grabbed the arm near him and hauled himself up.

'The police,' he said. 'Get ... me ... to Ryan.'

'The police?' the young man said to his companion. 'He wants the coppers. What'll we do?'

'Dunno.'

'Take me,' Lang panted. 'For God's sake take me.'

'Okay, mister,' said the youth. 'We'll take you. Panic not.' And they helped him solicitously into the van.

Ryan inched his chair across the rubberised flooring of the new wing of the cottage hospital, and McCaig too drew nearer from the bed end. The nurse, a young Jamaican, darted a malevolent glance at them and bustled forward to the patient. Apparently she could not understand that policemen had a job to do too, and resented the intrusion of justice into medicine with some bitterness. Ryan put his hand on the blanket and lifted his shoulders enough to watch Galbraith's mouth. The lips had opened, the tongue came forward, pus-yellow, like a strip of granny's flannel in the bone-white, black-eyed face. Bruises around the lips sat up scarlet, greasy with the unguent which the nurse had put on. The blankets were mounded over the cage, clear of the damaged gut. Probably operate, the doctor said, but granted them their request for one quick word with Galbraith before a hypodermic was brought into play again and his body stripped for the knife. The agent didn't look good; Ryan wondered at the violence which the two men had managed to inflict upon each other without the benefit of weapons. Hate, he supposed, was a good enough weapon. God,

Johnstone's face was torn to pieces. Even now he was lying senseless under the mask while rubber-coated hands and fine steel blades strove to repair the bloody eyeball.

The unit was excessively warm, and Ryan sweated. He glanced up at McCaig, but the Chief was as impassive as ever, letting none of the seething impatience which had marked his arrival at the hospital leak out now. What was it the matron had bellowed at him during their confab in the office – 'I don't care if you're the Archangel Gabriel, you're not going in there.' But they'd got in, and put her nose out of joint. In the County hospital it would have been different : these new people would have to learn the rules. Was it true, Ryan wondered, as Galbraith's mouth closed once more, that the agent and the farmer's wife had been knocking it off, or was it just a drunken masochistic boast? The agent and the farmer's wife; it sounded like a blue film, or a dirty joke – heard the one about the agent and the ... No joke to Johnstone though. They would get around to Johnstone later, settle the matter of who struck whom, and all the rest of it. Five witnesses, three dour farmers, a barmaid and a shrewd old mill-hand past retirement age : if they couldn't ferret the truth out of that lot then the police department wasn't worth its salt. Still, there were truths that a casual witness would know nothing about, which only Galbraith could illuminate for them. And these truths might be very important. Yes, Galbraith had been hiding something all right – Edna Johnstone – and he had done it with great skill. For all his thoroughness Ryan had heard no hint of gossip at that relationship. Did Johnstone have an inkling? Birnie's statement that the farmer beat up his missus, was possibly right. He would have to question Edna Johnstone about it. She was outside in the public waiting-room right now, but this was not the time. It was one thing to slide in a few questions to a man just coming out of consciousness, a sick man at that, but ... Galbraith groaned. His hands, lying dormant on the cover, slipped across to touch the ugly hump of the blanket cage.

'Nurse,' said McCaig.

'I see. I see.'

She busied herself, taking the pulse again, recording the figure in the form of a graph on the chart by the bed.

'How long now?' said McCaig.

232

The dark-skinned scowl was fiercely protective. Even unconscious, Galbraith was capable of making conquests : little use it would be to him now, with crushed testicles and a belly swollen up like a football. He had envied Galbraith once, and disliked him for rousing the emotion, but he didn't envy him now – not even for Edna Johnstone. Morality again, Ryan, the Inspector thought; you're a hide-bound, mothball-reeking Calvinist even if you haven't graced a church pew for twenty years. Maybe not such a bad thing to be – considering Jean liked him the way he was. Freedom was fine, but it hardened and turned sour with time. The fight against emptiness was only the struggle of the soul trying to find its fulfilment. God, he was lucky to have what he had, even with lousy hours and the grind of raising a family on a small budget. He admired the nurse's slender legs and tight buttocks under the striped skirts of the uniform. A coloured girl, but very pretty, civilised and efficient looking. Ryan, Ryan !

McCaig stepped aside to let the nurse pass, his hat brushing the nylon curtain which screened the bed, then came swiftly forward again as Galbraith's eyes opened.

Ryan stood too, staring down into the shocked pupils, waiting for them to fill up with pain or recognition, some discernible sign of awareness.

'All right?' McCaig asked.

'He's a sick man,' said the nurse. 'You leave him be.'

'Fetch the doctor,' said McCaig. 'Go on. I'll see he doesn't snuff it while you're gone.'

The coloured girl hesitated, then, because it was her duty, hurried through the curtain. McCaig moved up close to the bed head, opposite Ryan.

'Listen, Galbraith,' he whispered. 'What was it all about? The fight : you remember the fight.'

Galbraith closed his eyes again. For a despairing moment Ryan thought he was slipping back into unconsciousness, then he groaned loudly. His pale skin was beaded with sweat, every droplet looking distilled and very pure.

'Never mind your balls,' said McCaig. 'What did you mean when you shouted you'd killed her? Who did you kill? Did you kill anyone?'

'No, no,' Galbraith mumbled. 'No. I never.'

'Who did you kill?'

'Clare . . .'

'God!' said Ryan. 'He's raving.'

'Clare who?' McCaig said. 'Clare Hughes again?'

'Yes,' said Ryan.

'But he didn't kill her,' said McCaig.

'He just thinks he did,' Ryan said quietly.

McCaig grunted and put his nose down until it almost touched Galbraith's ear. The man in the bed was twitching now, his hands fluttering across the cage seeking for a grip, as if to pluck the pain out of him. Ryan knew it was hopeless. Maybe that was the only answer Galbraith could give – Clare Hughes; right answer too, fertilised by all the guilt and the despair which was in him.

'Listen, Galbraith,' McCaig said. 'What about . . .'

A doctor, the matron and the nurse came briskly through the curtain, and McCaig was pushed aside. They were all young; even the matron could not have been over forty. This was their domain, Galbraith their charge. Ryan stepped out through the curtain to give them room to work, hearing the mutter of instructions punctuated by Galbraith's uninhibited moans. After a moment McCaig joined him. Together they stood staring despondently at the blank wall and the unmade bed opposite.

'Well,' said McCaig at length. 'That's it.'

Ryan said. 'It looks like it, yes.'

'Damn the stupid bastard,' said McCaig. 'I thought we were on to something, and all he gives us is this tatty old claptrap about Clare bloody Hughes again.'

'It's all he's got, I think,' said Ryan.

The matron's head appeared through the curtain and both men turned to look at her inquiringly.

'Are you Inspector Ryan?' she said.

'I am.'

'There's a call for you on my office phone.'

'A what?'

'A call, a call, a telephone call.'

'All right,' said Ryan. 'Thank you.'

They began to walk up the ward, away from the mysterious sounds of suffering behind the screen.

'What now?' said Ryan.

'God knows,' said McCaig. 'Nothing good I'll bet.'

234

Ryan shrugged, went into the Matron's office and lifted the receiver from the table.

In the lounge of the ranch-house the stillness was total. The chemistry of combustion gave off sounds too faint for the human ear to detect, tobacco and paper joining with oxygen to change state to ash and smoke. The spiral went upward steady and straight, just discernible in the darkness, like a wisp of cobweb suspended from the ceiling over the hearth, tinted pink where it crossed the path of the gas mantel. The paper soon blackened and gave back to the burning cone in its sheath of granular ash, smouldering slowly down into the fibres of the rug. Then the rug caught too, gently, and the rim of fire, a thin crimson line, spread outwards, guttering in the whisky stain, eating patiently around it. Soon flame, spluttering and blue, scalloped the carpet, inching towards the spill of manuscript by the window and backwards over the litter of magazines for the fallen armchair's plump seat. After a while the room was quite bright with it and the smoke dense. Flakes of paper and cloth floated on hot currents across its surface. The table legs hissed with bubbling varnish, and the chair was enveloped in cheerful red, as if it welcomed the possessiveness of the fire. Later still, the separate legions united and rushed upon curtains and walls, swallowed up doors, poured into ceiling beams and out into other rooms, blasted from the exploding box of the gas fire like molten stars.

Ballentine choked. The clinging hem of the skirt was on him, darkness given faint definition by swirling smoke. He retched and coughed, his eyes streamed; he was not aware of the blood flowing down from his wounded skull. He was aware of nothing but his need to breathe, and struggled with the girl as if she was responsible for cutting off his air. In the acrid gloom, he fought with her as a child will mock a struggle with a doll, shaking and lifting and pushing the lifeless limbs, finding them clinging. Then, with the flickering glow from the wall ahead, he saw the narrow confines of the place and the girl's face clearly. Sparks burst in on him and the choking blast of flames spread up on him like a furnace. He seemed to be moving towards it, hugged by the body of the girl; she was slithering backwards into the holocaust and taking him with her. He waited for demons, but the demons were transformed into sheets of flame, spewing sparks from their mouths. He rose to his knees, his head splitting with the roar of the fiery place. Even she was spread on a bed of fire, laced and draped with it. Her hair glowed yellow as liquid gold and her eyes were like incandescent rubies. The rain of firedrops showered him with agony. He lifted his arms, spread his hands to stop himself being drawn into the blaze, but it was irresistible. He was melting, streaming into fire too. Finally he welcomed it; blackness again, the hiss and bubble of blood in his veins. Long before the roof broke in upon him and buried him, he was quite dead, never knowing that the fire and the girl embedded in it, face lit with a wild, welcoming, pure-white, innocent smile, existed in this cold world, and not the next. In his last second of life, he thought he had joined Clare Hughes.